THE
CHRISTMAS
VIRUS

BY
MICHAEL JOHN HOWELL

WINDENSE
PUBLISHING

A CIP catalogue record for this book is available from the British Library

Lines from The Second Coming by W.B.Yeats gratefully acknowledged.

Cover Design by Lawrence Creative, Glasgow

Windense Publishing
19 Grenadier Park
Glasgow G72 8EP
Scotland

Printed by CCB

ISBN: 978-0-9563512-0-3

To Bob, for his invaluable help and support; to my children, for whom this book was written; and for my wife, Linda, for everything.

What happens tomorrow is always fiction today.

ONE

Eleven seconds to go, and a sea-eagle wheels high above the ancient granite battlements. Two flags snap viciously in the salt-laden air.

The large window frames a grey and weathered fortress, glinting silver in the light of a weak winter sun. Five computers glow dimly on an antique Venetian desk, crafting an arrowhead of silicon at the window and the castle beyond. Watching them intently, a red-haired man stands immobile. The computers span a digital generation, dull grey monoliths to sleek silver icons. Each screen shows only a large analogue clock, second hand marching steadily towards the stroke of noon. The clocks are not perfectly synchronised, so there is a ripple as they strike the hour and dissolve into text. The text reads:-

"Please read this message carefully. Do not reboot your computer as it may not re start.

The heart of this computer now belongs to me. The heart of your colleague's computer now belongs to me. Soon the hearts of all computers will belong to me.

The civilisations of the West must answer some very grave charges. These charges will be made over the next several days. If the charges are addressed, then the computers will be released. Meanwhile, every day they will become less and less useful. This is day one of seven.

Again, please do not try to reboot this computer."

The red-haired man moves unsteadily from behind the desk to stand at the window. 'Let the dice fly high' he proclaims, and sinks to his knees.

1

The Ivy, London, a little the right side of noon. Andrew surveyed the table with a growing sense of anticipation. Crisp, starched linen, gleaming cutlery, a delicate vase of Thai orchids. A crystalline array of sparkling glasses that he did not intend to sully with mineral-laden water. Facing him Jacqueline, an elegant woman of a certain age, smart, amusing, sexy. And influential. Ahead lay an agreeable afternoon of good food, good wine and conversation. The crude tools of modern communications - mobile phone, organiser and laptop - lay blissfully dormant in his elegant Dunhill briefcase. Today required subtler forms of communication. Charm, finesse, a little chemistry. The softest of soft sells. Andrew had just settled on his starter when a white gloved waiter appeared at his elbow, holding a cordless phone with professional diffidence.

"I'm sorry, Mr Westlands, but he says it's very urgent?"

"Andrew here."

"A car is waiting. Leave now. Before the aperitif."

"Eldon? Since when does the Great One call his old friends?"

"Switch on your laptop in the car. Video conference is scheduled for one o'clock, your time. That gives you thirty-five minutes to prepare your plan."

"Plan for what?"

"You still there?"

"For the record," said Andrew turning sadly to the woman, "I recommend..." Jacqueline, however, smoothly interrupted.

"...the scallops with the Cloudy Bay to start. The venison with the Beaucastel to follow. More importantly, Andrew, just why would Eldon Harker phone *you*? And at lunchtime, of all things?" she teased, archly. Andrew acknowledged her with a smile, but no answer, and was gone.

Nature is not fair, and Catherine Connor was the perfect embodiment of that truth. Tall, blonde, blue-eyed and shapely, she had the kind of beauty that led men to greatness or foolishness or pretty much any place she chose. Catherine also had the quick yet deep mind of the truly brilliant. Those she could not captivate she could soon wrap in contradictions. Catherine knew that she was born for greater things, and that television was going to provide them.

Perhaps it might be today. At five minutes past twelve, Catherine had stopped using her computer with a rising sense of unease. By twelve fifteen they had decided the next bulletin would be done without the normal cues and prompts and backdrops. By twelve twenty they had known what the main item was going to be. By twelve forty they knew it would be that rarest of days, The Big One, the 'Where-Were-You-When' kind of day.

It was twelve fifty nine, and the adrenaline coursed as Catherine counted down to the stroke of one. Despite that, she was the very image of poise and confidence, and the adrenaline's only visible effect was to add passion to her eyes. The further enhancement was neither fair nor necessary. The summary headlines seemed to take forever, but when the autocue beckoned, Catherine's timing was perfect.

"Thank you, Richard. Now, today's main news item. There are reports coming in worldwide of a very serious computer virus attack. Our sources indicate that this virus targets the U-Sys operating system, produced by the U-Soft Corporation of Washington State, USA, and that the virus already affects a very large number of computers. There are some, unconfirmed, indications that an anti-western terrorist group may be responsible. U-Soft so far refuse to confirm or deny the reports, but have announced that a press conference will take place at their London office later this afternoon. A spokesman for Safeware, the world's largest anti-virus company, has suggested that all unnecessary computer activity should be suspended for the time being. Meanwhile, many City firms and most Government offices have

3

suspended work and sent their staff home. We have in the studio Dr Vasilevski, the world renowned expert on computer viruses and the author of 'Cyber Smart and Cyber Safe'.

Dr. Vasilevski, how serious do you think this virus attack might be? Aren't we all just a little too panicky?"

Dr Vasilevski was a tall, angular thirty-something, short dark hair, a clean shaven face framed by large brown eyes dressed in frameless eyewear. He waited until Connor had finished, but then replied immediately.

"I suspect that we might just get a lot more panicky yet. I have never seen anything quite like this."

"Surely not, Dr. Vasilevski. I am sure we all remember the Babylon virus, which infected twenty five per cent of the world's computers and caused billions of dollars of damage. Do you really think that this might be on the same scale?"

"This is different. By co-incidence, I received a new computer this morning and switched it on at eleven fifty. By noon, it showed the virus."

"Scary, I admit, Dr Vasilevski, but surely not unprecedented? In this day and age we all know just how fast a virus can spread."

"Quite, Catherine. However, this computer has never been connected to the internet. It has never seen an external disk of any kind. I switched it on and went for a coffee. When I came back, it was infected."

"Forgive me, Dr Vasilevski, I am not an expert but I do not see how that can be possible. Surely a colleague...?"

"No, no colleague. The only explanation I have is that the computer was shipped with the virus. Perhaps a bad batch of install disks. As you can appreciate, I'm reluctant to speculate."

"If that is the case, Dr Vasilevski, how do you account for the reports of older computers showing the same message?"

"I can't, Catherine. Like I said, we might just get a lot more panicky yet."

Andrew is seated at a large video console. The screen is filled with the unmistakable, startling features of Eldon Harker. A long, narrow, lined face topped with shoulder length, silver grey hair. One huge, continuous, silver eyebrow that frames luminous green eyes. The voice is characteristically brusque.

"Gentlemen, I am afraid it is again time for the U-Soft inner council to meet. We are under attack, and it is probable that this attack will be unusually severe. As always, we will meet this attack with intelligence and utter ferocity."

The U-Soft inner council was gathered, expectant, around their video consoles. Carl Sorensen, Head of R&D; Solomon N'Chenga, principal of internal security; James Downford, corporate vice president, legal; Eldon Harker, president, chairman, and chief executive officer. Carl Sorensen was a big, bluff Scandinavian, in his late thirties but perhaps older, dressed in an unspectacular blue suit with an open necked shirt. Solomon N'Chenga was black, tall, rangy; perhaps fifty but with conflicting cues that might mean as much as ten years either way. He wore a dark cashmere polo neck, dark trousers, and no jacket. James Downford was blue eyed and brown haired, of medium height and build, well-groomed with perhaps just a hint of sleekness. His black three piece suit was sharp, and his matching tie and handkerchief even sharper. Seeming to gaze straight at Andrew Westlands, Eldon Harker continued.

"Gentlemen, let me also introduce you to our new member; Andrew Westlands. You will all know Andrew as a vice president of corporate relations, but more as one of the founding members of U-Soft. Andrew has some unique qualities that we will require." Eldon paused briefly, but no one dared ask the obvious question. What qualities? Eldon did not stop to elaborate.

"OK, let me take it from the top. We need to scope the problem in terms of spread and severity. We need to understand it and we need to determine a solution. Given the indications of terrorist involvement, we need to find who is responsible, and fast. Meanwhile we need to hold off the press and the legal parasites. Let's start with you, Carl, what do you know?"

'Eldon has not yet lost his incision.' thought Andrew. 'Nor made much touch with his feminine side either.'

"We have one hundred per cent virus penetration here. Brand new computers, no outside interface, U-Sys4, all infected. Now testing U-Sys versions one through three. It is already clear that the virus does more than just issue messages. Among its other impacts, it has laid a minefield around the date changing functions, so we have not yet been able to fully test the date dependencies. Specifically, we do not yet know what the payload will bring in seven days time." Eldon interrupted.

"*Specifically*, Carl, you need to be more precise. The message said *day one of seven*. That makes it six days from now. Since today is the nineteenth of December, the virus will therefore deliver its payload on Christmas Day. I do not expect the virus to wish us a Merry Christmas."

The ensuing silence may have been long, but it was hardly an overreaction. It would have been much longer had not Eldon broken it.

"Let's move on. We've heard that we have one hundred per cent penetration, unknown payload, no date of origin as yet. None of this is good news. James, what is our legal position?"

"We have every kind of disclaimer going but the lawsuits are already flooding in. We have twenty billion dollars of indemnity insurance, the usual conditions re diligence, acts of God, the standard stuff. Terrorist involvement raises some unique issues. An inside source, terrorist or not, will be as bad as it can get. It is difficult to see how we can resist some measure of compensation."

Eldon interrupted, his voice coldly savage.

"James, if you feel you must surrender before battle has even commenced, then please leave now. Otherwise may I remind you of why we pay your wages, and those of your many colleagues in our legal department? It is because we do not pay so much as one red cent of compensation, to anyone, ever. Specifically not to the bottom feeders of the legal food chain. Are we clear, James?"

"Certainly, Eldon. I did not mean..." Eldon was not listening.

"You did not mean much, and you do not mean much, James. But please try and maintain some level of competence." Eldon paused just long enough for the barb to register. "Solomon?"

"Boss. Soon as we get the when, we can get the who. We know more about our senior coders and this has to be a senior coder than they do themselves. Assuming I'm given freedom to work properly, I'd hope on no more than a couple of days."

"Andrew, let's look at the P.R. issues. What should we do to minimise the damage?" Andrew's calm, confident demeanour betrayed nothing of his inner disorientation. Inner council? What on earth was that? But he would have time to think about this later: right now he had to focus. Andrew took a breath, and when the words came out they sounded cool and considered.

"We need to calm our customers down, which means we need to tell them what damage has been done and when we are going to fix it. We need to explain some of the difficulties we face and to ask for their patience. Oh, and we need to advise people, now, on whether to leave their computers on or not."

"Carl?"

"We know enough already to say that rebooting is unreliable. Unfortunately, our interim tests indicate that around ten per cent fail to reboot at all. There are two billion U-Sys computers out there. If we recommend that they are turned off we can expect two hundred million computers will never come back on. If we leave the computers on, then there is clearly a risk that the virus will inflict damage. However, thus far our tests show no trace of any such damage. Given that, I'd say we recommend that the computers are left on. People should exit all programs, make a backup of all their data, and leave the computer on, but with no programs running."

"Agreed. Two hundred million dead computers is not really an acceptable option." Eldon did not have to overstate it. Two hundred million dead computers was a lot more than not acceptable. It was a disaster on a grand scale.

"Andrew, draft a press release and run it past me for approval. Schedule yourself for a press conference, London, three o'clock. Carl, any resources you need, requisition them. I will need a progress summary every hour. A summary, no more. James, I need a full legal analysis of our indemnity cover, particularly in regard to the terrorism angle. Solomon, I want names, and quickly." Eldon looked up before he summarised.

"Damn, gentlemen, now is a good time to be on form. Anyone need me, e mail or video. I'll call the next meeting whenever it makes sense." Eldon's eyes gleamed savagely as he added a postscript.

"One last thing, gentlemen. I consider U-Soft to be at war. In war, U-Soft does not take prisoners. Good-bye." A click and the meeting was over.

By two o'clock the London, Paris and Frankfurt stock exchanges were already closed, but not before manual trades had dropped the indices an average of six per cent. U-Soft had dropped fourteen per cent. The shares of **Nexus** computers, which did not use any U-Soft software, had risen fifty per cent.

The banks had remained open, but only for the most basic of transactions. Automatic card cash was still available.

Many factories had closed and sent their staff home. Most local Government offices across Europe had closed. Airports and railways were largely unaffected. E-commerce struggled bravely, but was badly hit.

People gathered in the city centre coffee shops and bars. The virus was very much the hero of the hour, before the conversation turned, as always, to football.

American broadcasting stations were majoring on U-Soft. Most workers were being advised to stay at home until further developments. Stores remained open, those selling **Nexus** computers inundated for the couple of hours it took to sell all their stock. **Nexus** internet cafes were queued down the street, drawing people and hot dog vendors like a carnival.

In Cairo, Damascus and Tehran, crowds flooded the streets in celebrations. As always, 'Allu Akbar' was the dominant chant, closely followed by 'Guilty! Guilty! The West is Guilty!'

In Japan and China, people were being advised to come to work the following day. Stock markets, however, were not going to open.

The virus now had a name. 'The Christmas Virus'.

Three p.m. U-Soft London, Conference Room One. Gone are the familiar U-Soft robots who would verify your identity in an effortless digital blink. No robots to usher you in with a smooth cyber smile, endlessly patient, endlessly polite. Gone, presumed too vulnerable to the virus, or somehow inappropriate to a terrorist threat. In their place were U-Soft security guards, scowling in a genetic uniformity of neck, shoulders and steroids. The hard faces laboriously checked every journalist against their lists, insolently appraising the anxious faces against their digital images. Around the hall, most of the computer generated exhibits were silent and still, and the vast auditorium was empty of the usual hard-disk hum. A few of the journalists had **Nexus** computers, but the vast majority fidgeted nervously with pens.

More of the cloned guards were dotted around the arena, adding an edge of fear to the already expectant mood.

Sitting two rows from the front, Catherine Connor's attention was drawn to the inspirational posters that newly lined the walls. Posters that exhorted the benefits of 'team-work', and 'diversity awareness' and 'respect for your co-worker'. 'Admirable sentiments.' Catherine thought. Followed by, cynically, 'Pity they didn't pay as much attention to their products.' Just behind Catherine sat the odd couple: Peter Hawkins, of the London Times, Robert Perry of the Daily Telegraph. Sitting together, as they had since Beirut and Sarajevo and Baghdad. War-zone coincidences, transformed by habit into superstition. Today, even by their standards, Hawkins and Perry were unusually motivated, for they had had the misfortune to be born B.C. Before Computers, that is, and thus forever excluded from The Knowledge. In response, they hated computers with a deep, abiding, patient passion. This was their chance for a measure of revenge, and they intended to have their dish, and cold. In the expectant hall around them, many nursed similar grievances. The air crackled, as if with news of war, or an impending storm. But a digital storm, and a cyber-war, to be fought with bytes.

Precisely on the hour, three men strode onto the stage. The first two looked to be in their early thirties, of average height, one European, the other Asian. They dovetailed to the lecterns on the wings of the stage. The third man was in his early forties, tall, with greying blond hair that was longer than was good for him. A serious expression was written on a face that was better suited to smiling. He was the only one of the three to carry any notes.

"Good afternoon, gentlemen. I'm Andrew Westlands, vice president Corporate Relations, U-Soft Corporation. I'm here to make a short statement and to answer your questions as best I can. To my right is Brian Dempsey, European Technical V.P. To my left is Mohan Nehran, V.P. Customer Support. They'll help if things get too technical for me. Firstly, the statement:-

As far as we can determine, there is a defect with all releases of U-Sys4. The nature of this defect is not clear, but the most obvious symptom is the issue of a message. From the text of this message, it is clear that the defect is intentional, the introduction of alien code. It would appear that this code was created as a political act, by person or persons as yet unknown. All resources of U-Soft have been directed to the identification and elimination of this alien code.

In the meantime, we advise our customers to close down all their active applications, and to make a backup of their key files. The computers should then be left on, but unused. No-one should turn off their computer until we advise them to do so. We fully appreciate the problems that this causes to everyone. We offer our deepest apologies. We assure you that we will harness all our global resources to eliminate the alien code. Meanwhile, we appreciate your patience.

Questions, gentlemen?"

Bedlam. Chaos. Pandemonium. In a sea of shouts and waving hands, Andrew selected at random.

"You sir, in the second row, with the red tie." The red tie was quick, confident, professional.

"Peter Hawkins, The London Times. Andrew, what does this alien code do?"

"As far as we can determine, right now it seems to do very little. Let me bring in Brian to explain a little more. Brian?"

"The alien code clearly does something to stop the computer from rebooting reliably. It also erects defences to prevent detailed examination of what it is doing. Specifically, it blocks the points where we can insert debugging tools to break out the code instruction by instruction. Given that the message refers to a degradation of performance over time, we expect some features to negatively impact performance, but the effect is as yet too small for us to measure. We cannot yet test its future impact." A pause. "Because the code somehow stops us from advancing the date to find out." Somehow, as if by some unwritten law, the other half of the odd couple managed to but in.

"Robert Perry, The Telegraph. Firstly, Andrew, can't we just drop this 'alien code' formality and call it 'The Christmas Virus', like everyone else? Secondly, any idea how close you are to a fix?" Andrew nodded.

"I can't speak for the technical boys, but the Christmas Virus is OK with me. On what the problem fix is, no idea as yet, so no estimate on a solution. On how we will deploy the solution, let me bring in Mohan." Mohan began nervously but rapidly settled.

"*Everything*, gentlemen, we will use *everything*. We will distribute new code on CDs, on internet sites, and through e-mail. We will send supplies of disks to computer stores, supermarkets, even - given your proprietors' agreement newspapers. This will be the largest deployment of computer code in history."

"Jim Solomon, the Guardian. Andrew, how could a defect like this get through testing? How do we know that there are not other examples of alien code? An Easter Bunny, perhaps? After all, a virus is not just for Christmas." he added, acidly. It was a cheap line, and Andrew defused it with a wry smile and a pause, before he then answered. Confidently.

"Jim, I can assure you that our testing programs are unprecedented in their scope and thoroughness. No corporation in history has ever tested their products as we have. However, an operating system such as U-Sys4 is staggering in its complexity, and despite our best efforts, the only way we could be sure of zero defects would be to release zero product. In the real world, therefore, we gear up to address the defects that will inevitably make it though."

"Andrew, Tom Trenton, The Sun. What do you think of the

claims from Al Quaeda that they are responsible?"

"Not much until they tell us something to back it up. I'm sure they're not going to be the last to claim responsibility for this one."

"John Edwards, NetSentinel. Andrew, we're hearing reports of the Christmas Virus in U-Sys3. What do you know of that and what would that mean?"

"First I've heard of it. I won't comment on rumours. Let's please stick to the facts."

"Albert Rudolph, Rudolph Murray and Ferguson. Can you give us some indication of what and when you will offer your customers by way of compensation?"

"Albert, are you a lawyer?"

"Yes, and I suspect you're going to need one." Laughter rippled through the hall. Andrew chuckled, shook his head ruefully.

"Hell, another security failure. Gentlemen, this conference is intended for decent, honest, law abiding journalists. Security, give this man some money and escort him out." In the startled hall, several hundred jaws fell in unison. One of the muscle bound uniforms started towards the astonished lawyer.

"Only kidding, he'll sue us." Timing is everything, and Andrew's was perfect. Laughter rocked the hall. Waiting his moment, Andrew continued.

"Albert, I understand you intend to get rich on this. You, and ten thousand other lawyers. However, right now I want to address the problem, not your next yacht." The astonished Albert was still frozen on his feet as Catherine was next to get the nod.

"Andrew, Catherine Connor, the BBC. I am sure we all share your evident respect for the legal profession, and we do understand why." Most of the hall were happy to share Catherine's accompanying smile. "However the lawyer does have a point. How do you convince the people that you are genuinely sorry at all of the disruption this has caused, and will cause? That you really are sharing the pain? That you will fix this 'Christmas

Virus' without somehow making money from it? Again?"

Andrew paused, lifted the mike from the stand, and moved to the front of the stage.

"Ladies and gentlemen, this situation is serious. I know that, you know that, we all know that. I'm not going to hide anything from you. I know it is no consolation, but we are genuinely, deeply sorry for all the disruption this will cause. But I'm not going to make a lot of fancy statements that mean little or nothing. I'm going to tell you what we know, when we know. I'm going to work with you to minimise disruption and to restore normal operations as soon as possible. I'm going to be straight with you. You have my word on that. Right now, all we know is in the statement. I'm going to keep you informed every step of the way. When I hear something significant, I'll let you know. The next conference may therefore be called at short notice. Thanks for your time and cooperation."

It was a masterly performance. Sincerity, honesty, and a touch of humility. Fine ingredients, artfully combined, ending on the right note. Suddenly conscious of their deadlines, a torrent of journalists surged to the exits. Sheer glamour enabled Catherine to somehow defy the tide, and to make it to the stage in time. Her shouts turned Andrew just before he disappeared off stage.

"Andrew, Andrew, one minute please?"

"Catherine, you know the rules. I've made my statement. I can't do you any special favours." Despite his brave words, however, Andrew did not move away. Two paces ahead, his colleagues gestured impatiently.

"Sure, I know, Andrew." Catherine smiled winningly. "I also know you are going to have one hell of job getting the U-Soft message across on this one. Which is why I'd like to invite you onto 'News and Views', tomorrow night. You know my style. I'll be tough but fair. Think you could handle it?" Few males would have resisted the bait. Andrew saw no reason to try.

"Sure. When and where?"

"You'll be met at main reception, seven thirty. We go live at nine."

"Can't wait." said Andrew. "Dinner afterwards?"

"If I haven't ruined your appetite, you can ask me then." An encouraging smile.

"That I will." said Andrew, and rejoined his waiting colleagues.

Traffic was light and jaywalkers dense on the way back to BBC headquarters. Too many thoughts and too much data bounced around in Catherine's head. Flipping her pass at security reception, Catherine reached mechanically in response to their 'Package, Ms Connor'. It was of standard document size, dressed loudly in the livery of 'SwiftBike Express'. Clutching it under her arm, Catherine just made the rightmost lift and, two minutes later, her office.

Although much coveted, the office was hardly large, but it was comfortable. More than that, the privacy was everything. It was in this privacy that Catherine looked to see what someone was in such a hurry to send her. A typed sheet was wrapped around a hand labelled CD package. Unfolding the sheet, Catherine read.

The Christmas Virus. Underlined. *It is time to talk freely. Every day, I will release details of the next charge against the West. It may be some time before anyone is able to see those charges in advance of the given day. Except you.*

Please read carefully. The enclosed disk contains a program named Sesame.exe. When you run Sesame it will ask you for a password. If you enter the correct password it will reveal the statement that everyone will see the following day. The charge of the day, if you like. If you enter the wrong password more than once, your computer will be useless.

There are two e-mail addresses written on the label of the disk. The first address is my e-mail address, the second will be yours. Underneath these addresses is the first password. All passwords are case sensitive.

Catherine looked at the disk. The first address was 'BBC12@yahoo.com', the second 'CathBBC12@yahoo.com'. Clear enough. As was the first password - 'Behemoth'.

The first time you run Sesame it will create a file on your computer. This file will be called 'lic.txt'. You must e-mail this file to my address. If you do so, I will e-mail a new password to your address every day. Please do not add any new programs to your computer or otherwise change it in any way.

In return, I will expect you to use this information for our mutual benefit. Starting tomorrow, I wish you to chair a televised debate every night. The motion for each debate will be the charge we have made against the West that day. Each speaker should make a short presentation, on whatever side of the motion they choose. He or she is then open to question and answer from the other speakers. At the end, the invited audience will vote for or against the motion.

The audience must accurately profile the general population in age, sex, ethnicity and political orientation. You may choose a celebrity audience if that makes this task easier.

If you break this condition all communications will cease and I will choose a different resource.

The speakers at the debate will be chosen by you, from categories that I will nominate. For the first debate there will be a representative from U-Soft; an African politician; an American politician; an Indian journalist and a Middle Eastern journalist. Every speaker has the right to keep his place for the next debate unless I inform you to the contrary. Should a participant not wish to continue, the BBC may nominate a replacement.

The duration of the debate I leave to your discretion.

After the audience has delivered their verdict you will announce the motion for the next debate. If you have followed my instructions, you will already know the statement which we will make to the world the following day. The motion will be the charge at the end of that statement.

You must publicise this communication but you must not share this program nor reveal the e mail addresses to anyone. Other than providing the motion for the next day's debate, you must not share the statements the program reveals until they are already common knowledge.

If you break any of these conditions all communications will cease and I will choose a different resource.

You will see tomorrow that this is no hoax. If there is no debate tomorrow night, I will choose a different resource.

As I said, it is time to talk freely. People have not talked freely for a very long time. Encourage people to talk freely or I will find another resource.

Please make best use of this opportunity. Good luck.

It was some minutes before Catherine breathed again. Several more minutes before she came to a decision and inserted the disk in the drive of her laptop. Yes, she was glad she had kept it running. After a few seconds the screen cleared and a prompt appeared.

'Password?' it said.

'Behemoth' Catherine typed, checked it, checked it again, and pressed the enter key.

"Jeremy, it's Catherine here." Jeremy Wexham, Head of News and Current Affairs, was a busy man but he knew that Catherine never called without good reason. Well, from the obvious excitement in her voice, Catherine clearly thought she did have good reason.

"Shoot, Catherine."

"Jeremy, I need you to organise a meeting with the Director General. Now. It is about the Christmas Virus and that is all I can say right now. Tell him he can have my job if he thinks the meeting was a waste. Tell him that this might just be the biggest thing to happen to the BBC in a long, long time." A pause.

"This had better be good" growled Jeremy, but he made the call.

It was an elated Andrew who made it back to his desk after the briefest of breaks. Been a long time since his last all-day breakfast, but hell if cholesterol was his biggest concern of the moment. Pam, his long suffering secretary, had been waiting for him.

"Eldon wants you on video soon as you get in." she greeted him. "He said to tell you to cheer up, it'll be just you and him. Just like old times", she grinned. And Andrew groaned. However, less than a minute later Eldon's alien face filled the large screen.

"Helluva day, eh Andrew?"

"Yes, Eldon, rather special. You saw the press conference?"

"I did, nice work. You've still got the old magic. I'm damned, but I had forgotten just how good you can be."

"Thanks, Eldon, I appreciate it. However, we will need to do a lot more. We've got to maximise TV exposure, try and stem the tide somehow. I've signed up for a major live news show here, tomorrow night, BBC, 'News and Views'. It can be a little adversarial, but nothing I can't handle."

"Catherine Connor's show? You're not going to let that glamorous assassin do a job on you, are you Andrew? This is a bad one, Andrew. We are going to need all of your fine English charm. We don't need you losing the plot this early." Eldon had started to go on the attack: Andrew thought that a counter-attack might be his best defence.

"Talking of losing the plot, Eldon, why the call? What's

18

happening that you would call me twice on the same day?"

"Strange days indeed, Andrew. Strange days in more ways than one. There's been a lot of testing. There's not been a lot of understanding the answers. So far, every release of U-Sys, from version 1.1. to 4.2, exhibits this 'Christmas Virus'. We're now recalling archive backups from escrow companies, unpacking shrink wrap from the U-Soft museum, but everything so far shows the same thing. Unbelievable, but that's what we're seeing." Andrew gaped at the screen, and his mind went blank. Not the blank of enlightenment, but the blank of utter stupefaction. Then the thoughts flashed back and...

"I know what you're thinking, Andrew, but yes, it's true. It is twenty years ago, I know. Twenty good years, even if I have seen a little more money than you. You know the choice you made, you made your deal. Anyways, you've seen more money than most can count, and it's been your choice to fund so many casinos. You had no need to collect so many wives, either. Hell, let me get back to the point." Helluva day right enough. Andrew had never known Eldon to drift off the point like this before. It did not make him feel comfortable.

"Anyway, bottom line, there is still some code we never re-wrote. It was tough code, you know that, how many people could write that kind of stuff? How could we ever test a re write of that stuff? The kernel? How could we ever risk a fundamental error creeping in? And why would we? You know how the business works, Andrew. Nobody rewrites software just to go faster. Speed is the responsibility of the hardware people. *Speed belongs to the silicon.* No, the kernel worked, so there was no need to rewrite it. Fact is, some of the code you would still recognise. Some of the code is yours. Most of the code is mine. And then there is..."

"The kernel is unchanged? The kernel? You are kidding me, Eldon. Tell me the world is not ticking to twenty year old code?

19

Tell me that we at least went back and..."

"Yes, we did, we went back and re-wrote most of it. Most, but not all. Some original code survives, like I said. It makes no sense, but right now I'm looking like a suspect. And you. And...

"But you checked his work?"

"And he checked mine, yes. Thing is, you know how time was then. You know what some of his code was like. Can I claim I always checked every single line, no of course not. On the other hand, can I imagine how he could introduce some twenty year bomb? How even Michael could have found the time, when we were already working flat out? No, no way I believe it. When the data is conclusive, I'll still be struggling to believe it. Meanwhile, we're now looking for him. Damn, they were great days and I miss them more than I can say. I cannot imagine they are going to end this way. No way. We'll talk later."

"Hold on, Eldon, what are we going to tell people here? I promised them I'd be straight with them and that will not be an empty promise!"

"Tell them the facts. That right now it's looking like U-Sys 1 through 4 are all infected. That we do not know for sure, that we do not know how or why. I don't need to see any copy, it's your show."

"Connection terminated." the machine purred.

"Michael?" asked Andrew of the blank screen, "Michael, what have you done, you mad red-headed fool?"

It was eleven thirty before Andrew held a glass of Talisker 25 in the quiet of his Mayfair apartment. Talisker 25: in Andrew's opinion, the finest malt whisky that money can buy. Amber fire, soft salved by the dreamy peace of the Isle of Skye. Unlike Skye, U-Soft was still a hive of activity. Andrew was to be informed as soon as they made significant progress. It was several glasses later when Andrew put down 'Barbarossa' and closed the bed-side light. He did not, he realised, expect to be disturbed. Even with the Talisker, sleep did not come quickly, nor last long.

The President's Club, Newark, air-side, terminal 'C'. Ahmed Ali Khan stayed quiet and anonymous in the cluster around the large projection television. The six-thirty news, Eastern Time, had just finished. Ahmed was no longer thinking of the infantile security checks, fit only to suppress law suits. Lip service, nothing more. Ahmed was no longer thinking solely of what he must soon do. Ahmed was thinking of the U-Soft press release, the Christmas Virus, the Trials of The West. One hour later, even as Ahmed took his seat on CO-19, he was still repeating inwardly: -

"Mohammed, Great Father, I bow before your genius."

TWO

Frost had wrought sorcery on the high falls. Noon sunlight glimmered and glistened on a sculpture of ice and water. Great winter fingers shimmered and plunged into crystalline pools. At the edge of the largest pool, a red-haired man scooped water from a hole in the ice. Behind him, on a rock shelf, a laptop lay open, an alien artefact in the natural paradise. On the screen of the laptop was a simple text display. It read:-

I was asked:-

"How can you fathom the foolishness and greed of the West? They create computers and the software that powers them, the great machines of our age. They realise that there are great fortunes to be made, and that standardisation is the key. Blind with greed, they rush madly to standardise, but they regard only the cost, the cheapest option. The fools create a monopoly for one company. They have given control of their world to a single company. What will happen if they stop their computers? How can the West so disregard the future?"

... and I had no answer.

I charge the West therefore, with foolishness, with greed, and with disregard for the future.

The red-haired man closed the laptop, placed it carefully in his rucksack, and started down the mountain.

Five hundred miles away, a large, hairless man sat as still as a troll caught in sunlight. The director general of the BBC, Peter Bradshaw, was deep in contemplation. To his left was Jeremy Wexham: to his right, Catherine Connor. The three huddled in a tight cluster in the still vastness of Bradshaw's office. The large projection clock showed five past twelve. Bradshaw came suddenly to a decision.

"Jeremy, Catherine, it is high time that the BBC did its duty. It is high time that the BBC did the right thing." Peter Bradshaw turned his cool gaze first on Catherine, then on Jeremy Wexham. A look of astonishment started to flit across Wexham's face. Surely the director general was not about to turn down this opportunity?

"It is time to talk, freely. Democracy. Free speech. The BBC must stand up for that overriding principle. Jeremy, Catherine, this is a defining moment not just for us, but also for the institution of the BBC. We all need to rise to the challenge of this moment. I cannot tell either of you that this is going to be easy. The government is going to come down on us just as hard as they are able. I need to know that you are both clear on the path that we are about to choose. The path less travelled. I need to know that you both have the will to travel this path to the end."

Wexham's response was immediate.

"Absolutely, Peter! This is the story of the decade. We have the right, we have the means, and for once this government will get what's coming to it. Finally. We have waited a long time for this. No way am I going to lose my nerve now." Peter nodded his approval, slowly turned his gaze to Catherine. She rose slowly to her feet, moved towards the massive windows with feline grace. Turning, she spoke.

"Frankly, gentlemen, I'm scared. This Virus is serious. It is going to cause chaos: economic, political, social chaos. It has already started and none of us has a clue about where it is going to end. What if we are about to do the wrong thing? What if, armed with Sesame, the government could put a stop to this chaos? What if, armed with *Sesame*, some clever young hacker can crack this virus? You tell me that perhaps these debates are all these terrorists want and that anyway we cannot afford NOT to do what they ask. That we need to hedge our bets. You tell me that the debates are going to be a positive thing. A blow for free speech. That it's always our hand on the off-switch anyway." Catherine paused, as if to weigh up the arguments. Then came to a decision.

"I'm in, gentlemen. I've got reservations, but I'm going to accept the arguments you've made. I'm in the business and I believe in the business. To be absolutely honest, I'm also just too excited to let it go. I'm in, gentlemen, and I'll see it through." Peter Bradshaw, as always, appreciated Catherine's honesty, although he had never had any real doubts about her decision.

"Great, Catherine, I knew you'd do the right thing. Jeremy, bring over that draft press release and let's give it a last check. We release at two o'clock, special news bulletin, Alastair Smith on lead." Fifteen minutes later, and Peter Bradshaw was again a solitary presence in the vast and brooding room. He knew the implications of their decision. They had crossed their Rubicon. How would the attack come? Where was their weakness? He remained deep in analysis for some time.

U-Soft Video Conference: One p.m. December the Twentieth

The inner council has been joined by Brian Dempsey and Mohan Nehran. Eldon seemed more like himself.

"Gentlemen, let's focus solely on the determination and elimination of this Virus. We will not consider any other aspect of the circus, not the politics, not the economics, not the hysteria, none of it. Above all, let's keep our nerve. Let's assume that this

Virus really does kill our operating system and that the computers all stop. Let's assume we need at least two days to distribute a fix. That means we have four days, including today, to find the Virus, come up with a new kernel, and test it. Let's talk about just how we're going to do that. Carl, be as technical as you need to be. Anyone that does not follow can catch up later."

"Gentlemen, the first thing to note is that all versions of U-Sys are infected with the virus. The Virus has definitely been with us since Day One. I am afraid, therefore, that there are no safe versions of U-Sys that we can revert to. More specifically, we cannot just compare old and new kernels and see what has changed." Just exactly what they did not want to hear. Not a good start at all. A brief, pregnant pause that Mohan had to interrupt.

"Carl, surely this cannot be correct? In all these last twenty years of U-Sys, with all the dramatic advances we have made, you are telling me that the heart of our system is unchanged? How is that possible? How on earth can that have happened?" It was a fair question, at least for a layman. Mohan, however, was not a layman, and Andrew was surprised that he could be so naïve. So was Eldon.

"I will answer this. Mohan, please understand the nature of this business. Every new version of U-Sys adds new features to our software yet also makes it easier to use. The price for this magic is a loss of speed. People therefore need to buy a newer, faster computer in order to maintain an acceptable speed. They buy this new computer from our OEM customers: the people who make the computers. The end result: a better U-Sys and a shiny new computer. Everyone benefits. This is a very fine arrangement. On the other hand, a newer, faster kernel would not please our OEM customers. That would not help them sell new computers. They might just look for a new software partner. Nor would a newer, faster, *less reliable* kernel please our end-user customers. They might just look elsewhere too. So, we have made some changes to the kernel, but we have been very, very careful not to modify its inner heart. That we have kept unchanged. We might have kept it unchanged forever, were it not for this virus. Understood?" A nod. Mohan looked embarrassed. There was much to be embarrassed about, and not just his naivety. "Carl, let's move on." Carl resumed his thread.

"If the virus was new, we would have been able to find it by looking only at our new code, the code that has recently been changed. Unfortunately, since the virus has always been there, we must therefore examine all of the code. This is a good time for me to be very clear about terminology. When I say 'the code', I refer to the file of instructions that the computer reads. As you know, gentlemen, we do not work directly with this kind of code. It is not really human readable. We write our instructions in source code. Something that we can read and re-read. This is then transformed into the machine readable instructions -'the code'- by our compilers. When I say 'the source', I refer to the human readable source code." Carl paused long enough to verify that the clarification had not been necessary. Seemingly reassured, he continued.

"We have already verified that we have the correct source by compiling it to make a new kernel. The new kernel is identical to the old, therefore our source is good. That, gentlemen, is a plus." 'Really?' Andrew thought. 'Were we not even certain that we had the correct source?' Andrew would have to explore this thought later, as Carl had continued to talk.

"So what do we know of the behaviour of our virus? First of all, we know that U-Sys performance is now down by around fifty percent. We have tried looking in the source code for anything that would produce that kind of progressive performance degradation. That's a big task, because the kernel is large, extremely complex, and our source code is written in Assembler."

Carl seemed to hear the click of brains turning off. Ignoring

Eldon's warning, he quickly added a couple of lines of explanation.

"Assembler is the most basic of computer languages. It uses a set of arcane symbols that describe some of the most primitive operations of a computer chip. Basic, simple, laborious operations. Assembler code is typically a long sequence of very simple operations. The detail and the length make it very hard to follow."

Carl could see that he had everyone's attention again. And no murderous interruptions from Eldon. He pushed his luck.

"Assembler is also a skill that few nowadays have, as everyone is writing high level source code and relying on the compilers to make it work. Assembler source code is human readable but it is very basic. High level source code, however, is almost a form of plain English. Easy to read and to re-read. The compilers do so much of the work when they translate this down into code that the computer can read. I'll come back to this issue of source code. To summarise, right now we understand where we have to look, but we are still looking." No reaction, so Carl continued.

"We know that the Virus is not letting us change date, or is changing the date back. For example, on those computers that still reboot, we can change the computer date and time at power on, before our operating system kicks in. By the time the user sees the U-Sys login screen, the date has already been changed back to December the nineteenth. That means that there are calls to the 'set clock' function in the kernel. This function has a characteristic signature. We have searched for this signature in the compiled code but we cannot find it other than where we think it ought to be." Again, Carl decided to add some layman's explanation, just in case there were any listening.

"In layman's terms. There is only one way to change the computer clock. One unique sentence of instruction, if you like. We can therefore look in the code for that unique sentence." Carl was now certain that Eldon was happy for him to add his layman's guide. Because, if he didn't, he would certainly have told him by now. *Forcefully*. Beginning to relax a little, he continued.

"We have tried changing the date using all of the normal U-Sys clock functions. The date does momentarily change, but then gets set back to the correct date and time. That means that somehow the virus has set up its own internal clock. We have looked for signs of this clock in the compiled code, but again we have had no success." Andrew knew how important it was to get the date forward. That, like children, they could not wait for Christmas. They could not wait six days to find out what payload the virus contained. If the virus had set up its own clock, then that was not going to be possible. Bad news indeed. Bad news that they could not look ahead: bad news that the virus was smart enough to block them. Andrew refocused as Eldon came back with another approach.

"What about modifying the hardware?" asked Eldon.

"Hardware? In what way?"

"Change the clock/calendar timing circuitry. Change the crystal so that clock goes faster." No layman's guide was necessary. Everyone knew that the pulses of the crystal provided the ticks of the clock. A crystal with faster pulses meant more ticks. More ticks, faster time. Christmas would come sooner.

"Worth trying. I'll set up the tests, Eldon." Eldon was not finished.

"Let's also investigate changing the BIOS so that the interface to the clock is different and we take back control." Unlike Carl, Eldon did not supply a helpful explanation of the acronym. BIOS. Basic Input Output System. The way that the computer interacted with the outside world. BIOS. Alternatively, as translated from the ancient Greek: Life. In any case, Carl understood and immediately agreed.

"Done. I'll set that up too." Eldon pushed on.

"Any success in finding the text that the virus displays?"

"So far, we can find no trace of this text anywhere in the compiled code. That does not surprise us, Eldon. We are not dealing with an amateur hacker, so the text is bound to be encrypted. We are looking at various algorithms, but so far we've made no real progress." Eldon was flat, unemotional and brusque.

"If the text is encrypted, then it is a needle in a haystack. There is simply not enough text to go on. So where next, Carl?"

"We've got to look beyond the compiled code. As I mentioned earlier, we need to go back to the source. That means we need to start checking, line by line. We've examined our release logs and we do know how many lines of the kernel are unchanged, and what they are. The inner heart that Eldon referred to." A slight pause.

"In total, there are eighteen thousand and twelve lines which have not been changed." Silence, almost complete, broken only by the sound of people breathing, *deeply*. Several seconds, then Carl broke his own spell.

"It is common knowledge that the original kernel was the work of two people. As usual, the common knowledge is incorrect. The kernel was written by three people. Eldon is the biggest contributor, with twelve thousand and eight lines. Michael MacDonald contributed five thousand and forty one lines. The balance was written by Andrew Westlands." Andrew looked almost embarrassed. It was all so long ago, and he knew his work was nothing special. He was a journeyman, that was all.

"Eldon and Andrew are thankfully, still very much with us. Michael, however, left U-Soft some ten years ago. Regardless, we're going to have to check through the code line by line. Actually, not just the old code, but all the code. All of the kernel." Carl paused just long enough for Solomon to interrupt.

"Why, Carl? Surely the virus must be in the old code, not in the new code? Why do we have to check it all?"

"Because it may be in both." Eldon answered for Carl. "Because the virus may have been replicated in new code. Because a section may have been changed to GIVE it the virus. Or a different virus. Because we absolutely, utterly, cannot take the chance of any more viruses. Carl, please continue."

"We need more people, especially those with old language skills. We need more insight into the code. To be blunt, Eldon, we could really benefit from getting you at a keyboard."

"I can give you six hours a day. My assembler skills are somewhat rusty, but it's still my code - well, mostly - and it's still my company."

"Great. Morale is not what it should be and the guys could use a boost."

"Not surprised to hear it." cut in Solomon. "Whoever this is - and I'll find them - they have surely got us by the throat on this one. Surely, by the throat." Eldon cut back in, the light of battle in his alien eyes.

"I don't quite know how to put this, gentlemen, so I'll just come right out with it. U-Soft is going to emerge from this stronger than ever. Anyone not got the guts for this, anyone think we're through, let me know now." A few seconds dragged past in awkward silence. "OK. Let's assume we nail this virus. What's your test plan Carl?"

"There are several contingencies, none of them easy. Frankly, it all depends on how self-contained the Virus is. If it is a discrete block of code that we can just comment out, hell it's easy. If it's distributed, it gets a lot tougher. It's going to have to be an ad-hoc plan dependent on what we find. Seat of the pants stuff."

"Fair enough. Solomon, any leads yet on if and where Michael is?"

"Enough to get us started, boss. His life was an open book until two years ago. Until he left his wife, Karen, his three kids and went off by himself, places unknown. Vanished. Apparently, his wife thinks the world of him, kids too. Which is odd in the extreme since they've heard nothing from him in the last two years. I've spoken to all of them on the phone, and they appear to be concerned. To want to help. We'll soon see. I'm flying to Scotland today to meet them in person, get a feel for what they are not saying."

"Let me know how it goes. Otherwise, I think we've all got work to do. Andrew, I need a one-on-one. Half an hour." Eldon was gone with a click, and the meeting was over.

By one o'clock U-Soft was down twenty five per-cent in the day's unofficial trades. **Nexus** stock was up eighty per cent. OpenGUI - who supplied a similar type of operating system to U-Sys, but based on openly-published code - was up three hundred per cent.

Across Europe, the mood in the great capitals was still festive, but now laced with a hint of nerves. People gathered again in the city centre bars, but football no longer entirely dominated the discussions. There were isolated reports of attacks on mosques, but no-one yet seemed sure whom they should blame. There were isolated but persistent rumours of the involvement of an extreme eco-terrorist group, 'Paradise Lost'.

Children, sadly, went to school as normal.

In the U.S. the mood was largely sombre, although a significant minority thought the potential demise of U-Soft worth celebrating. Significant political reaction was conspicuous by its absence, although several leading political figures were rumoured to have been seen at U-Soft HQ. The President had promised an emergency statement for six o'clock Eastern Time. Generally, people expected U-Soft to come up with a fix. They always did.

The mood in Japan was strangely subdued, as if unsure if the news was good or bad.

Across Asia and South America, the mood was a complex brew: delight at the humbling of the West, but coloured by concern for their own investments.

In the teeming capitals of the Middle East, euphoria and celebration were the order of the day. Crowds flocked the streets, but the chants were unusual, especially in the world of Islam. 'Merry Christmas' rang out across Cairo, Damascus and Tehran. Beirut, more sophisticated, sang ' On the Seventh Day of Christmas...'

One thirty, and Eldon and Andrew are back in video conference, this time alone. There may have been an element of digital distortion, but somehow Andrew thought Eldon more relaxed than he ought to be. Eldon spoke first.

"Andrew, I wanted to get you before you had written today's press release. I am not too late, I trust?"

"Your trust is well placed, Eldon. I am more than ready to write it. It just seems difficult to get the peace to do so." A relaxed smile from Eldon. Why? Andrew was suspicious.

"I was hoping to announce for three o'clock. We are clear, Eldon, that I intend to fulfill my promise to our customers? That I intend to be as open with them as we both know we need to be?"

"Agreed. And not. What follows is just for you and I." Andrew felt his stomach tighten. His video image, cool and relaxed, betrayed nothing of his growing sense of unease. Andrew looked but did not respond. Eldon was not impressed.

"You need to think clearly, Andrew. To be open with our customers does not mean that we compromise our sources of information. That we cannot do, or our information will cease to flow. In order to protect our sources, the following has to be between you and I. Are we clear?" Seconds passed while trust and betrayal grappled for Andrew's heart, and head. Trust won, but narrowly.

"You worry me, Eldon, but ... agreed. We protect our sources. Anyway, source is not content." Eldon was satisfied enough to continue.

"We have heard that the BBC is planning a major statement at two o'clock. We cannot be precise about its contents, but we do know that it concerns the Christmas Virus. They know something, and it is big. I would wait until I heard what they have to say before doing anything about a press release."

"Makes sense to me. I'll wait until after their statement before I start to draft. I'll maybe aim for a conference at five, UK time. I'll copy you in before we go live."

"Not necessary, Andrew. I trust you and there is also no way I will have the time to read it." A strange expression on Eldon's face. "Tell me, old friend, how does if feel to be back at the centre of things? Did you miss the excitement?"

"Sure, Eldon. Just like I missed dying young."

As the screen blanked out, Andrew buzzed through to the redoubtable Pam.

"Yes, Andrew?"

"Time for my gin."

Pam was too experienced to hesitate.

The BBC has always known when the time is right for glamour, or for gravitas. This was, most certainly, a time for gravitas. Which was why it was the lined, patrician, features of Alastair Smith that greeted the expectant two o'clock audience. The audience was genuinely global, as the statement had been widely advertised and was being carried simultaneously on BBC One, BBC World, the major radio channels, the internet and anything else that the BBC could hook into. With luck, it would be the BBC's largest audience for many years.

Alastair Smith opened in his familiar, cultured Oxford English.

"A BBC journalist yesterday received a package which comprised a statement and a computer disk. This package purported to be from the source of the computer virus popularly known as the Christmas Virus. The statement read as follows:-

"The Christmas Virus. It is time to talk freely."
Alastair then read the entire statement slowly, carefully, dispassionately. He did allow his voice to become a little more upbeat as he reached the last few sentences.

"As I said, it is time to talk freely. People have not talked freely for a very long time. Encourage people to talk freely or I will find another resource.

Please make best use of this opportunity. Good luck."

Alastair paused, and sipped from a glass of water before he continued.

"From the password provided, we were able to correctly predict today's 'Christmas Virus' statement and our interim conclusion is that the statement is genuine. We believe that the communication has indeed come from those people responsible for the Christmas Virus. Following long and careful deliberation, the BBC are going to accede to the request and will stage the debates as requested. The BBC wish to stress that this is in no way a response to coercion or blackmail. This is a recognition that, as always, the BBC holds free speech to be of paramount importance. Free speech is one of the core elements of our democracy. A democracy that has nothing to fear, and everything to gain, from open debate. We hope that these debates will be a celebration of that democracy."

Alastair paused again. Long enough to let the audience understand the gravity of what he had just said.

"The first debate will take place tonight at nine o'clock Greenwich Mean Time. Catherine Connor will be in the chair. We are in the identification process for both participants and audience. We will issue a statement when that process is complete.

No doubt we will come under pressure from governments and security services because of the stance that we have taken. We trust that you, the public, will support us in this stance. We trust that you will help us maintain the secrecy of these codes, and to ensure that no government endangers our right to free speech. Thank you for your attention. This is Alastair Smith, from the BBC."

Across the world, a receptive silence soon gave way to a broad spectrum of emotions.

The Prime Minister expressed his in words which were initially unprintable. Several minutes later he had calmed sufficiently to call a cabinet meeting with the message:-

"It seems like the BBC intends to spend our tax-payers money on the support of terrorism. Let us see if there is any legal recourse left to us in this country."

Across the water, the President's emotions were little better, although his considered response was to call his erstwhile friend the Prime Minister. He was particularly vexed by the choice of spokesperson. Specifically, by who was to going to make the choice. The BBC was not held in high regard in Washington. Nor, for that matter, was Washington held in high regard by the BBC. The President had a bad feeling about just whom they might choose.

The great cities of Europe were abuzz with anticipation. Few knew what to expect, but clearly the entertainment value was high. Most TV stations were taking a direct feed from the BBC, and would supply real-time sub-titles or near-simultaneous translation.

Al Arabeeza promised the same. The programme was billed as 'The Trial of the West: Part One'. The fact that it would go out after midnight did little to curb the enthusiasm of the people. Some cynicism attached to the possible choice of spokesperson, but there was more trust in the BBC than people liked to admit.

The African and Indian media did not quite know what to make of the latest developments. The legacy of colonialism, curiously, did not make them suspicious of the proposed trial. They understood how oddly the British could behave, especially in pursuit of a principle. Frankly, there was nothing to lose, and everything to gain. The only worry was that somehow this was some kind of complex Western propaganda stunt, but few believed them still capable of such subtlety or precision.

Two fifteen, London, and a conspiracy of journalists huddle in the vastness of a penthouse office. The muted shadows of a bank of screens flicker on a far wall. The journalists are clustered around a vast boardroom table. At its head, the distinctive bald figure of Peter Bradshaw has just welcomed Catherine Connor, completed the introductions, and passed her the list of potential advocates for the first debate.

To her shock, Catherine sees that the list is complete! This was meant to be her show, yet has not been consulted! She struggles to swallow her shock and remain calm. Seeing her reaction, the director general starts to explain.

"For the record, Catherine, let me state some things that may be obvious yet are too important to be left unsaid. This is a unique opportunity; both for the BBC and for the World. Our audience will be global, our influence will be global. Whatever goal these terrorists may have in mind, it is in our power to turn this influence to the good. We agree it is time to talk freely. We will use free speech to defeat them." He paused and continued smoothly.

"You could not be part of the process of choosing the advocates or we would be accused of structural bias. You must be free to moderate the debates without fear or favour. In any case, it is not likely that you know too many African politicians or Middle Eastern journalists. Let me run through the choices and the basis on which they were made." A glance, a slight pause.

"Anwar Abbat is the foremost journalist in Egypt and probably the whole of the Middle East. He is committed to the Arab cause and will be a potent advocate for their constituency. We know he will be a popular choice for our Middle Eastern viewers.

'Except those in Israel.' thought Catherine. 'Still, I suppose that does make him broadly representative.'

"Krishnan Narajan is similarly pre-eminent in the Indian subcontinent. He is a distinguished anti-colonialist and a strong advocate of the knowledge economy."

"Anne Marie Sesoku you know as the former actress and former education minister for South Africa. She is known worldwide not just as a passionate champion of a free Africa, but as a practical and earthy character. She may also get us a few laughs to leaven the debates somewhat. That's something we need to remember: the audience. This is debate, but it must also be theatre. Yes, theatre. Our audience must be drawn in, amused and dazzled as well as educated. Which brings us to our fourth choice, Senator William Gladwin of the Commonwealth of Massachusetts."

Catherine resolved not to show her shock until she had time to gather her thoughts. Peter Bradshaw saw it, just the same.

"Yes, Senator Gladwin is controversial, of that there is no doubt. Senator Gladwin is not a mainstream choice, of that there is also no doubt. He is certainly known for his unconventional views on western culture and on minority rights. However, the Senator is a serious politician who has come far and is likely to go much further. He is known for his sympathies for the Third World and his desire to build bridges between the First World and the Third." The director general paused before he continued.

"Senator Gladwin is also uniquely qualified to speak on the issue of the Christmas Virus itself. He has been the official spokesperson for the Open Source Foundation for the last three years. He has advocated the open publication of computer source code long before the issue was on anyone's radar. He has campaigned for the recognition and break-up of the U-Soft monopoly for some time. Taken together, Senator Gladwin is in an ideal position to gain sufficient sympathy, worldwide, to get a hearing for the more liberal shades of Western opinion."

"Some very extreme shades of opinion!" Catherine interrupted. "What about a more representative opinion?"

"He does not represent all shades, Catherine, that is true, but he will present aspects of Western opinion and he will do so with some flair and no little theatre. In any case, the choice has been made. Let's move on to the last advocate. The representative from U-Soft. He - assuming it is a he - needs to be realistic enough not to push his party line too hard as his cause is, in any case, lost. He needs to be able to react to criticism in a sympathetic, yet positive way. Someone who can potentially win an audience, despite the weakness of his position. An employee of U-Soft, yet who will also make for good television." Bradshaw paused. He didn't have to. Catherine had already seen it coming. Bradshaw smiled.

"Yes, Catherine, we'd like to ask Andrew Westlands. Andrew projects an individual, yet sympathetic, profile that will appeal to many. He likes an audience. He is the main European P.R. for U-Soft. He was scheduled to be on your program tonight anyway. We think this to be a most fortunate set of circumstances. We are rather hoping you would be the one to ask him."

"What about the others? Have they been asked? Have they accepted? How will we get them here on time? We only have eight hours and most of them are coming a long way, surely?"

"They have already accepted and they are already here. The BBC still has friends of influence in the world, Catherine. More, I might add, outside this country than inside. I digress. What do you think, Catherine? Can you deliver Mr. Westlands?"

"I presume, Director, that I will be confirmed chairwoman for the duration of the debates?"

"Absolutely, Catherine. In writing, if you want."

"I do want. Yes, I will approach Andrew Westlands." She could not resist it. She ran her fingers theatrically though her hair and added "But I can promise nothing. After all, I am only a woman." Laughter broke the tension and the meeting ended on a high. Catherine did, however, keep some dark thoughts to herself.

The BBC statement was a bombshell and Andrew was still considering its implications when the call came in. Intuition overcame reluctance, and Pam put it through. Andrew was, surprisingly, happy to take the call.

"Catherine? I do hope you're not about to renege on our dinner appointment? Given your latest project, there may not be many chances left for you to dine with me. Not in this life, anyway." Andrew thought he sensed a smile, but perhaps not. Maybe a little too flippant?

"Andrew, actually I may just make dinner but the idea was that you would ask after the debate, not before. The reason I called is that while the debate is still on, it will now be a little different. It will now be the first of several, and you may just get the chance to embrace a little danger yourself. We'd like you to be one of the advocates. I can't think of anyone better to represent U-Soft, can you?"

It was obvious, and Andrew had seen it coming. There was no threat to his gin, which despite his reputation, was still almost full. However, he still took several seconds before he spoke. In an altogether different tone, as if it were a different Andrew entirely.

"It's a lot to give up. The anonymity, I mean. Anyone who appears on this is going to be famous, really startlingly, permanently, controversially famous."

"Seductive, isn't it?" Catherine asked, in a way that was more quiet statement than question.

"Seductive? Absolutely the right word, Catherine. Yes, seductive. Like the lure of sirens. Seductive, but deadly. Your anonymity gone for ever. You'll never be able to leave the house without swarms of paparazzi following you everywhere…"

" …Unless I'm in disguise, Andrew. Well, I've always loved dressing up…"

"What, the floppy hat, overcoat and thick glasses routine, Catherine? I rather think it's not you…"

" …and it's so last year, Andrew. No, I've always fancied a burka. Black, full-length, just the tiniest of eye slits. Designer, of course. You might want to think of one yourself, Andrew, You wouldn't be the first…."

"…Nor the last, Catherine, I'm sure. And under the burka, I wear what?"

"In your case, Andrew, make-up. Lots of it. And you will have to do something about the eyebrows." Andrew had to smile. She was smart, and fun. Unfortunately, he also had to keep trying.

"But let's be serious, Catherine. Because it's going to be. No more slipping into a corner pub for a quiet drink. No more vague wandering through town on a Saturday afternoon. Every visit to a restaurant or theatre or cinema becomes an exercise in stealth. No sure way to be private save to retreat behind the high walls like the rest of the poor celebrities. It's bad enough my venturing out, I'm a male who's seen lots of life and am certainly no oil painting. It's much worse for a glamorous young woman who might just want to spend the odd day in denims and bad hair." He should have quit earlier.

"Thanks for the advice, Andrew. And can you tell me why, exactly, you think I am still sixteen years old?" He really should have quit earlier: now it was apology time. For Andrew, an all too familiar routine.

"Forgive me, Catherine, that was stupid. You're no fool and you don't need me to tell you the blindingly obvious. Of course you've thought about it because you already deal with it every day. But it's going to get worse. No way back from this." Despite herself, Catherine's heart did sink just a little. She had not really wanted to consider that fame could be so negative. Nor had she found it so negative thus far, but then again she was not A-list. Mostly, Catherine's heart also sank because she dreaded a refusal. A refusal might meant U-Soft provide some corporate cyborg in his place. The kind of corporate cyborg that intoned teamwork and diversity and recycling and 'act local think global' and all the empty slogans of the age. A corporate cyborg that would deal death to the ratings. The debate, hell, the SHOW, had to be right.

"On the other hand, it's an opportunity to get some truth out there. An opportunity to say some things that probably most of my colleagues cannot say because they are too young to know or they now have too much to lose. The fame will be a pain. Saying things some people don't want to hear may be more painful yet." Another pause wrapped Catherine in doubt and yet more confusion. "Of course, there is also the prospect of dinner with your sweet self." Catherine struggled against the unexpected smile. "I am delighted to accept the BBC's offer on behalf of both myself and U-Soft. I look forward to the opportunity and to the audience."

Catherine breathed out slowly, more relieved than she would have expected. 'Why?' she wondered, briefly, before she brought the call to its conclusion.

"Great, Andrew. I am sure you will not regret this. Now, the practicalities of the arrangements. We will send a car to pick you up. All the advocates will be coordinated to arrive at the BBC at the same time. Preparation time, that is make-up and briefing, will be almost zero. Be ready to go from the moment you step outside the car. Understand that I will not, cannot, do you any favours. Good luck."

Somehow, that last statement made Andrew feel a little threatened. Mostly, however he felt an enormous surge of anticipation, and excitement. There was also much to consider, and it was five minutes before he had Pam place the conference call to Eldon.

Catherine also spent a quiet five minutes. The call was more thought provoking than she had expected. Andrew was more thought provoking than she expected.

It took twenty minutes for Pam to summon Eldon's image to the video screen. Eldon wasted no time.

"I already know."

"Know what?"

"Your invitation to the debate. You're off the press statement and on to preparation for the debate. That's not negotiable." Andrew was simultaneously angry, yet chilled.

"How? When? Didn't you think to warn me?"

"We only found out when you did. It's not *you* that's under surveillance, Andrew. Let's just say we have some people in the BBC who like to practise their reporting skills. Some of those people have expensive habits and some of those habits are not exactly legal. Of course, that is only speculation on my part."

"Of course, Eldon. Only speculation." Andrew was, however, a little mollified. "Talking about speculation, Eldon, what progress have we made on the main issue, this damned virus? Any ideas on what this '*Sesame*' program tells us?"

"Let's deal with *Sesame* first. This has either been written by the author of the Virus or by someone who knows what the Virus is. I'm deeply puzzled as to why *Sesame* exists. Who gains from these debates, trials, call them what you will? What is the BBC's role in all this? Intriguing, yes. Very intriguing. However, I think that we need to keep our focus on the author of the virus, because that remains the key. On that, I have now come to a conclusion." Eldon stopped and locked eyes with Andrew.

"I believe that, somehow, the virus is the work of that crazy red-head. Michael MacDonald. Michael had the opportunity, and, God knows, he had the ability. He could have written both the Virus and *Sesame*. More to the point, who else could it be? You, Andrew?" If it was a serious question, Andrew did not react. Eldon did not seem to expect a reaction, as he continued regardless.

"That's the real difficulty. It may have been someone outside U-Soft, but how? Most unlikely. No, Michael is the obvious suspect. Combine that with the existence of *Sesame*, and it suggests to me that there is a fix to the Virus which is not too disruptive. Something that everyone can do. Something that can be seen to be the fulfillment of this bargain that has been made with the BBC. Whomever wrote *Sesame* has to be in contact with your glamorous Catherine..."

"My glamorous Catherine? I wish!"

"...in communication through e-mail. That gives us a handle to work with. We need those e-mail addresses and we WILL get them."

"What about our own investigations? If I'm going to defend us, I need to know where we are! I need to have something to defend us with!"

"I will inform you if and when we have something significant. As I promised I would. You need to trust me, Andrew. Not keep second guessing."

"Point taken, Eldon. I'm listening."

"Thus far, there is no progress worth discussing." A silence that spoke of finality. The matter was closed. When it was clear that Andrew understood, perfectly, Eldon continued.

"Now, let's talk about the debate. U-Soft stock is now officially suspended on all world markets. Not that it matters very much, since most markets are now closed anyway. The bottom line is that you are pretty much free to say whatever you like tonight. So say it, and slay 'em dead. But watch out for the blonde."

"I'll slay 'em provided they don't slay me first. And, for the record, if I have to be slain, I'd rather it was by the blonde."

43

Eldon had already clicked off. Andrew gazed at the now-blank screen for a minute or so. 'What are you not telling me?' he wondered.

At five o'clock GMT the BBC made another newsflash. All broadcasts were interrupted by the stern figure of Alastair Smith, who read as follows:-

"This is an announcement from the BBC.
At nine o'clock this evening the BBC will host an international debate. The motion for the debate will be :-
The West is guilty of foolishness, greed and disregard for the future
The context of the debate will be the dominant market position of the U-Soft corporation, especially in the light of 'The Christmas Virus'.
The format of the debate will be as follows :-
There will be five speakers, whom we will term 'advocates'. Each advocate will make a short presentation and will then be subject to questions from the other advocates. The total time, including presentation and questions, that any advocate may speak is ten minutes. Once he (or she) has used his allotted time he will not be permitted to speak further in the debate, but will remain in the studio for the duration of the broadcast.
After the last round of questions the audience will be given a short period of reflection and will then be asked to vote on the motion. A formal count and announcement - the verdict - will then be made.
After the verdict, we will announce the motion for the next debate. This motion will be as exclusively revealed to the BBC by the 'Sesame' computer programme.
These debates will continue for the next several days.
Each advocate agrees to waive all rights of redress in respect of

alleged slander or conduct made during the course of the debate. Each advocate further agrees not to be interviewed nor to publish any articles until the BBC agrees that the series of debates has finished.

The chair of the debate will go to Catherine Connor, presenter of the BBC's 'News and Views' programme. The chairwoman will have the power to interrupt a speaker, and to take such measures as she sees fit, including suspension, to ensure that debates are conducted in a productive manner. Nevertheless, all advocates will be encouraged to speak openly and directly without regard to prevalent taboos.

The advocates will be as follows :-

Mr Anwar Abbat, Egypt.

Dr Anne Marie Sesoku, Africa.

Dr Krishnan Narajan, India.

Mr Andrew Westlands, Vice-President P.R., U-Soft Corporation.

Senator William Gladwin, the United States of America.

Thank you for attention. This is Alastair Smith from the BBC."

Worldwide, most people reacted to the advocate list with excitement and anticipation. In the United States, however, the appointment of Senator William Gladwin filled many of his countrymen with an acute sense of dread.

At eight o'clock, Catherine received the e-mail she had been waiting for. Gingerly, she inserted the *Sesame* CD into her computer and started the program. With exaggerated care, she typed and re-typed the password the e-mail had provided. Finally pressed the enter key. The screen cleared and a simple screen of text appeared. The last three sentences starkly identified the motion for the next debate:-

The West is guilty of the destruction of their heroes. The West is guilty of the promotion of weakness over strength. The West is guilty of failure to provide inspiration to their young.

'Just what have I got myself into?' Catherine asked herself, and made her way to make-up.

It had been a long flight, but it was excitement, not fatigue that illumined the face of Ahmed Ali Khan. His long form lay sprawled across a massive hotel bed. A huge bed, laid with the luxury that marked his hotel as five star, not four. Satin drapes framed a large, deep, bay window. On the left of the wall facing Ahmed was a large reproduction desk of walnut veneer and distressed green leather. On the centre of its elegant surface was a large Dell laptop, its display locked to the unmistakable U-Mail screen. To the right of the laptop was a large plasma television, and it was this which fixed Ahmed's gaze. The television was tuned to BBC World, and the debate was about to begin. The local time was nine fifty nine.

THREE

The lady in the mirror was not easy to impress. She stared steadily at Catherine, her assessment slow and careful. Light blue trouser suit by Donna Karan, pass. High-cut blouse by Yves Saint Laurent, pass. High-heels by Jimmy Choo, pass. Perfume by Chanel, pass. Hair by Raymond, pass. Face and figure by good genes and hard work, pass. The lady in the mirror smiled: Carpe Diem. Seize the day: yes, Catherine was indeed ready to seize the day.

Fifteen minutes later, at nine o'clock precisely, the first debate began. Catherine stood at a dais which faced the left of a seated audience of precisely one hundred. The audience was statistically representative of the adult British population. To most people that made it look odd, unusual, like something you would have seen many years ago. To Catherine's left, the five advocates were standing behind a narrow wooden table, long enough to provide each of them not just with space, but a hint of isolation. Above each advocate was a large motionless clock timer, hands frozen at ten minutes.

"Ladies and Gentlemen, welcome to the BBC. I am honoured tonight to be with you at a unique and historic moment in broadcasting history. Tonight we have the chance to start a debate which will be heard across the entire world. Tonight we have the chance to debate the first of the charges that have been made against the people of the West. Tonight we have the chance to demonstrate the power of free speech. Tonight we have the chance to make, and to change, history. Let us make the most of this chance. The motion before us is: *The West is guilty of foolishness, greed and disregard for the future*. I would like to now introduce our five advocates. William Gladwin, the senior

U.S. Senator for the Commonwealth of Massachusetts." William Gladwin was a tall, distinguished looking man dressed in an expertly cut three piece suit of dark blue, with a contrasting yellow silk tie and matching pocket handkerchief. His brown hair was flecked with grey, long enough to be worn swept back from his forehead. His clean-shaven face was deeply tanned, masking the many fine lines around his eyes and on his cheeks.

"Krishnan Narajan, the distinguished Indian physicist and journalist." Krishnan Narajan was a small, thin, ascetic looking man of perhaps seventy, dressed in a grey Nehru jacket, loose white cotton trousers and light sandals. His fine Brahmin features were topped by an impressively thick mane of silver hair. Despite his age, few lines marked his face, but those that did somehow hinted at an expression of mild disapproval. His large brown eyes were almost hidden by a pair of heavy-framed bi-focals.

"Andrew Westlands, the British face of the U-Soft corporation." Andrew was wearing a white linen suit, open collar black shirt, and brown cowboy boots. His still-handsome features looked worn enough to be interesting. His hair, though still too long, had at least been smoothed back and away from his face.

"Anwar Abbat, from Egypt, one of the most influential and widely respected journalists in the Middle East." Anwar Abbat was a powerful looking man of perhaps forty, dressed in a casual dark blue suit, open necked white shirt, black Oxford shoes. His bull neck and bulging shoulders were testament to the Olympic wrestling career of his recent past. His features were thick, sensual, and powerful, framed by a black beard. His black hair was tightly cropped. His look and bearing spoke of challenge, and combat, and a little of contempt.

"Anne Marie Sesoku, former actress, former education minister for South Africa and the current head of World in Hunger." Anne Marie Sesoku was a tall, striking looking woman, impossibly slim, impossibly black. She wore a long African style sleeveless dress of bright reds and yellows. Her hair was worn high, accentuating her long neck and the hint of a deep cleavage. Her face had been sculpted on classical lines, a long straight nose and the highest of cheekbones. Accentuated, as no doubt by intent, by the two tribal lines. They were two inches long, and ran down, exotic, from the top of both cheekbones. Long looped earrings matched the golden circlets around her neck. Anne Marie was officially forty five, but she looked at least ten years younger.

As they had been instructed, the five advocates sat down at the end of the introductions. Catherine moved on to outline the format of the debates.

"Each advocate will make a presentation and will then respond to questions from the other advocates. Presentations and questions will be made in sequence, starting from the left of the audience. Tonight, therefore, Senator Gladwin will make the first presentation, and will then respond to questions from Krishnan through to Anne Marie. Krishnan will then make his presentation and so on. The sequence was chosen at random and will continue to be chosen at random for all future debates. Each advocate is allowed to speak for a total of ten minutes, including his presentation, questions and answers. The clocks above the heads of the advocates will show their time remaining. The clock will start to flash to warn the advocate when he has reached the last thirty seconds. When an advocate has no time left, he cannot speak further or he will be expelled from both this debate and the entire sequence of debates." Catherine doubted they could enforce this clause, but also doubted that anyone would have the nerve to call their bluff.

"This is a unique opportunity, and a unique responsibility. Let us use it wisely." Catherine paused, giving the statement effect. "Ladies and gentlemen, our first advocate, Senator William Gladwin."

The Senator rose smoothly to his feet and paused for a moment to regard his audience. He was, by any standards, an impressive figure. Six foot three or four, slim, athletic build, thick brown, grey-flecked hair swept back from a face that belied his fifty one years. Clear brown eyes gazed steadily at the audience.

"First of all, ladies and gentlemen, let me say what an honour it is to have been chosen to represent the United States of America in this unique debate. No, let me say more, what an honour it is to represent all the citizens of this planet on this unique occasion. Before I move to the heart of this debate, before I move to consider the central allegation against the West, let me consider the simpler issue that we face today. Tax."

A wave of baffled expressions swept across the audience. '*MADMAN*', Catherine thought. It was the game she played. A means to maintain her professional detachment. When someone appeared on one of her shows they forfeited their real identity, became just characters in her play. As they spoke, so they defined their characters. Stereotypes, like cards from a Tarot deck. Gladwin's first words said *MADMAN*. Still it was early, and the Senator had started to continue.

"Tax. U-Soft Tax. We've been paying U-Soft Tax for twenty years and we're not going to pay it anymore! Let us all say it together. Out loud. 'We're not going to pay it any more!" The entire studio was now riveted on the Senator as he continued to gather pace.

"We've made these guys" - here he made a vague gesture in the direction of Andrew - "rich. Fabulously, outrageously, obscenely rich. Please, I beg of you, whatever else we decide here let's decide to end this now. Let's say it. WE'RE NOT GOING TO PAY IT ANYMORE!" This was Britain, and the BBC, and people just did not do that. But, Catherine thought, some of them looked like they weren't too far away. The few murmurs that she heard were, in their own way, hugely impressive. Outside the studio, in the warmer parts of the world, people were a little less inhibited. In the bars and souks and village squares, people stood up and cheered. A few even echoed "WE'RE NOT GOING TO PAY IT ANYMORE!" The senator lowered his tone an octave and continued.

"U-Soft people are going to tell you that you still need them. They're going to tell you that your tax is necessary. That they are only making an honest living. Hell, that's what they've been telling us all the last twenty tax filled years. And where are we now? Our computers have a virus and they are not sure how to fix it. We are going to hell in a handcart and there is nothing they can do!" Gladwin indulged his anger, letting his voice rage loud around the studio, then lowered his voice.

"And yet, the strangest thing. ladies and gentlemen. A glimmer of hope." The Senator paused, waited for the tension to build. 'Not madman,' Catherine thought. 'PREACHER.' Gladwin returned to his congregation.

"We have heard that U-Soft will announce tomorrow that they will test our emulators, in the hope that we have the key to fix their Virus. Emulators: you are probably asking yourselves what are emulators? Let me explain to you what I mean by emulators. We of the Open Source Foundation make an operating system that competes with U-Sys. We call it UNOS. Unified Network Operating System. But U-Soft have such a stranglehold on the market, that no-one will write software for UNOS. Virtually all popular software will run on U-Sys, and only U-Sys. That means that no-one can even start to compete with them. So, our people have come up with a very clever piece of software that *emulates* U-Sys. It makes a UNOS computer look and work like U-Sys. Pretend to be U-Sys, if you like. You can then run your usual software on a UNOS computer and it will not even know the difference. I am not the world's most technical man, so I hope what I've just said makes some sense to you?"

It did. Catherine was impressed. Not just a preacher, perhaps. Gladwin waited for the inevitable nods of agreement, then forged on.

"So, let me repeat. U-Soft will announce tomorrow that they will test our emulators. They hope that our software will run your programs without any sign of a virus. U-Soft people are now testing our products, our FREE products, in the reasonable expectation that we can fix their Virus. What did we pay our tax for? How did this ever happen? How are they going to compensate us?" A long pause, fertile ground for the growing anger. 'JUSTICE' Catherine thought. 'In the Tarot, his card would be justice.' As if on cue, Gladwin offered his judgment.

"Ladies and gentlemen, radical times require radical solutions. I think we have all had enough of U-Sys. Enough of their tax and their failures. I propose that we now make all fundamental computer software, the operating systems, open source products under international supervision. I propose that these key, strategic resources be placed under the control of the United Nations. I propose that all U-Soft source code, cash and assets be immediately given to the United Nations to provide not just compensation, but the means for us all to move forward from this. I propose that from the ruins of U-Soft we create an independent global software company, committed not to profit, but to world progress!"

Even in Britain, despite the reserve, if you hit the right chords then you will get a response. And Gladwin had. The audience rose in a thunder of applause, loud, raucous, and enduring. However, the Senator refused to milk it, but gestured to the audience to calm down, and raised his voice once again.

"Now we come to the central charge. That the West has been greedy and foolish and short-sighted. That the West, who gave us the colonial rape of Africa, of India, of South America, of most of the world, has been greedy. That the West that gave us two world wars, Korea, Vietnam, Iraq, has been foolish? That the West that gave us the atomic bomb, the hydrogen bomb, the neutron bomb, has been short-sighted? Ladies and gentlemen, do we have any time to waste on something so obvious? Let us say the word. GUILTY! Come on, say it with me. GUILTY!"

Unbelievably, many in the audience did. It started with a few, bolder souls, but others, encouraged by the swelling numbers, overcame their hesitation and joined them. Outside the audience, hesitation was not an issue. Millions, tens of millions of mouths took up the chant 'GUILTY'. Nodding in approval, it seemed that the Senator could, somehow, hear their chant. He gestured for silence again.

"I have no time to waste here, so let me quickly move on. The issue of guilt is beyond doubt. The issue that remains is compensation. Until it is addressed, the issue of compensation will never go away. I say that the time to address it is NOW!" As if suddenly aware of the anger in his voice, Gladwin lowered his tone, smoothed its edges.

"Let us dream that we have the grace, the honesty to face up to our responsibilities. Let us dream that the nations of the West admit their guilt and pay adequate compensation for their crimes. Let us dream of a great liberating force taking shape across the world. Wealth being used for good, and not for evil. That we meet to resolve these great injustices that still stain our history. That we meet in a great conference. A conference to resolve the issue of compensation. Compensation for the sins of history. Ladies and gentlemen, let me give you the title of that conference. *The Sins of History*. It is time for the West to confess those sins. It is time to unburden ourselves of our guilt. It is time to offer redress to our victims. Ladies and gentlemen, there will be no losers at this conference. We will lose our guilt. AND OUR GUILT CAN SET THEM FREE!" Roaring out the last sentence, Gladwin was finished, and sat down.

It was perhaps a little too far for the studio audience, but rapturous applause echoed around many parts of the world. Roars of approval rang from Cairo to Delhi, from Lagos to Rio. But not in the West. In Washington and London, in Berlin, Paris and in Madrid, the proclamation was met with a stunned silence. In the Fall River Diner, Massachusetts, the animated crowd of Gladwin's constituents was utterly stilled. Their silence was finally broken by a 'Huh?'

'DEMAGOGUE' Catherine thought. Yes, her first character was now revealed. Demagogue. The studio was still in shock, disbelief, confusion. How had they come so far, so fast? How far were they prepared to go? Catherine gave them ten seconds or so, but she had to move them on.

"May I remind you, ladies and gentlemen, that there will now be a chance for the other advocates to question the speaker. Questions will proceed according to the same sequence as the presentations. Dr Narajan, would you like to start the round of questions?"

Dr Narajan had a studious, scholarly air that spoke of his background in physics. He had only moved to journalism when age dulled some of the brilliance which had brought him his fame. Dr Narajan carefully removed his glasses.

"I applaud this man. I salute this man. Namaste." Narajan extended to the Senator the traditional Hindu greeting. "A wonderful presentation, Senator, and an act of great courage. Thank you. Since I welcome your suggestions, my questions are largely practical. How would this conference be organised? And who would be responsible for its organisation? Would you expect the conference to take place under the auspices of the United Nations?" Gladwin was quick to reply.

"Indeed, Krishnan, it would. Is this not what the United

Nations was created to do? As to how it would be organised? Each government will appoint a small team of lawyers and negotiators to represent them. These representatives will sit down together, for as long as it takes, to thrash out an agreement. They will sit and talk, but they will not talk forever, because we, the people, will not let them. It will be our force, the force of public opinion that will drive them to a rapid resolution."

"Thank you, Senator Gladwin. I will not use up your valuable time further." replied Narajan, and sat back.

"Mr Abbat?" prompted Catherine. Anwar leaned forward and looked directly at the Senator. There was nothing explicit in his expression, or his body language, but somehow Anwar exuded menace as he spoke.

"I am sure that many people are happy to have heard your words, Senator. Forgive me, for I am just old enough to be a little cynical. You offer us much but you are not in a position to fulfil what you offer."

"Not yet," cut in the Senator.

"Indeed," replied Anwar, "yet I would like to explore what you offer. According to what law would these 'representatives' reach agreement? American law? British law? Some new set of laws?"

"We already have a strong framework of international law. Would this not be an ideal platform to build from?"

"For me, Senator, perhaps. But you know that for many of my people that would not be satisfactory. For many of my people there can be only one law. Sharia law. The Law of Islam. I think, Senator, that this will present you with a very great difficulty." Stark, uncompromising. In a stroke, the mood was shattered. Senator Gladwin was an old pro, and moved quickly to recover the situation.

"Of course, there will be some issues to work through, Anwar, but, with good will, we can do this. Justice remains justice, regardless of the system."

Catherine waited a few seconds, but Anwar did not reply and the exchange was over. She prompted for the next questions.

"Mr Westlands?"

"Senator, I applaud you too. Quite a performance. I'm not going to go to the big question - the West - just yet, because I'm still puzzled by your first point, the, em, U-Soft Tax?"

"Your brain's probably addled with counting it all." quipped the Senator, to laughter. Andrew generously shared the joke and joined in the laughter. Undeterred, he then continued to his next question.

"As far as I understand what you're saying Senator, we're going to be replaced by some kind of official world software development company? Do I have that right?"

"Right. It's not so difficult, really just an extension of the good work some people are already doing."

"So, this company - foundation? - is started with U-Soft money, along the lines of some agreement that will be hammered out by lawyers?"

"Yes."

"Lawyers, OK. Who better to decide the fate of the world's key technology?" Andrew delivered the question with heavy irony. Gladwin declined to react.

"And this foundation continues to develop software, and to make it universally available, free of charge? Right? This foundation will continue to develop and innovate for the foreseeable future?"

"Yes, and for the greater good, not just to line some rich pockets."

"I'm sure. But I'm concerned about the funding. Who is going to pay for this foundation in the future? Just how will it be funded in the years to come?"

"The foundation is going to start with a great deal of money. However, it is a fair point. To be responsible, we will also have to have some kind of additional funding to cover contingencies. I would imagine there would be some kind of a levy, perhaps at a governmental level."

"A levy? You mean a tax, right? Instead of a U-Soft tax, we get an Open Source Tax, right?"

"Well, at least we know where the money is going, Mr Westlands, and it will not be to you."

"Yes, I'm struggling with that bit, Senator, I can't deny it." said Andrew shaking his head ruefully. "My croupiers will be too. And my ex-wives. Hell, that is a scary thought, because, believe me, you do not want to upset *them*." said Andrew, shaking his head in mock consternation. Some of the audience could not resist a chuckle. Andrew waited until the chuckles had died away.

"So it does seem like we will be paying tax, after all. That's why I'm really struggling with the bit where we all say 'WE'RE NOT GOING TO PAY IT ANYMORE!'"

Andrew's timing was always impeccable. Somehow, no-one had quite seen it coming. At least ten seconds ticked away before he repeated "WE'RE NOT GOING TO PAY IT ANYMORE!" Another five long seconds before Andrew continued.

"And yet it seems we are. Taxes, like death, are inevitable after all. Well, it sounded good, even it turned out to be complete and utter nonsense. I guess that's politicians for you, ladies and gentlemen. I'm finished, Catherine." and Andrew sat back. The Senator shook his head sadly at how his words had been twisted.

"Hell, I'd forgotten how smart you software guys are. It's just a pity you're not quite smart enough to find a cure for the virus. You're not fooling anyone, Andrew. No-one is going to put their head back into a U-Soft noose again." The opening point was a cheap shot, and would have been better left unsaid. The second part, however, was difficult to argue with. Andrew merely smiled. Catherine paused long enough to be sure the exchange was over. 'LAWYER' she thought. 'Perhaps Andrew is to be the lawyer?

Time for Gladwin's last questions.'

"We now come to the final question for the Senator. Ms Sesoku?"

"Anne Marie will do fine. And I'm going to call the rest of my new colleagues by their first names too. All right?" Anne Marie beamed a megawatt smile at the audience and none of the four other advocates was foolish enough to object. Nor wanted to, particularly.

"I too applaud the Senator's sentiments. Admirable. Wonderful. It would be fantastic if the West was finally made to confront and atone for its sins. To accept its punishment. And that gives me one question for the Senator. Is he suggesting that the West's punishment be purely monetary, or does he have some additional punishments in mind?" Silence. The silence of very deep water, and strong currents. 'Run silent, run deep' thought Catherine. Dispelling the silence, the Senator rose to the challenge.

"Believe me, Anne Marie, for the West, money is punishment enough."

The first round was over, and it had not disappointed. Catherine knew that even Peter Bradshaw could not be disappointed with such a start. It had drama, and theatre. A spell was being woven, and now was not the time to break it. She prompted for the next speaker.

"Dr Narajan, the floor is yours." Dr Narajan rose slowly to his feet. He had no notes in his hands. The Senator was a hard act to follow, but Narajan started well.

"Ladies and gentlemen, I am a child of the Raj. I grew up under the British Empire. I detested it then and I detest the memory of it now. Today is a very great day for me. Today is the first day I can really dare hope that the imperialists will be made to pay for what they did. I hope and I pray that compensation will be paid as the Senator himself has admitted it must be. I do not know when, but I hope it will come. I know that there are great many substantial issues between now and that day, but still, I hope it will come. I know that it must be a long road, but we have now taken the first step." Narajan paused and took a deep breath.

"However, in the meantime there is much we can do. There are practical measures we can take. Let us consider the issue of the U-Soft corporation. What is the U-Soft corporation? The U-Soft corporation is an instrument by which the West continues to rule us all. What is U-Soft but the ultimate expression of Western economic colonialism?" Narajan looked around the audience as he posed the question, but no-one responded. It was not his audience yet, so he went back to work.

"We have had no choice but to buy U-Soft products. As William had so succinctly put it, U-Soft has imposed a tax on us all. This tax has been paid to this man Westlands and to many like him. We must move now to complete the destruction of U-Soft. We must move now to create an independent software company devoted to the welfare of the world. I am in a privileged position today. As you no doubt all know, the principal economy of India is the knowledge economy. India has more programmers than any other country in the World. I know that I speak for all Indians when I say that we would be proud to put those resources to this great project."

Narajan's approach was different. Not Gladwin's quick flame of passion, but the slow burn of reason. Catherine could not help but listen as Narajan articulated his arguments, carefully, precisely, effectively. TEACHER. She had her second character. TEACHER. But then, against herself, she found her attention start to switch to the audience. The signs were starting to show. 'He's beginning to lose them' she thought. But she should not have doubted him, for his timing was good. At just the right moment, the magic word 'finish' snapped everyone back.

"Ladies and gentlemen, it is time to finish. It goes without saying that I support this motion and consider the West guilty of the charges. But I do not want to end on a negative note. Let's look at the positive: the new operating system. I am a Hindu and Hindus attach great significance to names. We believe that, in the right language, at a certain level, a name is more than just a description. It is the object itself. A name must be *right*. We need the right name for this great project. I would humbly like to suggest 'FreeOS'. FreeOS. The Free Operating System. The Operating System of The Free." Narajan paused and looked around his audience. He had hit the mark, but was not quite finished.

"Yes, ladies and gentlemen, this is about freedom. Freedom from U-Soft, certainly. But more than that. Freedom from the economic bonds of the West. Good people of the West, I hope you will help to set us free. Thank you."

It was well done, very well done. The applause was loud, and long, but Catherine sensed something was not quite right. The emphasis had been slightly wrong. Something had been missing. That was it: he did not come back to the issue of the Sins of History. 'He has no faith in it.' she thought. 'He does not believe that the West is going to part with one dollar. Why? What else is the physicist not saying?' Catherine waited until the applause had died down before she started the new round of questions.

"William, your questions?" The Senator was momentarily taken aback to lose his title.

"There is nothing I need to ask. Krishnan and I seem to be on the same wavelength." The Senator was acutely conscious that his talk clock was not healthy, and knew he'd need time for Andrew. And, probably, for Anwar too. Anne Marie he had no clue about. In fact, with ninety seconds left, his contributions now would have to be very carefully weighed.

"Andrew?" A puzzled look crept over Andrew's face as he turned towards Narajan. It reminded Catherine of the television detective with the bad clothes and the razor brain. Andrew's tone reflected his evident puzzlement.

"Forgive me, Krishnan, but I'm having too much trouble with some of the details to able to see the larger picture. Let me see if you can help me with my questions. I presume you know, Krishnan, that U-Soft is the world's largest employer of Indian programmers, both in India and in the U.S. Are you proposing that the same programmers who write for U-Soft go to FreeOS and do much the same thing?" A nod of confirmation.

"Why not? They have the skills and the knowledge. FreeOS would get off to a wonderful start."

"Then what makes you think that would make the cost of development any cheaper? Specifically, why would the FreeOS tax be any less than the U-Soft tax? Governments have a long and noble tradition of inefficiency. What if FreeOS actually costs more?"

"We are absolutely confident that we would be more efficient than a company such as U-Soft. Look at the vast bonuses and obscene wages that you pay. Who would not be more efficient?"

"It really is a funny old world, Krishnan, because we pay those wages and bonuses precisely because it makes us more efficient. We pay them to get the best work from the best programmers. In fact, we pay a lot of these wages and bonuses to Indian programmers. Which brings me to my last question. Given that you are going to pay them less, what makes you think our programmers would want to join you?" Narajan has seen the question coming, but just a little too late. He did, however, have some kind of answer ready.

"Perhaps they too would like to see the demise of the West?" Andrew looked coolly at Narajan, who was already starting to regret his remark as a little foolish, a little petulant. On the other hand, the issue was now out on the table. Who did *not* want to see the demise of the West? Andrew was content to let the silence build, until Catherine broke it before it went bad.

"Anwar?" Anwar Abbat sat forward then seemed to change his mind and sat back.

"No questions. I'm going to need all my time later."

"Anne Marie?"

"I have a simple question, Krishnan. Do you know how many African programmers there are in the world?" The question was unexpected. Narajan, to his credit, answered honestly, and quickly.

"No, Anne Marie, I don't know but I suspect the number is low."

"I don't either, Krishnan, but I know the number must be low because what else could it be when we do not have enough food never mind computers? Of course it's low!" Anne Marie rolled her eyes in impatience. "But do you think we are happy for it to remain low? Do you think that we do not look ahead to our time? The time of the *African Programmer*? Think about that, Krishnan." Narajan was stung, but offered no reply. Whose side was she on?

It did not take Catherine's feminine intuition to know this was compulsive viewing. It was definitely her feminine intuition, however, that rang alarm bells as she glanced across at Andrew's face. 'Don't blow it, Andrew' she thought, but obviously her concern was purely professional.

"Andrew, the floor is yours." Andrew rose slowly to his feet. His bearing was relaxed, his expression was pleasant, but his heart was racing.

"First of all, ladies and gentlemen, I'd like to apologise to everyone for the disruption caused by the Christmas Virus. Whoever or whatever is the source of the Virus, we at U-Sys are ultimately responsible. We will resolve this virus and we will do our best to ensure it never happens again." Andrew gazed steadily at the audience for several seconds before he continued.

"Ladies and gentlemen, I'd like to take you back to some recent history. Indulge me for a couple of minutes and I promise you I will then address the fascinating issues my fellow advocates have raised." Andrew paused again.

"Let me take you back twenty years. Three hungry men working in a window-less office in the bad end of town. Three men driven by the same dream. To create a piece of software so good that it would change the world. To write a piece of software that would make computers work better, period. Any which way we could do it. It was a blue-sky project: we got to define the problem, to decide what solutions were the most elegant, then to make them work. As Eldon said -'not programmers, but artists in silicon'. Three artists driven by the same passion, working on the same canvas. Two geniuses with me in the middle to stop them from killing each other." A wry smile.

"Yes, I was one of those men. Three men fuelled on coffee and cigarettes and passion. Three men battling against all the mighty computer corporations of that day." A slight pause.

"Let me take you back ten years. The three men are now a thousand. Now it's not coffee and cigarettes and code, it's strategy and market share and leverage. It's still about winning the game. More rules and less creativity, I might add, but still the same dream." 'DREAMER' Catherine thought. 'Is this his character?' Unhearing, Andrew continued.

"Let me take you to now. The three men are now ten thousand. It's not coffee and cigarettes and code, it's compatibility and legacy and viruses. It's lawyers and politics and regulations. I was there. I am still here. I've seen it all. The highs and lows, the triumphs and disasters. Twenty years of ferocious, relentless, competition. Quite a time." 'Quite a story' thought Catherine. 'But where is it going?' Andrew took it further.

"Were we foolish and greedy? Sure, and so were the competition. Did we fail to plan for the long term? No, we planned to have a long term. That meant we planned to win. If you don't win, there is no long term. Our old competitors would confirm that, if you could still find them. Could we have sat around the table with them and planned together for the future? No, we couldn't. Business is, by nature and by law, a competitive activity. Remove the competition and you have a cartel. And cartels are, rightly, against the law. No, we competed, *hard*, and I do not apologise for that." A murmur of disquiet from the audience, and Andrew paused until it subsided.

"Has the rise of the West been any different?" The question, delivered out of the blue, had maximum impact. 'Nicely done' Catherine thought. Andrew let the question hang for a few seconds before he continued.

"The West started small and fought its way up through hundreds of years of ferocious, relentless competition. Driven by greed and foolishness, yes. So were the competition. Driven also by the need to survive, by passion, by belief systems, by all the stuff that makes us people. Driven by greed and foolishness? Yes, but what human beings are not? What is the point here?" Andrew's gaze scoured the audience in challenge before he paused and slowed down.

"Forgive me my rant. If I have a pet hate it's hypocrisy. I'm trying to be honest with you, even if it's not what you want to hear. Time to move on. The Compensation Conference. What a fantastic idea! Truly fantastic. The Sins of History. It's a great opportunity so let's do it right, first time. Yes, obviously we have to pay for the sins of history. Let's be clear about dates, first of all. How far back should we go? Twenty five years? Too short, we would focus too much only on America and let Europe off the hook. One hundred years? Better, we not only get Europe, but we can now hold Russia accountable for the ravages of Brezhnev and Stalin. And Japan, for the Second World War. Five hundred years? Yes, we can now consider the empires of the Moguls and of the Turks. Let us go further, to include the Aztecs, the Mongols, the Huns, the Romans, the Persians, the Egyptians.

Ladies and gentlemen, why stop there? Let us go right back to the sins of those first ancestors who allegedly streamed out of the African plains to wreak genocide on our Neanderthal ancestors. Let us go back to Year Zero!" Andrew paused and looked up.

"Yes, ladies and gentlemen, this is a truly fantastic idea. A truly ridiculous idea. There is no Year Zero. There is no way to judge the long-dead by the standards of the present. This is an idea dreamed up by lawyers, for lawyers. Let's not waste any more time on such foolishness."

There was no doubting the power of Andrew's ridicule. He paused long enough to see the rueful shaking of heads in the audience, the half-smiles, the look of people who have just found out they have been a little foolish, but no harm had been done.

" Let's move on. FreeOS, as it has been termed. You ask me 'Why not FreeOS?' I've got to be honest, it's a good question, a fair question. Why not? Now might just be the right time for a FreeOS. This is my personal opinion, you understand, not that of the U-Soft corporation. But I am on the inside of U-Soft. I know what goes on. Personally, I think that it is now almost impossible for U-Soft to do good work. To make any real progress. It might well be time for U-Soft to step aside."

What? Catherine could not believe what she had just heard. Neither, to judge by their expressions, could the audience. Nor could much of the watching world. Time to step aside? For what? Andrew soon put their doubts to rest.

"Remember the three programmers? The artists in silicon? At U-Soft, those days are over. Nowadays, there is so much baggage that any progress is painfully slow. We have technical baggage. We can't write new code unless it works with all the old stuff. We have legal baggage. I'm willing to bet that U-Soft now spends more on lawyers than on programmers. Real programmers, that is, the ones who write real code. We have regulatory baggage. U-Soft can no longer hire and fire as we need to, nor hire whom we want to. The situation has become utterly ridiculous. Let me give you an example. Last week we were accused of not employing the right number of gays. The right number of gays? Has the world gone mad? How can we work under this kind of madness? Yes, it may be that the time of U-Soft is over. It may well be the time of FreeOS. However, a word of caution. FreeOS may just inherit the same baggage." Andrew paused briefly.

"As to the motion, guilty, obviously. Of course the West is foolish. No argument. Is the West greedy and short-sighted? Of course, no argument. However, ladies and gentlemen, we would do well to remember the warning. *Let him who is without sin cast the first stone.*"

In the studio, the confusion was palpable, but the initial silence gave way to muted murmurs of agreement and a couple of isolated cheers. No such cheers broke the silence that had swept over the souks and marketplaces of Islam. In the vast squares further East, no-one knew quite what to think. In the Fall River Diner, cheers swelled gratefully around the room. Not a dreamer. REBEL. Catherine had her third character. Smiling to herself, Catherine waited until the studio subsided back into silence.

"William, your questions?" The Senator's smile went no further than his mouth.

"Andrew, congratulations on your resignation from U-Soft. Perhaps FreeOS will be hiring ageing programmers, if you feel you are still up to it. However, I'm still waiting on your apology." Muted laughter greeted his acerbic delivery.

"Actually, William, I'm anything but resigned. I don't expect to be sacked either. I apologised at the beginning of my presentation. I'm not sure what else I have to be apologise for." William glanced around the room.

"Let me apologise to our audience on your behalf. In fact, let me apologise to the world on your behalf. In recent years the people of the West have worked hard for the rights of minorities. All minorities. I do not know quite what Andrew finds 'ridiculous' in the issue of the numbers of gays, but I can tell you it is anything but ridiculous to me and to the vast majority of the decent people of the West." Andrew, seemingly oblivious to William's outrage, almost smiled as he started to reply.

"You've lost me, William. I'm aware - we're all aware - of your keen interest in homosexuality."

"This is outrageous!" the Senator interrupted, his face red with fury. Andrew, however, somehow held the floor, helped by the fact that the Senator's clock just started flashing.

"Please, William, let me finish. I have nothing against gays or straights or bisexuals or anything and everything in between. I'm pointing out how ridiculous it is for us to be counting how many we employ."

"What is so ridiculous about it? What is it you are trying to hide?"

"It's ridiculous to ask our workers the question. Are people going to answer the question honestly? Are they going to answer the question at all?"

"You must at least give them the chance! Surely, in the fight against discrimination, any measure is better than none?"

"I disagree. Let us imagine that we do pose the question. Let's say two percent of our employees say they are gay. Is this a true number? What do we compare it to? What *is* the expected number of gays in the population? I don't know. Nor does anyone else. Let me summarise. You want us to make an unreliable measurement and then compare it to unknown standard. From this cartoon comparison you will then make a value judgement. And then, no doubt, enshrine that judgement in a law? And you do *not* find that ridiculous?"

"It is not ideal, Andrew, but it IS a step. These kind of

changes all start with that one step." As the Senator's clock went out, Andrew got the last word.

"It is indeed a step, William. A step towards madness. A step off the edge of a cliff. William, I think we should move on and let our workforce keep their privacy."

Andrew sat back with a gentle smile, and left the Senator to lick his wounds. Catherine decided it was time for a quick intervention.

"Ladies and gentlemen, as you can see, time really is an issue here. Let me summarise the positions. William is, unfortunately, out of time and can take no further part in this debate. Krishnan has three minutes left, Andrew has just over a minute, Anwar and Anne Marie have still over eight minutes each. Andrew, I'd advise you to be brief." Andrew nodded. Catherine turned to Krishnan.

"Krishnan, questions for Andrew?" Narajan spoke more to the audience than to Andrew.

"Andrew, I thought I heard you say two interesting things. Did I hear you say that you thought FreeOS might be a good idea? That it might be time for U-Soft to move over? I know you are short of time and I do not want to use all you have available, but can you please confirm this statement?"

"Yes, Krishnan, you heard correctly. Lawsuits and regulations make it very difficult for U-Soft to continue to make much progress. Not to mention this current little difficulty we face with the virus, and the legal battles that we will no doubt face afterwards."

"Andrew, I am sure that I speak for many when I say that at least *some* good may come of all this. I think we can confidently say that the world can get ready for a new era in software. But let's move on. I am sure I also speak for many when I say that I do not appreciate your refusal to accept the sins of colonialism. I accept your point about the difficulties around compensation and restitution. We were well aware of those difficulties, and did not find your ridicule at all helpful. In fact, as I listened to you, I could not help but think that you neither accept these sins nor express any regret. As an Indian who was born in your British Empire, I find that deeply regretful and offensive. I know you have little time, Andrew, but perhaps you can use some of it to set the record straight?" It should have been the standard political tango. They both knew the dance. Krishnan had just led, Andrew had only to follow. Andrew, however, was not for dancing.

"Krishnan, as it happens, I have an amateur's passion for history. Particularly the history of India. It is common knowledge that the British ruled two hundred and fifty million Indians with a tiny number of British soldiers. How was this possible? I think we should be honest enough to admit to the answer. It was possible because the Indian people permitted it. The Indian people permitted it because they perceived British rule to be better than that of the Moguls and the Maharajahs. Or any of the other alternatives. This was true of the British Empire in general. It existed not through the power of its guns but through the quality of its civil service. Much like the Romans, with their laws and their straight roads and their engineering. Or the Persians before them. It may not be palatable to you, but it is true. Of course, the British did some bad, but they also did much good. I can recognise, and apologise for, the bad that was done, but are you able to recognise, and acknowledge, the good?"

It was a critical moment, and Narajan's concentration was not helped by the flashing of Andrew's clock. The audience, absorbed in the contest, waited for him in silence. He was on the ropes, no mistake. It was several long seconds before he smiled and leaned back.

"It is difficult for me, Andrew, as I am sure you understand. But I can acknowledge at least one good thing." Krishnan gazed steadily at Andrew before he added. "At least now you can get a decent curry in this damned country."

Peals of laughter swept over everyone, Andrew included. It was the perfect response, he could not help but enjoy it. And the tension had become unbearable, everyone needed the release. It was a good thirty seconds later before things had calmed sufficiently for Catherine to resume the proceedings.

"Anwar, your questions?"

"I'd like Andrew to have the chance to question me. I'll pass."

"Anne Marie?"

"Andrew, you may just be the kind of persuasive rogue that is genuinely dangerous. I'm not sure what to make of you. Until I make my mind up, I think I'm happy if you're quiet. I agree with Anwar. I pass." Catherine noted the hint of sexuality in the tone, the provocation, and it somehow irritated her. She'd think about that later, but now she had to press on.

"Anwar, the floor is now yours."

Anwar Abbat was not a tall man, but on his feet he was somehow intimidating. The bull neck, the broad shoulders, the deep chest, the blunt features of a combative and formidable man.

"Ladies and gentlemen, as the man said, it is time to talk freely. It is also good to laugh. It has been good to laugh. It is right that we exercise all our emotions. However, ladies and gentlemen, I think we should now be finished with the laughter. Right now it is time for other emotions. It is time to be angry." But is was not anger his words created, but silence. Silence, tension, a little fear. 'WARRIOR' Catherine thought. 'We have a warrior.' Anwar continued, his voice shaking with intensity.

"I intended to speak to you of the foolishness of this motion. I intended to tell you that the World of Islam can live with the greed of the West. It is not important to us. We are used to it and maybe it is also the will of Allah that we have a little suffering. I intended to tell you that the World of Islam can live with the foolishness of the West. It is not important to us. In the end, the world has a way of dealing with fools. What I wanted to try and say to you was something more subtle, but I did not know how to do it. I wanted to tell you about what we really hate. What really is important to us. What really matters to us." Anwar paused and seemed to gather his emotion.

"It is your culture. It is your culture which we detest and despise and which we cannot accept. But I did not know how to make this point to you, ladies and gentlemen. By the grace of Allah, I do not have to. The point has already been made. William and Andrew have made the point more vividly than ever I could. They are asked to consider the greed and foolishness of the West. What do they have to offer to this charge? Arguments about lawyers and compensation. Arguments about counting the number of gays in the world. Arguments about how we protect their rights. Ladies and gentlemen, from the World of Islam, I could tell you what we think are the rights of gays, but I won't. I could tell you what use we have for lawyers, but I won't. It would be a distraction. The real issue is your culture, *all* of it. How can I summarise more effectively its emptiness? Lawyers and gays. How can I summarise more effectively its corruption? Lawyers and gays. Ladies and gentlemen, I am sorry if I disillusion you. The West does not mean democracy to us. The West does not mean freedom to us. What the West means to us is decadence, corruption, misery. Take our money, take our resources, take all these things that you want. But do not bring us your culture."

In the studio, the audience gasped at the ferocity of the attack, the anger. In the bars and streets of the West, there was a collective intake of breath.

"So, let me finish, ladies and gentlemen. As others have said, of course the West is guilty of greed and foolishness, no argument. I would even agree that the West is not unique in this, and that maybe we are all a little guilty. But I would like to add a more serious charge. I accuse the West of corruption and of decadence. I accuse the West of creating a culture which may one day corrupt us all."

As Anwar abruptly sat down, it was not just the streets of Islam which resounded with cheers. In Russia, China, India, even in Japan, people cheered. In Africa, South America, East Asia they cheered. The studio, however, remained in utter, disbelieving silence. WARRIOR, yes, that was definitely her fourth character. Catherine let the silence hang just long enough, then she broke its spell.

"Krishnan, any questions?" Krishnan was not ready. Krishnan needed more time to think this through. The consequences, where this might end up. The longer term.

"I appreciate the depth of Anwar's anger. I appreciate his honesty. I appreciate his insight. I think that it is not for me to dilute that anger, that honesty, that insight. I pass." Catherine turned to Andrew.

"Andrew, you have twenty-five seconds left. Your comments will need to be brief." Catherine sensed that Andrew had the guts to confront this. The BBC *needed* Andrew to have the guts to confront this. Catherine was just not ready, however, for Andrew's reply.

"You've got a point, Anwar. Hell, what *does* the West stand for today? A good question. I'm surprised that I should find that simple question so hard to answer. Certainly, the West is still a dynamic, creative powerhouse, maybe never more so. Science, art, music: who can deny the creativity of the West? And certainly, a little corruption is the price you expect to pay for that level of creativity. But I think it has gone a little deeper than that. Maybe that creativity is no longer *in balance*. Yes, maybe we have lost our way a little. I'm sure I'm not the only one here asking himself the same question." At that point Andrew's clock went out. While the audience tried to absorb what Andrew had just said, Catherine passed the floor to Anne Marie.

"Comments, questions, Anne Marie?" Anne Marie rose to her feet with the sensual and languid grace of the actress she ought really to have been.

"I think I'll pass on the questions, Catherine. I'd like to now go ahead with my own presentation. First of all, ladies and gentlemen, I'm sorry to tell you fine people that I agree with much of what Anwar has just said. Whatever you think of yourselves - and I'm sure you are mostly good people - from where I look the last thing I'd want for my people is a society like yours. I don't mean to condemn you personally, but what Anwar says is mostly true. But not all." Anne Marie paused and shook her finger.

"No, I don't think all that Anwar says is true. It *does* matter about your greed. I am a woman, an African woman, and so have to be doubly practical. We have mouths to feed. We need you to help us, not steal from us. Your foolishness *does* matter. We cannot afford for you to be foolish. Nor, for that matter, can we can afford Anwar to indulge in his anger. We women get plenty of experience dealing with the results of male anger, do we not? Is it usually productive?" Murmurs of agreement - and rueful smiles - flitted across the audience.

"I don't much care one way or another about your lawyers or your gay rights. It puzzles me, puzzles most of us, why you spend so much time and energy on these issues. But it is not my concern. No, my concern is the welfare of my people. Let me be practical. We need money and we need resources. The resources we need are the resources to leverage our greatest wealth. People. We need the means to educate our people so they can be productive. In education today, the key is computers. If we can get the computers, then the books are all there, on the internet, ready and waiting for us. We just need computers that work. We

73

need them today, not tomorrow. Africa is tired of all the tomorrows that never come. I did have a request for Andrew. Like most men, he's somehow found the perfect way to avoid answering the question. Well, maybe I'll ask it anyway. Maybe you can all help him to give me the right answer tomorrow? Will you help me to persuade Andrew? Are you fine people ready to help me do something good? Yes?" Anne Marie was magnetic, mesmeric. Between her looks and her voice, and whatever else it was, she was almost irresistible. British or not, a small chorus of 'Yes' echoed around the room. 'ENCHANTRESS' Catherine thought. My fifth character.

"Andrew, we know that U-Soft is going to fix this little problem. It might take you a little longer than you expect, but we have faith in you. When it's all fixed, will you ask your boss to provide ten million sets of software for Africa? While you are at it, can you also provide ten million free computers to run your software on? And will all you nice people in the audience, you kind viewers, will you all ask Andrew's boss for me too?" A collective gasp. Andrew cocked an eyebrow and hid his shock under a thoughtful look.

"You see, that would put today's motion in a practical context. I know, it's easy to forget the motion in all this extraordinary talking. Yes, the motion. Of course, the motion is silly. Of course the West is guilty of greed and foolishness and all the rest. Yes, of course, the motion is silly, ladies and gentlemen. Silly, but true. True but unacknowledged. I think it is now time for the West to make that acknowledgement, and to do something practical to make amends. Time for U-Soft, in particular, to make amends. Ten million working computers would make a very fine, very practical, start. Ladies and gentlemen, thank you." Anne Marie had used barely half of her allotted time. 'Still,' Catherine thought, 'if she gets the computers then who can argue with her productivity?'

"Questions, comments, Krishnan?" prompted Catherine. "You have forty-five seconds."

"Anne Marie, I'm disappointed. We have a chance to move away from U-Soft. To move away from proprietary, expensive software to something that is open, inexpensive. To something that we ourselves own. Surely now is the time to take that chance? Surely now is not the time to let U-Soft make cheap publicity gestures? You agree we need to move to FreeOS. While we wait for it to be completed, can you not move to UNOS or something open-source, not U-Soft?"

"Krishnan, this is not a gesture. Ten million programs and ten million computers is not a gesture. Not only will it give us something for today, but when FreeOS is ready we will have ten million computers to run it on."

"I accept that, Anne Marie. But why use U-Soft in the meantime?"

"Because it works. Well, today excepted. Because they will provide the computers. Because we need something today. Because the skills they give us will help us contribute to FreeOS tomorrow. Because we need to minimise our risk. Krishnan, if you were in my position, what would you do?"

"I would be very careful whom I chose for my friends", said Krishnan.

"But I am, darling, I am." said Anne Marie sweetly, and smiled. It was seven or eight long seconds before Catherine broke the ensuing silence.

"Last questions, comments, Anwar? You have forty seconds."

"Anne Marie, I agree with Krishnan. I appreciate your need for the computers and the software. But surely it also matters whom you work with? Surely you would not work with U-Soft on this?"

"Darling, I'd work with the Aryan Brotherhood if they gave me the computers I need." Anne Marie deadpanned. Then burst into the deep, rumbling laugh of a woman twice her weight. The audience roared with her – well, most of them, since quite a few were embarrassed, not sure how to react. Anwar did not share their laughter, but waited until it had died away.

"In that case, you will have a long wait." he said, softly, and no-one laughed, at all.

The vote was, of course, an anti-climax. Frankly, the audience, the world audience, were exhausted - and exhilarated - by the rollercoaster of ideas. Catherine announced the result - carried by eighty one to nineteen - and then once more spelled the audience into silence.

"Ladies and gentlemen. Your attention please. There is one more thing to be done. As you know, tonight is only the first of what may be many debates. Each night the BBC will announce the motion for the next debate. This motion will be based on the message that the Christmas Virus will display the following noon. The motion for the second debate is...

The West is guilty of the destruction of their heroes. The West is guilty of the promotion of weakness over strength. The West is guilty of failure to provide inspiration to their young.

We look forward to seeing you all again tomorrow."

The broadcast ended no more than ten seconds later. It was an exhausted, elated, Catherine that made her way back to make-up. She had her five characters. Demagogue, teacher, rebel, warrior, and enchantress. What would be the script?

It was a couple of hours and a couple of large Taliskers before Andrew started to come down. He had been left largely unscathed by the blizzard of flashlights and microphones that ambushed his exit from the BBC. A judicious choice of route had ensured that he arrived back at his Mayfair sanctuary unnoticed and untraced. Remarkably, Eldon Harker had left just one message on his private mobile - "Get some rest. Do not check e-mail. We'll talk in the morning. Have one for me." Which Andrew had proceeded to do, safe in the comfort that he termed his 'Maximum Batchelor Mode'. A generous sip of the Talisker, unfailing as always, constant as ... and Andrew's thought turned, surprisingly, to women, to a particular woman, to Catherine. Yes, she owed him a date.

Around the same time, Ahmed Ali Khan lay back on the massive baroque bed as sleep started to suffuse him. Even his exhilaration, his delight, his wonder, had to succumb sometime to the great fatigue. The righteous fatigue of a man engaged in great efforts for his Emir, his Prophet, his God. As sleep stole on Ahmed, his mind drifted to home. To the Great Cauldron of the North. To the barbarian city, the impossible city, the city of madmen, and anger. To Glasgow, Scotland. To home.

FOUR

Waves smashed the narrow promontory in a tireless and futile rage. Huge seas surged past on either side, roaring shingle up the beach. An anaemic sun flitted fitfully behind scudding clouds. At the head of the promontory a large rock formed a natural cave facing the shore. Spray illumined the entrance in a cold halo of liquid salt. Inside the cave the red haired man has just opened a small portable computer. On its screen is written :-

He said to me :-

In the West they have made a unique society. This society does not measure the good, only the bad. Not great deeds, but only weaknesses and faults. From these faults they derive blame. The King in this society is the lawyer, and the religion of this society is The Cult of The Victim.

Where now are their great heroes, their Spartans and Caesars and Churchills? All dead and denied, for heroes are, after all, only too human. Who then do they have to inspire their young? Without heroes, what will be their dreams?

I had to acknowledge his truth.

I charge the West with the destruction of heroes, the promotion of weakness over strength, the failure to provide inspiration for their young.

The red-haired man stood up, closed the computer and started back before he was trapped by the incoming tide.

Worldwide, the impact of the debate was remarkable, perhaps unprecedented. From the home to the workplace, from the newspapers to the television stations, virtually all conversation seemed to revolve around it. The morning headlines in the British press neatly summarised the response of their readership. The Times thought 'THE WEST LAMBASTED AS GAY RIGHTS ATTACKED'. The Telegraph asked 'LAWYERS, GAYS, CORRUPTION: IS THIS HOW THE WORLD SEES US?'. The Financial Times thought 'WESTERN VALUES MOCKED AS U-SOFT SEES ITS END'. Most of the tabloid headlines were tawdry, but the Sun showed its typical flair with 'GAY LAWYERS 0. BLACK BABE 10 MILLION'. In the rest of the world, the headlines ranged from the mild 'WORLD VOICES HATRED OF WESTERN VALUES' in China, to the 'THE WEST SQUABBLES AS THE WORLD ACCUSES' in India, to the 'THE HUMBLING OF THE WEST : DAY ONE' in Iran.

That the debate should already so dominate was doubly remarkable. The Christmas Virus itself was starting to bite deeper. People were starting to wake up to how deeply the computer was embedded in their daily life.

The banking system was on the verge of chaos. Most of the banks had suspended the use of automated tellers and had adopted a paper based system within the local branches. Of course, you could still withdraw cash, but only from your own branch. Herd instinct, the deep lure of the queue, meant that your branch was always lined right round the corner, especially since the shops no longer accepted electronic payments of any kind.

Supermarkets and restaurants were mostly still open, although they were starting to feel the impact of first shortages. Food supply remained good, but, inevitably, people had started to panic buy, fuelling shortages. Impromptu rationing was introduced, just like in some long-forgotten war.

Domestically, people soldiered on, but their computers were painfully slow, and they were beginning to encounter mysterious errors. Most of the new routines of daily life worked, but falteringly. E-mail, instant messaging, digital photography, internet based phone services: they worked, but only just. But not e-commerce. It wasn't just the speed of the computers that was the problem there. What other viruses lurked in their machines, waiting to steal their bank and credit card details? No, no-one was prepared to be that brave, or that foolish. Most E-commerce businesses had already closed, and few were certain when they would re-open. On-line was completely off-line.

Most professional organisations had stopped using their computers as a matter of prudence. If they could, they worked with paper. If not, people got an early Christmas. At the worst end of the scale, the computer business was devastated. Hardware and software. Unsurprisingly: what madman could possibly want to buy their products?

Most manufacturing businesses were also in deep trouble. The central principle of manufacturing was now based on 'Just in Time'. Otherwise known as 'Keep no Stocks'. Like the car industry, for example. There are minimal stocks of new cars, so when a car is sold, the factory needs to make another one to replace it. So it automatically generates and sends a vast stream of electronic orders to all the companies that manufacture its parts. Almost instantaneously. They, in turn, generate orders to their suppliers, and so on, down to the end of the chain. A vast chain of orders, sent and received almost instantaneously. The parts are delivered in the next few days and a new car is built. Unfortunately, without computers and electronic ordering, it just cannot work. Each link takes time, and there are just too many links in the chain. It was no wonder that even traditional manufacturers were hit hard and hit deep.

High street shops, waiting for the Christmas rush, faced an

even more serious issue than supply. After all, many of them were already fully stocked for Christmas, shelves piled high with the produce of the world. They had plenty to sell, and plenty of time to restock. Their problem was persuading customers to part with cash, or more accurately, credit. The big problem was not cash, but credit: credit cards and instant credit. But where could the customers find the credit? The banks had already closed credit card transactions. Now instant credit was closed too, because instant credit relies completely on instant verification. Without instant access to their credit histories, no-one could verify an application. No verification, no credit. Customers had to pay cash, or make a manual application for credit. The retail industry understood only too well that the fuel of the High Street was credit: easy credit made easy sales. Take it away, and the results were all too predictable. Manufacturers might be in deep trouble, but the high street shops were in even deeper.

Despite all this, excited children wrote Christmas lists much as they had since living memory. Parents, however, started to consider alternatives. Not alternative presents, but alternatives. Deep down, most people looked to Christmas with dread. In the towns of Bradford, Blackburn and Luton sporadic riots broke out between Islamist youths and police, as the youths torched cars in celebration.

As if in response, for the first time, a mainstream British newspaper carried a full page advertisement by the British Fascist Party. 'Unite to Save the West!' was its banner headline. In many poor urban areas, Fascist graffiti seemed to spring up overnight. How long would it be before the 'Christmas Virus' had blood on its hands?

The effects, and the panic, were not limited to the West, but were spreading to all industrialised nations. Some in the Third World were starting to see a familiar pattern, and were starting to fear a familiar fear. That, ultimately, it is always the poor that pay the highest price.

David Blenheim, the Prime Minister, addressed his inner cabinet grimly.

"I know I do not have to convince anyone here of the gravity of the crisis that we face today. This country, and the West in general, is under serious assault. We need to find out just who is leading this assault and we need to deal with them. We also need to deal with their sympathisers in the BBC. We need to do something, gentlemen, and soon. In an hour's time, I'm meeting with the Attorney General and then with MI5. We will reconvene when I've had time to digest their advice. Meanwhile, gentlemen, you have plenty to think about. I look forward to your counsel."

With that, the Prime Minister dismissed his cabinet and closed his eyes briefly. David Blenheim had the strong feeling that he should grasp any rest while he could.

In Washington, the President had scheduled a rather different meeting, a working breakfast with the Senate Minority Leader. Despite their deep mutual suspicions, somehow they both rapidly agreed that Senator William Gladwin needed some encouragement. They both felt that Senator Gladwin should be encouraged to perform just a little better. Should be encouraged to be clear about just whom he represented. The Senate Minority Leader was more than ready to speak to his colleague, and intended to do so, he smiled, just as soon as he had finished his waffles. Despite his levity, it was clear that he, like the President, felt the gathering storm.

Mayfair, London: Early, December the Twenty-First

As always, Andrew shed his dreams slowly, carefully, gradually. Shower was followed by ten minutes of the yoga exercises that he still preferred to keep a little private. Andrew expected that today might be a bit special. That justified a chilli omelette start:

peppers, tomatoes, onions, chillies, two eggs and dry rye toast. Orange juice followed by a double espresso. All through the omelette's short but fiery life, Andrew was distracted. Last night's tempestuous debate. His position in U-Soft, his upcoming meeting with Eldon. Tonight's debate, already demanding thought and preparation. The grim power that the Christmas Virus now seemed to exert, judging by the news in the background. Surely Michael could not be responsible? Focusing on the television brought Catherine into his mind, unaccountably. Catherine was beautiful, smart too, but why the special attraction? Why her? Nostalgic for another wife, or lonely, or genuinely interested? Somebody special or just another challenge? An empty espresso cup snapped Andrew out of his reverie, and back to the matters in hand. Catherine could wait. Eldon would not. Andrew needed answers, and fast, but today was not the day to panic. Andrew resisted the desire to rush, forced himself to stay poised and loose, to think logically and carefully. It was an hour later when a smiling Andrew walked calmly into the Lion's den, into U-Soft London. It was a further thirty minutes before Andrew and Eldon were locked in video conference.

"Well, Eldon, I'm ready. If you want my job there's not really much I can do about it, given last night."

"Want your job, Andrew? Hell, no! Thought you were great. Especially the FreeOS bit."

"You obviously didn't go for the superficial analysis, Eldon. Well, no surprise there. Willing to hazard a guess at the thinking behind my approach? Would you risk a bottle of red, perhaps?" Back in the old days, a bottle of red wine was the wager of choice. Perhaps the one wager of the year, and a victory to be savoured. In Andrew's case, a most infrequent one.

"A bottle of red, Andrew? I'm sorry, much too rich for me. I will hazard a guess, though. I think your reasoning is as follows.

You think that U-Soft is going nowhere with U-Sys. We are engaged in a constant struggle against the regulators, the legacy of our past work, our own bureaucracy, and a slavering pack of rabid lawyers. We get no real credit for any of it. Now this virus appears and we really do seem to have screwed up. So when we offer the job to some FreeOS foundation, at least we get the credit for being big enough to let it go. FreeOS, on the other hand, start to look at the magnitude of the task that faces them and begin to take fright. To make their job easier, they use some of their political assets to get some of the regulatory pressure lifted, but it is not enough. The task is beyond them, like it always has been. In the end, we get the work back, minus the regulators and their legal mercenaries. Not to mention that they finally accord us the credit we should have received the first time around." Eldon paused. "Well, is this close to your analysis, Andrew?"

"Very good, Eldon, I'm impressed. That would definitely have won you a bottle of red. Had you made the wager." Eldon made a mock grimace. Andrew saw his opportunity. "Perhaps I might hazard a guess at *your* analysis, Eldon. Another chance for a bottle?"

"I'm afraid the wager will have to wait a little longer, Andrew. It is too early to share my thoughts with you. You have got to be able to stand in front of the world and talk honestly. I cannot have you talking about issues that I've yet to fully resolve. While we're on the subject of honesty, Andrew, I must say that you took one hell of a chance with your political stuff. Compensation, gay rights, the British Raj? Any other taboos that you feel you really *must* break?" It was Andrew's turn for the mock grimace.

"Yes, Eldon, I certainly said a little more than I meant to. Who knows where some of those ideas came from, but, believe me, I was just as surprised to hear them as you. I did have to bait a trap for our woolly-minded Senator and his comfortable absurdities. He certainly took the bait and that part worked.

Perhaps too well. I did not mean it to escalate to become world headlines. On the other hand, the bit about the British Empire I did mean to say. The historian in me is just sick of hearing the same old crap trotted out, when it's so patently a nonsense. Not that it seemed to affect the result. No way our Western World came out of that debate on top. Anwar certainly saw to that."

"The West is strong enough and creative enough to take a little criticism. I agree with you that the West *needs* a little criticism. Maybe more than a little. What the West also needs is the chance to face down not just its faults, but also its critics. Maybe when we are finished with our faults, we can start to look at theirs. You might just be able to pull that off, Andrew. But not without some help. As a start, we've announced our agreement to the ten million African computers. That kind of positive P.R. is cheap at any price, a fantastic opportunity. Hopefully, that should help you to mount some kind of defence of our cause. God knows that our Senator is useless, and likely to remain so."

"I am not even sure of what the cause is, anymore, Eldon, so I most definitely am not going to try. Whoever has written the Christmas Virus has written the script, and I'm going to have to follow where it leads. No, I'm going to take it as it comes. Talking of which, how is the search for the virus coming along? What progress are we making?"

"In summary, progress has been poor. Some specifics? You remember I suggested yesterday that we change the timing crystal to make the clock go faster, and hence get us the messages sooner. Doesn't work. Assuming we get the computer to reboot, then time passes at the same rate as it did before we changed the crystal. The Virus has been timing its computer, and now effectively has constructed its own clock. The timing information must be written somewhere, so we decided to destroy the clock by reformatting, wiping the hard disk. We reformatted the disk, then reinstalled U-Sys4. Even less success. The machine performed like it was a model from twenty years ago, around the time we think the virus was written. Perhaps point one per cent of today's speeds, in fact. Needless to say, much too slow to run any of today's software. We've tried a number of other things, Andrew, but the fact is that the virus has blocked them all. It's way ahead of us." Eldon sensed that Andrew was thinking through the implications and paused long enough to let him catch up. Then continued.

"Moving on, as of this afternoon, the performance penalty of the Virus is seventy-five per cent. Data is still compatible, but the percentage of machines that will successfully reboot is now down to ten percent. We know what is going on: the virus is changing the active partition, so that the computer now tries to start from the wrong part of the hard disk. We can obviously reset it, but the operation is a little too complex for the average customer and..."

"...and does not address our major issue, performance."

"Exactly. We have released the fix but it is not going to do very much for us. There are, however, some positive developments that we can publicise. We can demonstrate our commitment to beat this virus, no matter what the consequences."

"So the Senator was right, Eldon? Emulators?"

"Yes, emulators. Emulation is the sincerest form of flattery, indeed, and U-Sys now has so many emulators. Well, we're going to start to work through them all. We've started tests of the **Nexus** U-Sys emulator and so far it shows no trace of the Virus. After that, we'll move on to the next most popular emulator, and so on down the list. We'll also look at the cut-down versions of U-Sys that we use for the phones and the hand-held organisers. All these efforts should make it absolutely clear to our customers that we are prepared to do whatever is necessary." Like the Russians, thought Andrew. Like the Russians burning Moscow so that Napoleon, too, would freeze. But he did not dare say it.

"I agree that it's better than nothing, Eldon, but surely the performance of the emulators is way down on ours? Are these emulators really going to be useful?"

"Their performance will be only a small fraction of ours, that is true. And emulators will only be useful for **Nexus** machines or new computers that do not yet have U-Sys and the virus. So useful, no, not very useful. It is, however, both a start and a way of marking time. And, as I said, a signal that, if need be, we are prepared to back the opposition. That we are prepared to contemplate our own demise."

"Our own demise, Eldon? Already? Do you remember the words of the poem?

My name is Ozymandias, King of Kings:
Look upon my works, ye Mighty, and despair!"

Of course he did: how could he not, when it had been pinned to their low-rent wall for so long. It had been their inspiration against the monoliths, their assurance that even the mighty do always fall. Smoothly, Eldon completed it:-

Nothing beside remains. Round the decay
Of that colossal wreck, boundless and bare
The lone and level sands stretch far away.

then continued, hardly pausing more than was respectful.

"Well, Andrew, our dreams are not yet over. No, *not yet*. Nor do we have time for any bouts of your romantic melancholy." A wince from Andrew. Barely perceptible, and anyway Eldon was moving on. "To continue. We're going to make a video presentation to a pack of journalists at noon, you can and should watch that on an internal link. People are desperate to know whom to blame for this. They fear that it is Al Quaeda or Paradise Lost or some other bunch of fundamentalists or eco-fools. It is time we gave them a different scenario. It is time they heard of Michael MacDonald."

"Red Michael." Andrew shook his head, as if to dispel unwelcome thoughts. "Are you sure you want to do this, Eldon?"

"No, not sure, but it is the best balance of the probabilities. Anyway, Andrew, I have another task for you. One more suited to your taste."

"Something tells me you don't need my coding skills?"

"Correct. It is your seduction skills we need, Andrew. We need to get a trace on the e-mails that Catherine is getting. We absolutely need to get a copy of *Sesame. You know what is at* stake here, Andrew. With *Sesame*, we can almost guarantee to save lives, not to mention billions of dollars. You can help Catherine to appreciate that, to see that there is more at stake here than just TV ratings. You can persuade her to help us, Andrew."

"You flatter me, Eldon. Maybe I could have pulled it off ten years ago. Maybe. But now? This is no baby blonde, and I am no longer quite the romantic prince I might once have been. Even if I did get some success with Catherine - which I doubt - do you really think that I could persuade her to give *Sesame* up? And if I did, what if word got out? How many dollars, how many lives would that cost? What will happen if Christmas comes and there is no virus fix under the tree?"

"You're assuming that we find no fix, Andrew, and that interests me. You're also assuming that the other side will honour their bargain. You're the amateur historian, Andrew. Was is it not Heinrich Himmler who said 'Who compels us to keep the promises that we make?' Yes, even if we are good boys, Andrew, Christmas may come but Santa may still bring us nothing. But I digress. I have some information which may greatly help you with the beautiful Miss Connor. Please listen carefully, Andrew."

Five minutes later, Eldon was gone and Andrew had much to think about. Yes, he was in the game. He had a hand, but how to play it?

Washington, USA: December the Twenty-First. Early.

Thanks to the God-send of the corporate jet, it was a refreshed and alert Solomon N'Chenga that sat down in Eldon's office on the forty-third floor. The office was huge, made even bigger by the minimal décor. A large world clock on the wall behind Eldon's desk. A dramatic original by Turner - 'The Fighting Temeraire?' - on the wall to his left, subtly and expertly lit. A huge silk Kashmiri rug on the wall to his right. A vast, cloud framing window directly facing him. Beyond that, nothing but blue sky and space. A window to promote awe, and humility.

"Boss." Solomon opened. "Karen MacDonald is an honest woman. And she does not know where her husband has gone." Genius is powered not by logic, but by intuition. Even the humblest computer has logic framed in its silicon, the poor dumb beast. No, Eldon respected not logic, but intuition. Eldon especially respected Solomon, for his intuition was extraordinary. Solomon had the uncanny ability to sense even the whitest of lies, to see just that little bit deeper. Solomon, perhaps, went a little further than intuition. Eldon never asked him how. Meanwhile, Solomon continued.

"No, Karen MacDonald knows nothing about where her husband is. She has not seen him, nor heard from him, in over two years. She's very definite, and I know she's not lying. She knew why I had come, seemed almost eager to answer my questions. She told me that she wanted to get this interview out of the way, so that she and her family could 'disappear' too, before the media storm broke. She was straight down the line, boss, no evasions at all. That tells me a great many things, including the fact that she knows nothing about where Michael is, or might be. Obviously, Karen is fabulously rich and Michael's disappearance has had no significant financial impact on her. It's purely an emotional issue. But she says that she and the kids always knew that he was going to do this, that he has not walked out on them. Two years ago he made an emotional farewell and left with his passport, his wallet, and an overnight bag. Two years can be a long time, so I'm guessing this Michael must be quite a character. This is a passionate woman and her passion for Michael is very evident. She told me that they all miss him terribly and that they cannot wait for him to come back. She says he told her, a long time ago, that one day he would be have to be gone for a while, that there was something that he had to do. Some kind of life mission. He would have to go, but he would come back. This is the really interesting bit. He told her when. He would come back in a little over two years. Of course there would be a risk, a danger, but, and she quoted him 'Deus Vult, I will be back in just over two years.' That is, boss, sometime around now."

"Deus Vult? She said that? His words?" Eldon knew the Latin. So too, he knew, did Solomon. The Jesuits got everywhere.

"Deus Vult. Not something you make a mistake over, boss."

"Is she sure he has gone on this 'life mission'? Is she sure about when he first talked about it?"

"She is sure. She expects him back soon. Is she sure when she found out? Yes, boss, she is. This is the bit that puzzles me. Seems like he told her this before they were married. That makes it twenty five years ago. That makes it some years before U-Soft."

Solomon sat back a little, as if expecting an answer to the question he had not quite asked. A question, a stream of questions, questions with implications. The expectation was not fulfilled. Eldon eased back and seemed to reflect for some thirty seconds or so, then gestured Solomon to continue.

"I asked her if Michael was religious, or committed to environmental causes, anything like that. Very religious, it seems, as is Karen. Catholics, although Karen said that Michael was 'also somewhat Hindu'. That was why they never went through with Opus Dei."

"Opus Dei?" Solomon nodded in assent.

"Yes, Opus Dei. Michael and Karen went some way down that road, it appears. Karen said that most of the tall tales about Opus Dei are just that, tall tales, but Opus Dei are certainly committed to a religious way of life. However, seems like Michael's 'somewhat Hindu' version of Catholicism made them back off. That may have been a smart move, judging by the statues of Shiva in their reception hall. Confusing. Not that Karen seemed bothered, either. Otherwise, neither Michael nor Karen is interested in the environment other than the normal concerns. Bottom line, religious, certainly. Opus Dei, possibly. Environmental fascists, no." Solomon leaned forward and held Eldon's gaze.

"You worked with him for many years, boss. Does this sound at all like the Michael you knew?"

"Sounds like he may have mellowed a little" Eldon remarked, dryly. "OK, let's assume that Karen knows nothing of where he went, nothing of where he is now. However, surely she has some way to contact him in an emergency?"

"No way at all. She was utterly definite. Michael had insisted there was no way it could be done safely. If she were not completely in the dark, then she would be in great danger. He said that it was a great thing that he had to do, a great thing and a good thing. He said he had great faith that everything would be fine, but that, ultimately, what will be, will be. We talked a lot more before we got to the question she knew I had to ask. Did she think Michael might be responsible? Responsible for the virus, the attacks on the West, the ensuing chaos?"

"And?"

"And she gave me a look that made me feel like the lowest kind of low-life scum. A look that said she was more disappointed in me than ever she could express. As you know, boss, I am not the shy and retiring type, but that lady got to me.

She has presence. Insight. Something special."

"That she does." Eldon agreed. "However, did you interpret her silence as a yes?"

"It was not a no. I think she believes it might be him. After she had withered me with her look she told me that Michael was not only a good man, but that he was 'a man of force'. That was her phrase, 'a man of force'. Anyway, we were finished talking within five minutes or so, it seemed like I had killed the conversation."

Eldon seemed to reflect for several seconds before he seemed to reach a decision.

"Well, Solomon, it seems that I have a new job for you..."
Solomon left U-Soft some fifteen minutes later, and was back on the corporate jet within the hour.

The red-haired man scrutinised his newly-bald reflection. Blue eyes, strong features, smooth skin, only the fine lines around his eyes to hint at his forty three years. Michael was of average height, but his massive shoulders made him look several inches shorter. The scalp was still reddened by the unaccustomed razor, but Michael could neither see nor feel any tell-tale cuts. He turned, picked up his suitcase and headed for the door. His pilgrimage had begun.

U-Soft Conference Room One, London: One p.m.
December the Twenty-First

Three rows from the front sits the odd couple, Peter Hawkins, of the Times and Robert Perry of the Telegraph. Their gaze is turned to the large screen facing them. The screen is filled by the familiar, alien-long face, the shoulder length silver hair, the continuous eyebrow. The luminous green eyes fix the audience sternly and Eldon Harker begins.

"Ladies and gentlemen. Thank you for your attention. For the benefit of everyone, I will make this statement as concise as is practical."

On the wings of the stage, Mohan Nehran and Brian Dempsey, exchanged inward groans. A statement deemed concise by Eldon was a statement likely to be deemed meaningless by anyone else.

"In this statement I will address five things. The nature of the virus, it's current and projected consequences, our recommendations to alleviate its symptoms, our efforts to determine a solution, and our analysis of its likely origins." Don't take a breath, Hawkins thought. One breath and you're likely to miss it. Eldon continued to read his own statement.

The virus is an infection of the kernel of the U-Sys operating system. By the kernel, we mean the heart, the centre, the core. This is the code that gives U-Sys its unique power and performance. The kernel was finalised in U-Sys release one, and this infection therefore dates back to then.

The current known consequences of the virus, aside from measures to protect itself, are a reduction in system speed and the issue of political messages. As of today, system speed is now one quarter of what it was two days ago. Some of my engineers consider this degradation to be binary, and predict that system speed will half every twenty four hours. If so, by Christmas Day, performance will be have been reduced by ninety-nine point eight per cent. The impact of the virus may not, however, be limited to these features. In any case, the performance impact of the virus will be effectively mortal to the computer.

We can alleviate the symptoms of the virus by the reinstallation of U-Sys onto a machine with a significantly earlier date. Naturally, this will have side-effects on date-sensitive applications, but it will make the computer usable. As of this moment, however, we are also working on software which will restore the computer to full usability. In effect, the intention is for the computer to be set at a date some years back, but for applications to deduce from this the true date. We expect to make a statement on this in twenty four hours, with a view to deployment in forty eight hours. I can also confirm that the portable implementations of U-Sys - those on hand-held devices and on phones - are free of the virus. We will publish a full list of these implementations. We are also working with our competition to validate their U-Sys emulators. We can confirm that the **Nexus** U-Sys Emulator Version Three is free of the virus.

In our efforts to determine a solution, we have verified that we are in possession of the correct source code. In layman's terms, we have the ability to recreate the kernel. That means we are able to modify the source code and hence to create a new, uninfected, kernel. It is our intention to check every line of source code in order to find the infected lines. This is necessarily a slow job due to the complexity of the code and the fact that there are now few programmers with the skills required.

There were also very few programmers involved when the kernel was written. Some of those programmers, like myself, are still at U-Sys and are working on this verification task. We are actively searching for those who are no longer with U-Soft, both for their skills and for their potential to shed light on this issue. Right now we have checked some fourteen thousand lines out of the total of seventy two thousand. It is too early for us to project from this to a future rate of progress.

Since the virus is present in all releases of U-Sys, it is clear that the virus was introduced when we created the very first kernel. The virus is categorically not the result of recent terrorist activity. If the virus is the result of terrorist activity, then the activity took place at least twenty years ago.

I have been brief in order to maximise the use of my time and of yours. I must still, however, assure you all that U-Soft utterly regrets this problem and are working as hard as humanly possible to arrive at a solution. Be patient and this will be resolved.

Thank you"

Eldon did not have the time to watch his own broadcast or any of the press conference. He was, indeed, working on code. Just like old times. In his stead, generally speaking, Mohan Nehran and Brian Dempsey handled the conference well. Some key questions reflected the main focus of the hundreds of journalists. Tom Trenton, of the Sun asked, to some laughter:-

"Brian, can you please explain how we can set the computer date back yet our programs will still work with the correct date? Can you please explain it in a way that a Sun reader might understand?"

Brian explained that they would set the computers to a date earlier than the real date. A date that was a precise number of years earlier: ten years, for example. Now, whenever a program read the date from the computer, it would automatically add on ten years. Bringing us back to the correct date, but without hitting the virus. The beauty of U-Sys was that every program used EXACTLY the same code to read the computer date. That pattern was as unique as someone's DNA. That made it possible for U-Soft to make a small program that would search all the software on a computer to find wherever that unique pattern occurred. Where it found the pattern, it would replace it with code that both read the date and then added on ten years. The whole replacement operation would typically take less than half an hour. The only problem was that you had to remove U-Sys first, change the date on the computer, and then re-install U-Sys. This was obviously feasible in the business world, but obviously less so in the domestic market. Still, it was potentially a life-saver, and the first real bit of good news since the virus first hit. Robert Perry, the more abrasive half of the odd couple, had two questions, and much scorn.

"How can you expect us to believe that the statements we all see on our computers were written twenty years ago? How can you really expect us to believe that these statements are not the recent work of some group of anti-western fanatics?" Dempsey ignored the incredulous tone, and answered politely and succinctly.

"Robert, that is not quite what we have said. The virus is in the kernel, that is a fact. The kernel has not changed in twenty years, that is a fact. If the virus has been written by anti-western fanatics, then they wrote it twenty years ago. These are the facts. Anything else is speculation."

It became obvious later that this statement was interpreted rather differently outside of London and the West. Exactly when had Al Quaeda appeared? When did the Russians invade Afghanistan?

Jim Solomon, of the Guardian demanded to know:-

"How is it possible for our most up-to-date software to be powered by a twenty year old engine?" Mohan tried to explain the enormous complexity of writing the code, and the even greater complexity of testing it. The monumental complexity and effort, the colossal cost. That no-one could justify such a colossal cost to fix something that was not broken, and something that they might not be able to significantly improve. Not broken until now, he had to add, wryly.

Peter Hawkins, the more thoughtful half of the odd couple, posed the last significant questions.

"Is it true that a large part of the source code was written by the legendary Michael MacDonald? Is it also true that Michael has disappeared?" Mohan Nehran had to reply that, to the best of his knowledge, both statements were indeed true.

Those were the key questions. The journalists now had a name. The conference came rapidly to an end as the hounds now had scent of their quarry, and were straining at the leash.

David Blenheim, the Prime Minister, was what was termed a conviction politician. Not that he had been convicted of anything, yet, but he used his hands a lot when he talked. He also furrowed his brows a lot, especially when he thought, and he rarely made a public joke. In the five minutes he had before the MI5 meeting, the PM reflexively furrowed his brows. He furrowed as he tried to think through the implications of what he had just learned from the Attorney General. Actually, appearances were deceptive, for, despite the theatrics, thinking was something David did very well, very well indeed.

Put simply, a judge could legitimately instruct the BBC to hand over the *Sesame* programme and all communications with the supposed terrorist organisation. There was little doubt that it was a clear case of the national interest. There was also little doubt that the BBC could probably be charged with furthering the causes of international terrorism, so legally they were in an untenable position. Unfortunately, it was not so simple. There was no doubt at all that, if the BBC refused to comply with the instruction, then all hell would break loose, and probably not to the benefit of law and order. He had to find some kind of a reasonable approach to the damned BBC, ask them for co-operation before compulsion. He needed to find out what kind of attitude this Director General, Peter Bradshaw, was likely to take. He had, naturally enough, met him several times in the past. The memories did not fill him with confidence. David Blenheim added yet another item to the MI5 agenda, and invited them in.

The Director-General of MI-5, the legendary 'M', had said he would bring a 'geek' with him to explain the technicalities. 'M' was a study in the specimen known as English Eton Gentleman. Tall, poised, distinguished, an erect and trim figure around which was draped a grey Aquascutum pin-stripe suit, topped with a black cashmere Crombie coat. 'M' was, in fact, a study in the deception of spy craft, for he was a working-class boy from the Liverpool Eight, an area that had yet to provide much in the way of Etonians. 'M''s double first at Oxford was real enough, as were his deeply classified days in the field. The 'geek' that 'M' brought with him could not, surely, be what he seemed either. The man 'M' introduced simply as 'Hector', was six foot three of the kind of male that keeps romantic fiction popular. Dark, handsome, saturnine looks, a slim athletic figure and a skin that advertised health and fitness, 'Hector' was the very image of a young James Bond. "Geek', indeed, thought David, "I'd think twice before I let him anywhere near my daughters. Or my wife, for that matter. Well, let's see what he has to say, at least."

In response to the PM's curt nod, 'M' opened the discussion

"Prime Minister, the key thing for us is to get access to Catherine Connor's computer. If and when we get access, we can achieve three things. Firstly, prior knowledge of the messages and the so-called charges. This will enable us to mitigate their effects. Secondly, the potential to find, and eliminate, the virus. Thirdly, the means to track down and capture whoever is responsible. Hector, would you please explain, in layman's terms, some of the technical issues?" Hector wasted no time.

"Prime Minister, the *Sesame* programme is able to provide advance knowledge of the virus messages. That means it either contains the messages or reads them from the U-Sys files. Either way, we should be able to see the same messages. The first problem we have is that *Sesame* needs codes to operate. The second problem is that we think the codes are specific to Connor's computer. That is the logical explanation of why Connor had to send a file back. Put bluntly, the codes will work on Connor's computer and on no other."

"Surely we can get our hands on the same make and model of computer? The same hard disk?" the PM interrupted.

"It would not be the same in two key respects, Prime Minister. As the computer is used, routine information - for example, about whom it belongs to and how it is set up - is written to an area called the registry. Very soon, the registries of two identical computers become very different. More than that, every modern computer has a unique address stored in its network card. It's called the 'MAC address', and is absolutely, globally, unique. So, in order for us to use the passwords that Connor receives, we need to make an almost identical copy of her computer, and we need to create a network card with the same Mac address."

"Which ought to be impossible, since these addresses are absolutely, globally, unique?" David prompted.

"Ought to be sir, but obviously we have the means to get round that little difficulty. I'm confident that, if we can get access to Connor's machine, we can - as we say - clone it. We also need to make sure we can get a copy of the *Sesame* program. This may not be stored on the computer, but may have been left on the CD for security. We'd guess that Connor only inserts the CD when she wants to run the program. Again, with access to the machine, we can install a sniffer program. A hidden program that will hunt for Sesame, and will send us a copy of it as soon as it is detected. I am sure that, with an hour's access to the computer, we can do all that we need to do. I've skipped over some of the details, but does any of this make much sense to you, sir?"

"Yes, it does, Hector, so far so good. However, what about the e-mail addresses? How do we get the addresses and how do we use them?"

"We will get the addresses by running Connor's e-mail program. Once we've got them, we can then lean on the service providers. As you know, they are obligated to store all messages and to provide them to us when required. They can also be asked to alert us every time someone tries to send a message to, or read a message from, these accounts."

"But how do we know where they are being accessed from? How do we know where the computer is?"

"Good question sir. In a sense, e-mail is not that different from ordinary mail. People talk about the electronic world, the cyber world, but the world is *always* physical. Sooner or later a message has to end up on the computer that asks to see it. Information that the computer requests must come back to it. The road back is through the phone point, or cable point. Let me expand. The computer is a physical object. When the computer logs on to the internet, it is given an 'IP address'. This identifies the computer on the internet. The service provider -for example, the phone or cable company- has to know which phone number each IP address relates to, otherwise it does not know which phone point to send the information to. In reality, the IP address means a short-term *physical* address. There are complications where there are multiple computers using the same connection, but it still brings us into a specific building. The IP address can also be a long term address, but that is highly unlikely to be true in this case. Bottom line, it represents a town, a street, a number. If we can trace fast enough, we get them while they are still sending - or composing - the message."

"Excellent, Hector. You almost make me feel like an expert. Now, tell me how we are going to get access to Connor's computer? What is our way in? What are the risks to us?"

"Prime Minister, let me answer that, if you will." 'M' cut in. "We have a name for the most effective route into the BBC: 'The Golden Triangle'. Otherwise known as 'money, honey, and cocaine'." 'M' permitted himself a quick smile before enlarging.

"Money is self-evident. 'Honey' refers to the traditional honey-trap, the romantic liaison. Cocaine remains the drug of choice for many in the BBC, and in Colombian volume.

Generally speaking, their security will rarely resist a couple of pretty girls, with a couple of grams, in a BBC pub." David Blenheim's face flushed red with anger. His anger was due more to the tone than the content, but his anger was real nonetheless.

"Amusing, 'M'. I'm impressed you can be so confident. So flippant. I presume you have these pretty girls to hand, not to mention sufficient quantities of a Class 'A' drug to put us both in jail?"

"I apologise, Prime Minister. I did not mean to sound flippant." The words were right, but somehow there was little in M's manner that suggested apology, as he continued. "Those operations all belong to the past. To a previous Government. In any case, it is not necessary. We already have the assets in place within the BBC. We already have the people who can give us access to Connor's computer. Give me the go-ahead, and I will expect that you will have a running *Sesame* by this time tomorrow."

David Blenheim, the Prime Minister, knew when to stop and think. He had yet to speak to the BBC. They may yet comply with his request. Just like there might yet be a cold day in Hell. No, they would not, and their security, however poor, would be stepped up. There was much else to consider. A full half-minute had passed before he replied.

"Use your assets, 'M', *immediately*. Obtain *Sesame* as soon as possible. Let me know as soon as we have it. However, please understand that we may be called to account for this sometime. Thank you, 'M'. Thank you too, Hector."

If 'M' felt any threat, there was nothing in his relaxed exit to betray him.

Dubai: Four p.m. GMT, December the Twenty-First.
Eight p.m. local time

"La llaha illa illah wa Muhammad rasul Allah" Or in English:
"There is but one God and Muhammad is His Prophet"

Few TV stations included the full text of the Al Quaeda message. Al Arabeeza did. Certainly, the sacred introduction was obligatory. The rest of the message was short and stark. The key sentences were in the middle. No translation is precise, but the message was not ambiguous.

"By the grace of Allah, the most merciful, very soon we will strike a mighty blow against the Crusader-Zionists. Very soon, the World will see the Crusaders struck down in their pride. After this blow, I call on all the faithful of the Ummah to do their sacred duty, and to join us in this last jihad, the Final War. By the Grace of the One God, Allah the Most Merciful, we will make this the Last Christmas of the Crusaders."

Catherine had taken the phone call just five minutes before.

"Catherine, I just wanted to see if you had any preference for tonight? Any special restaurant?" Andrew inquired brightly.

"Certainly, Andrew" laughed Catherine. "My preference is for a light meal and a long bath. No restaurant at all, special or otherwise."

"But we had a deal, Catherine! You promised me a date, remember?"

"Nice try, Andrew, but I expressly remember I used the word 'might'. I'm actually amazed that, given everything that's going on, you'd even think to find the time? Or that you'd imagine that a young woman like myself would even consider going out with a man with three ex-wives?" she added. And immediately cringed at her involuntary coyness. She should have been colder, much colder.

102

"Surely you must be a little intrigued by a man who is still best friends with all of three ex-wives?"

"...and probably still sleeps with them, too, Andrew?"

"Wouldn't be much point. They've all had headaches ever since the wedding day." Catherine couldn't suppress a smile.

"Seriously, Andrew, I'd be more than happy to have a drink with you sometime. I'm sure you're great company. But do you really think that I'm going to compromise my position in the debates by having dinner with a participant? Can you just imagine what the tabloids would do with that story? I'm amazed - flattered - that you'd risk your position, Andrew, but the answer is 'No'. After all this is over..." Andrew interrupted.

"If your door is not closed, Catherine, close it. If anyone can overhear you, get rid of them. This is serious." Andrew's tone changed with unexpected suddenness.

"Andrew, the door is closed and no-one can overhear. And I'm not finding this funny. I have not got time for foolish games."

"I'm afraid this is no game, Catherine. You must trust me now and I will explain later. If you want to remain as the presenter of the debates, you need to go out with me, tonight. I cannot explain why to you now, over the phone. Meet me tonight, after the debate, and I can explain. Do not meet me tonight, and tomorrow you will be off the programme. Replaced. This is not a date, Catherine. A date will have to wait. This is business." Catherine was stunned, incredulous, furious at the threat. How - and why? - could he threaten her like this? Colour rushed to her cheeks.

"Andrew, are you out of your mind? This has got to be just the cheapest trick I've ever had pulled on me. A man of your age and experience trying to threaten me into a date?" Andrew, to his surprise, could not hide his irritation at the jibe.

"Catherine, I'm sorry you think so little of me. This is neither a silly game nor a cheap trick. Nor am I making a threat, but trying to do something for *your* benefit, not mine. Not just yours, in fact. However, I am not foolish enough to assume that other people's welfare would do much to get your attention." There was a note of disappointment, disapproval, in Andrew's tone, and now it was Catherine's turn to be stung. Andrew let it hang for several seconds.

"Catherine, if you want to chair any more of the debates, if you want the BBC to keep the debates at all, then you need to meet me tonight. I'll be outside the Horse and Lion, Bayswater Road from around ten forty five." She knew it. "I'll be in a silver Mercedes SL500, and I'll flash when I see you. Given the curiosity of the average London cabbie, I suggest you take a taxi to the Drum and Monkey and walk the last hundred yards." She knew it too. But Catherine was utterly confused. Surely Andrew would have to be mad to dream up a ridiculous stunt like this? Surely, however improbable, this had to be on the level?

"I'll think about it, Andrew, but..." The line clicked dead before Catherine had a chance to finish her sentence.

Catherine thought long and hard but the only impression she made was on her brow. Catherine was still thinking when she saw the Al Arabeeza news feed. The Virus was real. The chaos was real. The debates were real. It was the idea of romantic stunts that now seemed unreal.

In the City of the Infidels, a fully clothed Ahmed Ali Khan lay on his back on the vast bed. His heart was still racing but his sweat had started to cool. He still could not believe his own incredible stupidity. He still had no message on his contact. He still waited on his codes. He needed to run the *Caliph* software to decode them both. Yet he had let his laptop run out of charge, and switch itself off! True, he had one backup laptop. But surely not just the one sole laptop to trigger the last jihad, to condemn the crusaders to dust! Allah be blessed, for, somehow, the laptop had rebooted, against all the odds and truly a sign of Allah's will. But not before Ahmed had gone through a hell of fear and dread. Now Ahmed Ali Khan must calm down, and wait. There were only five days to go. He still did not have what he needed, he still did not know where to go and whom to see. There was still so much to do, so much pressure to withstand. Allah be merciful, let the computers not fail him! Ahmed Ali Khan knew only one reliable way to relax, and opened his Koran. At Surah Forty Eight, Al Fath, the Surah of Conquest. The familiar opening *'Inna fatahna laka fathanmubeenan.'* Or, in English: *'Verily We have granted thee a manifest Victory.'*

Back in London, Peter Bradshaw, the Director General of the BBC, had expected the call. It had started well enough, but now the pleasantries were exhausted.

"Peter, I am sure you know why I'm calling. This Christmas Virus is a matter not just of national interest, but of global interest. It is an attack on democracy everywhere. My people assure me that a working copy of the *Sesame* programme would be an enormous help to them in neutralising this virus. With your co-operation, we can do this without the terrorists knowing anything about it. Can I take it we will work together on this?" Peter Bradshaw was, fortunately, ready. He had done his homework, and his notes lay before him, in sixteen point type. He would get only one chance, and he wanted to get it right.

"Prime Minister, we are absolutely agreed on the need to protect democracy. That is why I must, unfortunately, decline your request. Please let me explain. The BBC has only agreed to using *Sesame*, and abiding by its terms, because the end product is free speech. By staging the debates, we graphically demonstrate to the world the unique, liberating power of free speech. Of democracy itself, because democracy and free speech are inextricably linked. If we were to grant your request, and it were discovered that we had given you *Sesame*, what would be the consequences? We would lose *Sesame* and the debates would stop. Perhaps they would be staged elsewhere, but perhaps not. Further, it would send a message to the world that the BBC is more concerned with the approval of government than with free speech. The BBC, which has been an icon of democracy since the very beginnings of broadcasting, would be forever tarnished. It would be the beginning of the end. I am sorry, Prime Minister, but I cannot allow that to happen."

"Peter, free speech is not democracy. Democracy is a system that uses free speech. Free speech is itself neutral. Do not confuse the tool with its task. Free speech can be used for good or ill. That is why we need laws to protect against its misuse. Laws to protect against libel, slander. Defamation. Laws against incitement. You deal with these laws every day. We also have laws to compel the disclosure of any information that the State needs in order to protect its citizens. I am sure you agree we need them too. Now you have asked me to consider the consequences if the terrorists discover that you have co-operated with the government. Your own government." the PM added, tartly. "Firstly, I can see no reason why they would find out. Secondly, and more importantly, surely the potential benefit outweighs the minimal risk? Surely we both accept the gravity of this attack on the West? Surely we both agree that we must use every weapon to defend ourselves from this assault on our culture?

"The most potent weapon we possess, Prime Minister, is free speech. You are asking me to risk losing it. You are asking me to be the one to allow the destruction of one of the greatest institutions of this country, indeed, of Western civilisation itself. Is this not exactly what the terrorists want?"

"Peter, I am asking for your co-operation. You know that this is matter of national security. I would rather do this amicably, but

I will do what I have to do for the sake of this nation. You know that there are other measures available to me. Do not force my hand on this."

"Prime Minister, this call is no longer productive. I will not compromise the BBC and the principle of free speech. Do what you have to do, certainly. But you can expect that the BBC will defend itself vigorously."

"No doubt it will, director. No doubt you will defend your narrow interests against those of the nation. Well, you can also expect that I will do my best to defend us all."

FIVE

The wardrobe of any television presenter is no small affair. The wardrobe of a female presenter, known for her glamour, is most certainly not. Catherine was, however, a practical and organised woman. Her wardrobe was grouped into sections to reflect the impression she would make. Within a section, she had many outfits of great similarity - and several exact duplicates. Today, the lady in the mirror should have again worn Karan, St Laurent, Choo and Raymond. Different items, of course, but subtly the same. But she did not. Catherine's face was still flushed with anger at the thought, the *presumption* of it! She had received the *Sesame* code in e-mail, run *Sesame* and seen tomorrow's message, God forbid! She was just getting ready to move when Jeremy Wexham had appeared. Catherine had appreciated his words of encouragement, even if she was anxious to get going. The conversation had, however, then gone to some unexpected places.

"No doubt you are anxious to get going, Catherine, so I'll be brief. It's just a small thing. There's a feeling among senior management about *respect*. Even the BBC has never had an audience this global. We want to make sure we show *respect*, you know, for all cultures?"

"Jeremy, I have no idea what that just meant. Perhaps you would prefer to use a different language?" Catherine had not meant to be so sharp, but hell, she had better be sharp tonight!

"Modesty, Catherine. We want to make sure nothing you wear will upset anyone's standards of modesty, show them any disrespect. Or distract people from the serious nature of the debate, you know? There is a feeling that last night you were maybe a little too... *Western*?" For fully twenty seconds, Catherine was too shocked, too angry to say anything at all. For Catherine, that was a very long time to be speechless. The length of the silence was reflected in her parting words. As she headed down the corridor.

"Couldn't agree with you more, Jeremy. Tonight it'll be a grass skirt and topless. Bye."

Well, she had taken his words on board. Tonight she still went with Karan and Choo. And the Divine Raymond, of course. The blouse, however, was from Mikie, and it somehow just showed a little more *shape*. As she made her last critical inspection, her mood suddenly lightened. "Quite the glamorous woman, aren't you?" and she smiled. "But the grass skirt is *so* not you."

Nine p.m. GMT, December the Twenty-First.

Across the five continents, millions, no *billions*, of people gathered expectantly around screens large and small, private and public. Their focus is a small to medium-sized studio, BBC headquarters, London.

Catherine had brought the studio smoothly under control and made a brief recapitulation of the rules. An expectant silence had prevailed as Catherine read the charges.

"I charge the West with the destruction of heroes, the promotion of weakness over strength, the failure to provide inspiration for their young"

The sequence of speakers was to be Anne-Marie, Krishnan, William, Andrew and Anwar. Catherine had just prompted Anne-Marie.

Anne-Marie rose smoothly to her feet. If anything, she looked more beautiful than the night before. All attention switched immediately to her. As, perhaps, it always did. SORCERESS again, Catherine thought. Do the same spells work twice?

"Ladies and gentlemen, I would like to ask you all to salute the greatest hero in the world today. A hero not just to me as an African woman, but to us all. Ladies and gentlemen, I ask you all to salute: Nelson Mandela!" As she bowed her head, many followed her.

"Ladies and gentlemen, modern Africa is the creation of heroes. Jomo Kenyatta, Kwame Nkrumah, Kenneth Kaunda, Joshua N'Komo, Robert Mugabe, Nelson Mandela - I salute you all! Through your bravery you have liberated my continent, and I thank you. Believe me, ladies and gentlemen, without these heroes, the world would be a very different place." Many of the names were unknown to the audience, but not all. There was no disguising the disquiet that greeted some of them. They were names that were synonymous with corruption and cruelty, and on a grand scale. Anne-Marie was happy to acknowledge the disquiet.

"I understand your reservations. In a way, you are right. These are not necessarily the names of saintly people. Not necessarily even good people. But they were heroes, nonetheless. People who would fight and die for others. For a principle, a cause. Idealists. That does not mean they did not have feet of clay. I am afraid that heroes usually do. Even Nelson is not *perfect*, you know?" and Anne Marie executed the most perfect wink. To be instantly followed by her trademark, high-voltage smile. The spell was working already: the audience was captivated as she continued.

"Yes, I think we need heroes, although we must be prepared for them to be a little less than perfect. Yes, I even think that the *existence* of heroes might be essential to a healthy country. All countries, all cultures, have had their heroes. Including the West. Except that in the West you no longer believe in them. Like the Tooth Fairy, you think. I knew a very famous historian once.

When I was younger and men were still interested in me." she added with a smile. A hard smile to resist.

"My clever man could make history come alive. He could hold your attention like a child's to a bed-time story. I remember once that he talked about heroes. About how you could link the decline of the West to their rejection of heroes, and of heroism itself. He even told me he could put dates on when it had happened." Anne-Marie paused, to gather her breath, to let the tension grow, the expectancy build.

"He said that the French lost their heroes on the fourteenth of June, nineteen forty. When they surrendered Paris to the Germans. Without a fight. When they decided their beautiful city was more important than their liberty. When they decided that architecture meant more than ideals. When they decided that they were too civilised to fight the barbarians." 'Not sorceress,' Catherine thought. 'TEACHER.'

"He said that the Germans lost their faith in heroes a little over two years later. In another city, almost three thousand miles away. In a ruined city, a city of utter destruction and death. In Stalingrad. The Germans lost their faith in heroes on the thirty first of January, nineteen forty three, when the Sixth Army chose to surrender rather than die on the banks of the Volga." Another pause.

"He said the British lost their faith in heroes on July the seventeenth, nineteen forty five. When they voted Churchill from power right after of the victory he did so much to win. When they decided that they no longer needed their heroes. That they were just too tired for any more heroics." Anne Marie looked up and paused. GOVERNESS Catherine thought, finally. A teacher of small children. Is that how we appear?

"Finally, my clever man came to the Americans. They were different, he said. It is not really true to say that they have lost their heroes. He did not think that they lost them after Vietnam, as many people did. No, they had a uniquely American reaction. Since they lost the war, their soldiers could not be heroes. Yet they could hardly make heroes of the Vietnamese, who, apart from being the enemy, seemed both faceless and cruel. So, whom did they choose? Who else were the victors? Answer: their very own anti-war movement. Why not, since they had won? But, of course, these were hardly conventional heroes. So they decided to change the meaning of hero. From now on, the anti-hero became a hero. The age of the anti-hero had begun. Not traditional heroes, but their opposite. The time when a six became a nine, as in the song." For some reason, Catherine felt a shiver. 'When a six became a nine?' The pull of the Tarot. Who but the Magus turned a six into a nine? Meanwhile, Anne-Marie had continued.

"Since then, so my clever friend told me, deep down, America has been in decline. Ladies and gentlemen, I wish I could talk as he could, but I cannot. But believe me, I was convinced. We need our heroes and their heroism. Without them, ideals fail and we start to decline." Anne Marie paused and took a sip of water. Her time clock was still healthy, her audience still captive. Catherine was not happy. 'She is using someone else's words', she thought. How can I choose her character when she is hiding behind some else's words?'

"So we come to lawyers, and this so-called 'cult of the victim'. Well, I really do find the whole Western compensation thing to be utterly ridiculous. Utter bullshit." Anne-Marie did not follow this unexpected earthiness with a smile. "Really. If you reward weakness you will cultivate weakness. We all know that. We also all know that to make progress you have to take chances. When you take chances, things can go wrong - otherwise it would not be a chance, would it? But there is no way you can take chances, if you have a pack of legal hyenas waiting to profit when chance goes against you. Waiting for things to go wrong. I know there are times when people genuinely need compensation, but this is so not what we are talking about. What the West has is compensation sickness. An irresistible desire to seek personal injury and misfortune, and someone to blame it on. A madness, in other words. No, ladies and gentlemen, you are most welcome to your compensation sickness. Just do not bring it to my country, *please?*" Anne Marie's winning smile took the sting from the barb.

"I really did not mean to talk so long, kind people. Let me just finish with two things. Firstly, for the record, I vote for the motion. I think the West is guilty of the destruction of its heroes. Secondly, and more importantly, Nelson Mandela." Puzzled looks accompanied her pause.

"Yes, Nelson Mandela. Heroes are real. And like Nelson, they are not saints either. Yes, believe in them. Try and find some new ones before it is too late. Thanks to you all for your attention." Anne-Marie sank gracefully to her seat. The applause was long and genuine.

Not exactly a teacher, thought Catherine. GOVERNESS. With a hint of parent. Doing her best for the small children, but they have so much to learn. She let the applause die down before she turned to Krishnan.

"Krishnan, your questions, please?"

Ahmed Ali Khan's concentration had been total. Heroes and heroism, ideals: by the Grace of Allah, his fate. It took him several seconds to register the alarm that signalled an incoming message. He leaped from the bed to the laptop and clicked on the 'view message' button. The computer seemed to take forever to respond. *Forever.* Allah save them all if things were going to get slower! Despite the air-conditioning, beads of sweat ran down his forehead. By the time Ahmed turned back from the Spam, in disgust, the round of questions had already reached Andrew.

Not that Andrew was making much use of it.

"Wonderful speech, Anne-Marie, although I expected no less." Andrew opened, with a roguish grin. However, Anne-Marie, I must say that I am surprised that everyone accepts as heroes people with so much blood on their hands," Andrew opened. "and so much cash in Switzerland. Perhaps you seem to have frightened everyone into submission. Or charmed them?" he added with a smile that was immediately, and challengingly, answered. "Anyway, I'm charmed, too." he added, to laughter, and sat down.

Anwar brought the round of questions to an end when he politely declined his opportunity. Krishnan heard Catherine's invitation to speak, and prayed that he was ready. He rose a little nervously to his feet.

"Ladies and gentlemen, as Anne Marie said, Nelson Mandela is the great hero of our time. Anne Marie is proud that the liberation of Africa could produce such heroes, and many like him. She should be. I also am proud of the heroes of *our* liberation struggle. The liberation of the Indian continent. I am proud to talk about the man who was the greatest hero of the *previous* age. A uniquely Indian hero. I am proud to ask you to salute: Mahatma Gandhi." There was a reaction in the audience, certainly some recognition. But the audience was, had to be, a cross-section of the British population. Well versed in the stars of soap opera and sport, pitiful in history beyond that version served by the BBC. Gandhi was so long ago, and his character so difficult to understand. However, if Krishnan was disappointed, he did not show it, as he continued.

"A uniquely Indian hero. The great apostle of non-violence. A man who did not consider that heroes necessarily had feet of clay. A hero and, yes, I say it, a saint. Ladies and gentlemen, we *can* ask everything of our heroes. Bravery, yes. Idealism, yes. But also

114

goodness. Like Gandhi. Like Mandela too." Krishnan took a sip of water while he gathered his thoughts.

"Mahatma Gandhi was not only unique in his opposition to war, but in another respect. He was a lawyer. Gandhi considered the law his most potent weapon in the war for liberation. We must understand that heroes can be lawyers. That the law can be a weapon as potent as any bomb."

Ahmed Ali Khan had been riveted to the screen. At these words, anger swept blood to his face. "What madness is this man talking? What use are lawyers to our faithful in Afghanistan? What use are lawyers to our people in Palestine?" Ahmed seemed to be compelled to run through the familiar arguments, his constant debate. It was several minutes before Ahmed refocused on the debate. Krishnan had moved his theme on.

"So let us come to this idea of the 'Cult of the Victim'. Let us consider the merits of using the law to fight our battles for justice. The American system has gone mad, it is true. The British are following, as they always do. Obedient to their masters. There is no doubt that some people are abusing the system, and that some fraud is taking place. However, despite that, there are a great many genuine cases. A great many Americans, and British, can now get compensation at a level appropriate to the injury they have suffered. That is just and fair. There is only one thing wrong. One thing *very* wrong. *In the Western world of compensation, their lives are worth more than ours.*" The audience within the hall were visibly startled. They seemed to freeze for a few seconds as they tried to digest what Krishnan had said. 'LAWYER. PRIEST. Which is it?', Catherine thought.

"Ladies and gentlemen, there are American and British multinationals all across the developing world. *Western* multinationals all across the developing world. In many cases they are there because the local regulations are - shall we say - *freer* than those in the West. Accidents and tragedies can and do happen, and more of them. Our people are being injured, poisoned, polluted. Yet what compensation is paid to our people? Little or none! Of course, it is true that a dollar may go much further outside of the West, and that awards should reflect that. But the compensation that is being paid - when it is paid - is derisory, insulting! No, it is not the existence of compensation that is the problem. It is not the existence of lawyers that is the problem. The problem is the *inequality* of the compensation. The problem is that the West still treats us as lesser peoples. They still *see* us as lesser peoples. I am sorry to say that to you, ladies and gentlemen of the audience. I do not accuse any of you here of being directly involved. But what I say is true nonetheless, and it is my duty to speak." A pause, a last gathering of breath.

"So, ladies and gentlemen, to the motion. Yes the West has destroyed its heroes, that is true. Yes, the West has created what was termed 'the cult of the victim', that is also true. However, I do not think that the so-called charge is important. It is not the real issue. The real issue is, as Anne-Marie said, that heroes are real. Can anyone deny Mandela? Or Gandhi? Not only are heroes real, but they may also be good people. Perhaps not just good, but saintly. Seek and you may just find. Seek your heroes, and you may just find again your culture. And with that, your soul."

Applause swelled around Krishnan as he sat down. 'GANDHI', Catherine thought. 'He's playing GANDHI himself. And well.' Outwardly, Catherine was the image of cool professional poise, but, inwardly she was impressed. Not sold, but impressed. She gave the audience ten seconds before she passed to the first questions.

"Questions, comments, Anne-Marie?" Anne-Marie looked as if she would pass, but then could not resist.

"Krishnan, a very moving speech, and I thank you. There is much we agree on, we both know that. However, I'm sorry, but I cannot accept that this non-violent way works. Yes, there is clearly a place for non-violence - did not Mandela show that too? - but it cannot be the only approach. Wolves eat lambs, I'm afraid. They are not impressed by their meekness. Anyway, Krishnan, I want to ask you about the compensation issue. What do you think would be the effect of forcing the multinationals to operate to Western standards in the developing world? Western standards of safety and compensation?"

"Fairness. Equity. Equality." Krishnan replied swiftly.

"Really?" Anne-Marie mused. "Not equality with the conditions in our local companies, that's for sure. They cannot afford it. Hmm, little outposts of Western laws dotted around our countries. I wonder which country will be the first to try it?" The question hung in the air long enough for Catherine to know it was time to move on to Gladwin. The Senator briefly congratulated Krishnan on his speech and was silent. "Andrew?" she asked. Andrew seemed to look at some notes he had made, and then started to speak in an unusually diffident tone.

"A moving speech, Krishnan, and some things in it that I agree with. However, you'll need to forgive me, Krishnan, for my bluntness. Gandhi. It is difficult for anyone to speak objectively of Gandhi. It is maybe too early, or already too late. Too many myths, too many taboos. But I'm going to try. Yes, Gandhi may have been part saint, but many think he was also part madman. How else could he insist that his people reject any kind of industrialisation? That all Indians spin their own cotton? How else could he tell his people that it was better for them to be exterminated by the Japanese than to take up arms in resistance?" This was unexpected. Like most of the rest of the world, Krishnan was shocked, angry. His reply was immediate.

"Your disrespect does you no credit, Andrew! You should be

ashamed. Gandhi was a very great man, a very holy man - who could deny it? He had some unusual beliefs, it is true. The spinning wheel, I admit, but that was only a symbol. But to suggest that his own people choose death before resistance, no, Andrew, I do not believe he ever said that." Andrew thought differently

"But he did, Krishnan, and no doubt people who are interested can confirm that after we go home. Or even while we speak. And I am not ashamed of speaking the truth, nor will I ever be. Anyway, the point is, I would expect a hero to defend his people, not to lead them to extermination." Andrew then addressed the last remark directly to Krishnan.

"I ask you the question, Krishnan. What kind of hero would knowingly lead his own people to oblivion?"

"You have twisted the truth, Andrew. You should acknowledge the greatness of Gandhi, and not demean his memory!" countered Krishnan. Andrew did not answer, but he knew he had made his point. Just enough, but not too much.

"Anwar?" prompted Catherine. Anwar was brief.

"Krishnan, I do not understand what you propose for these Western multinationals. You say that they should apply Western social and compensation standards wherever they are, correct? That we would have little outposts of Western law dotted around our countries?"

"Yes." Krishnan confirmed. "They must treat their local workers as they would their American or British workers. That is the definition of justice." The shake of Anwar's head spoke sadly of disagreement.

"But surely, Krishnan, that means that our workers will become infected with the compensation madness of the West? The corruption of the West? How will our workers ever again work for a local company? Worse than that, what if they infect the rest of the workforce? What if they spread their Western disease to everyone else? Surely, Krishnan, this is not an equality that you want?" Krishnan shook his head in turn.

"That will not happen, Anwar. Our people will not expect our local companies to work to Western standards. They will not want them to. They only want the multinationals to treat their workers the same everywhere."

Anwar did not look convinced, but he did not look to Catherine like he was going to reply either. It was time to move on. Senator William Gladwin had been compulsive viewing yesterday, even if things had not gone well for him. It was with a keen sense of anticipation that she prompted him and waited for the fireworks. Would the demagogue make a second appearance?

Senator William Gladwin rose slowly to his feet, carefully placing his glasses on the table beside him as he did so. Nothing in his calm, confident bearing hinted at the nerves that shot through him. His had been a traumatic twenty four hours. Americans are a patriotic people, and expected the senator for Massachusetts to be at least a little patriotic too. As a minimum, to represent the basic interests of his constituents and his countrymen. No-one seemed to understand what he had tried to do the day before. Least of all the leader of his party, his key campaign contributors, or his wife. Not that he had succeeded, he had to be honest with himself. Today would be different. Had to be. Senator William Gladwin began boldly.

"Ladies and gentlemen, our heroes are alive and well and living in the West. Let me repeat. Our heroes are alive and well and living in the West. Let me also say that we have no so-called 'cult of the victim'. What we do have is a 'cult of the just'. We are not guilty of the crimes because no crime has been committed." Catherine was not disappointed. Judging by his opening, Mr Gladwin was not about to let her down. 'Once a demagogue, always a demagogue' she thought.

"Ladies and gentlemen, we have already heard much today of

119

heroes. Heroes of liberation struggles, good men mostly, some bad men perhaps, maybe even a saint. These were the heroes that answered their people's need in desperate times. These are the kinds of heroes we used to have in the West. That we do *not* have any more. Not because we do not have heroes. No, because our needs are now different, and so now must be our heroes." The Senator paused for a few seconds, giving the audience some time to consider, and absorb, then he resumed.

"The West has fought many wars, that no-one can deny. Our heroes have been defined by those wars. As we have progressed, as we now seek peace above all things, so has our need for heroes. Our heroes now are those who would preserve and strengthen the peace. Our heroes are those who would rather the pen than the gun. Krishnan was not wrong. Lawyers can be heroes. I would put it more strongly. In a mature society, it *must* be the lawyer who is hero. It must be the warrior who is villain. No, ladies and gentlemen, the West has not destroyed its heroes. The West now seeks heroes for *today*, not yesterday. The *right* kind of heroes. Let me be a little less abstract. According to the values we have heard today, there are plenty of old-style heroes in the world. People of courage, principle, idealism. People who are also responsible for one of the greatest threats that civilisation has ever faced. I am talking, of course, of suicide bombers."

The atmosphere in the studio, already tense, intensified. Hairs stood up on the back of Catherine's long elegant neck. Senator William Gladwin paused long enough to take a slow, careful breath, and deepened his tone.

"Yes, ladies and gentlemen, it is not crazy to see suicide bombers as heroes. In some ways they are. They are also responsible for brutal, senseless, mass murder. For the killing of innocents, men women and children. For the disregard of even the most basic qualities of humanity. Is there anyone here that thinks what they do can be justified? Is there anyone here that does not believe that some people think them heroes?" Catherine stole a glance at Anwar. He was staring straight ahead, jaw clenched, a slow pulse beating visibly on his bulging neck.

"Ladies and gentlemen, that is why we need a different kind of hero now. A hero that brings the pen, not the bomb. Lawyers can be those heroes. I don't mean all lawyers, obviously, but the great ones. The ones who make a difference. Do not be confused by all this 'cult of victim' nonsense. As Krishnan said, lawyers are the ones who protect the little guy. The ones who stand up against the large corporations that would trample on your rights. Compensation does not cultivate weakness. Compensation cultivates *respect for the law*. It is the law that will bring us peace. That is what it is designed to do. Can we dream of a time when it becomes impossible to go to war - for legal reasons? When it is too hard to justify it in court, too hard to avoid 'collateral damage'? Too hard to ensure the well-being of your troops? Think of it. Wars become impossible because they are too impractical. Not worth the risk." Gladwin lowered his voice once more, deepening the tone and increasing the intensity.

"Ladies and gentlemen, do not doubt that a lawyer can be a hero. A hero with a pen, not a gun nor a bomb. Ladies and gentlemen, you *will* not doubt that a lawyer can be a hero. *Not when he brings an end to war!*"

Senator William Gladwin was already seated before the audience reacted.

Exploded, in applause. Catherine was, despite herself, impressed. Who could not be? 'Without doubt,' Catherine thought, 'demagogues are dangerous. Perhaps more dangerous than lawyers. And do demagogues also bring an end to war? Or a beginning?'

Ahmed Ali Khan had been as absorbed as he could remember. Yes, he had heard the insults. That was no big thing, and to be expected from an infidel. He had also heard the word 'hero', and it made him feel strong, confident, *important*. Even the infidel had called them heroes. Back in the studio, Anne-Marie was first in line to ask questions. Her time clock showed over two minutes.

"William, a wonderful speech, some wonderful thoughts. Hmm, I just don't know what to make of you?" She almost made it a question. Then asked a different one. "I guess my only question is a simple one." She looked directly at the Senator. "Are you sincere?" A simple, unexpected, question. Direct. Potent. William Gladwin paused long enough to make it clear he took the challenge. That he did not need to bluster. That nothing in his answer could condemn him.

"Yes, Anne-Marie, I am. And I thank you for giving me the chance to say it." It was clear. Clear from his tone, his words, his manner. No-one in the studio, nor anywhere, could reasonably doubt the sincerity of the Senator for Massachusetts. At least this time. Catherine let the silence build before prompting Krishnan. He spent a minute or so to stress his broad agreement with the senator, before Catherine passed the questions to Andrew. Several seconds passed slowly before Andrew spoke.

"William, I respect your sincerity, and I admire your sentiments. However, I do have a couple of questions. You associate compensation with justice, and with making future wars impractical, correct?" William nodded his assent. "That was exactly the position taken by the allies at the end of the First World War. They imposed punitive reparations - compensation by another word - on Germany. To punish her, to repair the damage she had caused, and to make it impossible for her to invade again. Yet, William, she did. And the cause? Those very reparations. Historians are not a breed to seek agreement, but all serious historians do agree on that. *That the biggest single cause of the Second World War was the reparations imposed after the*

First. The reparations, and the German sense of injustice at their size and severity. *Put bluntly, William, compensation did not prevent the Second World War, it caused it."* If the Senator was shaken, he certainly did not show it . He did, however, seem to take plenty of time to compose an answer.

"I regret, Andrew, that my duties do not allow me as much time to indulge in history as I would like. However, I know that you do have the time to indulge in such things, so I'm going to assume that what you say is correct. It is an intriguing question, but the answer is mundane. The reparations were obviously at a level that the Germans thought was unfair. That is the consequence of having negotiations *after* the war has been fought, and lost. When you are *forced* to agree. When lawyers negotiate *before* the fact, not after, then the result will be fair to both sides or no agreement would be reached." Andrew seemed to expect the answer as he did not hesitate.

"...and if no agreement were reached, the result would be what, William? War?" William Gladwin took longer over this answer than the previous one.

"If no agreement is reached you keep talking. And talking. You keep talking until you get agreement. Any good lawyer knows that, Andrew." The Senator paused, then, with impeccable timing, added a last line. "It doesn't do any harm to the bill, either." The audience roared, and Andrew laughed with them. To Catherine, his laughter looked absolutely genuine. She waited for it all to subside, and for Andrew to indicate he was happy enough to leave things be.

"Questions, Anwar?" Anwar had a question.

"William, you have great faith in the rule of law. You must know that not all countries share it. Not even your own, I might add." Everyone sensed that Anwar was about to say something *big*, to step over a line, but he seemed to pull himself back. "Anyway, let's not digress. My question is, what happens when countries do *not* respect the law? When, for example, they start a war? Who enforces the law?"

"IF it happens. In time, I think it will be impossible. Too many laws within a country. Between countries. But, to guard against any eventuality, we would have some kind of a supra-national force that would come in and keep the peace."

"Something like the United Nations?"

"In essence, yes. But more powerful."

"Something like the United Nations? Which we have had for how long? And for how many wars? I think that most people will need to see the current United Nations work before they will believe in another one." Anwar had made his point and William was not about to dig deeper. Still, Catherine waited until the exchange was clearly over. The audience needed to gather their thoughts, surely? She certainly did. Andrew was next. Quite the enigma. Thoughts of their proposed meeting - only a couple of hours away - surfaced, unwelcome. Catherine refocused. She could sense Andrew's tension. Not exactly tension, in fact, more a kind of expectancy, a buzz. 'Good luck, Andrew', she thought, to her surprise.

"Andrew, the floor is yours." Andrew rose and gazed pleasantly, almost ruefully, at the audience. When he started to speak his tone was tinged with regret.

"Ladies and gentlemen, I am sorry that tonight I have to be the one who seems a little negative. The one who has to pour a little cold water on things. I hate it, but it has to be done. I want to believe in much of what I have heard tonight. As you do, no doubt. But we know that, deep down, there is something wrong with what we have heard." Andrew paused and looked around the audience.

"War will always be with us. *Believe it*. I'm sorry, but it's true. We'd all love to believe otherwise, but we all know different. Does anyone here really think we do not need our armies? Does anyone here really imagine a day when we will give them up? Yes, respect for the law is a noble principle. But how strong is this respect? Does it stop common criminals? No, I'm afraid not. How then can it stop the tyrant or dictator bent on war? I'm sorry to have to say it, but laws are respected only by the good guys. To deal with the bad guys, we need people who fight." Some people in the audience nodded involuntarily.

"Yes, war will always be with us. Bravery will always be required. That is why we have heroes. Heroism is related to war as medicine is to disease. War is the illness, heroism is the cure. Heroism is not what causes wars. Appeasement causes wars. Weakness causes wars. Heroism helps convince the bad guys that it is not a good idea." Andrew took a sip of water.

"I hear that we have redefined heroes. That we really do have heroes, they are just different. More mature. As if. As if human nature has really changed. No, I am sorry, but the West is guilty of the accusations. We stand accused of ignoring the good, measuring only the bad. Not being concerned with great deeds, but only weaknesses and faults. We are guilty as charged. This is *exactly* how we have killed our heroes. In Britain, Nelson became not the saviour of his country, but an adulterer. Churchill became not the saviour of his country - perhaps even of Western civilisation itself - but a cigar-smoking drunk. Why? What is this disease that we seem to have, where we want to diminish people, humble them, bring them down? When did we get so mean spirited that we must make everyone ordinary? No, ladies and gentlemen, we have heroes - we had heroes - we just got to be too small minded to give them the recognition they deserve." People in the audience started to shift uncomfortably. 'PROPHET' Catherine thought. 'John the Baptist, preaching in the wilderness. Calling on people to repent.'

"In any case, war or no war, heroes will always be with us. From as soon as they can walk, children look for heroes. What father has not been a hero to his son? At least briefly?" Andrew added, to a curious ripple of nervous laughter from the back right of the audience.

"Ladies and gentlemen, let's admit it. Even as we get older we still have heroes, even if they are only the sporting kind. What is it that makes a hero? What is we look for? Courage, yes. Willpower, yes. Without will you can achieve nothing. Idealism, some kind of unconditional commitment, yes. Something that cannot be bought. But not just that. A hero must also bring success. In the broad sense of a real hero, their actions must succeed, they must benefit other people. It is not enough to be brave and idealistic. You must also succeed." Andrew paused and looked around the audience.

"That is why suicide bombers are not heroes. They are not heroes because their actions do not bring benefit to those whom they love. Brave, yes. Idealistic, yes. Good for their people, no. Let me come back to the central point, which is heroes, real heroes. Basically, I agree with Anne-Marie. It is not that complicated. We need to give our heroes a chance. We need to measure their greatness, the benefits they have brought to us all. We need to remember that they are not saints. We need to stop being so small-minded." Andrew paused over another sip of water. The audience waited in utter silence before he continued.

"Can lawyers be heroes? Maybe. But only if they stop being lawyers. Think about it. A lawyer is someone for hire. Someone you pay to represent you. Someone who is happy to do whatever he has to do, to talk as long as it takes, whatever is good for the bill, right?" No-one was looking, but a brief and rueful smile came to the face of William Gladwin. Andrew continued, as if oblivious.

"A lawyer is someone who will fight for you, whether you are right or wrong. Ladies and gentlemen, we do not call that a hero. We call that a mercenary. *And with a mercenary, ladies and gentlemen, you had better pray that you do not run out of money."* Many heads in the audience nodded in assent.

"I don't even want to waste time on the 'cult of the victim'. We all know that it has stolen its way into our lives. The whole 'no win, no fee' mentality. Compensation and settlements. I had an idea last night that is probably crazy, but I'm going to tell you anyway. It seems to me that most of our laws are old. We need lawyers - and judges - to interpret them for the present day. To these old laws, we add new laws. These additions create interactions, complications, and, inevitably, contradictions. There is also the continuing problem of precedent. No matter how hard we try, as time goes by, we need more and more lawyers and yet still the whole legal system becomes less and less efficient. It is inevitable." Andrew paused again, as if to assess his audience, then continued.

"However, ladies and gentlemen, unfortunately, it is worse than that. Every election we get to vote for parties on broad, vague, headline issues. The economy, health and welfare, crime, those kind of things. But we do not get to vote on the laws the politicians actually pass, which seem to always present a very different agenda. A social agenda." Andrew took a deep breath, before delivering his next words were with a ferocious intensity.

"Ladies and gentlemen, in one generation the politicians have turned this country from a mildly Christian, traditional British culture into a nihilist, multi-cultural, social experiment and I do not remember ever getting to vote on any of the key issues. Do any of you?" The audience was visibly shocked. Yes, Andrew did have a point, but what kind of man dare say these things? Did this make him a fascist? Or a racist? Surely there was a name for this kind of person? Some kind of 'ist'? 'BARBARIAN.' Catherine thought. 'A barbarian at the gates, sensing the Empire is ready to fall.' The audience were still in shock. They needed time to absorb this sudden, impassioned, bombshell. Andrew gave them a few seconds before he continued.

"Yes, ladies and gentlemen, I am one of them. A democrat. In the true sense of the word. I believe in democracy. I think that means that the laws reflect the will of the people. I do not believe that we have this today. *Because the politicians are happy to let us vote on slogans, but never on laws.* They reserve that right for themselves. *Yes, ladies and gentlemen, we get the slogans but the politicians get the laws."* Andrew delivered the words with a fierce, angry intensity, and gazed deliberately around the audience. Long enough for the phrases to register. Then a little more, just time enough to let the tension ease a little, before he resumed in a more relaxed and reasonable tone.

"Anyway, through time and the trickery of politicians, it comes to the same thing. We do not have a set of laws that are suitable for a healthy society. That is one reason we are in decline. Ladies and gentlemen, I'd like to suggest two things. Firstly, that we agree on a new, simple set of laws, and throw all the old ones out. Start again. New laws, no precedents. A simpler, modern system with a minimum of laws *that we, the public, have agreed on.* Yes, that we have agreed on. That we have been able to vote on. We have the technology now. Why not?" The studio seemed to murmur agreement.

"I'd also like to suggest a second thing. I'd like to suggest that all laws get a 'sell-by' date. That they automatically lapse unless they continue to be useful. Why not?" Again, a murmur of agreement. Andrew gave the audience long enough to let the agreement register, then continued.

"Ladies and gentlemen, I've been the one here who has tried to be practical. To stay away from dreaming. But, damn, sometimes we need a dream. Let me give you a dream. *Not of an end to war…but of an end to lawyers!"* Cheers resounded around the Fall River diner. The studio, however, didn't buy it. They were confused. Where were they going now? 'The barbarian has gone too far! These are civilised people.' thought Catherine. Andrew waited a few seconds to let their confusion, and tension build.

128

"That's right, ladies and gentlemen, that kind of talk is always foolish. The indulgence of children. We all know that lawyers will always be with us, just like war." A pause, nods of agreement, relief from the audience. But Andrew was not going to let them get comfortable again. His next words were delivered almost in a shout.

"So let's make sure they deal with the laws we actually want." This time, the audience really got the point, many heads nodding in agreement. 'Nice timing' thought Catherine. Andrew acknowledged their reaction, and glanced at his time clock.

"Ladies and gentlemen, I need to finish. Let me come back to the point, heroes. I'd like, as Anne-Marie and Krishnan suggested, for the West to find some heroes. Of course, we do not have far to look, because we can find many of them without much effort at all. They are in our own history. We can welcome back our old heroes, whom we disowned in an age of pettiness and jealousy. Welcome back, Nelson and Churchill. However, it is not enough. Right now, I think the West is failing. We are lost. Today, the West needs someone to have the courage to stand up and tell the truth, and to hell with the consequences. Today, the West needs someone to have the courage to stand up and demand change. Today, the West needs leadership. Ladies and gentlemen, today the West needs a new hero."

Andrew sat down. Catherine was as stunned as everyone else. Not just barbarian. HERO. BARBARIAN HERO. She was stunned, for she had not seen it coming. Everyone else was certainly stunned too. What had they just heard? Just what was Andrew Westlands suggesting? Should they be applauding, or what? Silence stole empty seconds from the time clocks. This was the kind of silence that can build, and last. No, this was still a show, still theatre. Her show. The silence needed broken. "Questions, Anne-Marie?" Catherine asked.

Anne-Marie's eyes were wide and her face showed a mixture of shock, amusement, fascination.

"Andrew, darling, you might just be my hero." she breathed, without a hint of embarrassment. "Just a pity they're going to lock you up if you stay here. Why not come back to Africa with me? We still welcome heroes. And I'm sure I can find someone to look after you." she finished, with theatrical coyness. It broke the spell and the studio laughed. 'Hands off, witch!' thought Catherine, and immediately wondered why? Andrew joined in the laughter but let it go at that. Catherine was glad to pass the questions to Krishnan. He did not seem quite so amused.

"I am glad you are someone's hero, Andrew. I rather think you need to be. I do not share your enthusiasm for the heroes of your imperial past. I suspect you may just have read more comic books than history books. However, there are more important issues and our time is short. Did I hear you correctly when you said that we should abolish all laws and start again? That we have the technology to do this today? How on Earth do you start again?" Andrew paused for several seconds before he replied. It mattered, and he wanted to get this out right.

"The purpose of Parliament is to pass laws. But it is the people's right to choose the laws they will pass. Parliament has not respected that right. So let's imagine that the next election is fought not on what new laws we are going to have, but on something more than that. On the laws we are going to have, period. Let's start again. Let's imagine that the political parties nominates one hundred laws on which they will fight the election. The parties will be defined by their choice of laws, not the other way around. People will be voting for their laws first, and their party second. The less important laws can be approved, or rejected, by a random cross-section of the population, perhaps voting electronically. It's possible to do everything else on the internet, so why not on this too? Ladies and gentlemen, sometimes you just need to start again with a blank piece of paper. I'm suggesting that this is such a time."

"There is a word for such a time, Andrew. *Revolution.*"

"That may indeed be the word, Krishnan. However, I would use a different word. *Renaissance.*"

"You may just need that African sanctuary, Andrew." finished Krishnan, darkly.

Revolution. Renaissance. These are words that can travel at impossible speed. It was already too late to stop them: they were out, already weaving their seductive spell. *Revolution. Renaissance.* Catherine felt it, they all did. She tried to shake it off by prompting the Senator from Massachusetts.

"Questions, William?" William, however, was not under the spell, and he certainly had questions.

"Andrew, it is clear that you have a love of heroes. It is also clear that you have no love for lawyers, as far as I can see?"

"Yes, William, that is true."

"But can you not acknowledge the good that lawyers do? That they are essential to the law? That the law is essential to the keeping of the peace? That the lawyer is the best defence of the little man against those of greater wealth and power?"

"I can recognise the good, William, in theory. But, in practice, we have left so much of that behind us now. The system is corrupt. To me, William, and to most people, lawyers are associated with compensation claims and the 'cult of the victim' that we are here to debate. Your description of a lawyer is not one I would recognise. Outside of a cheap novel, anyway."

"Perhaps you have a better definition of a lawyer?" prompted William, and immediately regretted it.

"A lawyer, William? A lawyer is...." Andrew paused for dramatic effect.

"A lawyer is a machine for converting hindsight into money."

The statement seemed to hang in the air for several endless seconds before the penny dropped and the audience dissolved into laughter. Speakers included. Even Catherine, despite her best efforts, could not help but join in. Andrew, however, theatrically halted the laughter with an upraised hand. And continued.

"Except that most of the money never seems to leave the machine."

It was fully a minute before the studio settled down. Catherine let it happen, why not, the tension had been well nigh unbearable anyway. What an extraordinary character this Andrew was. BARBARIAN, HERO, REBEL? Dangerous. Well, so was she, for that matter. Later, for right now she had a show to run.

"Anwar, any questions?"

"Yes, Catherine, I have, but please give me a minute." Anwar replied. He was still wiping away the tears of laughter. "Andrew, a most wonderful definition. I appreciate it." Anwar visibly composed himself, took a deep breath. "Andrew, we must now be serious. I think you may just be an honest man, even if I utterly disagree with much of what you say. I also think your discontent with your society is obvious. You think that perhaps a new set of laws might be the answer. Might I make a suggestion? Rather than try and formulate a new set of laws - an impossible task - why not choose a set that already exists? That already work? Why not join with us, and live under a just set of laws. The set of laws that have worked for the World of Islam for over thirteen hundred years? Yes, Andrew, Sharia Law." Tension again gripped the audience, just as if the laughter had never been. Andrew took some seconds to think.

"Why not, Anwar? I'm sure many of the laws are fine and fair. However, some I could not agree with, and I am sure there are many here who feel the same. I would not stone a woman to death for adultery, for one. Nor a gay person, for that matter."

"You disappoint me, Andrew. I thought you did not share

William's passion for gay rights?"

"I do not, Anwar. I think being gay is certainly a problem for the individual and probably for society as a whole. God knows how it got to have the status it has now, but, to me, being gay is clearly not a blessing, but something unfortunate. Even for the non-religious, it is clearly an evolutionary disaster. At least for those individuals. However, it is not for me to judge what adults do in the privacy of their homes. That is a private matter for them, and no concern of mine nor the State. Anyway, I'm only expressing my opinion here. The fact is, we should *all* get the chance to express our opinion. Our laws need to reflect those views. If that turns out to be Sharia law, so be it. However, I'll not vote for stoning anyone to death because they're gay. Or unfaithful. For that matter, rather than Sharia law, we could also start with the ten commandments. The point is that we start again, with a clean slate. We get to vote *directly* for our laws. What else, ladies and gentlemen, is the point of democracy? Do we still have the courage to use democracy as it was meant to be used?"

Anwar seemed happy to have made his point and Catherine was more than a touch relieved. 'It's time to talk, freely' she thought. 'Interesting how uncomfortable we are when the taboos are lifted. How many taboos we seem to have acquired? Is this sensibility, or indoctrination? Focus, woman!' she snapped to herself. She did.

"Anwar, it's back to you. You have the floor."

Anwar Abbat nodded his head, took a deep breath and stood. His shoulders were bunched, his jaw was clenched: he seemed to have steeled himself to face some dread fear. It was a surprise, therefore, when his voice opened soft and low.

"Ladies and gentlemen, I want to talk to you briefly of blood money, before I move on to my main point. Heroes. So let me start with blood money. In the world of Islam, blood money is the system of compensation we have had for a thousand years. A fair system, that has stood the test of time, and has not been abused. Why? It is based on personal responsibility. If someone deprives a family of the services of a breadwinner, in whole or in part, then they must replace what has been lost. Personally. Not the company that employs them, but the individual. That means that any settlement is limited to the damage that has been caused, and the ability of the offender to pay. No crazy settlements, no punitive damages, nothing technical to debate, not enough money for lawyers to get rich on, no 'cult of the victim'. You all know - well, most of you do - that you have a problem. Are you big enough to accept a solution from the world of Islam?" Anwar's bearing had softened as he spoke, his muscles relaxed a little, his jaw softened. As he now paused and sipped some water, all the tension returned. And then some. He replaced the glass of water and now spoke with a barely controlled ferocity.

"Now, let me come to heroes. If the West chooses to think heroes are not required, then that is their problem. If they think lawyers are heroes, that is their madness, and is at least amusing. In the world of Islam, we know heroes are required. We have them, many of them. However, sometimes that can be a problem." Anwar stopped, took a deep breath, and continued.

"Ladies and gentlemen, I need to say something now so that there is no misunderstanding. In the past, I was a great friend of the West. In the future, God willing, I may again be a great friend of the West. But today? Today, everyone knows I am no friend of the West. Everyone knows how I feel about its corruption. Everyone knows how I feel about the injustices done to the world of Islam. However, enough is enough. To our heroes in Palestine, Afghanistan, Chechnya and Britain, I say this. Please, you must stop. Not the struggle, but the suicide bombs. No more suicide bombers, I beg you. Your bravery, your courage, your sacrifice, is bringing nothing but disaster on all our heads. It is true that some of us agree with your methods. Most of us do not. Most of us think you will not be forgiven for the innocent deaths. Whatever your belief on this, I tell you it is not working. You must see this. You must stop!"

Anwar stopped and visibly struggled to compose himself, to control the emotions that raged all too visibly on his face. Not one sound was heard until he resumed.

"Ten years ago, the Palestinians had the sympathy of the world. Well, except America, where the media is controlled by the Zionists. But the rest of the world was on our side. We were the David against the Goliath of Israel. Now, everyone is against us. Not just Palestinians and Iranians, but all Muslims. Now, Muslims everywhere are objects of hatred. Suicide bombers have turned every Muslim into a legitimate target for racism, discrimination, injustice. The more devout a Muslim we are, the more they are entitled to harass us, imprison us, even kill us. To be a Muslim in the West is to be a suspect. To be a devout Muslim is to be a prisoner. How did we let things get so bad?"

"I know you are thinking, heroes, that I am wrong, and that we are winning. I beg you, think again. Since you brought down the Twin Towers, what have we won? You have brought the infidel into Afghanistan. You have brought the infidel into Iraq, near to our very borders. Will you not stop until you have brought the infidels to the gates of Mecca itself?"
Anwar paused, took another sip and still took the best part of a half minute to compose himself. MARTYR. Catherine could not help but admire his courage. MARTYR. Please God it is only his stage character. Please God he has not signed his own death warrant. Meanwhile, finally, Anwar was ready to continue.

"Forgive me, ladies and gentlemen, that was something I had to say. It is done. Let me be again the journalist. That the West is in the grip of lawyers and their 'cult of the victim', is too obvious to be worth debate. Guilty. It is also obvious, as Andrew admits,

135

that the West has become too small-minded, too envious, to recognise its own heroes. The West is therefore also guilty of this charge. But I ask you, ladies and gentlemen. I beg you." A slight pause, an expectant hush.

"As you begin your search for new heroes, please do not seek to build them from the dead of Islam."

Anwar abruptly sat down but the studio remained silent. The silence was total, the audience inside the studio, and the audience outside. A strange thought stole unbidden into Catherine's head. 'Has there ever been a larger audience to witness an act of bravery?' Andrew's thought was more direct. 'Will they silence him?' Outside the studio, other, colder, minds considered their best strategy. His statements were unacceptable. A price must be paid. Should he live or should he die? Back in the studio, Catherine took back control.

"Thank you, Anwar, for a most sincere and courageous contribution. Anne-Marie, questions?"

Anne-Marie kept it very simple. She knew what had just happened. "Anwar, thank you." and she was done. Krishnan, Andrew and the Senator followed her lead. Their respect for Anwar's bravery was clearly genuine. More importantly, no-one wanted to dilute his message.

The debate was over. The audience were deeply impressed with Anwar's bravery. But that was not the only thing that had impressed them. Acts of bravery are powerful, but ideas are more powerful still. They were more focused on what Andrew had said. Had said *about them*. They had heard the magic words for the first time. *Revolution. Renaissance.* They wondered where they were going. They wondered if they should.

In any case, Catherine smoothly pulled the studio together for the anti-climatic vote.

"Ladies and gentlemen, the motion before us was:-
The West is guilty of the destruction of their heroes. The West is guilty of the promotion of weakness over strength. The West is guilty of failure to provide inspiration to their young." Catherine paused for several seconds, mechanically, as if there was tension to build. But there wasn't: this was a sure thing.

"Ladies and gentlemen, the motion has been carried by ninety-seven votes to three."

Immediately, the audience exploded in spontaneous approval. 'Why?' thought Catherine. 'Approval of what? What was on their minds? The verdict? Lawyers? Heroes? Renaissance? Dare she think it? Revolution?' The audience were still ringing out their approval. Catherine indulged them, waiting until their applause came to its natural end. They'd earned it. Choosing the right moment, she again took control.

"Now ladies and gentlemen, I come to tomorrow's debate." Catherine had memorised the words, had no reason to read from any of the large screens that lit the studio walls.

"The motion for the third debate is ...
The West is guilty of the failure to protect their own, the inability to act for the greater good.
We look forward to seeing you all again tomorrow."

Five minutes later, as Catherine neared make-up, she considered her cast. Governess, demagogue, barbarian, martyr. And Gandhi. What kind of script does that make?

Two thirty in the morning, Mayfair, London, and a large glass of Talisker is helping a sleepless Andrew with his analysis. He'd moved on from the debate, too tired to generate any more insights. Now he was on to the meeting, and Catherine. She had made the meeting, as he knew she must. Not that he initially recognised the creature in scarf, robe and large glasses. It had not taken long for him to make his well-rehearsed pitch. Her reaction was still utterly fresh.

"Let me get this right, Andrew. You are telling me that the BBC plan to replace me with a more 'heavyweight' presenter. Tomorrow. How you know, you cannot divulge. But you do have a solution and you are going to ride to my rescue. Out of chivalry, I presume? Are you offering to be my hero, Andrew?" A hint of light mockery in the tone. And more. A slight upturn of eyebrows, a deliberate widening of the eye. And something else again, something further. Andrew saw it. Inside every woman is a little girl, it is just that the wrapping is different. There are moments when you can almost see through to that little girl. Key moments. But Andrew took too long, and the moment passed.

"No, Andrew, I am afraid that we both know that there is more to it than that." Andrew was not giving up.

"Catherine, I can't tell you everything, but what I have told you is true. The BBC want a more heavyweight presenter. They want a man to give the debates more gravitas. They are going to manufacture a reason to get you off the programme. Tomorrow."

"Yes, Andrew, and your solution is that I share a romantic dinner with you, tonight? Just you and me, an intimate restaurant, your favourite candlelit table in the corner, and what else? Ah yes, just to make the evening complete, a couple of hidden tabloid journalists? Don't you think that perhaps that would just manufacture a perfect reason for the BBC? Save them any awkwardness?"

"Catherine, listen to me. The BBC do not control this process, these debates. The terrorists do. They decide. If they send no code, there is no debate. They want maximum publicity, otherwise why else would they want the debates at all? For no-one to watch them? With a soap-opera romance between the glamorous presenter and the maverick panellist, we can bring them the last of the audience segments. What is the downside for them? Or for the BBC? Remember the terms of the debates. No-one gets to change personnel other than the terrorists. Are the BBC going to take the chance of losing the debates? Would they risk everything to replace you with a tired old hack? No, Catherine, the terrorists chose you. They want *you*." Catherine interrupted.

"You are right, Andrew. They did choose me and they did stipulate no changes. And I think you are right about the plans to replace me. I've already had a run-in over dress standards and they've yet to see me in a basque and stockings." Andrew could not resist a smile. Well, a bit more than that. It wasn't the worst image of his day. Catherine did not acknowledge his reaction, but continued.

"But you are right, Andrew. For some reason, I was chosen. I'm going to stand my ground and dare them to take the chance. The romantic dinner is not necessary, Andrew. I can handle them perfectly well without it. However, I do appreciate the warning - and I do owe you a dinner, perhaps when all this is over? Now Andrew, please, can I ask you drop me off at the nearest taxi rank?", Catherine had finished, flashing Andrew her most irresistible smile.

Well, Andrew thought, they had known it was a long shot. Unfortunately, Catherine was as smart as he feared she might be. She was also, close up, even more attractive than he had realised. Much more. In the close confines of a sports car, there was something deeply chemical, deeply potent. Which was why the Talisker mocked him tonight, for it was it not sleep he wanted.

Andrew Westlands was not the only one unable to find sleep. Ahmed Ali Khan had continued the debate long into the night. His internal debate. How was this possible? How could one of their own not see? How dare he say such things to the Jihadis? But then, what if he were right? What if this is all a terrible mistake? What if he were not forgiven? As sleep eventually stole over him, he went back, as always, to Glasgow. To Pollokshields. To the death of his first infidel. McCulloch Street, the border line, the disputed land. They had counted seventeen stab wounds on the infidel's body. He could still count them all, replay them slowly, see the life ebb from the dying eyes. Forgiveness? There is no need for forgiveness in war. Sleep stole in behind the reassurance.

SIX

Starched white linens shroud an ancient marble altar. Medieval windows dapple reds and yellows on its solemn surface. Dust motes dance in the shafts, caught in captive reverence. Beneath the feet of an altar-side Madonna, guttering candles whisper ceaseless supplications. Incense hangs in the air, as natural as bees in a glade. At the front of a side altar, a bald-headed man is kneeling. A tiny laptop is cupped in his hands. On its screen is written:-

She spoke softly, her voice soft with puzzlement.

"Do you know what is the biggest fear in the West today? They live their lives in fear of criminals, fear for themselves and their defenceless ones. So much wealth yet so much fear? Let me tell you what I think. They are too weak to make a difficult decision. They pretend to themselves that it is possible to live life without making difficult choices. For fear of making one wrong conviction, they will let a hundred innocents die. What kind of society will not protect its weak and defenceless for fear of making a mistake? What kind of society is so lost it will not protect its own? Better the death of one unfortunate criminal than that of one hundred poor innocents!"

I had no answer. I charge the West therefore with the failure to protect their own, the inability to act for the greater good.

The bald man closes the screen and renews his prayers.

The headlines of the Twenty-Second of December spoke of nothing but the debate. As if somehow unsure of themselves, the broadsheets all asked questions. The Times asked 'RENAISSANCE - OR REVOLUTION?'. The Telegraph mused 'THE RETURN OF THE HERO?'. The Independent led with a large shot of an impassioned Andrew Westlands, and the headline 'RENAISSANCE MAN?'. The tabloids had a field day. The Sun continued its recent theme with 'LAWYERS: 0 HEROES: WANTED'. The Express led with a huge cartoon, suitably titled 'THE HINDSIGHT MACHINES'. The Mirror sang 'NO LAWYERS, NO CRY'. In the rest of the world, headlines reflected different concerns. The Washington Post wondered 'HERO OR ANTI HERO?'. The Delhi Times had 'GANDHI DEBATE RE-OPENS AS WEST SEEKS HEROES'. In Iran, the headlines asked 'INFIDELS AT THE GATES OF MECCA?'.

Unfortunately, the debate was not the only impact of the Christmas Virus. In Western Europe, industry was now largely at a halt. A few businesses still soldiered bravely on, but with their computers taking eight times as long to do anything, and supplies uncertain, it was a struggle. Food supplies were still reaching the shops. People had adapted to the routine of queuing for cash at the bank, then taking real cash to the shops to pay for their food. It felt odd, like things were beginning to unravel, like maybe soon they would be bartering in some market. Thankfully, the banks could still process credit card cash advances, but only inside their own branch. For a remarkable number of people - and by no means all poor - that was their only way to get cash. How odd was that? Coffee houses, pubs, restaurants - all were open, and busy. People had time to talk, and things to talk about. The parks were full too, and the squares, even the shopping malls where little other than food was being bought. Everywhere you looked there were animated groups of people talking long, and passionately. Not always in agreement, and rarely of the weather.

Remarkably, internet usage had increased from the day before. People were so desperate to log on that they would queue outside the internet cafes for hours. Talking as they waited. Most internet cafes had introduced some kind of rationing system, fifteen minutes being a typical maximum time on-line. Some people were also continuing to use their own computers, despite the obvious risk and the excruciating speed. Somehow, despite everything, thousands of new web sites were springing up and rapidly becoming the place to go, the place to make your contribution. Many, like 'LetstalkFreely.com', mixed replays of the debates with on-line participants. Others, like 'WesternHeroesToday.com' and 'ItsGoodToTalkFreely.com', were focused on some of the issues that had caught the imagination. A significant number were much more sinister indeed, but no-one had the time nor the means to close them quickly enough. Among the most sinister were 'AnarchistVictory.com', and 'Fascistdawn.com', and the people that knew, and cared, were worried indeed. The owner of 'WesternRenaissance.com', however, found nothing sinister in the offer he received. He took the millions, sold up his site, and began to party.

Not everyone was on the streets to talk. Riots ringed the Asian districts of almost every large European city. In Britain, Bradford, Leeds and Luton were in flames. In France, large parts of Paris and Marseilles were war zones. In Spain, Madrid and Barcelona burned. Two flags started to sprout from the flames. The black flag of the anarchists, and the unmistakable geometry of the swastika.

The U.S. reacted much like Europe, although with fewer riots and fewer flags. Two of the riots seemed to centre around the premises of prominent law firms. Whatever else, lawyers are not known for their stupidity, and their reaction was muted.

The rest of the world mostly watched in fear. The Middle East, however, was in tumult. Everyone had heard Anwar Abbat.

Sheik Mohammad Unshal Basri had immediately issued a fatwa on his head, and added a price of fifty thousand US dollars. But people were talking, and freely. Yes, 'Infidels at the gates of Mecca' was on the lips of many. But, surprisingly, 'How did we let things get this bad?' was also on their lips. The debate was vigorously underway, and the body-count was beginning to rise. Sheik Basri was among the first, the single exit wound at the back of his head a testament to the sniper's deadly art.

The BBC statement was first released at the end of the eight o'clock news. It was short, dignified, and political dynamite.

The BBC wishes to confirm that they have received a request from members of Her Majesty's government to release to them the Sesame computer program. The BBC fully recognises issues of national security, but considers that, in this instance, the issue of free speech is paramount. Accordingly, the BBC will not release this program to the government, nor indeed, to anyone. The BBC recognises that this position may not have the full protection of the law. Accordingly, we ask the public to show their support for our position, and to help to persuade the government to withdraw their request.

The public reaction was swift and emphatic. MP's phones rang off the hooks. Somehow, and despite the deadly bite of the Virus, the Houses of Parliament was engulfed in a blizzard of e-mails. People started to gather on the streets of London. Within the hour, a human cordon ringed Broadcasting House. Impromptu citizens' road-blocks had been placed on the surrounding streets, checking all traffic, mechanical and human. Despite the burgeoning traffic chaos, no police had as yet dared intervene. Uniformed BBC security staff moved to the road blocks, providing a first line of identification for employees. Camera phones forwarded pictures of all visitors for verification. One road-block seemed to be manned exclusively by well organised young men in hoods and ski-masks. Above the road block billowed a prominent black flag. A polite request to respect the non-aligned nature of the protest was not well received, and the man was savagely beaten. No-one needed this kind of hassle, so people just left them to it, and migrated to friendlier groups. In general, other than the one group of anarchists, the atmosphere was friendly, animated, somehow virtuous, like at a garden fete or a local charity event. Watching journalists wondered if they had yet grasped the real story line.

Impromptu banners were everywhere. Most were unimaginative: 'Hands off the BBC', 'Free Speech!', 'Death before Silence' and many depressingly similar. One large banner, however, caught the imagination and rapidly multiplied. It was written in large red letters on a yellow cloth, and it said 'It's Time to talk freely'.

The internet buzzed with conspiracies, rumours and the occasional fact. Not surprisingly, the search engines were not fed their usual fuel. The most notable new search was 'Renaissance', and that, curiously, they all directed to www.WesternRenaissance.com. Beneath the surface of the mainstream search engines, the dark sites were like black holes, drawing many that came too close. Predictably, the Islamist sites were the busiest. Theirs, however, was not the only brand of fundamentalism. For the first time, many were drawn to www.AnarchistVictory.com. Others heard rather different sirens, and ended on the shores of www.Fascistdawn.com. As in the words of the song, there was something in the air.

Although it was still early, it had already been a long morning.
Peter Bradshaw, the Director General of the BBC, leaned his large
frame back from the desk and rubbed both hands back over the
smooth contours of his scalp. An historic time for the BBC,
certainly, but so much work for him to do, and so little time. The
BBC had always had much political power, but nothing ever
quite to this level. Politicians were falling over themselves to
present their compliments, to offer their respect and support.
Looking for an opportunity. Ah, the power of patronage. But it
took time. So, too, did the licensing deals. Everyone had to have
footage of the debates, live or not. Everyone had to screen and
re-screen them. The money being generated was quite simply
staggering. The money *and* the influence. Too important for him
not to be involved. The affair with the government over *Sesame*
was starting to need attention, now: the issue just could not wait.
Unfortunately, now it seems, neither can Catherine Connor. It
was surprising that she had taken the initiative, but she was
unwittingly giving him an opportunity. Peter Bradshaw intended
to take it. No time like the present.

"Catherine, come in my dear, take a seat. Let me tell you how
much we all appreciate your performances: great work. I'm
delighted to get the chance to thank you personally. Now what is
so urgent, Catherine, that you needed to see me this morning?"
the Director General asked, his tone rapidly altering.

Catherine was wearing, somewhat improbably, a full length
light blue cashmere coat. 'Women,' thought Peter. 'always feeling
the cold'. Catherine made no attempt to sit, but immediately
started to speak.

"Director General, I do appreciate you are busy, but I have

two serious problems and I urgently need your help."

"Glad to do what I can, Catherine. In any case, it's maybe time we had a chat. But let's deal with your problems first."

"Thanks, Peter." Catherine smiled, and paused for a second or so. "It is a little embarrassing, however. You see, the first problem is my shape." At that, Catherine slipped smoothly out of her coat, draped it over a chair, and stood back, hands on hips. Peter Bradshaw's jaw dropped, his eyes bulged, and his face flushed a deep heart-attack red. She did look good in the low cut black basque, red suspender belt, and high heels. Full breasts, narrow waist, swelling hips and long legs: yes, Catherine looked rather more than good. She did not wait for Bradshaw to recover his poise before continuing. Life was too short.

"Yes, Peter, my shape. Somehow it must have changed in the last couple of days. When I was invited to chair these debates - by the kind Mr. Virus, whoever - then I was most definitely a woman. With a woman's shape. But now, I fear my shape has changed. It must have. Please Peter, can you please reassure me that I still have a woman's shape?" The Director General had not recovered his poise yet. His mouth moved, but nothing came out.

"I'll take that as a 'yes'" continued Catherine. "Good. Of course, I can see why Jeremy would have been worried. These virus people would not hesitate to move their debates if they thought someone had broken their conditions. They have made that very clear. What a disaster that would be for all of us, would it not?" Catherine paused and gazed directly at the Director General. One way or another, she certainly had his attention. She continued.

"Then there must be some other explanation. If my shape has not changed, I'm puzzled as to how Jeremy Wexham now thinks it's a problem. A problem serious enough to come between a woman and her wardrobe? Perhaps it's not really just a problem with my shape, but with the shape of women *in general*? Maybe that's the problem? In that case Jeremy should take up his complaint with a higher authority. In any case, Peter, perhaps you could speak to Jeremy on my behalf? Advise him that I still do have a woman's shape, that he's not to worry himself any more." Catherine picked up her coat from the chair and, to Bradshaw's relief, slipped it back on.

"Now, Peter, my second point. I need my computer moved out of my office, into a secure room, under my sole lock and key. I also need it taken off the BBC network. I am no longer willing to bring *Sesame* into the BBC, nor to access *Sesame* when I am on a BBC network. For security, you understand. Mr Virus was very insistent that *Sesame* remain secret. Now I know that you would never, *ever*, co-operate with the government, Peter." There was a soft edge of irony in Catherine's tone. Not too much, but there. She continued.

"But you cannot vouch for everyone else. As long as the computer is on the BBC network, *Sesame* is at risk. I cannot imagine what would happen if the newspapers got hold of some story about a BBC technician selling *Sesame* to the government. And as long as the computer is on the BBC network, who could say that the story is baseless? I'd have to make it clear that I had expressly warned against it. That I, for one, took the conditions of the debates seriously." Catherine paused and looked directly at a stunned Peter Bradshaw, then continued.

"Right now, it is true, I *am* the only one to have the password to the e-mail account." Another pause. "However, with the computer off the network, and in a secure room, I'll feel a lot safer. I am going to go now to wait in my office, Peter. I do appreciate you giving me so much of your time. None of this is going to be a problem, is it?" Catherine smiled sweetly. There were several seconds of high quality silence.

"I do hope you know what you are doing, Catherine." Bradshaw said, finally.

"Oh, but I do, Peter, I do. I just wanted to make sure you did."
With that, Catherine made her exit. It took a great deal of effort
to suppress her laughter until several floors below. She could not
wait to get Andrew's reaction, nor would she.

Peter Bradshaw took several minutes to recover, then decided
it was not too early for a stiff drink.

U-Soft London: Eleven Fifty Five a.m.
December the Twenty-Second

Andrew Westlands felt more tired than heroic. Few could deny
the potency of the Talisker 25, nor its enchantment. Assuming
female form was, however, a little beyond it and Andrew's night
had been long and sleepless. Not that female company need be a
problem for him, so it would seem. Andrew was, it seemed, a
popular man. On this morning's evidence, extraordinarily
popular. As he leaned back from his desk, Andrew watched the
redoubtable Pam leave with the last of the cards and unsolicited
gifts. The vast majority of which were from women, and not all
of them shy, it would appear. Yes, Andrew was in demand, but
not just from women. Politicians too. Notes of congratulation,
and invitation. Many from well-known mainstream politicians,
but also some from rather more shadowy figures. Most of whom
Andrew had heard of, but never yet met, although it appeared
they wanted to address that issue. In demand, yes, and with Eldon
too. It was a scant five minutes before the scheduled conference
call, and Eldon of all people did not favour the tired nor the
stupid. Right now, Andrew required a lot from his espresso. The
continental roast was, however, highest quality, and inside a
couple of minutes Andrew's eyes yet again hinted of intelligence.
Eldon's eyes screamed of it, as did the whole of the alien silver
image that filled Andrew's video screen. Andrew braced himself,
and reassembled his features into something more positive.

"Ah, Andrew, you are wearing your brave face. I would expect nothing less from a hero. Sleep well, did you, my Renaissance Man?" Eldon did have a way of saying a lot without actually using many words. Andrew saw no point in beating about the bush.

"Not exactly, Eldon, as you might have guessed. It was a rather long and busy evening, but, hopefully, productive. I thought the debate went well, although there was probably little in it that directly concerns you. I also think things went well with Miss Connor. She believed what I told her about the BBC's plans, and I'm pretty confident that she will do what she needs to do to safeguard her position. However, that's the limit of my progress with the lady. The next stage will have to wait for another day. Sorry, boss, but these things are never straightforward, and women, well?" and Andrew executed a perfect Gallic shrug.

"Sorry, Andrew? No need to be. You struck a fine blow for common sense last night, and any blow for common sense is good for business. While we're on the subject, Andrew, the debates. Please be reassured that you are absolutely a free man there. You may say anything you like: it's about time someone did. In any case, the bullet is going to have your name on it, not mine." Eldon smiled.

"Thanks, boss", Andrew deadpanned.

" ...so I'm upping security on you, Andrew. That's not debatable. I spoke to Solomon last night, it's already in hand. Anyway, it seems you are making quite a name for yourself. Maybe you're the coming politician, Andrew? Well, good for you, and it certainly takes a little of the pressure off U-Soft. Which is just as well, since progress is steady, but hardly spectacular." Eldon's tone hinted of frustration, and he seemed happy to respond to Andrew's arched eyebrow.

"Let me summarise, Andrew. We have four main activities: mitigating the impact of the virus short term: identifying whomever is responsible: finding and fixing the virus ourselves: and surviving the fallout from the whole sorry mess." Eldon was clearly building up a head of steam, and Andrew offered silent thanks for his espresso.

"Firstly, mitigation of the impact. We are assessing the alternative operating systems - **Nexus**, UNOS, the smaller versions of U-Sys we use for mobile phones and the like. That's going OK, no problems. The date-set program - SafeDate - is done and performing well under test. We expect to make it available for download later tonight. We're going to tell the public it's a Beta, still in evaluation, but in reality we think it is ready for release. We are also working on something completely new, something rather more radical. Designed to harness lots of computers, to compensate for the reduction in their individual speed. When you invoke a program, our new software will determine which one of a cluster of computers is least busy, then runs the program on that computer. An adaptive form of pseudo parallel processing. A product which will be useful after the Christmas Virus has gone away. I gave it a name: Hydra. Marketing have nothing else to do, so they've even come up with a slogan: 'Many heads are better than one'. A wry smile. "At least they have not lost their sense of humour. I've insisted on a very small team and minimal documentation until we have Hydra working. No more committees. I've also removed the requirement for Hydra to work with the older U-Sys versions. We might think about that later, but right now I think it is about time that we stopped making everything we create automatically crippled at birth." A pause, and a sharp look. "Please note that Hydra is totally confidential, Andrew."

'Hydra?' Andrew thought. 'A many-headed monster with poisonous blood? And marketing liked it? ' However, Eldon was already moving on.

"Secondly, identification of those responsible for the Christmas

Virus. Most suspicion is falling on Michael MacDonald, and the searches are underway. It appears that almost everyone is looking for him now. Us, governments, the media, not to mention the bad guys. Solomon is shivering in Scotland as we speak, looking at castles. A most unlikely tourist, I might add. Anyway, at this stage we do not think this looks like eco-idiots or Islamists or any of the other usual imbeciles. However, data is limited, and that view might change." Eldon paused to let Andrew catch up.

"Thirdly, finding and fixing. Progress is slow. We are around thirty three per cent checked, no bug detected. Difficult to extrapolate, but going to be tight. Damn tight. And I'm getting damn tired, as it happens." For the first time, Andrew thought he saw signs of wear and tear on Eldon. Signs of mortality.

"Finally, U-Soft 'after the deluge'. Well…" Eldon seemed to frown. "Difficult. Challenging. Sooner or later people are going to notice that all those glitzy presentations in corporate fonts and embedded this that and the next thing are not really necessary. As they work around the virus some behaviour is going to change. People just might ask themselves if all that computing power is really being put to good use? Folks might just get a little more pragmatic. We'll see. Like I said, Andrew, you may be doing better than we are. Anyway, Andrew, I'm out of time. Good luck tonight." The screen was blank before Andrew could muster a response. Andrew glanced at the large wall clock. Yes, it had been a lot of information in a very little time. Some things never change. Andrew reached reflexively for a cigarette before he remembered that he had given up ten years before. Some things never change, but really all things do.

Solomon N'Chenga looked down onto the storm-tossed loch, eyes drawn to the jagged causeway, and onwards to the stark, forbidding battlements of the island fortress. Eilan Donan Castle: majestic home to the Macrae Clan, and improbably beautiful.

The castle that had been in the photograph. The expensive photograph. Horribly expensive. The more-than-lucky shot of a paparazzi on holiday. Eilan Donan castle, but with a red-haired man in the foreground. Yes, Eilan Donan, star of countless movies, but not this one. Eilan Donan, but a gull's high cry from the Isle of Skye, on the rebel road to the Isles. Which was where he was headed now. Stereotypical images of the Bonnie Prince flitted across Solomon's mind - from where? - dispelled instantly, but not entirely. He'd come back here someday, take his time. But today there was work to be done. Ghosts the place might have, but today the spooks were more evident. How did the news get out so soon? Solomon signalled to his pilot to start up the Lynx. Perhaps he would beat them to Skye. Perhaps they were already there. Either way, no way to stop them following him. Well, he could at least make them work for it.

"Colin, Skye. You know where. But let's make these journalists work for their money. Land somewhere a couple of miles away, somewhere awkward, and have a Range Rover waiting for us. With a bit of luck our disciples will have themselves a wet walk."

"Understood, sir. Weather's coming up, anyway. That should help." Solomon knew that it wouldn't. He thought the trail was already cold, and the weather would only make it colder. Damn if that wind did not go right through you.

The press were, indeed, looking for Michael MacDonald. The lunchtime Evening Standard was the first to inform its readers. The headline on page four teased 'U-Soft: Riddle of Missing Software Guru'. The accompanying photograph was at least ten years old, but the hair and beard made it well worth printing. By early evening, the public had plenty to read and hear on 'Red Michael', especially when Scotland Yard confirmed that they wished to eliminate him from their enquiries. Which meant, when you stripped out the police jargon, that he was the prime suspect. Paparazzi set up their camps around the MacDonald family home, their vigils fuelled by soup and optimism. But it was in vain, entirely in vain, for Karen MacDonald was long gone, and far gone, and did not intend to return.

BBC Headquarters, London: Mid-morning, December the Twenty-Second

Catherine Connor had to calm down, and she was deliciously aware of it. Exhilaration still gripped her like an unexpected windfall. It was not just the image of a red-faced, gulping, Peter Bradshaw, desperately trying to regain his composure. It was not just the sense of a crucial victory won. It was the sense of rebellion, the heady scent of freedom. She had tumbled the dice and fortune had smiled on her. However, now she really had to calm down. Yes, and she also had to thank Andrew, because there was no doubting, from Bradshaw's manner, that Andrew had been right. She had been deemed *unsuitable*. The wrong shape. Catherine knew it was a good time to go slowly. She had to be careful. She sat back in her new chair, and gazed around at the bare cream walls. Then decided, abruptly, to tumble the dice once more. She punched in the numbers, and found, to her pleasant surprise, that Andrew was not so hard to get hold of. Andrew had expected the call, but he got much more pleasure from hearing her voice than he had expected. Much more than he usually got from being proved right.

"Catherine, nice to hear from you. Before you ask, I'm still available for dinner tonight. I'd be quick though, because I got at least two firm proposals in this morning's mail. Of marriage no less." Andrew opened.

"A date with me would be much cheaper, Andrew." Catherine laughed back. "Well, since I don't go out with married men, it

154

does sound like I'd better be quick. How about tonight then, Andrew?"

"Tonight, Catherine? You're serious? What happened to all the stuff about the tabloids, the risk to your job? All the issues of last night? Of course, I'm delighted to go out with you, but I don't want to push you into something ..."

"There's no issue, Andrew." Catherine interrupted. "You were right about my bosses at the BBC. Yes, I think they had plans. But not any more. I've dealt with them: their bluff has been well and truly called. As a matter of fact, Andrew, I rather enjoyed it. There is nothing quite like humiliating the boss, especially when he is a man. I think I might just develop a taste for it. And it's *so* important for men to know their place, Andrew, don't you think?" and Catherine laughed lightly.

"I do agree, Catherine. And mine is normally on top," shot back Andrew, and this time they both laughed. Catherine, however, was grateful that Andrew could not see her unexpected blush. Andrew continued.

"How about our usual place then, Catherine? Outside the Horse and Lion, Bayswater Road, around ten forty five?"

"Sounds good, Andrew, I'll be there. And bring that nice car again. There was something about it." And then Catherine was gone, before Andrew could say anything stupid. Then again, maybe it would be better to get the stupid stuff out now. It had no place in his preparations for the debate. Andrew desperately wanted to make some time this afternoon, if only the 'little chat' that the mysterious Mr Chamberlain wanted. Yes, but the debate came first, and Andrew knew it. Twenty minutes later, and Andrew was still searching for inspiration. That was unlike him, and Andrew was suddenly conscious of the rising pressure. That made him happier, for he thrived on pressure, or so he thought. Well, *liked to believe* might be more accurate.

If David Blenheim, the much-derided Prime Minister of Great Britain and Northern Ireland, felt under fire, he did not show it. In fact, he began the meeting on a highly positive note.

"Congratulations, gentlemen, well done. I can't tell you how pleased I am at your news. Delighted. I'm also relieved to discover that at least some of my people can still get things done." David Blenheim, 'M' (whose real name was John Nightingale, although convention forbade it to be used) and 'Hector' were seated around a small oval table, in a windowless, nondescript room, several levels below Downing Street. Magnolia walls, racing green carpet, and three or four vaguely nautical prints said all that had to be said about the design budget. Which was not much. It was not that the room did not have a budget, because it most certainly had. Budget enough to buy a large London house. But this budget had gone on security, electronic, and state of the art. Here, it was not only time to talk freely, it was also safe to talk freely. And the Prime Minister, was, certainly, talking freely.

"The Golden Triangle. Money, honey, and cocaine. I have to say, a memorable trinity. Tell me, Hector, which of the three worked?"

"Actually, Prime Minister, we used all of them. I did not consider this to be a time to be overly economical. Especially since the only opportunity to get at Sesame is the one time each day when Connor inserts the disk into the drive of her computer. Yes, we gave our man a very good evening. I'd say he's very much looking forward to working with us again."

"So, we have a working *Sesame* computer, Hector? Are we now able to get a trace on these e-mails?"

"If you don't mind, Prime Minister, I'd like to take a minute to explain some of the technicalities. I think you might need to know a little more of how things work to better understand what we already have, and what we have yet to get."

"Absolutely, Hector. However, please try and use plain

English. I detest jargon."

"Certainly, Prime Minister. We have a copy of the *Sesame* program. As we had deduced, what Connor sent back to the terrorists enabled them to construct a configuration code for *Sesame*. When Connor entered this, *Sesame* changed to make itself operational. It is our guess that this code would work on Connor's computer, and *only* on Connor's computer. If we wanted to use the same code, then we would need to construct a computer almost identical to hers. We now know that our guess was correct. We also think that we have now constructed the computer that will let us run *Sesame*." Hector paused for a breath but the PM broke in before he could continue.

"*Think*, Hector?" he asked, letting the words hang in the air menacingly.

"Prime Minister, we took a spare computer from stores and ran *Sesame*. It wiped out the computer. We then ran *Sesame* on a JetPC12, exactly the same computer type as Connor's, same amount of memory, same hard disk size, same programs installed. It also wiped out that computer." Hector sensed the PM's impatience, but knew his job and would not be distracted.

"We took a second JetPC12, but now used our technical wizards to make a network card with the same MAC address as Connor's. *Sesame* now starts and asks for a password. Since nothing got wiped out, we are confident that we can now run *Sesame*. However, we need a valid password to be sure." The Prime Minister cut in.

"Remind me, Hector. MAC address?"

"Almost every computer has a network card. Each network card has an absolutely unique address worldwide. We call this the MAC address."

"Ah yes, I remember now. Now, I thought that we would get a password from Connor's emails. Each one should have a different one, right?"

"Yes, that is true, Prime Minister. However, our man could not get a copy of the e-mails. It seems they are on an on-line account, and she never downloaded the messages to her BBC computer. He did, however, get a copy of the e-mail account details. Apparently Connor had to convince the Director General that it was not a hoax. To be convinced, he insisted that she access the account on his computer. Seems that when she entered this unusual internet address it triggered a keystroke-logger - something that gives a record of all keystrokes pressed. Every time you press a key, it is recorded and written to a keystroke file. So our man got a copy of the keystroke file, found the account name and password, and tried to access the account. But he was too late, it would seem. Connor has obviously been smart enough to have changed her password, making sure that there was no way for the Director General to follow in her footsteps. Normally, hacking into an on-line mail system would be child's play for us, but this system is unusually, suspiciously, secure. Password entry is over a secure connection, and all passwords are a minimum of ten characters. I know, I opened an account myself. Anyway, Prime Minister, we know the account name. Unfortunately, the account provider is located in Dubai. Outside of our official reach. There is nothing legal we can do to compel them to give us copies of the e-mails. We can monitor most of the traffic to her e-mail address, depending on where and how it originates. That means that there is a decent chance that we will be able to intercept her future e-mails. However, it is by no means certain. If we want to be certain, we must use..."

"Whatever it is, it had better not be The Golden Triangle," the Prime Minister growled. "In an Arab country, that is not a risk I am prepared to take."

"Of course not, Prime Minister," 'M' cut in smoothly. "This is a job for local assets. Dubai assets and Dubai methods. I am told they do things a little differently over there. Things are a little, shall we say, more robust. Of course, as you know, Prime Minister, the details are decided at an operational level, and are quite outside my scope. I do know that we have a good relationship with the authorities in Dubai, and that they are happy to give us considerable operational latitude. I took the liberty, Prime Minister, of assuming that you would permit this meeting to be interrupted, should we hear anything definitive?"

"Correct, 'M'. I want to know the moment we have something. Now, let's assume we can get access to the Connor's existing e-mails. What happens next? Can we ensure we get all future messages? Can we get a trace on where they are coming from? Quickly enough to do something useful with it?" A brief pause before 'M' responded.

"I'll keep it brief, Prime Minister. When we get the existing e-mails, we will get the passwords that will enable us to confirm that we have a working *Sesame*. The next step will be to intercept any new messages the terrorists send to Connor. The earlier we get the messages, the earlier we can get the codes and put *Sesame* to work. That will give us some time to assess the probable impact of the virus messages, and time to plan for the debates. It also lets us hunt more effectively for the virus, to try and find where the virus text is being hidden on the computer. The e-mail messages will also give us considerable additional information, including where they were sent from, and when and how they were sent. That information will certainly be of value to us. However, getting the messages *while they are being sent* is the big prize. If we can home in on the sender's location while they are on-line, then the chase would be on. Then we can really set loose the dogs."

"So, 'M', how do we get the messages? *Specifically*, how do we get them while they are being sent? Educate me a little, please." 'M' exchanged a glance with Hector, who took the hint and took over.

"Prime Minister, every e-mail message contains lots of information on where it has come from and how it was sent. When we get copies of the two messages that Connor has already received, then we will see that information and can put it to some use. However, there is no guarantee that the terrorists will send future messages in the same way, so its value is limited. To understand how we can get future messages, either when they reach Connor's mail-box, or while they are being sent, we need to understand a little about how e-mail is sent." Hector paused for a second, and looked to the Prime Minister as if for approval.

"Go on, go on." Blenheim prompted. "I'm waiting."

"In general, e-mail is despatched from computers to clearing centres that send the e-mail on to their destinations. The type of program that sends the e-mail to the clearing centres is termed a sending client. The precise jargon is 'an SMTP client'. 'SMTP' is an acronym for Simple Message Transfer Protocol. The jargon for the clearing centres is 'SMTP servers'. Basically, the client asks the server to accept a message for delivery to a specified address. The server then becomes responsible for delivering it. We have arrangements with the mainstream SMTP servers, like those provided by Mahoo or Oogle. We can instruct them to send us a copy of any message addressed to Connor. They will set this to happen automatically." The Prime Minister interrupted.

"Hector, I think you said '*the client asks the server to accept a message for delivery to a specified address.*' It seems to me that this is a most unusual kind of mail clearing system. Normally, you would just leave your sacks of mail. Instead, you say that each person has to come forward to the server, and show him the address of each item they want to send. A very personal, interactive arrangement, really. Is my understanding, correct, Hector?" Hector was surprised at the question; and impressed.

"Yes, Prime Minister, very much so. That is an accurate assessment. Shall I continue, sir?" The Prime Minister's impatient

160

gesture provided Hector with all the answer he needed.

"As I said, Prime Minister, we will instruct the mainstream servers to send us a copy of any message addressed to Connor. We will receive the copy *immediately*, while they are still on-line, and we will also get the IP address of the sending computer."

"IP address?" the Prime Minister cut in. "The address that locates a computer on the internet?"

"Exactly Prime Minister. An address that is globally unique, but is also usually only assigned on a temporary basis. With the help of the phone and cable companies, we can resolve the IP address to a physical address. In other words, we find out which phone or cable line, which real physical address. That's when we can set loose the dogs." Hector paused again. Again, the Prime Minister impatiently gestured him to continue.

"The problem is, the terrorists may not use a mainstream server. We will see what they have been using when we get copies of the first two messages. Not that that is any guarantee. Unfortunately, whatever they have done in the past, they may not choose to do the same thing in the future. They might use a server outside our sphere of influence, or they might set up one of their own. In my opinion, we need to assume this eventuality. We can still deal with the situation. It just means that Dubai becomes critical."

"You're making me nervous, Hector. I am rather conscious that Dubai is not Britain. Why does Dubai become critical?"

"Because, Prime Minister, that is where Connor's mailbox is, *physically*. Sooner or later, the messages have to go to Dubai. They have to be received by a mail server there. That might be a POP server or an SMTP server: the precise details and meaning of the jargon are irrelevant, Prime Minister, as it all comes down to the same thing. We need to get control of their mail servers, period. When we can get control of the mail servers in Dubai, then we can definitely get copies of the messages. Not only that, we get the chance to activate the on-line tracing. There are several different scenarios to consider." At this point, Hector paused briefly, as if mentally enumerating the scenarios, before he then continued.

"The ideal scenario is that messages are being sent *directly* to Connor's account. In that case, the Dubai server software - with our modifications - would automatically, and instantly, give us the address of anyone who connects with a message for Connor. It will also deliberately slow up the process, keeping the sender on-line much longer than normal. The terrorists will have no real reason to suspect anything: internet speed is always variable and delays occur all the time. If the messages are being sent *indirectly* to Connor's account, for example being automatically forwarded from another account, then an on-line trace will still work, provided that they are being forwarded by one of the mainstream servers. In that case, as soon as one of the mainstream servers sees Connor's address, they - we - will start to chase the message up the chain. To where it started."

"...and if they use their own mail servers to do the forwarding?" the Prime Minister interrupted.

"Even if they use a chain of their own mail servers to do the forwarding, when we get control at Dubai we will receive all the messages, plus an on-line link to the last forwarding server. That means that not only do we get the messages, but we have a fighting chance to get our hands on one of their home-grown servers. That, Prime Minister, would be quite a catch. One of their servers would be a treasure trove to us. Of course, they may not use a chain of their own servers. The worst possible scenario is that they forward messages using some third-party server that is located somewhere unfriendly. In Teheran, for example. In that case, our on-line trace would end in Teheran. But we would still have copies of the messages." Hector took a breath and pulled it all together.

"In summary, Prime Minister. The bottom line is that control

162

of the Dubai server gets us Connor's messages. It will give us on-line tracing that may, or may not, lead somewhere useful. Without control at Dubai, we have to rely on the terrorists using a mainstream SMTP server if we are to get anything at all. Specifically, we may get neither any messages, nor any means to trace the terrorists on-line."

David Blenheim did not react at all, but sat silent, his brows as furrowed as a ploughed field in winter. The wall clock slowed as it metered the long seconds. 'M's patrician features were a mask, but Hector had no doubt that 'M' understood. The rumours suggested that 'M' had a mind that was as comfortable with particle physics as it was with medieval poetry. Hector had every reason not to doubt those rumours. The silence thickened, and deepened, yet still the PM's brows stayed furrowed. Hector focused on the clock, improbably slow now. *He* would not be the one to break the silence. Suddenly, David Blenheim brightened, and unfurrowed the famous brows.

"It really is not like a mail clearance centre. It's more like an old-fashioned telephone exchange, and the SM-whatever server is an operator. The operator talks directly to the caller. She takes his message, but she goes slowly, to keep him on the line while the police run a trace. And she gives the police a copy of his message. Yes, I think I'm clear. I guess we now have to wait on news from Dubai before we do any more. In the meantime, gentlemen, let's move on. How do we stop the BBC from finding out that we have *Sesame*? How do we know our man in the BBC is not talking to anyone else?"

As 'M' started to speak, Hector could not help but admire the PM's analogy. Why hadn't he thought of that?

It was fully thirty minutes before 'M' and Hector ascended back to the surface levels of Number Ten, Downing Street. It was a further twenty minutes before they were back at their lair in

Thames House, at the end of Lambeth Bridge. It was a further fifteen minutes before the news came in from Dubai. 'M' placed the call immediately. It was one o'clock, and in London the now traditional U-Soft Press Conference had just begun.

U-Soft Conference Room One, London: One p.m.
December the Twenty-Second

The room, the people, the format were much the same as the days before. Or the days after, if you looked at it that way. The days after the Christmas Virus. Familiarity may have been in the air, but not complacency. Again, the striking image of Eldon Harker filled the video screen, the not-quite alien face forming the opening words of his statement.

"Ladies and gentlemen. Thank you for your attention. For the benefit of everyone, I will continue to make my statements as concise as is practical. In this statement I will address three things. The current known consequences of the virus, our efforts to alleviate its symptoms, and our efforts to find and eliminate it.

Unfortunately, the current known consequences of the virus have increased. System speed continues to degrade in a binary model and is today one eighth of optimum. We expect this binary degradation to continue. Eyes in the audience were already starting to glaze over, before Eldon's next statement refocused them.

In other words, each day computer speed will be one half the speed of the day before. There are some entirely new consequences of the virus. As of noon today, it would appear that all stored computer data is no longer compatible with that of uninfected computers. The electronic image of Eldon Harker could not have heard the gasps in the conference room, but nonetheless he seemed to have anticipated the reaction, as he paused and then restated the information.

I repeat that something in the virus is now altering stored data so that uninfected computers cannot read data from infected computers. It would appear that the virus is spending some of its idle time in converting all stored data to a new format. Whenever a program requests data, it restores the data to its original format and then presents it to the program. When the program stores the data, it is automatically converted to the new format again. As a consequence, it is likely that backups made from today onwards will not work with uninfected computers. We are able to characterise this format change, but there is clearly the possibility that there will be further changes in format. We will be able to provide you with more information tomorrow. Eyes again started to glaze over, before Eldon provided a less technical explanation.

To put the above in layman's terms. The virus has now locked all the data. When a program needs data, it unlocks it. When a program stores data, it locks it again. An uninfected computer cannot use the data as it does not know how to unlock it. We also think the virus may change the locks regularly. Eldon paused briefly, as if to indicate a return to his technical mode.

The virus is now also causing computer crashes. These appear to be random but are not. We would estimate that there is now a one in a million chance of a clean U-Sys computer crashing at least once per day. This crash is not random but is the result of the deliberate instruction of the virus. We expect this probability to increase. To most people in the room, 'one in a million' sounded like an increase in reliability, not a decrease. How could U-Soft suggest such a low number? And think it a problem? Eldon, however, was not waiting while they thought.

We have been successful in some of our efforts to alleviate the symptoms of the virus. U-Soft is now ready to make a beta release of a program which will allow new computers to run without any impact from the virus. As discussed before, this program will allow all programs to infer the correct date when a computer which is set to a date prior to the effect of the virus. The name of this program is SafeDate, and it can now be downloaded from the U-Soft web-site. In twenty four hours we should be able to state, with confidence, that SafeDate presents a workable short-term solution while we find and eliminate the virus itself. We can also confirm that USOS, the U-Soft emulator for UNOS, is free of the virus. Software for U-Sys versions 3 and above can therefore run on computers using the UNOS operating system. An almost imperceptible pause to signal the end of the section. Then immediately on to the next.

Our efforts to find and eliminate the virus are concentrated on two areas. Firstly, we are searching computers for hidden text, particularly any text which has appeared in the virus messages. We have met with a measure of success. Specifically, we have found text hidden in what is known as the directory of U-Sys, the area used to indicate what files are stored, and where. It would appear that the directory of infected computers contains reference to many files that are marked as deleted, although these files have never actually existed. The file names are encrypted, but if we apply three variants of the same encryption method we can identify all of the text that has been displayed by the virus to date. We are working on the determination of the variants which will enable us to predict future text. We are also looking for any areas in the U-Sys kernel which makes reference to those hidden directory entries. Eyes started to glaze for that third and final time, but again Eldon provided a layman's synopsis.

Put simply, we have uncovered lists of files that have never, ever existed. The names of the files may be put together to create the messages that the virus displays.

Finally, our teams have now inspected and validated around twenty five thousand lines of the kernel source code. That represents around thirty five per cent of the total seventy two thousand lines. It remains our belief that we will find the virus

code in the remaining sixty-five per cent. We remain unwilling
to extrapolate our current rate of progress to estimate a
completion date.

Again, I have been brief in order to maximise the use of my
time and of yours. I must again assure you all that U-Soft utterly
regrets this virus attack and are working as hard as humanly
possible to arrive at a solution. Be patient and I am confident this
will be resolved.

Thank you"

The assembled journalists had expected bad news, but the form
and scale of it was unexpected. They were transformed a
seething, turbulent clamour of oaths, outrage, and questions.
Given that, you could argue that Mohan Nehran and Brian
Dempsey did not do so badly. They survived, at least. However,
there was little doubt that they got a rough ride. It was a fine day
to have been born Before Computers. Certainly, The Knowledge
no longer seemed quite so precious. Reflecting afterwards, these
were Dempsey's main recollections:

Jim Solomon, of the Guardian, started the ball rolling when
he wondered aloud:

"Given these new bombs from the virus, does anyone at U-
Soft have any idea what might be coming next? Can anyone at
U-Soft explain to me how this much malicious code can still
remain hidden from the people who are supposed to have written
the software in the first place?"

Robert Perry, was the first of the odd couple to get the nod.

"What happens if U-Sys are unable to check all the source
code in time? Is there an alternative plan? If U-Soft cannot find
the virus themselves, why do they not put the source code on the
internet and let us see who can?

Peter Farnham, of the Mail, asked, without a hint of irony:

"How can the virus be doing so many things, yet we cannot

167

find it? Is it true that the virus was a deliberate creation by U-Sys, and that U-Sys cannot admit to it? What do U-Sys say about the rumours of U.S. Government involvement?"

Jim Higgins, of the Mirror, suggested, acidly:

"Why do we not all turn off our U-Sys computers now, and never switch them on again? How can Eldon Harker and the other fat cats of U-Soft expect to stay out of jail after this?

Peter Hawkins, although clearly delighted with the humbling of U-Sys, was perhaps beginning to get past the revenge stage. Could he already have had his fill? Anyway, he was more thoughtful:

"Given the variety of effects of the virus, surely some bad code would have shown up in the thirty five per cent of the code that has now been checked? Are we certain that the virus really is in this so-called kernel? How can we be convinced that the virus is twenty years old, and not the recent creation of terrorists, like Al-Quaeda?

James Taylor, of the Independent, raged:

"How we can trust U-Soft to make an assessment of the emulators? As I understand it, the Christmas Bug evaded the Millennium testing because it was triggered on an ordinary date, several years later. What is not to say that the emulators have the same bug, but that it is just triggered on some later date?"

Perhaps the most interesting question came from Tom Trenton, of the Sun, who asked:

"Have U-Soft had any success in finding Michael MacDonald? Have U-Soft any reply to the claims that he is responsible?"

In Dempsey's recollection, those were the key questions. Certainly, Dempsey and Nehran did their best to first defuse them, then answer them. Unsuccessfully. Their answers were, at best, met with derision. At worst, with downright disbelief. It was obvious to all the journalists that things were getting worse, and their mood had turned ugly. To Dempsey and Nehran they seemed little better than a baying mob, clamouring for blood. At one forty five, it was with relief that the U-Soft men brought the conference to a close, and left with their limbs intact. The mob streamed out to file copy. But it was clear that a lynching would have been more to their taste.

The two o'clock news bulletins carried the disheartening message. People had convinced themselves that they could tolerate the slowing of their computers, and that U-Soft would sort it out in time, as they always did. The knowledge that their data was no longer safe was a body blow. A crippling blow, even more so for being unexpected. It was clear that the virus was intensifying its attack, and their defences were already down. Anger was easy to kindle, and scapegoats easy to find. The streets burned, while the dark flags flew.

Ahmed Ali Khan had wakened still dreaming of the infidel, and of his father, Mohammed Ali Khan. Of his father, and of his terrible anger when he had heard of the killing. His father was well known in Glasgow – and beyond – as a community leader. Very well-known, for he was the first, and most influential, of the Asian businessmen who had also carved out careers in local politics. He was also many times a millionaire, through business interests that had started in import/export and had then spread to include restaurants, taxis, fast food and internet cafes. Yes, Mohammed Ali Khan was the embodiment of the multi-cultural ideal, the passionate Glasgow man who also happened to be a devout Muslim, and who still remained close to his Pakistani culture. Few knew that there was much more to his father. Among all his many cash businesses, the greatest by far was drugs. Mainly, but not exclusively, heroin. Heroin, born as opium in the poppy fields of Afghanistan, destined to wind its way down the Taliban Trail, and over the wild Pakistani border.

Opium that was reborn as heroin in labs of his Turkish friends, and heroin that was finally despatched by sea to the port of Dundee, Scotland. His father's business, indeed. Even fewer knew that his father was not just a devout Muslim, but a long time follower of the Jihad path. One of the very first to plan for the Jihad that was to come. Even fewer still knew that Ahmed had been raised to be his fiery right hand. All the teaching, the training, the subterfuge. His father's life work, and his salvation. No wonder that his father had flown into a terrible rage when they told him of Ahmed's murder of the infidel. Had he not endangered his father's great plan in that one foolish moment? By the grace of Allah, his father had been able to buy two witnesses, and a confession of guilt. Poor Rashid, his closest friend, had also cost much blood money. There was no choice. They dared not let him live long enough for the bleak walls of his cell to loosen his tongue. No, Rashid's tongue was now forever silent. Ahmed had shivered with the memory, still fresh, perhaps forever fresh. But then Ahmed swelled with pride as he remembered just why that had to be - just who he was, and the honour that was to come to him. It was then that he had noticed that he had mail.

U-Soft, London: Five p.m. December the Twenty-Second

Andrew sat back from his desk and vainly tried to rub the fatigue from his eyes. He had finally finished his analysis, prepared the list of key phrases that summarised his arguments, and was ready for the debate. Well, he would be, after a half-hour's nap. No time for Mr Chamberlain tonight, but at least they were scheduled to meet tomorrow at one. Mr Chamberlain, apparently, was going to bring a friend.

Half an hour later, and braziers ring the BBC in a glowing amulet of fire and rumour. People have flocked to the barricades, to the excitement, the gossip, the welcoming heat. The atmosphere is charged, vibrant, intoxicating. One enterprising soul has rigged a web-cam to a car battery, and feeds the output to *ItsTimeToTalkFreely.com*. Within the hour, virtually every brazier feeds a webcam and a growing internet audience. Already, the celebrity game is in play, as stars are born in the fiery brazier light. *ItsTimeToTalkFreely.com* is the site of choice for most of the broadcasts, its many threads providing an intoxicating array of newly-born stars and earnest, impassioned monologues. However, a small but growing audience are drawn to other stars, and to other sites. To one site and to one star in particular. The name of the star is Daniel D, to give him his full street name, and the name of the site is AnarchistVictory.com. Daniel D is a tall, powerful man in his mid twenties, large eyed in a broad face topped with fierce blonde dreadlocks. His monologues alternate between harangues and poetry, between rage and tenderness, and his hypnotic power entraps many who had thought they knew better. Nor do the television cameras seem immune. As they pan around the fires and the flags that dance in their glow, no fire seems so bright and no flag seems to dance so seductively as the anarchist fire and the anarchist black. Still, the amulet holds all safe. It is this amulet of fire that will also save the life of Anwar Abbat, but he does not yet know it.

At the same moment, Peter Bradshaw is caught in thought as he surveys the amulet from his lofty eyrie, his earlier discomfort now all but a deniable memory. Truly, he thinks, the BBC *is* now the news. Not the observer, but the player. The singer not the song: the medium not the message. How strange a time, how intoxicating a time! A time to be careful, for the dangers are as new as the role. The debates are the key: above all else, protect the debates. Does that mean the BBC must protect the participants? Not from the viewpoint of the ratings, he thought. No distant sniper's bullet will frighten off our viewers, nor will many hesitate to fill an advocate's place, to make the leap to fame and lifetime fortune? Does that mean the BBC has a moral duty to protect the participants? Yes, Peter thinks, for with power goes responsibility. Duties. The BBC must discharge its duties, and must be seen to do so. Rubbing his bald head, Peter calls his good friend. There is no problem, he is told. The police are only too happy to oblige, and will make available one of the large, armoured black vans used for transporting prisoners. That is why, an hour later, three assassins wait in vain for Anwar's car. He has gone by another route, to another destination, where he has boarded the armoured van with the last of the advocates. A little later, in a scene of the highest televisual drama, the juggernaut arrives at the barricades. A noisy phalanx of police outriders shield it on all four sides, their blue and red lights strobing its sheer black panels, while yards away the cheering crowds are hidden by a white blizzard of camera flash. All is captured by the TV cameras and the webcams, each endlessly reporting on each other like the infinite reflections of facing mirrors. The stage is being set for the debates. Expectancy is rising. So far, the amulet's protection has held.

Three and a half thousand miles away, in Dubai Internet City, a rather more select web cast is about to go live. John Nightingale, otherwise referred to as 'M', knows just enough of the operational details to exercise his management role, but not enough as to be embarrassing. Apparently, Dubai centre had identified a suitable target, and had traced the unlucky man to the luxury of a suite in the Bab Al Shams, a twenty-first century oasis some fifty kilometres deep into the desert. The sole hotel at the end of a long road, a desert road, a black surface forever shimmering with water, yet forever dry. A long and *deserted* desert road. One way in, and one way out, making the Bab Al Shams the ideal extraction point for the hard men who were charged to bring him back. Apparently the married gentleman was not alone, nor with his wife, which was just the kind of behaviour that had got him selected in the first place. It did not take long for the technical director of Al-Mail – for he was the unlucky romantic – to become desperate to please. Less than an hour later, he arrived at his offices in Dubai Internet City, in the company of two sharply suited young men and a black Range Rover Sport. The two external consultants were hurriedly introduced to the surprised assembly of multinational geeks, who were amazed and dismayed to discover that their servers had been compromised and that urgent disinfection was required. Still, the consultants radiated a calm competence, and the day off they were all granted was always welcome. In the privacy of the now deserted offices, the Dubai servers were at their mercy, and the three had wasted no time in getting to work. Back in London, in the nondescript, subterranean room, 'M' was the image of professional patience as he did what he did best. Wait. Everything had been prepared as best they could. Specialist teams of MI5 and Special Branch were poised at all the major cities: London, Birmingham, Manchester, Liverpool and Glasgow. It was not ideal, but probably the best gamble they could make with the available resources. Surely not much longer to wait? As if on cue, a technician stopped clicking, leaned back from his laptop and beamed. The large wall screen now burst into life. A clean display, almost blank. Little more than a thin frame around an empty expanse of text. The title of the frame: 'E-Mail trace enabled. Status: Waiting for activation'. 'So far,' John Nightingale thought, 'so good. Please let it continue. Insh'Allah.'

Back in Dubai Internet City, the same screen danced in almost perfect synchrony, yet always that blink ahead. The first, therefore, to show 'Mail-box Request Detected', followed by a flurry of lines. 'IP address 213.171.193.5', 'UK address', 'BT', 'Glasgow', 'Govanhill', '21 Charles Edward Street'. By the time the last line appeared, three thousand six hundred miles away, three cars of Special Branch police had already hurtled from their base, and were speeding the four miles to Govanhill. As they drove, it was obvious that no-one was surprised at the destination. Govanhill had a long background as an immigrant community, starting with the Irish that fled the great famine, through to the Polish Jews that had fled the Nazis and holocaust, and now to the Pakistani immigrants that today dominated its tenements and streets. While very much a mixed community, Govanhill seemed free of racial strife, all races seeming happy to live together in the fragile harmony of mutual poverty. Yes, an ideal choice, the perfect place to hide. But no longer, for now the chase was on. The time in London was six thirty,

Number twenty-one, Charles Edward Street is an empty ground floor retail unit in a care-worn block of a dozen four-storey Victorian tenements. To the left of number twenty-one is 'The Oasis', which describes itself, in Urdu and English, as an Islamic community centre. 'The Oasis' was presently dry, doors locked and padlocked. To the right of twenty-one, 'O'Reilly's Free House' is also a community centre, of sorts, and continues to provide beer, sanctuary and racing tips, much as it has done for the last two generations. On both sides of the street, the pavements are carpeted with litter and dog turds. The kerbsides are filled by cars that are not worth stealing. Despite this, the width of the road, and the pavements, make it clear that Charles Edward Street was born in more optimistic times. At one end, Charles Edward butts into Victoria Road, once a prestigious shopping street, but now dominated by charity shops and fast food outlets. Large concrete bollards seal the junction from cars, and around the feet of the bollards swirls a rainbow nation of children and mongrels and litter. At its other end, Charles Edward crosses Georgic Road, beyond which the tenements unexpectedly blossom into large Victorian villas. On a practical level, however, Charles Edward Street is not the easiest of streets for three police cars to enter discreetly. A fight, however, is always a compelling distraction. This fight was particularly compelling, as a small Chinese man rained spectacular roundhouse kicks on a large, black-bearded bear of a Sikh. Initially, the Sikh seemed impervious to the blows, repeatedly lunging forward, grasping for the Chinese, looking for the one hold that would be all he needed. Just as the Sikh seemed to be losing heart, worn down by the torrent of kicks and elbows, a car screeched to halt in Victoria Road, and two more Sikhs leaped from its rear seats. The martial artist rapidly re-assessed the odds and fled, sprinting down Victoria Road and out of sight. Meanwhile, as all eyes were elsewhere, the Oasis had briefly opened, just long enough to admit two specialists and the tools of their trade. Their trade is surveillance, and the tools of their trade are electronic, mostly sensors, and utterly state-of-the-art.

Just five minutes earlier, as three cars had bulleted down the Pollokshaws Road straight, the IP connection had been broken. Computer off-line, still a minute or so from their goal. Damn. It had not been a popular decision, and a short but fierce debate, but Dubai insisted that they could not slow the e-mail any longer without arousing suspicion. Still, DCI Bendle was optimistic they had got there before anyone could leave. Senses on maximum, he reflexively scanned the street. It was now two minutes since the specialists had disappeared inside the Oasis, so swiftly and unobtrusively that it almost could not have happened. Inside, they were already well underway, the silence and precision of their movements a study in the silence of their art. Within ten minutes the bulk of their sensors were operational: heat, motion, sound, network. Five minutes later and they knew several things. Number twenty-one, Charles Edward Street was empty of people, of motion, of network signals and heat, save that generated by a small laptop in the small bedroom at the rear. They also knew it was safe to install visual surveillance. Ten minutes later and they had installed a sophisticated array of microscopic, wireless transmitter cameras, and number twenty-one was theirs to view. Not that it took long. Lounge, kitchen and bathroom were all empty. Junk mail was heaped below the front letter box, hinting that no-one had been in for some time. Perhaps deliberately so. Only the small bedroom at the back had any signs of life, and that was the Sony laptop that sat on a small, otherwise bare, desk. The power light indicated that the laptop was on, although its screen was blank. A cable ran from its back to a phone point. Five minutes later, just twenty five short minutes from gaining entry, the lead specialist called his DCI. Bendle listened to the whispered report with some disappointment, and told the specialist to keep working until they both knew, personally, the name of every spider that still stalked the dusty floors of number twenty-one. And then to figure out how they could get in, and onto the laptop, without any prospect of detection, by humans and spiders alike.

They were not the only ones who had been busy. MI5 now had all of Connor's e-mail, three code-words, and, perhaps, a *Sesame* computer. John Nightingale -'M'- had felt he was in a position to provide at least some of the answers that the PM clamoured for. The meeting was to be at Number Ten, and he was to bring Hector. Naturally; and no problem. John Nightingale needed him just as much as did David Blenheim. 'M' has also been instructed to bring the *Sesame* computer. It was time to put it to the test, the PM thought. And its message was for their eyes only. 'Understandable,' John Nightingale thought. 'but I wonder. Just what exactly will *Sesame* open?

SEVEN

London: Seven-thirty p.m. December the Twenty-Second

'No,' Catherine thought. 'Now is not the time to be unfaithful. Jimmy Choo it is. I still love you, Jimmy Choo.' In the mirror, Catherine smiled at her shoes and her hair and her blouse and her skirt and the sheer delight of being a glamorous woman. 'Just where does all this good humour come from?' she wondered. When she thought about it she had rather a lot to feel good about. A marvellous, *delicious*, day, and the world at her feet tonight. Yes, she was ready for her audience. And, maybe later, Mr Westlands.

Such frivolities would have shrivelled in the subterranean depths below Number Ten. The atmosphere at the small meeting was one of focus, concentration, intensity, and the famous Blenheim brows were spectacularly furrowed.

"So, tell me, John", he opened. "Tell me all I need to know about Glasgow." John Nightingale was disturbed at the use of his real name, the breach of protocol. 'A good sign or a bad?' he wondered. His face betrayed nothing of his unease, as he collected his thoughts and summarised as requested.

"We have located where the last message originated from, an immigrant area in the south side of Glasgow. Unfortunately, we arrived just after the message was sent. It is possible that we missed the sender, but, if so, it must have been very tight. Right now we have the flat under highest level surveillance. Nothing enters, nothing moves, nothing happens without our knowing. Not just physical traffic, internet traffic too." David Blenheim interrupted.

"How do we know that, John? Are we sure?" In response, John Nightingale smoothly brought in Hector.

"Hector, perhaps you would like to take over here?" From his immediate fluency, Hector was obviously well prepared.

"The phone in the flat is registered with BT. They also provide the flat with its internet dial up service. From their records, an internet connection was initiated and terminated yesterday at times that precisely match the transmission of the message to Connor. We are therefore certain that this computer sent the message, and that it used the BT dialup internet service to do so. We have talked to BT and we will now get copies of anything, *anything*, that this computer sends or receives through this internet connection. That means we have the physical and electronic ins and outs covered. Now, Prime Minister, the question is: where do the messages actually come from?" Hector paused and gazed at Blenheim, who gestured in impatience. Hector took the now-familiar cue.

"Prime Minister, there are three possibilities. One, the messages are already stored on the computer and are automatically sent at a pre-defined time. Two, someone sends messages to the computer, and it picks them up and relays them. Three, someone enters the flat and manually sends them. If we don't examine the computer, then we have to wait for the next message to know which of the three it is. So, either we wait, or we make the decision to enter the flat and to take a look at that laptop." Hector paused. David Blenheim took his time.

"Guess, Hector. If it were you, what method would you use?" It was Hector's turn to pause. But not long enough to suggest that he had not seen the question coming.

"If the messages are already stored on the computer, then the terrorists need an off switch in case the BBC give up Sesame or otherwise break their deal. That would not be easy to do, given that we might already have possession of the computer. Too easy for us to disable. Too easy for us to remove the off switch. No, I would not take that route. I would not even consider manual entry. Why take the risk? No, Prime Minister, I would take the second option. I would send messages to the computer and have it relay them." John Nightingale, to Hector's surprise, cut in.

"There is absolutely nothing that these terrorists have done so far that is stupid, Prime Minister. If Hector considers that the relay option is the smart one, then I am prepared to back his choice and his advice. I'd recommend that we act on that basis."

It was David Blenheim's turn to be shocked, and even his politician's skills could not mask his surprise at such clear, unequivocal advice. Surprise, and also pleasure. Unmistakable signs of leadership, as well as teamwork. Not a common occurrence in such a politically-charged situation. Or was there more to it? He had no time to reflect, right now he had to press on.

"In that case, John, am I right in thinking there is no reason why we should not discreetly enter this flat and look at the computer a little more closely?" John Nightingale, however, did not agree.

"Actually, Prime Minister, that will not be necessary, as we can now intercept the messages anyway. There is also the chance that the computer is booby-trapped in some way. I would recommend that we continue to monitor the premises, but let's not enter them just yet."

"Recommendation accepted." agreed David Blenheim. He then sat back and unexpectedly smiled. "So, gentlemen, are we now ready to open Sesame?"

Four hundred miles away, and Solomon N'Chenga felt he had more than earned his rum. Somehow, from the beguiling, desolate beauty of a winter Skye, he had conjured a result. Ah, rum, God bless you for the warmth you bring to an African's heart in this cold white world. Let's not forget the whisky too, for it too had its heat and the key to a man's tongue. A quiet, desolate bar, with

179

a clientele that wrapped themselves in salt-laden silence the moment he entered their murmuring domain. Quite how the gnarled, white-haired fisherman had known he was looking for Red Michael he could not say. On second thoughts, perhaps not so hard to guess. Even if Michael had lived here two hundred years, rather than two, he would still have been an outsider, a strange outsider, to these people. Like me. No, for a whisky or two, he and the fisherman had had a fine chat about the other stranger, not as dark as you, mind. Sometimes he took a whisky or two, even though he was a religious man, the elder church, if you please. A very clever man he was too, and well travelled. Brought me back a fine book once. From a place that he used to talk about, a beautiful place, a fine watery place for a man with salt in his bones. Too many of those grand churches, mind, to be for honest folk. Ah, but beautiful, and the gentlemen seemed to visit there often. Ah rum, God bless you, Solomon thought as he finished with a flourish and a fiery swallow. That's the last I'll see of you for now. I'll need a clear head for Venice. The rotors of the Lynx were soon spinning, and Solomon was heading East. Strangely, as he had left the warmth of the Eilann Airmann Inn, he could have sworn he heard the first bars of 'Will Ye No Come Back Again'. Must have the fiddler in the corner, what else? Solomon shivered a little, and not with the sudden cold.

Ahmed Ali Khan tapped his spoon on the top of the espresso cup, placed it casually on the tiny saucer, and leaned back into his customary, languid, playboy pose. Young, handsome, lithe and muscular, Ahmed immediately attracted admiring glances from the bolder of the passing women. Even - Allah curse the abomination! - from some of the men. The City of the Infidels, what else could you expect? No matter, today Ahmed's joy was unassailable, and the playboy mask sat easily on his broad shoulders. For the countless time, Ahmed replayed the message in his mind. All was well. He had been chosen to strike the deadliest blow. The meeting with his local jihadi was set for tomorrow. What relief, what joy had surged through Ahmed! His laptop was rapidly becoming useless and he had begun to fear he would never be able to get the message, never be able to read it, never be able to answer the call of his Emir. This afternoon, as he had seen the message come in, his heart had surged. How had his hope then turned to despair when the *Caliph* software took forever to decrypt the attachment? How long did it take? Five minutes? Ten minutes? Almost forever, but not quite. Contact was established. He would be met tomorrow. Judgement was coming to the City of the Infidels. Ah, life was sweet. And short, he thought, with a sudden jolt of fear. Raw fear, stronger than before, a chemical burst that quickened his heart. However, Paradise is a powerful anaesthetic, and soon Ahmed was strong again. He finished his coffee, left a generous tip, and was gone.

Nine p.m. GMT, December the Twenty-Second

Across the globe, people are again expectant. As before, their focus is a small to medium-sized studio, BBC headquarters, London. But it is not their only focus. As news creates news, many cameras are focused on the braziers, on the newly erected screens that flicker in their light, and the volunteers that are tensed around them. And the webcams that send the echoing images out into the dark and alien ether.

Back in the BBC studio, Catherine had brought the audience smoothly under her spell as she made a brief recapitulation of the rules. There was complete silence as she read the charge - or motion, as some insisted on calling it.

"The West is guilty of the failure to protect their own, the inability to act for the greater good."

The sequence of speakers was to be Anwar, Krishnan, Andrew, William, and Anne-Marie. In her professional capacity as presenter, Catherine was grateful that the sequence was clearly different, that no-one could make groundless allegations of bias. In her personal capacity, Catherine was a little disappointed that Andrew was in the least effective position, and wondered how he would cope. But only momentarily, for Anwar had already risen to his feet.

'He has already played the martyr, and lived.' Catherine thought. 'Does that mean the return of the warrior?' Anwar started to speak with his familiar, unsettling intensity.

"Ladies and gentlemen, I would like to ask you some questions. Some simple questions." Anwar Abbat's combative features looked almost sympathetic.

"To the parents in here, let me direct this question. Do you feel that your children are safe? Safe from crime and criminals? To everyone here, do you feel safe as you go about your daily lives? Can you walk the streets at night without fear? Do you also feel confident that your country can keep the terrorists from your shores, the suicide bomber from your cities? Can anyone here tell me that they live without these fears?" Anwar paused and scanned the faces of the audience. Their response, however, was to avoid his eyes, and to remain silent.

"Can anyone here explain to me how a society can spend so much on security and yet get so little? More money than any society has ever spent in history? Can anyone here explain to me how this can be?" Anwar again paused and scanned: no response. In the clusters around the braziers, the rainbow audience watched the mute response of the studio in comradely silence. No disagreements were voiced: no explanations were muttered.

"And yet," Anwar paused, "and yet, you do *your* part. You pay for police and lawyers and jails. You buy locks and alarms and security cameras. You hire security guards for your shopping malls, bouncers for your pubs and clubs. You buy tanks and guns and aeroplanes. You pay for soldiers and airmen and seamen. You fund rockets and missiles and bombs. What more can you do?" Again, Anwar paused and looked around. People shook their heads sadly, in the studio, around the braziers, and in the countless squares of the West. Well, not all the braziers. Above the anarchist black, a new banner had just been hoisted, and it read 'No laws, no punishments'. The other brazier people were too caught up in the debate to have yet noticed. Or so it seemed. Meanwhile, Anwar continued to lay bare their failure.

"Yes, ladies and gentlemen, the West is *absolutely* guilty of the failure to protect their own. The West is failing in its duty to protect the innocent. We are agreed, are we not?" More shakes of the head; more nods.

"Yet, I think there is no mystery to this failure. At a practical level, I think the answer lies in the words that I saw on my computer today. That we have probably all seen today. The words that said *They pretend that it is possible to live life without making difficult choices. For fear of making one wrong conviction, they will let a hundred innocents die.* You are so concerned with the criminal and his rights that you cannot protect the victims. Because you cannot bear the burden of making a mistake, you let the criminal go free. Go free to harm more innocents. You consider this the fairest course of action. Is this fair to your innocents? You even have the madness to pride yourself on this, your humane penal system! A penal system that is paid for by the suffering of innocents. You refuse to get your hands dirty. You will not risk the occasional mistake. Because what matters most to you is your own image. That you look like a good, humane, caring human being. Such hypocrisy! Consequently, inevitably, *automatically*, you condemn your innocents. And, of course, you yourselves, because they are your children, your loved ones that suffer. Even if fear of crime is the extent of their suffering, it is suffering nonetheless. Is it not?" Anwar looked around, gauging the reaction. Judging by the nods, few in the studio disagreed. Around the braziers, clear expressions of support were being heard. But not around the black flags. Anwar waited a few seconds, before he continued.

"Is there are an answer, you ask? Your politicians tell you that there is not. That this is as good as it gets. Ladies and gentlemen, they are deceiving you. They know the answer, but they are afraid to tell you. Let me, a good Muslim, give you the answer." Anwar paused, letting the anticipation build. Catherine watched seven seconds tick away before Anwar continued. Yes, the warrior was back, and about to deliver a killing blow, surely?

"The problem lies at the heart of your society. No amount of money is going to fix it. The problem is that you worship life. You respect life too much. *You love life too much.*" Anwar saw the looks of the puzzlement in the studio. Had expected them. Continued.

"It is like falling in love with a beautiful woman. A beautiful, virtuous woman. You worship her, put her on a pedestal. Make her your Princess. Then, later, you wonder why your marriage does not work?" Anwar paused, and took a breath.

"You must not worship life. If you worship life, for what reason can you possibly sacrifice it? And if you will not sacrifice life, your life, someone's life, how can you keep your innocents safe? How can your soldiers fight if they are not prepared to die? And how can they be prepared to die if they worship life beyond all things? If there is nothing beyond it?" Around the braziers, more and more heads were beginning to nod. Whispers of assent. Murmurs of understanding, and agreement. Anwar was becoming more impassioned, his voice dropping deeper even as it became louder.

"A balanced person does not worship only life. A balanced

person worships *life and death*. You must see this greater picture. You must have some values that enable you to put life in its proper context. If not, the preservation of life becomes a conundrum, a paradox. Your attempts to preserve life at all costs can only result in the greater loss of life. You do not kill murderers, so your innocents must die. You do not remove criminals from society, so they continue to prey on you all. Your love of life has been taken too far. It is out of balance. It rules you, and leads you to disaster. Of course, as a Muslim, I can go further. I *will* go further."
Anwar paused again, and everyone sensed it was for the last time. 'Not warrior,' thought Catherine. 'PROPHET.'

"Once you had a Christian world, but now that is gone. Now you have created a Godless world. My friends, it is God, Allah, who provides balance. Allah who puts life and death in perspective. Without Allah, your world will fail. Your world is failing, for are we not already agreed that you cannot protect your innocents? That you cannot look after your own? No, the West as you know it is over. Your day is done. Let me tell you an ancient Persian proverb." Anwar paused again, but only slightly, and for the last time. His last words were delivered in a slow, deep, rhythmic pulse.

"Try to grasp happiness tightly between your fingers and it will escape you. Try to grasp life tightly between your fingers and it, too, will escape you.'"

'PROPHET' Catherine thought. 'Yes, prophet.' But the prophet was not quite finished. He shook his head, sorrowfully, and scanned the faces in the audience. His last words.

"It is so, my friends. Continue to worship only Life and you will find only Death."

Anwar sat down to a stunned and sombre audience. In the silence that gripped the braziers, 'It's Time to Talk Freely' banners flapped in mute mockery. In the Cabinet Room of Number Ten, no-one moved, and no-one spoke. In his hotel suite, high in the City of the Infidels, Ahmed Ali Khan sank to his knees in joy and gratitude. What wisdom Allah had shown in preserving the life of this brave Muslim! How wrong had Ahmed been, that he had not seen the subtlety of Allah's works? Strength, courage, and resolution flooded through Ahmed, swamping the fear that had begun to gnaw at him constantly. The fear they had warned him of. By the time Ahmed refocused on the screen, the questions were already underway, and Andrew Westlands was about to address his question to Anwar.

"A powerful speech, Anwar. And I do not disagree with you when you say that there is something wrong at the heart of the West. Many of us think so too. However, it does not seem to me that anywhere else is much better. In particular, in the Muslim countries of the world, is crime any better than it is in the West? Do your citizens live in peace and security? Not from what I have seen. In your Islamic world, your idealistic world, there are crime and security problems every bit as bad those in the West. So tell me, Anwar, how can you expect us to accept your explanation?" It was a fair question, and a bomb at the heart of Anwar's argument. However, Anwar had obviously anticipated the question, for he did not hesitate.

"Let me be completely frank with you, Andrew. Forgive me if I say exactly what I think." Anwar paused for effect, then continued, his tone deep, strong, and uncompromising.

"I am afraid that the lure of the West is too strong. The promises of the West are too beguiling. People always have moments of weakness, and they can be seduced by the these false promises. I am afraid to say it, but as long as your society exists, it corrupts everyone. As it stands, as long as the West exists, no-one can be safe."

186

In the silence that followed, the earlier silences seemed like a celebration. In the City of the Infidels, a rapturous Ahmed almost whooped with glee. What clearer definition of the problem could they make? What part did these infidels not now understand? Surely everyone must see that the Jihadi path was right and just? Lost in delight, interspersed with prayers of thanksgiving, for several minutes Ahmed was oblivious to the drama that continued to play on the large plasma screen.

Back in the London studio, by the time Ahmed's attention had returned, much had happened. Andrew had long ago shaken his head in disbelief, and declined to question further. William and Anne-Marie's questions had been posed and brushed aside. Krishnan's speech had been and gone, and Catherine Connor was about to prompt Anwar to ask the first question. Despite herself, Catherine could not help but feel a twinge of sympathy for Krishnan. At any other time, she thought, Krishnan's speech would have been judged to be a fine piece of work, elegant, intelligent and powerful. It had certainly begun strongly.

"A society that cannot protect its own members is certainly a failure. However, a society cannot protect ALL of it members, because resources are never infinite. If society seeks to protect everyone, inevitably it is everyone who will suffer. Choices must be made, and some people must be unfortunate. This is the truth that the West refuses to recognise." However, everyone, advocates included, still seemed to be gripped in a collective shock. *As it stands, as long as the West exists, no-one can be safe.* There, it had been said. It was out there. And how did you follow that up? Not with Krishnan, unfortunately for him. It was not that Krishnan's speech had not been good, because it had. Good, but just too cerebral, and the audience was most definitely not in a cerebral place. *As it stands, as long as the West exists, no-one can be safe.* Yesterday's hero, the courageous voice of moderate

Islam, could not have been more explicit. He could not have spelled it out more clearly. Islam would not, *could not*, tolerate the West. At their core, the secular West and religious Islam were not compatible. However, *compatible* was not the word in everyone's mind. In their minds the word was *exists*, and it was no wonder that Krishnan's speech was almost over before their attention had returned. Most had refocused by the time Krishnan delivered his last few sentences.

"The West is guilty of the failure to protect its own. The West is in this position because it considers the legal process to be a hunt for perfection. The West is proud to devote more and more resources to the protection of criminals, to protect against the possibility of any miscarriage of justice. The West seeks for the goal of perfect justice: zero mistakes, zero doubt. Zero, ladies and gentlemen, is for mathematics, not for real life. There is never a zero and you will never find it. In your arrogance, however, you cannot admit this. You consider yourself above the laws of nature, free to act with infinite power and resource. Meanwhile, your society crumbles, and your innocents suffer. Ladies and gentlemen, you may not agree with the analysis I have just made. You may not agree with the analysis that, God forbid, Anwar has made. However, I am sure that you do agree with one thing that we have said. I am sure that you know that your system is broken and you need to do something about it. If it is not already too late."

With that Krishnan had sat down.

Yes, a fine speech,' Catherine thought, 'a PHILOSOPHER'S speech. But the wrong speech in the wrong place at the wrong time. A philosopher can never follow a prophet.' However, Anwar was to be first to question, and as he rose the wheel of drama turned again. The prophet was back, and the audience snapped back to the ongoing debate.

Back in Number Ten, David Blenheim had another distraction to deal with. A **Nexus** lap-top had been hurriedly placed in front of him. Images from a live web cast filled its small screen. The title of the screen identified the site as www.AnarchistVictory.com, and it struck the horrified PM that the site might indeed be well named. The images came from the anarchist braziers outside the BBC. Dominating the screen was a demonic looking Daniel D, eyes flashing, blonde dreadlocks streaming. In his hands he held aloft a long staff, its tip tightly bound in flaming petrol soaked cloths. Just behind him was a large mound, arranged in the celebration of a bonfire. Suspended above, loomed a huge red banner, whose large black lettering read 'No laws, No punishments, No religion'. The anarchists had clearly done their homework, had correctly guessed the direction the debates would take, for it would have taken many hours to stockpile the books that now lay heaped high in the brazier light. Just on the far left fringe of the camera shot, a last can of petrol was emptied onto the incendiary mound. 'Whatever else you can say about them, they've got guts,' David Blenheim thought, as the web-cams slowly and deliberately scanned the books, lingering long on the titles. Hundreds of Bibles and Korans were heaped there, but they were by no means the only fuel. Pretty much any religion was represented, from the teachings of Mahayana Buddhism to the Gathas of Zoroaster. Crying a last, belligerent slogan, Daniel D thrust the flaming staff into the mound, and answering flames immediately leapt high into the night-sky.

David Blenheim watched in silence for a full minute before he finally came to a decision. By the time he had issued the necessary instructions, Krishnan's questions were over and Andrew Westlands was rising to his feet. Good timing, thought Blenheim. He felt his colleagues' expectancy, their anticipatory buzz. He shared it. But he had more at stake on this speech than they did.

Ahmed Ali Khan was also expectant, almost fearful. In some ways, Westlands fitted all the Western stereotypes that he so despised. Rich, corrupt, sure of his power. Yet his acknowledgement of the faults of the West disturbed Ahmed, raised the spectre that talk, and argument, might still have a role to play. But today Ahmed felt more secure. Today, Anwar Abbat had thrown down the gauntlet. Westlands had no more easy choices. Acceptance of criticism is one thing. Acceptance that you must be annihilated is another. Just under a thousand miles away, Andrew Westlands calmly cleared his throat, seemingly oblivious of the babble of thoughts that everywhere assailed him. Andrew opened in a clear, strong, calm tone.

"Ladies and gentlemen, it is time to talk freely. Then again, sometimes it is just a waste of our time." Andrew paused to gaze around his slightly puzzled audience, then continued.

"This motion for example. We said yesterday that our laws were worthless, that it was time to start again. We already know, *and admit*, that our laws do not protect us. We agreed yesterday that we do not inspire heroes any more. So we already *know* that our soldiers can never fight as effectively as they should. As they need to, for their sake and ours. We could talk about the underlying reasons for the problems our society faces. Both Anwar and Krishnan have already offered their insights into the deeper issues. I even agree with some of what both of them have said. Not all of it. I think that people will fight and die for principles other than religion. Communism proved that. And people will always be prepared to fight and die to defend their children. But, those comments aside, I agree with much of what they have said, and tonight I'd like to be more practical. So let's move on and talk about something constructive. *When we tear up these foolish laws we are saddled with, what are we going to put in their place?"*

At the anarchist barricades, silhouetted against the belligerent background of the bonfire, Daniel D leapt to his feet and bellowed "Nothing! No laws!" The rest of the anarchists immediately picked up the chant, following their leader as if in conscious parody of their own principles. In the BBC studio, half a mile yet a world away, Catherine Connor felt a surge of adrenalin, a jolt of anxiety. 'Be careful, Andrew,' she thought, 'You are going too far...' Thankfully oblivious, Andrew continued, still calm, still conversational.

"Ladies and gentlemen, it sounds so wild when you say it, does it not? Tear up these foolish laws we are saddled with? It's easy to forget, ladies and gentlemen, that we live in a democracy. That they should be *our* laws. That if we do not like them then we can change them? It may sound wild, but it is our *right*. That is the meaning of democracy. Hell, it is not just our right to tear up these laws, it is our duty. It is our duty to protect our innocents. We are not fulfilling that duty. We must *do* something about it. So I ask you again. *When we tear up these foolish laws we are saddled with, what are we going to put in their place?*" On the other braziers, away from the anarchists' thudding chant, a lone voice shouted 'Tell us!' Others immediately echoed its call. In the studio, Andrew seemed to be was gazing around the audience, as if waiting for a response. Strangely, however, he was more in tune with the braziers, and, somehow, he reacted to their unheard call, their distant request.

"Yes, I asked the question, so it is only fair that I make the first attempts at an answer. Yes, I will make the first suggestions. Now." In the Cabinet Room, Blenheim could not help but admire Westlands. To show his cards at this stage? At the braziers, on the amulet that circled the BBC, shouts of 'Now!' drowned out the anarchists' 'Nothing!' David Blenheim took subliminal note of that, even as he focused intently as Westlands continued.

"Ladies and gentlemen, before we can write our laws, we

need to decide on their purpose. We need to decide on their guiding principles. We have already seen, to our cost, how laws can get complicated, very complicated, even self-contradictory. So we need some practical, guiding principles. Some principles that we can use to restore sense when we start to get buried in complexity. I am going to suggest some key principles. These are the honest thoughts of a layman, but we have to start somewhere, so someone has to set the ball rolling. Let me start with the first principle." Andrew paused, excited now, forcing himself to take the deep, deliberate breath of the experienced speaker.

"*The purpose of laws is to protect the innocent: laws have nothing whatever to do with punishment.*" A pause to let them digest it. Then an expansion. "The overriding function of any set of laws is the protection of the innocent. In all the complexities of real life, it is easy to forget this. Protection of the innocent is the primary goal of all laws. Full stop. The courts deny criminals their liberty in order to remove the threat to the innocent. It is not about punishment. The duty of the courts is to protect the innocent. Full stop. The consequences for the criminal of these protective actions is secondary. It's about *protection*, not punishment. Let's never, ever mention punishment, for it is irrelevant and only confuses the issue. The protection of the innocent is the whole of the issue." A pause. The audience were with him, so far anyway. He knew he had to keep up the momentum, not let their thoughts wander at this early stage.

"The second principle. *Those who observe our society's laws should receive more of its resources than those who do not.*" The pause to let them digest the principle. Now the clarification. "Our society does not have infinite resources. No society does. Yet we spend more of those precious resources on criminals than on the sick or the old or the needy. We spend more to keep a criminal than on a young child. *This is ridiculous.* We cannot continue to deny help to the young or old or sick in order to fund

192

jails. No innocent should ever receive less from society than criminal. The cost of keeping a criminal in jail must never exceed the cost of the humblest innocent of society. I don't know how we can do this, but we must." A pause, and Andrew scanned his audience: still with him.

"The third principle. *Our society provides rights to everyone, but those rights are reduced by the failure to observe our laws.* A glance around: heads nodding; still with him, or at least most of them. Keep up the momentum. "Membership of any society involves both rights and duties. The rights that a person has should be conditional on their observance of those duties. One of those duties is to respect society's laws. If someone breaks the law, they should forfeit, for a period of time, some of those rights. If they continue to break the laws, they forfeit more of those rights. An innocent *must* receive greater rights than someone who continues to break our society's laws. A law-abiding member of the community must deserve more respect, and protection, than a career criminal. Everyone starts with equal rights. But, in the end, you get what you have earned." More nods. About to start the last lap, and they were still with him. Strike while the iron is hot …

"The fourth, and final, principle. *Our society reserves the right to expel those who continually refuse to respect its laws and values.* Why should society be obliged to devote resources to keep, and protect against, those who have shown they will never respect its rules? Why do we take resources from the poor and needy to spend on those who only prey on them? No, membership of our society is not guaranteed forever. Whether that means death or exile, we have the right to expel those who endanger us all." It was done. Deeply, utterly, lock-you-up words that could never be unsaid. But, looking around, they were still with him. But he had to bring things together, to wrap it up tightly. Glancing at his time-clock, Andrew was acutely conscious that his time

ith a calmness that belied both his words and
is heart, Andrew started on his summary.

gentlemen, these are my layman's thoughts. They
ı   ı pretty radical in the light of where we are today.
But ı   that, while they are radical, they are not crazy. They
recognise that society is like a family, where we must all act for
the greater good. Where resources are limited, and we must use
them wisely. Where the rights of the individual are secondary to
those of the whole."

In the Cabinet Room, as he looked around at his rapt colleagues,
David Blenheim was struck by utter disbelief. 'Surely,' he thought,
'surely he cannot be about to pull this off?' Andrew paused for
the last time and then wound up with the last of his thoughts.

"Ladies and gentlemen, it's time to talk freely. But sometimes
you must act. This is one of those times. Our innocents are
suffering, our society is failing. Change has to come. Change *is*
coming, whether we want it or not. We can adapt, or we can die.
Ladies and gentlemen, Renaissance or Revolution. Those are our
only choices."

With that, Andrew Westlands sat down.

The studio audience rose in spontaneous, thunderous
applause. At last, something positive! Prolonged, thunderous
applause. In the Cabinet Room, to his colleague's astonishment,
David Blenheim joined in. Outside the BBC, at the barricades and
braziers, the watching activists and volunteers erupted in wild
cheers. Not quite all of them, however. At the anarchists' bonfire,
a tall anarchist expertly launched the first petrol bomb, arcing it
lazily towards the cheering crowds. There it landed, showering
the unsuspecting victims in fire, petrol and screams.

Back in the studio, Catherine had no difficulty with her third
character. None at all. 'REVOLUTIONARY' she thought.
'REVOLUTIONARY, HERO. Andrew, what a dangerous,

194

dangerous, man you are.' It was fully a half a minute before she thought it the right moment to bring the audience back under her spell, not *his*. 'Dangerous' still echoed, as she invited Anwar to start the round of questions.

Anwar's eyes sparkled and his combative features wore a slightly rueful smile.

"Congratulations, Andrew. You have now most definitely joined me on the assassins' lists. There is now also a bullet out there with *your* name on it." Andrew acknowledged him with a rueful smile.

"No doubt, Anwar. Well, at least I am in brave company." Anwar returned his smile.

"Thank you, Andrew. Likewise, I too am in brave company. However, that does not mean we are on the same side. But let me come back to the point. You do realise, Andrew, that they cannot let you continue. They cannot let you continue to talk of Renaissance, or Revolution. They will not let it happen." Andrew smiled grimly.

"Actually, Anwar, I think they are already too late."

David Blenheim did not let himself be distracted by one petrol bomb. He made the time to hear out the exchange, before he then switched his attention to the carnage unfolding at the barricades. By the time he returned to the debate, the sequence of questions was about to finish, as Anne-Marie Sesoku had just declined her opportunity. She seemed distracted, caught in some train of thought she dare not leave. Andrew did not even merit a smile. Catherine could not help but be nervous as William Gladwin rose to his feet. 'Fireworks for sure,' she thought, and was not disappointed.

William Gladwin looked, as always, impressive. But he had looked impressive before, yet had failed to deliver. Tonight, however, his bearing was perhaps a little sharper, perhaps a little more focused. Was this, finally, going to be his day?

"Ladies and gentlemen, listening to Andrew just now, I could not help but be reminded the famous line one of my colleagues used some years ago. He was asked to comment on the speech made by a highly charismatic, highly inspirational member of the opposition. In reply, he said *In your heart, you know he is right.*" Gladwin paused. "*But in your guts, you know he is nuts.*" The audience *were* hit right in the guts. Gladwin paused to let them gasp.

"That's right, ladies and gentlemen. And my apologies, Andrew, but someone has to deal with this nonsense. *In your heart, you know he is right. But in your guts, you know he is nuts.*"

It was a great line and Gladwin knew how to milk it. But while the studio audience had been stunned by the line, as yet it was not much more than that. A good line. 'He's taking a new approach.' Catherine thought. 'He's going to let Andrew be the charismatic, inspirational speaker. The idealist. He's going to be the realist. This time, he's letting Andrew be the heart, while he is the head. STATESMAN. He's going to be the statesman.' Catherine was right, as Gladwin soon made clear.

"I have just heard what Andrew has to say, so I've not had the time to study it in any depth. But, how long does it take to consider ideas like 'exile'. Exile? What are talking about here? Penal colonies? Please tell me, Andrew, that you are not suggesting that the West start a new colonisation program? That the West starts to turn the clock back to the days of penal colonies and prisoners in chains?" The Senator gazed directly at Andrew, his words dripping in ridicule, his body language an echo of contempt. Andrew, somewhat surprisingly, seemed utterly unaffected. The Senator continued.

"Ladies and gentlemen, this is not the only madness we've heard today. Or yesterday, or the day before for that matter. The fact is, this whole circus has been started by terrorists who despise the West, who seek its destruction. They want us to believe that it deserves to be destroyed. Ladies and gentlemen, pardon my language, but it is a bunch of crap. A nonsense. As it stands today, the West is the fairest, most just, most inclusive society there has ever been. It is not perfect, but it is better, by far, than anything else out there. We should be proud of it. Actually, ladies and gentlemen, now is the time for us to show our courage, and to defend it."

There was no doubt that some in the crowd were swayed, albeit with reservations. As Gladwin expanded on his theme, outlined all the social advances the West had made, more were swayed. Some in the Cabinet Room echoed 'hear, hear'. David Blenheim, however, listened in silence as Gladwin rehearsed all the classic arguments. Explained the complexities and conundrums that are inseparable from a just and humane society. Exposed the foolishness of thinking that we could somehow do it differently. Blenheim listened intently to the familiar arguments, brilliantly assembled, brilliantly presented. The world listened, and for most of them these were arguments that they had never heard. Potent arguments, even if unwelcome. As Gladwin finally came to his closing address, the world was listening, intently.

"Ladies and gentlemen. The West looks after its innocents better than has any other society in history. The West also has time to look after the rights of its minorities, its handicapped and its unfortunates. Even the rights of its criminals. Because yes - and let us never forget it - even criminals have rights too. What is more, the West does this while it still manages to remember that people are innocent until proven guilty. No, ladies and gentlemen, we should not be dismantling the laws of the West. We should not be looking to create a new Dark Ages. *Now is the time to celebrate the justice of the West, not to destroy it.*"

Cheers and applause resounded around the Cabinet Room. For those who were interested - and who was not? - the Prime Minister did not join in. He was busy looking at the web-casts from the barriers. There the only spectators were of the unconscious variety, as everyone else was either fighting or fleeing in panic. That surprised David Blenheim. Surprised him that the anarchists, well drilled in their art of riot, should not already have the battlefield to themselves. Blenheim switched the laptop to a police web cast. This came from one of the dark helicopters that hovered above the battlefield, searchlights criss-crossing the battlefield. 'Light sabres,' he thought, 'impotent light sabres. As worthless as so much of our new weaponry.' A line of charging red ski-masks suddenly halted as it impacted an opposing charge. A charge that was also well-drilled, that also wore ski-masks. However, their ski-masks were black, not red, and the banner they carried was a swastika. A swastika! The edge: they were over it. Yes, it was time to act - he had to act! - and the Prime Minister spent the next several minutes in frantic, whispered instructions. And then, just as soon as it was humanly possible, he switched back to the debate, settling down once more as Andrew accepted Connor's invitation to question Gladwin. 'Fine timing' he thought, as Westlands started to speak.

"William. Let me be sure I understand you correctly. The West has never spent so much on the prevention of crime, the detection of crime, and the penalties for crime. Yet we have serial killers, murderers, paedophiles and junkies in numbers never seen before. Yet none of us feel safe. Yet none of us *is* safe. You, however, *think there is no problem?* Come on, William, you really cannot be serious, can you?"

"Serious, Andrew, which is more than I can say for you. There are problems, yes. I am a realist, I can admit that. But that is life, and I can tell you that life is sweeter in the West than anywhere else, or anytime else before now. You, Andrew, exaggerate the problems beyond all proportion. You tell us we must start again. You even have the nerve to tell us how to do it. And how are we going to do it? 'Exile'? Exile to where, Andrew? To penal colonies? Australia, perhaps? And you ask *me* if I am serious?" It was a wounding reply. Andrew, however, did not seem wounded.

"I'm talking about principle, William. Principles have to come first. Solutions then follow. Do I know the solutions today? No, of course not, but that does not make me too frightened to be honest about the principles. Uncomfortable, yes, scared a little, yes, but I know we must do something. We cannot pretend all is well because we are frightened of change. We cannot *afford* to be too frightened of change, William, for it is coming." William was low on time, and this did not demand a reply, so he let it go. He knew he had done well, finally.

Anne-Marie rose to her feet in a graceful flow of ebony, red and gold: skin, red trouser suit and high carat jewellery. '*I've* got problems with my shape?' thought Catherine. 'What about her? She *definitely* has problems with her shape!' Anne-Marie certainly did, and the glamorous picture that she presented would certainly have caused offence to many. Then again, would probably bring pleasure to more. Anne-Marie, however, was not there to pose but to speak. As she started, her eyes were bright, her easy smile unforced and natural.

"Ladies and gentlemen, we all know that the world is starting to make more sense when a woman gets the last word. Is that not true?" It may not have been quite the world's wittiest line, nor was it strictly accurate, but it did serve its purpose. The tension eased, a few smiles appeared.

"And ladies and gentlemen, it is certainly time for some sense, is it not?" Anne-Marie paused only briefly to register the odd involuntary nod. "Well, let's start to try and make some sense of what we've heard so far. To summarise: William thinks the West has no problem with security. Anwar and Krishnan think the West does, and they offer us reasons why. Andrew also thinks the West does, and he wants to offer us solutions. Rather radical solutions. How do we sort the confusion? Let's start with William, because if he is right there is no point in wasting time on anyone else." Anne-Marie paused and took a breath.

"William, I'm sorry, but you cannot bury your head in the sand. The West is riddled with crime. All kinds of crime. From serial killers to murderers to rapists to petty thieves. Look around you when you leave this studio. Take a late night tube. Or a bus. Even better, walk. Then tell me, tomorrow, that you felt safe. And I'll bet you don't. No William, darling, I don't buy it and I'll bet none of us do. All those locks and keys and guards and cameras and guns and lawyers and jails are not working. Face it. Now, perhaps you want to tell us that this is the best it gets? That, despite everything, it is still safer than anywhere else. It is the best we can do. Perhaps many of you feel that? Perhaps many of you do not believe things can be any better? That you should just stop whining and accept it?" Anne-Marie looked around the audience and registered the tacit agreement. She shook her head sadly, then shook a finger.

"Ladies and gentlemen, you need to get out more." And Anne-Marie laughed, heartily.

"Ladies and gentlemen, I arrived in London from Japan. From Tokyo, in fact. There, the streets are safe. The late night trains are safe. Cars are left unlocked, with the keys in the ignition. As you probably know, ladies and gentlemen, space is precious in Japan, and houses tend to be a little small. Sometimes very small. In these very small houses, to lay a bed at night, they have to move their possessions out on the pavement. And leave them there overnight. Can you imagine trying to do that here? OK, Japan is not zero crime, that's true: but crime is low, very, very low, and a

200

universe away from the cities of the West. If you don't believe me, go there and see for yourself. Then tell me that this is as good as it gets: because you won't. Believe me, ladies and gentlemen, you *can* do better. I'm sorry, William, but things really can be much better. You are asking these people to settle for too little." The audience wanted to believe her, Anne-Marie could see that. However, they were not there yet. Time to move on.

"So, let's think about what Anwar and Krishnan have had to say. They are agreed that the West has a problem. That you truly cannot protect your innocents, and never will. Because the West has no values, no heart, no core. That the West is a mad dog, and a danger to us all. Maybe they are right. And yet Andrew has the nerve to think about solutions. And what thoughts, ladies and gentlemen?" An edge of ridicule had started to creep into Anne-Marie's voice. Andrew managed to look unconcerned, but Catherine was not the only one who felt a twinge of sympathy for him. Anne-Marie continued.

"Exile, ladies and gentlemen? Spend less on criminals than on children? I can only be blunt, ladies and gentlemen. Do you know what my response to Andrew is? My rather *American* response." Most of the audience cringed a little. They knew what was coming. Andrew had struck a chord with them, and they empathised with him. He had at least tried. It was painful, but Anne-Marie made them wait, let it hang several interminable seconds. Then answered, all pretence ripped from her voice.

"Send us your criminals. Send us your murderers. Send us your evil." Anne-Marie paused to look round a silent sea of blank faces. And beamed her siren smile. "We will turn it to good."

David Blenheim, three quarters focused on the heightening battle for the barricades, switched his focus back to the debate. 'What!?' he thought. He did not have long to wait for clarification.

"That's right. Send us your criminals, and their budget. We

will guard your criminals. As a business. We will feed some of our own people from the money it will generate. We will turn your evil into an instrument for good. We have the space. Why not? We can provide the security. We need the money. Why not?" No-one had yet recovered enough from the initial shock to even begin to answer the question. Even - especially - Senator William Gladwin looked utterly dumbstruck. But Anne-Marie was in full flight and was not for stopping now.

"Ladies and gentlemen, before anyone here dares talk of human rights, let me make one thing absolutely clear to you. We will not mistreat your criminals. Not at all. They will receive the same food, the same medical treatment, as our own people. If it is good enough for us, why not for them? Why do they deserve better? What makes your criminals deserve better than our innocent children?" The entire cabinet room listened in utter silence while the madwoman - or was she? - continued to expand on her idea. The guarantees necessary, the long term commitments, the sheer rightness of using bad as an instrument for good. 'SIREN' Catherine thought. 'No, not exactly. QUEEN. SIREN QUEEN. AFRICAN SIREN QUEEN. SHEBA. QUEEN OF SHEBA. Yes, an African Queen to meet the West. To dazzle the West. To entrance the West. Yes, the Queen of Sheba' Meanwhile, the Queen had started to draw to a close.

"Ladies and gentlemen, are these thoughts not interesting? Are they not worth pursuing? The chance to feed innocents from the proceeds of crime? You have to admit it, " Anne-Marie shook her head ruefully. "It is time to talk freely." And laughed. And gathered herself for her conclusion.

"Ladies and gentlemen, the motion. The charge. Is the West guilty of failing to protect her innocents? Today, yes. Guilty, of that there is no doubt. As of today, you have certainly failed in your duty to protect your innocents. But tomorrow? Tomorrow is another day. I would like to think that tomorrow you *will* protect your innocents. I would like to think that tomorrow you will *also* help us to protect our innocents too."

Anne-Marie let the statement hang in the air, as if a cloud, or a mist that permeated them, seeped into them. When she finally sat down, the applause was spontaneous, prolonged, and emphatic.

Not in the Cabinet Room it wasn't. The interminable silence was finally broken by a loud 'Good God!' from the Home Secretary. David Blenheim said nothing, his mind in overdrive. He needed to see Chamberlain. Tonight. Unfortunately, his thought process was broken by a whispered 'Prime Minister', and his attention was led back to his laptop, and the images from the barricades. Things there were now at least orderly, in a way. Brazier light, bonfire light. Black flags and swastikas. The arcing of petrol bombs. A long line of mounted riot police, long batons in hand, ranged in front of a line of ski-masks. One half black, one half red, their junction marked by two overlapping flags. On some hidden signal, the cavalry started forward. 'Good God, indeed' Blenheim thought. "Campbell, get me the Commissioner." He barked. "Now."

Back in the City of the Infidels, Ahmed Ali was still exultant. The West now knew they were a mad dog. The West must *know* what happens to mad dogs. He, Ahmed Ali Khan, would be the one to wield the knife, to do what needed to be done. Now they start to think of change? Tear up their foolish laws? Better late than never, perhaps? But too late. It would come to nothing anyway. The idle chatter of the West. Reality TV, nothing more. Change is coming. Judgement *is* coming. Soon, Insh'Allah, soon.

David Blenheim had been assured that the Commissioner had never actually intended for there to be a charge. Had always understood that the barricade people would unite in the face of the police, their common enemy. In any case, it had had the desired effect. Order, of a sort. The special kind of order that only fascism can bring. By the time David Blenheim could get back to the debate, all questions were over and the result had been announced. He was just in time to catch the finale.

"Now ladies and gentlemen, I come to tomorrow's debate." Catherine looked just as cool and collected as she did an hour ago. Before mad dogs and penal principles and exile and 'send-me-your-evil'. The debate was over and her cast was again complete. Prophet, philosopher, revolutionary, statesman and the Queen of Sheba. Quite a cast, and quite some drama. Yes, Catherine was satisfied. Who would not be? Time to deliver the finale in her best calm, clear, BBC voice.

"Ladies and gentlemen, the motion for the fourth debate is: *I charge the West with dishonesty, the failure to admit to their own beliefs.*

Thank you, ladies and gentlemen. We look forward to seeing you all again tomorrow." Then she improvised, adding "It's time to talk freely."

"Indeed it is." echoed the bald-headed man. 'Indeed, it is." Less than a minute later, his leather shrouded figure walks briskly into the watery night. The alleys are narrow, confusing, but he knows where he is going, and he knows he has little time. 'And yet,' he thinks, 'Time enough'. Soon he is shrouded deeper in layers of mist, and is gone.

Two hours later, London, La Fiorentina, London. A corner table, shielded on three sides by Chianti-laden shelves. A red table cloth, a small white rose, a large amphora from which flickers an olive candle. On the sides of the amphora, two laughing nymphs have seduced a satyr into eternal chase. 'Not this time,' thinks

Andrew, 'I'm too old and too tired.' As if she had heard him, Catherine laughs.

"Don't worry, Andrew. You'll feel better after something to eat." As he reached for a bread-stick, Andrew felt that familiar sinking feeling.

At the same time, in the City of the Infidels, Ahmed struggles to sleep. The next day's meeting fills his thoughts. So soon now! He knows the meeting place, what could be easier? He will be contacted, he will be given the recognition signal. He need do nothing. Just sit. Who would not recognise him? The playboy. The prodigal son. The multi-cultural icon. The adopted son of Mohammed Ali Khan, the first of his multi-racial kind. The first gift to the jihad from the pathetic, doctrinaire, commissars of Glasgow. The first fruit of the long plan of his devout and brilliant father.

Sleep would not come, and Ahmed knew it. His Koran beckoned: which verse? Surah Three, Al Imran. Most appropriate. Rising to retrieve it from beside his laptop, he paused at his reflection in the full length mirror. Playboy, indeed. Tall and powerful, with long blonde hair and cornflower-blue eyes. Yes, he certainly looked the part. But no, it is not real. It is only a part. Not a *playboy. Jihadi. Martyr.*

EIGHT

Lapping wavelets dance sunlight on the under arch of a medieval bridge. Faded mansions press tight and tall to the ageing canal banks. Distant conversations tantalise with waterborne confidences. In the background, the deep chug of marine diesels, the light slap of waves against stone, the sudden peal of a pair of church bells. A bald headed man sits on the edge of deserted steps, a laptop open on his knees. On its screen he reads:-
Explain this to me, he asked:-

"They say they believe that we have evolved from raw chemicals through the laws of chance and the interaction of the environment. It would be easier to drive from Moscow to Paris at night with a blind driver, no map and no destination, but still, they say that this is what they believe. However, ask them about genetic engineering and they are utterly opposed. How so? Do they believe that the best efforts of their best minds, with the best of intentions, will be worse than raw chance? That a sighted driver with a map is more dangerous than a blind one without? Of course not. They say that they believe these things, but really they do not. They only pretend to. Why will they not admit what they really believe?"

Again, I had no answer.

I charge the West with dishonesty, the failure to admit to their own beliefs.

The bald-headed man smiles, closes his laptop, and starts towards the sound of the bells.

The headlines of the Twenty-Third of December again spoke of nothing but the debate. The Times thundered 'SEND US YOUR CRIMINALS!' The Independent asked 'THE ALCHEMY OF EXILE: EVIL INTO GOOD?' The Telegraph, in an editorial stance, proclaimed 'CHANGE IS COMING.' For once, the tabloids were more grounded. The Express waved 'BYE-BYE, BAD BOYS!' The Mirror asked 'DEATH OR EXILE?' The Sun delivered its now customary score line, with 'INNOCENTS : SAFE CRIMINALS : EXILED'. In the United States, the Washington Post echoed the Times, with 'SEND US YOUR EVIL!' However, in India the Delhi Times had 'THE CORRUPTION OF THE WEST ENDANGERS US ALL!' In Iran, the headlines proclaimed starkly 'THE WEST A MAD DOG!'

Not all of the inside pages were devoted to the debate, however. 'The Battle of the Barricades' was big news, too. As was Daniel D. Already his dreadlocked image was appearing everywhere. "Day of the Dread?" one article mused. "King of the Streets?" asked another.

Away from the headlines, the world was one day older, and the virus bit one day deeper. Unfortunately, the virus bit much deeper than U-Soft had confidently forecast the day before. Computers were much more than twice as slow. They were so much slower that few people cared exactly how much. Most of those who did care were probably certifiable. Or seeking God. '... or working for U-Soft.' the comedian quipped. Another brave comedian renamed U-Sys to U-Heat, since a U-Sys computer generated far more in heat than it did in results.

Certainly, people did have plenty of time for comedy, plenty of time to kill as they queued for their cash, and to buy food, and to get on the internet. Talking and joking were no longer the indulgence they somehow had grown to be. No, more of a necessary skill, especially for the now essential art of bartering. Bartering was *the* growth sector of the economy. The art of exchanging what you did not need for what you did. And at an advantageous rate. Impromptu stalls sprung up everywhere, but especially around the traditional shopping areas. Besides advertising their own goods, each stall usually had a board where they listed what they were looking to exchange for. Enterprising youngsters - and many of them not so young - ran between the stalls, spotting potential trades, and negotiating a small share of any deal that was struck. Handshakes secured bargains, new friendships, and food on the table.

In the traditional business world, people were starting to talk tentatively of a world without U-Sys. They were starting to ask themselves just how important all those spreadsheets were? Just how detailed need a sales forecast be? Just how much animation and music was necessary in a simple presentation? Did we really have to give the average salesman more computing power than a NASA moon landing, just to help him cheat on his expenses? Those who really needed numbers crunched, or heavy database work, could still use the **Nexus** or UNOS emulators. Or the mainframes, none of which had any taint of U-Sys, never mind the virus. Or, at the other end of the scale, much of what people needed could be done by their electronic organisers or their high end phones. As always, there were ways.

On the surface, so much had changed, and most of the that for the worse. However, these were the first tentative indications that people were starting to adapt. The first signs that people were beginning to settle in to the new way of doing things. Socially, it clearly had a lot of positives. It was time to talk, freely, and it was good to have time, and reason, to do so.

However, as always, there were negatives too. People sensed the growing anarchy, the gathering storm. People talked of *Renaissance*, and of *Revolution*. People talked of the anarchists too, and of Daniel D. Of his 'Bonfire of the Bull****', as AnarchistVictory.com termed it. People also talked of the fascists.

Around the major Muslim areas, people talked *with* the fascists, as they poured in by the thousands. As they *marched* in, to ring the Muslims in barricades and braziers, defining their ghetto, sealing them, entombing them. To those who knew their history, it was like Warsaw all over again. Time and time again, police broke up the baying crowds and dismantled the barricades, but it was futile. No sooner were they dismantled than they were soon back in place, and stronger. As the struggle intensified, *FascistDawn.com* listed the areas where they looked for 'volunteers'. Clearly, the stigma of being fascist was being dissolved, for many heeded the request, swelling the numbers and deepening the cordon. In response, the Police requested military backup. It was not clear that the backup would be forthcoming. It was no longer entirely clear who was in charge.

Most of Europe was little different to Britain. The same adaptations. The same confrontations between anarchists, fascists, and Islamists. North America and the rest of the West were little different, although the U.S. had too few Islamists to build much in the way of ghettoes. Or the enthusiasm to do so. For most of the people of the West, the overall mood was dynamic, complex, a sense of great forces finely balanced. A sense of threat, but also of opportunity. Above all, the mood was *expectant.* Something was about to happen, the sensation was almost tangible. It was now only two days to Christmas, but not even the children were now thinking of presents.

Ten, Downing Street, London: Six a.m.
December the Twenty Third

David Blenheim has yet to go to bed, nor does he intend to. Not today. Anyway, his cabinet room armchair always did a magnificent power nap. There would be time later, but right now things were moving too fast to dare blink, let alone sleep. 'Well done,

Chamberlain!' he thought. 'But just how the hell do you do it?'
Well, he'd have time to ask before the meeting. His High Noon,
but at two o'clock in the afternoon. A fragment pops, unbidden,
into his head - 'Do not forsake me, oh my darling'. 'Coffee and
adrenalin will not forsake me,' he smiles to himself, 'but my
darling just might.' The strain of the last four days is beginning
to tell, and David Blenheim is tired. Perhaps there will be time for
the armchair afterwards. Perhaps. Right now it was time for 'M',
and the bad news. David Blenheim rises wearily to his feet.

Less than two minutes later, the PM surveys the dreary,
familiar setting of the subterranean magnolia room. To his left is
Campbell, his secretary. Facing him is John Nightingale, the spy
formerly know as 'M'.

"Well, tell me, John, what is happening with my country?"
Blenheim opened. "Please reassure me that things are not as bad
as they appear to be?" Nightingale takes a little time to respond.

"Things are a little *interesting*, Prime Minister. Let me try and
set out the facts, at least according to our best information."
Nightingale sat back and fixed a dispassionate gaze on a point
somewhere between Campbell and the PM.

"The barricades outside the BBC are now being replicated
across the country. Anywhere there is a television or radio
station. But also around all the major Asian areas of our large
cities. Specifically, London, Birmingham, Manchester, Liverpool,
Newcastle, Leeds, Bradford and Glasgow. The barricades are the
principal battleground of the anarchists and the fascists.
However, in the face of their common enemy - police or Muslims
- they immediately unite. Prime Minister, the police tell me that
the extremists are too many and they are too few. They build
faster than our police can dismantle. On the other side of the
barricades, the Islamists are in control. They have opened their
arsenals and we are now seeing the first AK-47s on the streets. In
Leeds and Bradford, Islamists have already proclaimed the

imposition of Sharia law." The Prime Minister cut in savagely.

"The anarchists and fascists only stop fighting to unite in the face of their common enemies, you said? Yet still somehow they build faster than our police can dismantle? How is that possible, John?"

"A good question, Prime Minister, and one that I posed myself. It would appear that the battles of the barricades are not equal. One side is strong to enough to both fight and build." A pause. It appeared that 'M' was almost teasing the interruption.

"My God, John, what's in a hairstyle? Are our people so superficial that Mr Danny whoever wins just because he is photogenic?" Blenheim cut in, not bothering to mask his contempt.

"Actually, Prime Minister, to be blunt, the real issue seems to have been more basic. The anarchists are mostly rebellious, middle class kids who are desperate for *attention*. Comfortable with long distance bombs and ritual clashes with police. The fascists, on the other hand, are mostly disaffected, classless thugs, who are desperate for blood. Comfortable with the boot and the fist and the blade. In terms of the street-fight, it has been no contest. The fascists have control already. Not only that, but their move on the Muslim areas has been hugely popular and they are attracting new 'volunteers' in droves. No, it seems that the anarchists might already be beaten. It has been suggested to me that the fascists have kept the battles going as a propaganda ploy. A recruiting tactic.

"Are you telling me that we are losing control of our streets to a bunch of swastika wielding street thugs? That's ridiculous, John!"

"It's not quite as simple as that, Prime Minister. As long as they wield swastikas and Nazi salutes then they will lose. We will beat them, even in these days of crisis. But we are starting to hear of subtler forms of the same theme. New flags. New salutes. And respectable politicians." A pause, and 'M' now fixed his gaze directly on the Prime Minister.

"I am sorry, Prime Minister, but you know I cannot be more specific on names. They are mainstream politicians, and that means I cannot help you against them. The last thing this country needs at the moment is our own Watergate. The Government cannot be seen to use the security services against their political opponents. Right now, it is clear to everyone that we are dealing with a threat to the nation. However, if things continue to move in the same direction, we may yet end up with something entirely different. Something political. Something legal. At that point, Prime Minister - and I stress to say it is not now - at that point, it will become difficult for me to advise you. I'm sorry to seem disloyal, Prime Minister, but I am obligated to make the point. I am sure that you appreciate the complexity of the position that I am in."

David Blenheim stared balefully at Nightingale. He could read nothing from Nightingale's demeanour. It was too professional, too mandarin, too inscrutable. There was nothing, therefore, on which to focus Blenheim's bitterness as he spat:-

"I am not entirely sure why we are talking of the protocol problems that you may potentially face in the future, John. It seems to me that we do need to face rather more urgent ones today. I do trust that you do still feel able to advise me on the imposition of Sharia law? On the appearance of Kalashnikov-wielding Islamists on our streets? And I trust that you have considered that the Islamists might just be keeping the barricades going as *their* propaganda ploy?"

It was a bright morning in Mayfair and Andrew Westlands had woken early and well. A half-full glass of Talisker 25 still waited patiently by the *Berlin* on his bed-side table. Despite that, or perhaps because of it, Andrew was still a little intoxicated as he stretched luxuriously, cupping his hands behind his head. Intoxicated, as in charmed, happy-for-no-reason. As in the early endocrine grip of a familiar chemical spell.

Nothing surprising there, then, to anyone who had seen them together last night. Nor could Andrew hold the wine responsible, either, although plenty had been consumed. No, it was Miss Connor who was intoxicating, captivating, *bewitching*. Sure, they could take it easy - and hell, he certainly would, especially at this time and at his age - but the script was in no doubt. If he was in with a chance, he'd take it. What else was life for? But what on earth made her attracted to him? Sure he was charming, and good company; and rich and old enough to know that these things did make a difference. But not that much, really. No, luck - or whatever you called it - mattered more. Talking of which, Andrew knew it was time to make some more luck. Time to invest in a little hard work. What was it the Skye proverb said? 'If you wish to be lucky, then you must use your own dice.' Suppressing a grin of involuntary good humour, Andrew rose to face the day. Half an hour and a chilli omelette later, Andrew was no longer quite so intoxicated. Images of Catherine had led him to the evening's debate, as yet unprepared. Before the debate, the small matter of Eldon Harker, U-Soft, and the progress of the Virus. After that, Mr. Chamberlain, the man of mystery. Andrew shivered. 'Too much coffee', he lied to himself, unconvincingly.

The Piazza Navona, Rome. The ancient stadium of the Emperor Domitian, the thunder of the chariots now but a distant memory. Home to the church of Sante Agnese in Agone, and to Bernini's exquisite Fontana dei Quattro Fiumi. Beauty beyond price, yet free of cost to anyone who cared to visit. An impromptu circus of artists and street peddlers perform in front of ordered ranks of tables: much as they have done for over two thousand years. The Piazza Navona, the City of the Infidels, home to some of the finest espresso in the world. Despite that, on the front rank of the Café Navona, Ahmed Ali Khan sips water, blind to the tableau before him.

'Did they ever really believe it? Senatus Populusque Romanus?' Ahmed Ali Khan rolls the words on his silent lips. 'SPQR. For the Senate and People of Rome. A four letter spell, potent enough to conquer most of the known world. A four letter spell, deep enough to propel the legions to the four corners of the earth, spreading law and order by the fire and the sword. Two thousand years and an Empire later, and they still engrave it on their drain covers. Did they believe it? Do they believe it now? What *do* these people believe?' It is a little after nine in a bright but cold Rome morning, and Ahmed is early. Dark shades protect his weak blue eyes, and hint at a hangover that he does not have. A sudden flash immediately to his left, and Ahmed wakes from his reverie with a start. But it is too late, for the small ball has landed under his table, bounced around between his briefcase and his feet, and come to rest. Ten seconds later, and the boy appears, a tiny whirlwind of pumping limbs and streaming hair. As the boy screeches to a halt, Ahmed can see that he is perhaps four, five at most. A blonde-headed boy with blue eyes and the utterly direct gaze of the truly innocent. A little blonde boy, with a ball. Ahmed felt a physical jolt as he looks back across twenty five years, into the perfect image of his own past. And hears, in a broad and perfect Glasgow accent:-

"Please Mister, can I have my ball back?"
Ahmed, dumbstruck, nods, unable to tear his eyes from the boy's face. The boy ducks swiftly under the table and emerges with a small red ball.

"Thanks, mister. Are you here to see the Pope too?" Ahmed shakes his head.

"I am. My mum and dad are taking me on Christmas Day. And Julie, although she is only two." A distant shout of 'Lewis' and the boy glances back over his right shoulder. Across the square, Andrew can see a blonde-haired woman waving. Her other arm is attached to a pram.

214

"That's my mum, mister. I've got to go." And he did, and he was gone, and the door into Ahmed's past was closed. 'Why now?' he thought. 'Why here?' He was still absorbed in whys when she appeared. Tall, auburn haired, slim figure and perfect teeth. The one he had been waiting for.

"Hi, Phileas, I'm Sandra Connelly, from the New York Times. Sorry I'm late." But she wasn't. And she wasn't Sandra either. But the accent was unmistakable. She was an American girl. What was it the song said? Brought up on promises. Well, we would see about promises.

Fifteen minutes later they leave together, heading down the Via de Canestrari, turning right down the Corso Rinascimento, and heading in the direction of the Colosseum.

U-Soft Headquarters, London: Nine p.m.
December the Twenty-Third

The alien face seems longer, gaunter, than usual. Fatigue is etched in the face, and the eyes, while still hypnotic, are noticeably dimmer.

"Congratulations again, Andrew. Quite a performance. 'Tear up the laws'? 'Renaissance or Revolution. Those are our only choices'? Well, so far Solomon's people have managed to keep you alive. And with enough time and energy to start another romance. God help us, however, if they ever get smart and send a female assassin. Andrew, we greatly appreciate your bravery on-air, but is there any possibility we can see a little more caution otherwise?" Andrew nodded his head gravely, and put on his most rueful smile.

"Things do seem to be a little eventful, Eldon. You might just have a point. Maybe I'd be better off doing something safer. Like checking code."

"Like hell you would, Andrew." Eldon had been too tired to register the irony. Wound too tight.

"You've got the wolf by the tail, and now is not the time to let go. Which you know full well without any reinforcement from me. Anyway, this meeting you have with Chamberlain." Andrew did not register even the slightest surprise. Of course Eldon knew of the meeting. What did he not know? "Be ready. This is not a meeting to be taken lightly. You know that I do *not* have the luxury of talking, freely. I can only tell you, old friend, that this man and this meeting are important." Andrew nodded.

"I appreciate the warning, Eldon. Don't worry, I'll be ready." As he said it, a sudden wave of doubt hit Andrew. Would he? Ready for what? He ignored it. "And if I am wearing my U-Soft hat, Eldon, how are we doing? Is the Fixdate release going as planned? How far have we got with the code checking?"

"Right now, Andrew, I'd say we were dead men walking. The news is all bad, uniformly negative. Let's start with the Fixdate release. We've got big problems. It looks like the virus got there ahead of us. On our test machines, Fixdate worked just fine, for a while. Then the whole operating system fried. Looks like the virus anticipated our attack. Our best guess is that it had already found all the programs that had date calls, and was just waiting for us to change them. It let us waste our time for a while and then fried the machines. That kind of behaviour casts doubts on our entire testing methodology."

Andrew was, despite everything, still a programmer. He had known that the virus could also look for all the programs that used the date function. He had known that it could detect whenever those programs were changed. But to let the 'fix' work for a while, let them get their hopes up before dashing them again? Would Michael do that? Would there be more such defences, and if so, how the hell could they deal with it?' Eldon seemed to sense that Andrew's attention was wandering.

"Moving on, Andrew. I am beginning to fear that we might have lost control of the machines. Permanently." The sense of defeat was palpable. Defeat? Since when did Eldon Harker admit defeat?

"The machines are slowing even faster than we thought. Crashes are getting more frequent. We're now also seeing regular incidences when data appears to be saved, but is not." Andrew interrupted Eldon's pause.

"What about the code checking?"

"Going too slowly. I'm afraid your three men and their cigarettes were just too good. The code is just too fine. Even with the comments, I'm struggling to check even my own code. You know what it's like, Andrew, when you're in the zone." Andrew knew exactly what Eldon meant. 'In the zone'. Was there any other way to write real code? He said nothing as Eldon continued.

"Yes: eating, sleeping, breathing code. Under the spell. Well, we sure as hell were. I look at my code and, believe me, I'm impressed. Once I've managed to understand it again. Unfortunately, no-one else here seems to be able to follow it. As for Michael's code? Fantastic work. Fabulous. But compact, opaque, dense. Almost impenetrable."

"But I remember that Michael was religious about making comments in his code? We used to laugh at his dedication when there was so much new code to write!"

"That's true, Andrew. There are lots of comments but they may as well be written in ancient Babylonian for all the sense they make. As it stands right now, Andrew, I'm the only one making progress and I've slept four hours in the last three days. I'm going to get some overdue sleep, and then we will see where we are with a little more clarity. It might be time for Plan B."

"Which is, Eldon?"

"Which is nothing I can talk to you about. Not as yet. Anyway, Andrew, please remember the point of my call. You've got a wolf by the tail. Prepare for this meeting or you might just get bitten. As might we all. Good luck, my old friend."

Click, and Eldon was gone. His call had served his purpose, however. Any hint of romance was as fried as Eldon's computers. Andrew was back to business. He was just not sure what business it was anymore. The long suffering Pam was told to field all calls, without exception.

Catherine Connor's call was one of the first to be fielded. At first she took Pam's assurance at face value, and accepted that Andrew was taking no calls for the time being. It was not as if he did not have much to prepare. Still, the early stages of romance are always fraught with insecurities. The unspoken understandings are desperately fragile, and can rapidly distort, or evaporate, in the heat of the day. One phone call can be all it takes. It was not long before Catherine felt the first pangs of doubt, and started to wonder. Just exactly what was she getting herself into? Thankfully, there was no time for Catherine to indulge her anxieties. The U-Soft conference was scheduled for one o'clock, and it was already twelve fifty. That meant that the world had little more than forty-eight hours left before it found out just what the Christmas Virus was going to do with their computers. With their economies. With their lives. People were angry, and looking for scapegoats. There were strong rumours that fireworks were expected at the conference. Catherine switched her large screen to BBC One, and settled back to watch. On a sudden afterthought, she reached back over for her phone, and set it to divert all calls.

U-Soft Conference Room One, London: One p.m.
December the Twenty-Third

The large screen is again filled by the familiar, alien face, the silver hair, the continuous eyebrow. Although the image is frozen, somehow the green eyes are as luminous and hypnotic as ever. Standing at a small dais in front of the screen, is the familiar figure of Brian Dempsey. Mohan Nehran, equally familiar, stands to his left. In third row of the audience, Peter Hawkins and Robert Perry, the odd couple, are again seated together. Old adversaries, old friends, the old routine. 'The old routine?' Hawkins thinks. 'But how on earth can this be *routine*?' On the stroke of one, Dempsey begins to speak.

"Ladies and gentlemen. Thank you for your attendance. I'd like to open this conference with an overview of our current status. Eldon Harker will then make a short video presentation on the way forward. Afterwards, there will be a brief period of fifteen minutes for questions."

"Fifteen minutes?! You have got to be kidding!" a voice bellowed from the back of the hall. Hawkins exchanged a glance with Perry. The glance said 'No. Not routine.'

"Ladies and gentlemen, today is a critical day for all of us. It is important that we all keep a cool head. It will be obvious from our statements that we have much to do today. Believe me," and Dempsey looked up with a wry smile, "believe me, you will have plenty to write about, questions or no questions." Dempsey waited for his words to have the desired impact. The mood in the hall swiftly switched from anger to expectancy, and the hall was silent as Dempsey continued.

"Today we had hoped to be able to announce that the Fixdate program was ready for release, and that we therefore had a temporary solution to the Christmas Virus. Unfortunately, that is not the case. The Virus is more sophisticated than we had hoped, and it has blocked the approach we have taken. It is also reasonable to expect that it will block any similar approaches. However, as a matter of diligence, we will still continue to explore them all. We would have released this information sooner, had the virus not deliberately misled us into thinking that the Fixdate software had been successful. Our test machines did run successfully for almost twenty four hours, before they all suddenly and simultaneously crashed. As you can appreciate, the nature of this delayed response makes any further tests very difficult to evaluate." There was stunned silence in the hall as the audience digested the information, the disappointment. Their hopes had been so high, and so much had been riding on them. 'Where the hell do we go from here?' Hawkins asked himself. 'What the hell do we do next?' Oblivious, naturally, Dempsey continued with more bad news.

"Unfortunately the impact of the virus is also more severe than we anticipated. As expected, in the last twenty four hours system speed has degraded in a binary progression. Unfortunately, it has degraded by a factor of eight, not by the factor of two that we had hoped for. Given the changed rate of degradation, we can offer no meaningful guess as to its future progress. There are also a variety of new behaviours that negatively impact the system, such as occasional failure to store data, disappearance of programs, corruption of hard drives." Brian Dempsey looked around the punch-drunk audience. 'And the good news is?' Hawkins thought. Dempsey resumed his onslaught.

"Ladies and gentlemen, I will not continue to enumerate all of the issues. Things are bad, and getting progressively worse. You may all wonder just how we come to find ourselves in such a desperate position." 'Whose side is this guy on?' Hawkins thought. 'Is he trying to minimise the problems or maximise them?' He had no time to answer his questions, as Dempsey proceeded to answer his. They were all in a 'desperate position' because ...

"We are all the victims of a deliberate terrorist attack. An attack of extraordinary sophistication, planned over twenty years ago. Virus code of remarkable subtlety has been implanted deep within U-Sys and our only effective response is to identify and remove this virus from the source. I am afraid that there are no other options. As you know, our best minds have been engaged on this, day and night, for the last four days." Dempsey paused to survey his audience. They were silent, waiting. Waiting to hear the message of their progress, of the breakthrough, perhaps. 'Come on, man!' Hawkins thought. 'Get on with it!' Dempsey, however, did not.

"Ladies and gentlemen, as I said. The attack the world faces today has been long in the planning, and sophisticated in execution. We will all need to work together if we are going to have any chance to defeat this attack. I will let Eldon Harker take over to explain what he has in mind." Dempsey pressed a button on the dais, and the frozen image of Eldon Harker sprang into life.

"Desperate times, ladies and gentlemen, require desperate measures"
The electronic image paused as if somehow it was able to assess the impact of its words.

"Ladies and gentlemen, two weeks ago the U-Soft kernel was considered to be one of the great intellectual achievements of the century. Not just a great intellectual achievement, but also a great commercial achievement. The foundation of U-Sys and of the computer revolution that has reshaped the world. Our golden child. Unfortunately, it seems that our child has been infected since birth."

"In the last four days we have worked, day and night, to find the source of the infection. Unfortunately, the kernel is written in assembler language, which is a language that U-Soft seldom uses any more. Consequently, U-Soft now has very few programmers who possess the required skills. Thus far, we have verified around sixty-five per cent of the code. Our rate of progress is, therefore, too slow. Fatigue is now beginning to slow us further. Nor have we yet found any trace of virus code. There is no prospect, therefore, that we can complete our task in the next two days. We will not be able to verify the kernel in time. We therefore have to think the unthinkable." A pause, and silence. 'Which is what?' Hawkins thought. As if on cue, Harker answered.

"We need help. We need to enlist the help of anyone who has the assembler skills to help us find and eliminate the virus. To do that, I can see no alternative but to let our child go. We have now uploaded the source for the U-Sys kernel to the U-Soft web-site. It may be freely downloaded and distributed by anyone." Hawkins and Perry exchanged glances of utter incredulity. 'He's giving it away!' Hawkins thought. 'He's giving away the kernel! Eldon Harker is surrendering U-Soft!' Perry ran a hand across his throat. Harker brought the short pause to an end. Not nearly enough of a pause. Too much to assimilate.

"We have also uploaded all related documentation, together with a report on our progress to date. Finally, we offer a reward of one hundred million dollars to the first person to find and eliminate the viral code. Ladies and gentlemen, the task is urgent. I will not waste any more of anyone's time. Thank you for your attention."

'A *ransom*.' It hit Hawkins in a flash. 'He's talking about a *ransom*.'

Fifteen minutes of bedlam later, Hawkins fought his way through the exit scrimmage, desperate to file copy.

The Sanctuary, Whitehall, London WC1. It existed because it had to exist. Everyone understood that the government of the day required the very best security that the taxpayers could provide. But what happened when a fickle electorate voted the government into the opposition? Or what had to happen before the opposition were able to become a government? All the major politicians needed protection from the bomb and the bullet. They always had. In power or out of it. They needed a secure place to meet, both with themselves, and, sometimes, with their political foes. Meetings that were secure even from the prying eyes and ears of their own colleagues. That place was the Sanctuary. Staffed by MI-5, its secrecy guaranteed by their oath to the State and to the Crown.

The administration of the Sanctuary was very simple. A handful of senior judges, preferably - but not necessarily - rather anonymous, were authorised to arrange meetings on behalf of senior politicians unknown. By tradition, this authority was granted sine die: for the lifetime of the judge. Only one group could use the Sanctuary at one time, so the judges were expected to filter requests to eliminate the wheat from the chaff. This they did with brutal efficiency: for much of the time the Sanctuary lay quiet and empty, endlessly murmuring its secrets to itself. Officially, of course, the Sanctuary did not exist.

"Let's get down to business, Mr Westlands. In political circles, I am what is termed a power-broker. Please let me explain to you a little of what that term really means."

Andrew Westlands was seated on an olive green chesterfield, worn smooth with age. His chesterfield looked to be the youngest of the six that were arranged in a vague rectangle around a spectacular Bokhara rug. Three crystal chandeliers were aided by the red lantern wall-lights that were dotted regularly around the walls. Rich, heavy cream wallpaper provided a discreet background to several large oils, well executed and vaguely familiar. A single large oak door, deep studded in brass, provided the sole entrance. The far wall that faced it was dominated by a large, ornate marble fireplace. The room was around thirty foot by forty, and it's confident masculinity was the very image of the Victorian club. It was, however, older and yet more modern than

223

that. Facing Andrew a large man sat back in apparent relaxation. A very large man, dressed in dark blue three piece suit. His grey hair, although thinning, was well groomed, while his face put his age at anything between fifty and seventy. A large, confident, prosperous man. As he had suggested, Mr Chamberlain now started his explanation.

"As you are well aware, Mr Westlands, politicians are not the only people of influence in this country. Politicians are made, and unmade, by the people of real, enduring power. People with money, or decision makers in the large corporations, or owners of newspapers, radio, broadcasting. Sometimes even senior policemen, retired military figures. You know the kind of people I am talking about. I like to refer to them as sponsors. These sponsors trust their politicians to operate within certain parameters. By parameters, I do not refer to their political party. A political party is a grouping of convenience. An arbitrary grouping, little more than a label. Many of our politicians would be comfortable in either of the main parties. Provided they do not stray from them, that does not concern their sponsors. What does concern their sponsors is that their politicians listen to what they have to say. Provided they do that, they will not interfere too much. However, if a politician strays too far from his sponsors' wishes, then they will most definitely run into problems. As you know, Mr Westlands, it is the easiest thing in the world to ruin a politician. As a breed, they are particularly prone to indiscretions. The power goes to their heads. In any case, the sponsors have many other cards to play. If need be, they can *make* whatever facts they need. To answer my own question, Mr Westlands. A powerbroker is a go-between. The man who keeps our politicians aware of their sponsors' wishes. You do understand, Mr Westlands, just why I should be telling you all this today?"

Andrew was not ready to make such an admission.

"I'm afraid not, Mr Chamberlain. I have no interest in politics."

224

"Only, it would appear, in revolution." Chamberlain shot back immediately, smoothly. "Please, Mr Westlands, I must ask you to be frank with me. In the Sanctuary, one is guaranteed privacy and discretion. It is a convention in here, therefore, that we take advantage of this to speak clearly and directly. As you might say, Mr Westlands, it's time to talk, freely."

"Mr Chamberlain, I'm flattered by your attention. However, I am not a politician, and most definitely not sponsored - as you term it - by anyone. I'm sorry, but I can see no reason why you should be talking to me." Chamberlain did not buy it.

"Mr Westlands, you are standing up on a public stage and making political statements. That makes you a politician, de-facto. That brings you to our attention. You say that you are not sponsored by anyone, Mr Westlands? You are being a little disingenuous, are you not? Not sponsored by U-Soft? Not by Mr Eldon Harker?" Andrew, despite himself, immediately rose to the bait, and retorted angrily.

"Mr Chamberlain, my opinions are not sponsored by anyone, least of all Eldon Harker. They are mine, and mine alone. Honestly thought, and honestly expressed." But Chamberlain did not back off.

"Really? *We need more heroes. Revolution or Renaissance, those are our only choices. Tear up our laws and start again.* Do you honestly mean to tell me you are sincere about all of this? Do you even begin to understand just what you are doing? You're an educated man, Mr Westlands, are you not? Perhaps you are familiar with these lines:-

Things fall apart; the centre cannot hold;
Mere anarchy is loosed upon the world,"

Andrew was. Who was not familiar with the dread lines of William Butler Yeats? A hesitation, then he continued.

"The best lack all conviction, while the worst
Are full of passionate intensity.

225

Is that your fear, Mr Chamberlain? Do you think I am the one full of passionate intensity?" Chamberlain took a few tense seconds to reply.

"Perhaps, Westlands. Or worse. Do you remember the ending?
And what rough beast, its hour come round at last,
Slouches towards Bethlehem to be born?"

Silence. Silence, deep and chilling like the still potent words. Not a silence to be dispelled in impatient haste. Only when he was sure that his thoughts were clear, and that he was ready, did Andrew speak.

"Actually, Mr Chamberlain, I fear that you may be right. I fear the rough beast is already on its way. I guess that is the point. The rough beast is on its way, and I, for one, am at least prepared to face it. However, I don't need nor expect to convince you of this." Andrew rose to his feet, half angered, half sad. Chamberlain rose too, towering above Andrew. Surprisingly, his manner was not threatening, but conciliatory.

"I apologise, Mr Westlands. Sincerely. I have a job to do and these are questions that I must pose. We had to test your sincerity, and I am pleased to say that you have passed. We are all aware that you have been a lone voice in the wilderness. Saying some things that desperately need to be said. There are some people who would like to add their voice to yours. Hopefully, before your head ends up on a plate. As I said, Mr Westlands, I am a go-between. Someone who also makes introductions. I'd like now to make one." Andrew had not noticed the phone in Chamberlain's hands. The signal was obviously pre-arranged, as the large oak door swung open almost immediately.

"Mr Westlands, let me introduce you. Mr David Blenheim, the Prime Minister." David Blenheim immediately strode in, right hand extended in automatic professionalism.

"Great to meet you, Andrew. I think we have much to talk about."

226

NINE

The long alien face was a canvas designed for sadness, sorrow, madness perhaps. The features moulded reluctantly into joy, or exhilaration: yet so moulded they undoubtedly were. The image of Eldon Harker was bright, shining with enthusiasm and good humour.

"Good afternoon, Andrew. I'm sorry to disturb you when I know you are so busy. I just wanted you to know that reports of my suicide are a little premature."

It was four o'clock, the twenty-third of December, U-Soft headquarters, London. Andrew was simultaneously trying to assimilate his extraordinary meeting with the Prime Minister and the dramatic news announcement by U-Soft. At the same time, he was also trying to somehow gather his thoughts for the looming debate. Unsurprisingly, he was not doing well, and the unexpected summons to video conference was almost a relief. If it were not for the coming debate, the redoubtable Pam would have been requested to provide gin, large, with lime, not lemon. Instead, it was a responsibly sober Andrew Westlands that faced the Great Man. Thankfully.

"I'm glad to hear it, Eldon. However, I am sure that there are many U-Soft shareholders who may not be too pleased to hear that. There must be many of them who would be only too happy to speed your passage into the next life. Now you'll also have to watch for that assassin's bullet, Eldon."

"No change there then, Andrew. Anyway, to continue. Reports of the company's demise are also a little premature. Very premature. For the first time in many years, I can see the prospect of work that is worthy of us. Although I understand that you might be

227

otherwise engaged, Andrew?"

Just what did Eldon know, exactly? How much did he know, and how much did he almost know? How much was based on deductions, and intuitions? Well, Andrew wasn't – couldn't – going to help expand his knowledge.

"That is probably correct, Eldon. It does appear that I may also have some work that is worth doing. But my involvement with U-Soft is going to have to end. You obviously know that there are some political things going on, and there is probably little I could tell you that you don't already know. In any case, I'm no longer really free to speak any more, Eldon. All I can say is that I will be submitting my letter of resignation later today. It's been a long road, Eldon, a long road and a marvellous journey, but my time at U-Soft is now over." Eldon hardly reacted to the news at all, feeding Andrew's suspicions. Why? Did he already know, or…? Andrew had to ask the obvious question.

"You're not going to tell that your time at U-Soft is also over, are you Eldon?"

"Not at all, Andrew. Anything but. I am convinced that we have been presented with a great opportunity. I would strongly advise you not to sell your U-Soft shares just yet, Andrew."

"But I don't have a choice, Eldon." replied Andrew, quickly. Too quickly: act in haste, repent at leisure. 'Damn. Eldon would not miss the implication. He had a conflict of interest. Which meant…'

"Not at all," smiled Eldon. "Put them in a blind trust. It's standard practice."

'He knows.' thought Andrew. 'He probably already knew.' Well, if he didn't know before, he certainly knew now. But Eldon was speaking again, his interest clearly elsewhere.

"Anyway, Andrew, I would very much like to outline to you just what I have in mind for U-Soft. You've not resigned yet so you are still covered by our non-disclosure terms. I'd like to get the reaction of my old friend one last time: indulge me. Five minutes, then you can get to your speech. Inspired, perhaps." A long, slow alien smile.

"Go ahead, Eldon. Let's spin the wheel just one more time." Eldon sat back and began, vibrant, confident and smiling. An Eldon that had miraculously shed ten years in the last six hours.

"Let's look at the short term issues first. Tactically, when we released the source code we largely neutralised the only weapon the open source community has. That is, the ability for anyone to validate, modify, and enhance their software. For the development process to be fully open. We have now stolen their thunder. More importantly, we help solve two of our more serious problems: the legal parasites and the drop in our brand value. Consider the legal issue first. The more obvious it becomes that the virus is the result of sophisticated terrorist attack, the smaller becomes the target for the legal jackals. What could U-Soft possibly have done to protect against infection by computer viruses before such viruses were known to exist? How could we possibly have thought to protect against something that no-one had even imagined *would* exist? The argument that we were negligent makes no sense, and pretty soon the public is going to see this. Then, instead of U-Soft being the proud, arrogant bully that they all love to hate, U-Soft becomes the innocent victim of a colossal conspiracy. U-Soft deserves just a little sympathy. Maybe even a second chance."

"That's all very well, Eldon, but what do you have a chance with? If the kernel is out there, free to everyone, who now needs U-Soft? Releasing the kernel is a tactical gain, that is true, but strategically it looks like a disaster. What am I missing here, Eldon? What is the bit that I don't see?"

"What you are not seeing, Andrew, is that the personal computer, as it is today, is finished. It is the dinosaur of another age, somehow still clinging to existence." A pause. Andrew did not react. Where was this going? Eldon did not give him long to ponder.

"Let me ask you a question, Andrew. Apart from U-Soft, what sector of the software industry extracts the most revenue from the personal computer?" Eldon hardly bothered to wait for an answer, barely pausing before he answered his own question.

"The anti-virus industry. And after them, the backup and recovery industry. For the vast majority of people, their computer comes - courtesy of U-Soft - with all they want. After that, it is all downhill. From then on, our poor customers have to devote an inordinate amount of time, money and effort just to preserve the computer in the state that they bought it in. To protect it from viruses, to protect their data from corruption, and to restore their computer to health after they have configured it just that little bit too much. For most of our customers, the everyday reality is a constant maintenance struggle. Not only that, the performance of their computers is poor. All the efficiency that we put into our code is irrelevant, as the average personal computer spends over ninety per cent of its energy in its futile efforts to protect against viruses. The personal computer was already mortally wounded, before the Christmas virus came along to administer the *coup de grace*. Thankfully, in this day and age, there is a better way. The personal computer is dead, Andrew. There is a new way of working. Let me give you a new name, Andrew. The OmniBox."

Eldon's excitement was evident, and infectious, but Andrew resisted, made no comment. A quizzical raise of his right eyebrow signalled Eldon to continue.

"Imagine a box that contains software but no data. A computer that is protected from change by a physical switch. In normal use, nothing can be written to it. No viruses can infect it. There is no data on it to be lost. Everything that makes the computer individual, from your documents and data all the way through to your favourite screensaver, *everything* is external. On a U-Soft server, maintained and backed up by U-Soft. All you have to do is connect. Using the OmniBox in your house or in your hotel room or *wherever*. This is the new model for the new age. The age of connectivity. We assume connectivity, and we embrace it. We use connectivity to be more reliable, more efficient, more secure. We have now moved far enough forward that we can now see clearly that the road is curved. In reality, as always, we are moving in a circle. In a sense, we are moving back to the days of the mainframe. But a mainframe that, effectively, contains a personal computer for everyone." Andrew could still vividly remember those days. Mainframe computers were great monoliths, tended day and night by dedicated teams of reverent technicians. Buried in some deep vault, hermetically sealed, guarded, hidden from the prying gaze of the common man. He, Eldon, and Michael had changed all that. *Forever*, he had thought. How could Eldon think it was going to be possible, or desirable, to turn that clock back? There were so many issues, so many questions, so he started with the first.

"What about security, Eldon? And how do you *guarantee* connectivity?" Andrew knew Eldon had to have answers. And he knew that the answers would be good, because they *had* to be.

"Security." Eldon paused. "OK, let's start with security. Security and identification need to be considered together. Everyone knows that every personal computer is already unique through its MAC address. An OmniBox will use a similar unique identification, but will couple it with a two hundred and fifty six bit public encryption chip. The input and data streams to the OmniBox will be entirely secure. Designed *from the ground up* to be a secure platform. How does our server know which virtual computer to reproduce? How will we achieve this local characterisation? A U-Key. Imagine something like the portable USB drives that were so widely popular, before they became the source of yet more viruses. The U-Key will contain personal information, again coupled with further encryption keys. The U-Key will be made secure by a fingerprint, or a retinal scan. A lost U-Key would automatically be worthless to anyone else." Andrew had to interrupt.

"It sounds great to me, Eldon, but would not, I suspect, make much sense to our average customer."

"How would we summarise it for the layman? *We keep your personal computer safe on our U-Soft servers. Whenever you want to use it, just plug in your U-Key to the nearest OmniBox.* Or a slogan? *Your U-Key. Make any OmniBox yours. Anywhere, anytime. Always.* I think, Andrew, that the customers are going to be more than happy with the concept. The principles are sound, and consequently there are many downstream positives. No more driver disks. Every driver is on our server. There, and only there. No more security updates, nor version incompatibilities, nor any of the countless complexities that come from maintaining a billion different software sources. To quote the movie, Andrew," and Eldon, improbably, smiled. "There can be only one." Andrew was too excited, too impatient, to be amused. He wanted answers, not quips and smiles. Now.

"So how do we replace the software revenue that comes from a billion licenses, Eldon? How do we generate revenue from updates? Are we really going to go for pay-per-use?"

"Absolutely, Andrew. Pay-Per-Use. In this day and age, why would we ever do anything else? The world is more than ready for pay-per-use software. People would be delighted to no longer have to buy our programs, and to only pay a charge when they use them. Certainly, it's a more equitable model than today. More importantly, one that we can automatically tune to generate stable, long-term profits. We know the usage volumes, and we can therefore price accordingly. Profits will be, almost literally, guaranteed." Andrew was not yet convinced, was about to interrupt, but Eldon waved it away, and continued.

"Yes, it is time to address the issue of connectivity. What issue?

Is there an issue? Do we not already have wireless connectivity everywhere? Does the modern house not rely on it for entertainment sources, for e-mail, for cheap telephone calls? Wireless connectivity is already an everyday reality. But U-Soft may still choose to do something directly. Why not? Why not have a U-Network that people can log onto, certainly in the big cities at least? Our own masts providing our own network access to our own servers? Just in case there is a connectivity issue, and also as a fine potential source of revenue in its own right? Connectivity is a given, Andrew, or at most, a minor problem from which we can generate rich streams of easy revenue." However, the last issue remained, and it was the most difficult, the most intractable of all.

"I love it, Eldon, but how on earth will we get the processing bandwidth? How do we keep adding processing power to satisfy the demand for all these hundreds of millions of OmniBoxes. Every time you add a OmniBox, you ..." Suddenly, it slipped into place.

"*Hydra*. Every time you add a OmniBox you add a new processor. Hydra. My God, Eldon." Andrew was, suddenly, silent.

Eldon smiled indulgently, as if pleased with his bright pupil. It was, by any standards, a dramatic, staggering, vision, and Andrew now stopped to gaze. In wonder. A great leap backwards, to the days of the mainframe, and a powerful box maintained by professionals. But yet providing the user with all the benefits of having his own computer. That always had virus protection and the latest drivers and compatible versions of whatever. That might cost as much or as little as you chose to use it. Andrew knew Eldon was right to be excited. The concept was brilliant. Andrew knew only too well that most people hated their computers. They thought them more fragile than the ornaments on the fireplace. More hassle to run than their cars. Took so long to start, and to stop, that you just had to leave them on, whirring away malevolently day and night. Not even to mention the whole virus issues, never mind the Christmas Virus itself. No, nothing would stop people from making this transition, to fully embrace the connected world. Whatever else, at least revolution was coming to the world of computers. Or was it really revolution? Was it not, perhaps, a *Renaissance*? Andrew was reeling, and yet acutely conscious that he must not get sucked into this. Not at this critical time. He heard the hypnotic pull, the familiar lure. The stirring explosion of his creative energies. But no, he had another future entirely. A very immediate future, tonight, at the debate, and he was not even remotely close to being ready. The OmniBox would have to be for later. It was too big a wave, and he was already in a stormy sea. It was time to ask the question. A last disbelieving shake of the head.

"Congratulations, Eldon. Truly a breathtaking vision. However, I need time to do your OmniBox justice, and time is something I don't have right now. Forgive me, Eldon, but I need to get to my own issues. Just one, unrelated, question. The hundred million dollars." Saying it fast, Andrew thought, somehow it just didn't seem like so much.

"The hundred million dollars." Andrew repeated. "We both know it must have been Michael Macdonald who created the Christmas Virus. How, I don't know, but who else could it be? What if Michael provides the fix? If you pay Michael, surely we cannot call this a *reward*? Surely, Eldon, we have to call this a *ransom*? Eldon thought for a second or two. Somehow, he did not seem uncomfortable at the question.

"Until we know how the virus was created, we cannot know for sure that it was Michael Macdonald. Even then, there are other possibilities. For example, someone might have changed his source code without Michael's knowledge. Not only is it possible, but it has also happened before now. However, for the sake of argument, let us assume that Michael is responsible. Let me answer your question: yes, I would be more than happy to pay out a ransom of one hundred million dollars. However, that is all no more than wishful thinking. I do not imagine for a moment that Michael, or whoever, would settle for so little. Would you, Andrew?" A slight pause, an almost question hanging in the air. Then gone, as Eldon seemed to switch gears.

"Anyway, Andrew, thanks for letting me share my U-Soft thoughts with you this one last time. In any case, I'm sure I'm going to see plenty of you in the future. Good luck tonight, Andrew, give my regards to Mr Chamberlain, and stay alive." Click, and Eldon was gone.

'The Slovakian': The Corner of Georgic Street and Charles Edward Street, Glasgow: Five p.m. December the Twenty-Third

A red-rimmed DCI Bendle gazes out of an upper window of the rundown Victorian villa, eyes fixed on number twenty one, Charles Edward Street. It's been a long night, and despite himself, Bendle is lost in thought.

'How can this area have so many mosques and yet no barricades? No braziers, no Kalashnikovs? Is this a new definition of multiculturalism: mosques, but no madmen? DCI Bendle smiled to himself a little ruefully. 'Aye, a definition good enough to lose you your job, idiot. Anyway, who knows what goes on here. This is Glasgow: intractable, belligerent, violent. The crucible. No-one here needs additional excitement. It might just be as simple as that.'

The original builders had named the villa 'Glencairn', picked out in a fine copperplate on a proud brass plaque. 'The Slovakian' had conquered the plaque, obscuring it all but completely with its crude hand-painted letters. Not that refined artwork was necessary: the nameplate was quite good enough to guide the latest wave of immigrants who'd come in search of work and a better life. Normally, a dozen or so men would have slept here last night. But quiet words had been exchanged with Jan, their unofficial landlord. The law would remain happy to turn a blind eye, but his premises were needed for a night, or four. Jan was a realist, and a businessman. That was enough for him to get the word out. Bendle's people had set up their equipment in the tired and faded lounge. Behind him, in the centre of the room, a quartet of technicians were glued to two screens. At the rear of the building, in the car-park that had obliterated the landscaped gardens, a rapid response unit had been caged all night in two unmarked vans.

Further down Charles Edward Street, the stealth specialists had not moved from their vigil in the Oasis. Its landlord, like Jan, had also received a discreet visit. Unlike Jan, he had also been detained under the Emergency Powers Act. Quiet words are wasted on some people. In any case, the end result was the same: the specialists were now secure for the next three days. They did not have that long, anyway. No-one did.

A few wandering thoughts later and Bendle is snapped from his reverie by a muted shout. "Incoming! Incoming!" "Finally!" he growled, and in two swift paces was with the quartet behind him. The left-hand screen showed the now-familiar view of the bedroom in number twenty one. The table and the laptop. Nothing seemed to have changed, although Bendle thought he could just see the hard disk LED flickering. Not clear enough to be sure. The right-hand screen showed a plain text box, where cascading lines of text homed in on their quarry.

'Mail-box Request Detected'

'Delivering message'

'Resolving IP'

'IP address 213.171.193.5',

'UK'

'BT'

'Glasgow'

'Govanhill',

'21 Charles Edward Street'

'Permitting message acknowledgement'
'Sender acknowledged'
'Sender disconnected'

Whatever details the left-hand screen might contain, a man was not one of them. The room was defiantly empty of messengers. The message was being sent remotely. Their quarry was not going to appear. The disappointment hit Bendle like punch in the gut, and, winded, he sat down. He was not alone: the disappointment in the room was palpable. The gathering silence was broken by the tentative voice behind him.

"What next, sir?" Bendle turned to the voice. 'Funny' he thought. 'I've been cooped up with her all night and this is the first time I notice how pretty she is. That's professionalism for you.' He had his cue.

"Professionalism. What's next is we show some professionalism. Let's start by having a closer look at that laptop. If the messages are getting sent from this laptop to Connor, then perhaps this laptop contains them, right? Time we found out what it knows. Brian, initiate discreet entry. And I mean *discreet*. Somebody tell our lads out back they can stretch their legs. Hell knows they've earned it. And a beer, or two, on me. Heather, you're coming with me." Adding purpose to his words, DCI Bendle turned and strode to the door.

Five minutes later, Bendle is one of a trinity of special branch clustered around the small laptop. Its screen is entirely blank, but the power LED confirms that it is on but in power-saver mode. To Bendle's left is Heather; to his right is Brian, a young man of medium height and universally nondescript appearance. Except that, right now, Brian is much too animated to be nondescript, and is the very image of an impatient young man.

"Sir, if the word comes through that mail was only sent, not received, then that means the messages are embedded in this computer. Surely we're going to get a crack at them? Give me half an hour with this computer, sir, and you'll not regret it." Bendle growled his response.

"IF the word comes that no mail was received. And an even bigger IF, Brian. IF the computer is not booby-trapped. Not primed to send a message the moment anyone presses the wrong key. Or primed to fry itself, perhaps." Bendle wondered, no, *hoped*, that Brian was not so wet behind the ears that he had not considered the risk. Oblivious to Bendle's hopes, Brian continued to press his point.

"With respect, sir, that simply is not possible! This is U-Sys, remember. Who knows when a dialogue is going to pop up to remind you that your virus subscription is out of date, or that you need to register your applications, or any of the crap that happens? It's too risky, sir. Anyone who knows U-Sys would know he could not take that chance."

OK, Brian was, thankfully, not that wet. Bendle continued to look like he was listening.

"Think it through, sir. If no message was received, then we know for sure that the messages are all already here. That means we cannot intercept anything coming in. All we need, and all we can get, is already on here. Sir, I agree that there's a chance that we might fry the computer. But that is a small chance. More than that, sir, if we don't look at what is on this computer then it might as well be fried for all that we will learn from it. If it was my decision, sir..." Somehow, Brian caught himself, but it was too late. Started to blush and to look for a hole in the floor. There was no hole, and nowhere to hide. Bendle did not miss him.

"Which it isn't, son. Thankfully. Nor is it even up to me. Let me remind you how it works. I wait for the decision from my superior. You wait for the decision from me. If you are still lucky enough to be on the force, and the decision still, somehow, concerns you, I might just let you know what it is. And you will then jump, smartly, before I kick your backside. Are we clear on that, son?"

Out of the corner of his eye, Bendle thought Heather looked embarrassed. Nice girl, as well as pretty.

Four hundred miles away, Hector was about to make his decision. Hector was an oasis of calm in the frenzy of the surveillance room. Everywhere, people were hunched around terminals - mainframe terminals, thankfully, not personal computers - talking quietly, urgently. Many were looking up at him as he so obviously struggled to arrive at the right decision.

The analysis of the internet connection had been completed. The laptop had sent Catherine Connor the next code. They had already entered the code into Sesame, and it had worked. The laptop had not picked up any messages of any kind. Ergo, the laptop already contained the message it had sent. Not only that, but it was obvious from the progress of the connection that the laptop - the Glasgow Laptop - was free from the virus. What was the secret behind that? Oh yes, there was a clear gain. There was also a clear risk. A software booby-trap. Something that sent out a warning message to the terrorists, or subtly changed the ones being sent to Connor. Perhaps even fried the computer. On the other hand, that kind of booby-trap, on a U-Sys computer, was rather more than likely to blow up in your face. Hard to believe. No, on balance, the gains were worth the risk. Hector reached in his pocket for his phone. Somehow, the hubbub of the room had now been supplanted by an expectant silence. Hector was conscious of his audience, but he was not a man uncomfortable in the limelight. Suddenly, from the back of the hall, a shout.

"Sir! Sir! There's something you need to see!" It was no more than ten seconds before Hector's long stride brought him to the far end of the long hall.

"This had better be good, James." Hector took pride in knowing all his staff. They thought highly of him, and he tried to reciprocate. James was older than most of the technicians. Older, more experienced, but perhaps past his best.

"It is sir. You see, I was listening carefully to the audio feed from Glasgow. I am something of an involuntary expert in modem connection sounds. You know, sir, the 'EEEHAAAAAAHUUUUM' that happens on a dial-up connection. If you listen carefully, it can tell you a lot about the capabilities of the modem, the speed of the connection..." Hector did not have much time; had to interrupt.

"Time, James. Brevity, please." James swallowed

"The sounds were wrong, somehow. I've gone back and replayed the scene. There were no connection sounds. The connection was set to quiet mode. However, I knew I had heard sounds, because I am attuned to them. I went back to the scene and replayed it again. From five minutes earlier. This time I heard the sounds, sir. The sounds happen three minutes before the internet connection was made. The sounds were the sounds of an modem answering a call. A modem allowing a remote computer to make a connection. I think, sir, that our terrorists have used an old-fashioned technique to send data to the laptop. Data from which it then constructed a message that contained today's code. It then used the internet to send that message on. I am afraid, sir, that this laptop will contain no further codes."

Hector did not think for very long. Two minutes later, a disappointed Bendle delivered the message.

"We've missed a trick, ladies and gentlemen. It seems that we have become a little too modern, and have forgotten that there are other ways to send messages than just the internet. We've monitored the internet traffic but we've failed to put a tap on the phone line. Hopefully, we will get one more chance. I want the tap on within the hour. After that we have another nice long wait. Oh, and if anyone comes within three feet of that laptop, they're dead."

Bendle turned and strode into the hall. Pausing only to trample the junk mail heaped on the doorstep, he wrenched open the outside door and was gone. Brian and Heather soon followed in his wake. No-one bothered to make good the junk-mail. Junk is junk after all.

Around the same time, give or take, Andrew's mobile received the text he had been waiting for. The timing was good: he had, somehow, managed to put Chamberlain and OmniBox into his mind's quarantine zone, and to get down to some serious preparation for the debate. He had even made a little progress. The text, however, could not be quarantined. He fought it for ten minutes but then he made the call. Thankfully, she answered on the third ring.

"Andrew, they're wonderful! I can't tell you how surprised – and delighted – I was when I opened my door and there they were. Whoever delivered them really missed one hell of a photo opportunity, because my face must have been a picture! His – or her – loss, because for some reason he only knocked once, and then just left the flowers outside. But how on earth, Andrew, with the barricades and chaos and everything going on, *how on earth* did you manage to get *flowers* delivered? Never mind find the time to think of it?" Catherine Connor was, clearly, delighted. Andrew was happy to bask in her delight.

"I'm so pleased you like them, Catherine. I really meant to phone you earlier, but it has been one of those days. Well, that does not begin to do it justice, actually. Anyway, I thought I'd better do something to thank you for our date last night?" Somehow, just saying the words, made it all seem more real. Real, like they were in La Fiorentina, and it was last night, and no Chamberlain nor OmniBox nor anything but the sound and scents and intoxication. Andrew knew there was no fool like an old fool, but it sure beat the alternatives. Catherine, however, was more focused. On the flowers.

241

"But the flowers, Andrew! Who on earth is still selling flowers, never mind delivering them?"

"Well, it was a bit unconventional, Catherine. I'm just glad you like them."

"Unconventional, Andrew?" Catherine was, suddenly, suspicious. "What exactly do you mean by *unconventional*?" Catherine was on the trail. Like all married males, Andrew knew that meant it was only a matter of time. Escape was longer a realistic option: best to tackle it head on.

"The BBC internal flower delivery service. Only available to the most select of outsiders. The price, exorbitant: a bottle of malt whisky, rare and old." A slight pause, an answering silence. Best to continue. "I'm afraid, Catherine, that you were right. Interflora is quite out of season. The only flowers available were those already within the BBC. Let's face it, there are so many arrangements there that they will hardly miss the odd flower or two." Andrew's bright words were met with a stony silence.

"Andrew, do you mean to tell me these flowers are *stolen*?" Catherine's tone was incredulous.

"Well, yes, Catherine. Every last petal, I'm afraid."

"And the delivery man, or should I say, thief?"

"An old friend in the BBC."

"And the bottle of single malt whisky?"

"Talisker Twenty Five." Silence.

"Talisker Twenty Five? Talisker Twenty Five and a bunch of stolen blooms? Andrew, you *are* a romantic devil." With that, they both burst into laughter. It was half a minute later that Andrew, wiping away his tears, thought he really ought to quit while he was ahead.

"Catherine, I'd love to do the same again tonight, but some other things have come up." Andrew did not want to say too much. For all kinds of reasons, not the least being that he wanted to keep it light. A counterbalance to everything else that was going on. Please God that she is as smart as I think she is. "More importantly, I thought it time we had a decent cappuccino. How about we meet tomorrow, maybe midmorning-ish? I'll give you call around ten?" Unexpectedly nervous again, despite the laughter.

"Certainly, Andrew. A cappuccino would be just fine. After all, you do make me laugh." A click, and Catherine was, maddeningly, gone. *Make me laugh?* Really? What the hell did that mean? Women, damn them! But Andrew smiled to himself, and was still smiling right up until the next phone call. After that, things were, indeed, serious again. Did he really mean to go through with this? Could they pull it off? What if they failed? A sharp burst of sheer terror surged, lanced, through him. 'Fight it!' Andrew thought. 'What was it he said in that movie? *What we do in life echoes in eternity!* Eternity. And how far away was that, now?' Despite it all, Andrew fought down his fears and went back to work.

Venice: Six p.m. GMT, December the Twenty-Third

'I have measured out my life in altar stones.' An unexpected homage to T.S. Eliot surfaces, unbidden, as Michael emerges from the incensed gloom into the twilight vastness of the square. Yes, a *pilgrimage* of altar stones, and yet more to do today. Pausing at the outer face of the ancient portal, Michael MacDonald gazed around the splendour of St Mark's Square, the spiritual centre of Venice, the archipelago empire. Surely nothing less than an empire could have dared such utterly unreasonable, reckless displays of boundless wealth? What price these arches, and towers and gilded mansions? Beautiful Venice, long fallen from hub of empire to clichéd haunt of tourists. Sic Transit Gloria Mundi, indeed. True, but at least Venice had had its day and what a day it must have been? A day of wealth, and power, and even piety. Perhaps some greatness from those days lingered yet?

As Michael now crossed from the cathedral to the Quadri restaurant and the arches beyond, for once his amateur tradecraft let him down. He was too absorbed in his thoughts, forgot to make the routine checks, the glances, the pauses to catch whomever might have somehow got onto his trail. By the time he has reached the Mercerie, he remembered his tradecraft too late. Turning, he caught a tourist head whipping back to admire the elaborate Venetian masks in the boutique window. Ten yards later, as he spun round in a sudden sneeze, the tourist head turned again, their two heads in sickening synchrony. Two hundred yards further, as he now stoops to tie his lace, and there is no longer any shred of doubt. The young man in the denim jacket is not shopping for masks, but faces. His face. No, there is no longer any pretence of doubt. Not for him, nor for the man in the denim either. Two thumb clicks, and the denim man has sent the pre-prepared text on its way. He has summoned the rest of his pack. The chase is on.

'Don't panic! Think! Have Faith' Michael forces himself to focus, to fight off the suffocating paralysis of panic. 'God speed me!' as he puts his head down and strides for the Rialto Bridge. Michael knows, instinctively, that his tail is professional, dangerous, and probably one of many. As he bulks his way through the milling tourists, he knows that raw speed will not be enough. He needs a plan. Well, if he can make it to San Pantalon, in the Dorsoduro, then he has a chance. God speed indeed!

Despite himself, Michael cannot resist the impulse to flee. The brisk walk accelerates into a trot, then a half run. By the time Michael has traversed the Ruga Dei Oresi, turned right down the Ruga Vecchia San Giovanni, and turned left into the Cordaria, all attempt at concealment has vanished, as he barrels through the startled tourists, scattering them to left and right and howls of outrage. His heart pounds with his feet, as he stretches, stretches, seeking for the relaxed speed of his youth. As Michael turns suddenly left, he slackens his pace just enough to look over his shoulder, and see the denim man, for all his youth, losing ground, falling back. However, someone else has joined the chase. Someone tall, rangy, black and intimidating. Someone Michael recognises from the photographs. 'God speed me!' Michael pounds, forcing his pace to the beat. 'Deus Vult!'

Solomon N'Chenga had been at the Calle Sturion, no more than six hundred yards away, when he got the text message. A quick glance at his hand-held tracker and he can see the Peter's red dot as it blinked towards the Rialto Bridge. Too many tourists, he'd never intercept him there! Solomon forces himself to wait, wait, wait: not to run blindly! He sees Peter's dot turn right into San Giovanni. 'He's going down the fishmarket.' he thinks. 'He'll use the stalls and tourists and then out, into the Campo San Cassano, and into the labyrinth of the San Croce. After that? So many ways to the open bay and onto a fast boat. Solomon knew he now had time only to gamble, and he did not hesitate. Turning and heading right into the upper end of the San Giovanni, Solomon sped down the Giovanni towards the market, turning left into the Ruga Spezier, and forty yards later veered right again and down the Calle de la Donzcla. He gambled well: as he burst from the Donzela into the Campo Pescaria, he was just in time to see Red Michael, scattering tourists to the four winds, at a dead run no more than thirty yards ahead. 'I've got you, Red Michael!' thinks Solomon. 'I've got you. Soon.'

Fear speeds Michael as he crosses the small bridge over the Riva de L'Ogio, left into the Calle Dei Botteri, right down the tiny street and the Campo San Cassano. But it is not possible. He is not built for this. Now he can hear the thudding steps of his nemesis, and Michael knows he is not going to make it. Pound, pound, pound the beat in his feet and his heart and the breath in his lungs. Pound, pound, *it is not over until it is over.* A sharp right at the end of the Campo, and then, ahead on the left, the small hump-backed bridge over the Rio de San Cassiano. The *very* small bridge, and approaching it from the other side a large, and bulky, crowd. 'Pound, pound, must pound!' and Michael charges headlong for the bridge. From the other side, a grim faced theatre of shaven bodyguards shepherd a tiny blonde woman. 'They will block the bridge, please God! Give me speeeeeeed!' and, seeing his one chance, in a last desperate leap, Michael makes the bridge, and over, just an instant before the first hooves of the steroid herd.

Anger had given Solomon wings, but not quite enough time. The muscle factory were now on the bridge, and starting to react to the sight of a middle aged black man hurtling towards them and their charge. The bodyguards did not see this one no-longer-young man as a threat, but more as an opportunity. A chance for a much-needed workout. Deploying to centre, left and right, three large bodies tensed in readiness, while a fourth, their leader, bellowed a warning.

"Back off! Back off *immediately*, old man!"

"Out of my way, fools!" bellowed Solomon. "I'm a police officer, let me through!"

In hindsight, Venice did not have that many plain clothes African policemen, but, on the spur of the moment it was what he came up with. It was not good enough, Solomon realised, as the left and right giants seemed to simultaneously launch their huge bodies towards him.

There is a difference between gym trained and street trained and, anyway, Solomon had the benefit of both. And motivation? Yep, it might even have been the 'Old Man' that did it. For whatever reason, Solomon was a blur of fierce precision. Suddenly leaping left at the final closing yard, Solomon then re-spun back on the balls of his feet to deliver the textbook blur of a left hook. Then followed it up with a right cross that might have impressed old Stone Face Liston himself. The pumped up giant on his left

246

went down, down to stay down. All his life Solomon had been a rebel. Not for him the easy adulation of Muhammad Ali or Sugar Ray Leonard: no, Solomon liked Joe Frazier, and Big Bad Sonny Liston, and Thomas 'The Hit Man' Hearns. Real fighters, not dancers. Fighters, like him, and they would be proud of his work today. In his element now, Solomon followed up with a right and left combination to the head of the second giant, then a ferocious left to the gut, and a right uppercut to the chin, and the brain, and an early night. Now, just the one to his right, the one in front and a gap to burst through. And the sound of a large calibre pistol, deafening, immediate, near, and very compelling. Solomon froze.

"DOWN! HIT THE FLOOR NOW! DOWN ON YOUR FACE NOW!'

The pistol was too convincing. A wave of sheer fury swept Solomon, but he hit the floor, just like they asked.

"CUFF HIM!"

Beefy hands grabbed his arms and cuffed them, behind him, *tight*. A female voice, a tone of command, and the centre bodyguard then moved aside, to reveal an almost familiar blonde face. Some kind of actress, not quite current: middle aged going on tired and bored and lonely. The actress positively dripped with jewellery, but nevertheless Solomon's gaze was irresistibly drawn to the blaze of her left hand. There she sported a diamond, a huge diamond, big enough and bright enough to have a mine named after it. Hence the bodyguards, and the theatre, and the desperate waste of maybe the one chance that they would get to stop the world going to hell. Diamonds? Always the same thing: trouble. Bodyguards? Same thing. Some protection this lot provided. Solomon could almost see the irony, but when he spoke there was absolutely no trace of humour.

"Gentlemen, you surely have utterly, *utterly* screwed up. Cuffs? By the time I've finished with you, you'll all be wearing a leash. And I'm going to walk you round St Mark's Square till you've long forgotten what it's like to stand on two legs."

Across the small bridge, a brightly lit shop window swarmed with glittering Venetian masks. To Solomon, from where he lay, cuffed, on the cold wet stone, they all wore but one expression: mockery, silent and superior.

It was ten minutes and much adrenalin before the denim man, and his colleagues, and the Venetian Police, and the other baleful, anonymous figures were able to sort it out. Ten long minutes. Time enough for Michael Macdonald to reach the San Pantalon, and its dark, awe-inspiring ceiling. And to reach the small, locked, Chapel of the Holy Nail, that lay within the Pantalon. And to enter, again, its sacristy. Time enough to still his pounding heart, and to don his new vestments, and his large, wide-brimmed hat. By the time Solomon N'Chenga stood in the harbour, and gazed out over the fading gloom of the lagoon, Father Thomas O'Donnell had already been helped onto the speed-boat, one nervous hand clutching his hat, the other his cane. And then he was gone, just another anonymous priest in a country ridden with them. Anonymous, because, outside of the church, no-one likes to look at a priest full in the face. They might just look at you right back, and who knows then what they might see?

TEN

The hundred million dollar reward. One hundred million reasons for a programmer to download the kernel source code. Plus one: *Glory*. Above all else, it was glory that all the top programmers wanted. The hundred million dollars was cool, no-one said it wasn't, but to be *The Man*? More than cool, and the money just made it even cooler. However, Robert Alexander Scott was too obscure to have attained the status of legend, and he was, most certainly, not cool. Forty one years old, Robert was of medium height, brown eyed, dark Mediterranean complexion, with curly, unkempt salt and pepper hair, ill-fitting, ill-matched clothes and a modest but growing paunch. He was also a walking cliché, so brilliant as to appear to most of the world as awkward, inarticulate, unintelligent to the point of defect. Not that Robert Alexander was much interested in what people thought of him: his interests lay in software, puzzles, and whatever was the latest in electronic gadgets. He was good enough at the first two to be able to pick and choose his occasional paying projects, and for them to pay well enough to more than satisfy his modest financial demands. Just occasionally, Robert Alexander yearned for a little more challenge, and a little more recognition, and this was one of those times. Robert Alexander wanted a shot at the puzzle, and the glory, so he downloaded the kernel, and got down to work. From the window of his modest sea front apartment, the Mediterranean seas rhythmically pounded the municipal beach, much as they had done since time immemorial. Robert was working to a rather tighter timescale: hours, not millennia. However, as always, he

249

remained calm and composed. Because, deep down, Robert
Alexander was cool, very, very cool.

BBC Headquarters, London: Seven Forty-Five p.m.
December the Twenty-Third

Caught in the silhouette of the still smouldering bonfire, Daniel D,
blonde dreadlocks snaking in the bitter breeze, hurled his arms
skywards in an unmistakable gesture of triumph and victory. The
war of the barricades, he said, was over, and the war of the
streets was about to begin. Not all of his people looked happy,
but still, to most of them it was clear enough. Anarchy was not
exactly *no* laws. More an issue of no *artificial* laws. Natural
laws, on the other hand, were, by definition, *natural*, and must
be obeyed. Natural laws, as reflected in the Laws of the Tribe.
Really, the position of those who wore the red ski masks was not
so very different from those who wore the black. The Laws of the
Tribe: The Laws of the People. Was that not what they both
really wanted? He, Daniel D, had recognised that, as had some of
the more enlightened of the black masks. They'd put their egos to
one side, tried to see the bigger picture. They'd worked on it
throughout the night, desperate to break the impasse, to seize the
great opportunity. To answer the Call of History. They'd finally
made the breakthrough, exhausted, yet elated. Now the war was
over, and they stood united, and *strong*. They also had a new
name to go with their new-found strength: The British People's
Party, dedicated to the natural laws of their tribe, the People of
Britain. Daniel D was proud to have been confirmed as their
leader, to have won the privilege to stand at their head in the
battles that were to come. And they had a new flag to go with
their new name. Just as Daniel D locked his arms in the
exultation of victory, two large flags were snapped free to either
side of him. Caught in the stare of a thousand broadcasts, the

flags unfurled into black, deep black, rent by a jagged red lightning bolt. The flags were greeted by thunderous roars of acclaim, and hundreds of arms were hurled skyward in matching, jagged salutes. Beyond the amulet of braziers, some undead fears began once again to awaken.

Ahmed Ali Khan should have been one of the viewers, but he paced the ten paces, as he had for the last two hours. Ahmed tight caged in his hotel suite, was desperately trying to impose order on his thoughts, but especially his emotions. Today he should be happy, proud, ecstatic, should he not? The American Girl, full of promises, had fulfilled them. His luggage had arrived. He had seen the weapon, the Sword of Islam, and it was *real*. The focus of his life, his *most privileged* life, was so very close now. His most privileged *death*, for was he not to be the Wielder of the Sword, the bringer of Allah's punishment to the infidel? It should have been joy that filled him, but it was not joy, but fear, and anxiety. Fear, yes fear, the robber of peace and reason. His mind reeled from the dread images that assailed him: images of slaughter, and chaos, and death on a global scale. The guilty, and the innocent. Those he knew, and those he did not. The old and the young. Children, yes, perhaps millions of them. Including the little blonde boy, and his sister. Was all this really the Will of Allah? *Could* it be the Will of Allah? And if it were the Will of Allah, there was still so much he needed to do. And he now desperately needed a code, which they have now told him is coming by e-mail. By e-mail?! Were they crazy? He needed an e-mail and the *Caliph* software to decrypt it, and his laptop was now as slow as an infidel's prayers, and even less reliable. Allah, be merciful! No, Ahmed Ali Khan was not happy, but anxious, fearful, distressed. Still, tomorrow his father arrived. Insh'Allah, at least tomorrow his great teacher would be here. Father would lend him strength, shatter his doubts, and renew his resolve. As always. Come, father, your chosen son needs you, and as never before! Gradually, progressively, Ahmed slowed his pacing, brought his mind and heart to focus. The training: in times of stress, the training always pulled you through. Finally, Ahmed was able to sit down to watch the debate which would soon start. 'Are you ready, infidels? Are you *really* ready?' he asked, to himself.

Venice: Eight p.m. GMT, December the Twenty-Third

Solomon N'Chenga was used to running on intuition, it was just that he usually had some data to back it up. Running on intuition, yes, but not running so far, so fast. Then again, what alternatives did he have? Not making a guess sure as hell wasn't going to do shit for him, because guesses were pretty much all he had. If he guessed wrong, then he guessed wrong, but at least he'd have the guts to make one.

He did have some facts. One of them was this: pretty much everything Michael did was never very far from religion. That was the constant theme: religion, and churches. Christmas was coming. The Virus was coming into its Hour. If Michael was its author, where would he choose to spend this Hour? Not Venice anymore, he was sure of it. Solomon felt in the deep marrow of his Zulu bones that Michael was gone. Where would you flee to, Michael? Where would a devout believer go at Christmas? Somewhere big enough to get lost in, yet near enough to get to, without risking discovery by the dogs who sniffed at his trail? The answer came, *swiftly*. Rome, *obviously*. Where else would the devout Catholic go for the Appointed Hour? Bethlehem? No, he would be too conspicuous, Michael could never have set up a bolt hole there without arousing way, way too much suspicion. Jerusalem? The battleground of the Orthodox and the Islamists? Could there be a worse place for a red-headed Christian? No, it was not Jerusalem, and it had to be Rome. Where else would a

Catholic go to make himself ready as Armageddon approached? 'Armageddon?' Solomon, pricked sharply by the unexpected name, immediately started to rouse from his muse. 'Armageddon? Why Armageddon?' There was no answer, so Solomon slowly sank back into his half dream, his divination 'Yes, Rome it must be. That is where you have gone, Christian. After all, everyone knows that, sooner or later, all roads lead to Rome.'

And Solomon ducked under the blast of the rotors, entered the impatient helicopter, and headed South.

'Cathedrals,' thought Michael MacDonald, 'are the forges of humility. Who is not humbled at such wealth and artifice? Who could not be conscious that men, richer and more powerful than himself, have here humbled themselves before eternity, in fear or in love, but humbled themselves nonetheless? After all, what is God? God is Great. Brahman is Greatness. God is the beginning and the end. Here a man, no matter how dull or bright, weak or powerful, poor or rich, can get a sense of that greatness. *Those whom the Gods would destroy, they first drive mad with pride.* Well, in a cathedral like this, even the proud must be humbled by your greatness, and know that they are nothing, and be freed from their pride. Forgive me, Lord, if I have been guilty of the sin of pride. Now, on the eve of battle, I humbly beg for your forgiveness.'

Michael MacDonald is kneeling in the second row in the nave of a vast cathedral. Facing him is a gilded altar of silver and gold, and art beyond price or catalogue. All around him, marble and granite vault high towards a distant heaven. To his left, a side altar flickers with candles, offering wax and mothers' prayers to a medieval Madonna. Michael rises, pauses to genuflect in the aisle, and starts to leave the vast cathedral. Soon he starts down the many steps towards a late dinner. It is time.

BBC headquarters, London: Eight fifteen p.m.
December the Twenty-Third

Peter Bradshaw, the director general of the BBC, sat at the head of a small table in the impromptu meeting room, barely twenty yards from Catherine Connor's office. Waiting. 'The trouble with power is that you never quite know how much you've got, until you use it. You can't just sit and count it, like money, or touch it, like a rich fabric. No, you have to use it to measure it. Well, we've found out this week just how much power the BBC has. Now, I think, we're about to find out just how much power The Cause has.' Bradshaw is roused from his meditations by the opening of the door, as an impatient-looking Catherine Connor is ushered in. The wait is over.

To Bradshaw's left was Richard Ferguson, the informal leader of the BBC group known as The Cause. Ferguson is a small, neat, clean-shaven man with short, well-styled brown hair. His hands and nails are well-groomed, and he wears a black Gucci shirt with a striking, bright red tie. Catherine Connor, clearly in a hurry to get to make-up and the debate, sits down facing Ferguson. She had watched the Daniel D theatre for too long, and now her schedule was as tight as a kettle drum. This unexpected meeting placed her at a disadvantage, just as Bradshaw had planned. She would learn the hard way that he, Peter Bradshaw, was not a man to cross. Since it was not really his meeting, he let Richard Ferguson get things underway. Ferguson's tone was pleasant, but as neutral as a lawyer's.

"Sorry to call a meeting at such short notice Catherine. I will be as brief as possible. You do, of course, know who I am, and whom I represent?" Not really a question, more a gambit. Despite her impatience, Catherine responded sweetly enough.

"Only by reputation, Richard. You are, unofficially of course, the leader of The Cause. What can I do for you, Richard?"

Richard smiled. Of course, Catherine knew who The Cause were. How could she not? She knew, they all knew, that the BBC was a magnet for people of conviction and passion. Those who fought for gender equality, and against racism, sexual stereotyping, and homophobia. The warriors for animal rights, and the sanctity of the single parent family. The educated, who battled bravely against the superstitions of the religious. So many worthy goals, but so difficult to co-ordinate, and so easy for them to degenerate into mutual conflict. It needed co-ordination to ensure that gay rights, or gender equality, did not come into conflict with respect for Islam; and that respect for animal rights, or contempt for religion, did not result in cultural intolerance and racism, and so on down the line. The Cause provided that co-ordination, that unity of purpose. It was never really formally a name, more something that came into usage from their discussions. The acceptance that, in order for everyone to get what they wanted, it was necessary to make sacrifices ...to make compromises ...*for The Cause*. Not so much a name, more the defining fragment of an argument. In any case, at the high levels of leadership, the people of passion were united, informally, in The Cause.

Although its existence was shadowy, people knew The Cause by its fruit: success. Without doubt, The Cause were the most powerful engine of change in Britain, responsible for a generation of social engineering on the national scale. The BBC was a living microcosm of that success. Diversity abounded, a kaleidoscope of races and beliefs, in which every shape and shade of opinion found a voice. Although this was still Britain, they had managed to keep white males to a minimum, and most of those tended to be unnaturally muscular, or perhaps excessively slender. Power? The Cause had, almost single-handedly, transformed the social fabric of Britain. How could Richard *not* be confident of his power?

"Tonight's debate, Catherine. We'd appreciate it if Senator William Gladwin is the last speaker." There, straight to the point.

A moment of silence.

"I'm sorry, Richard, I cannot do that. The draw has already been made, and it was made fairly."

"Please think carefully over your answer, Catherine. The Cause do not ask for a favour twice. And you will still need a career, after the debates are over." There was no disguise over the threat: none at all. Why should he bother, when her time was so short? Catherine paused, but she did not answer directly.

"Well, it might help if you tell me, Richard, just why we should favour the Senator?"

"He's our kind of politician. You're a very smart woman, Catherine. You know exactly what I mean."

"Yes, Richard, I do. I've spent many years interviewing them. I think I can summarise his kind perfectly. Senator Gladwin is... *the kind of politician who somehow weaves the threads of contradiction into a badge of personal goodness. If the world is not the equal of his beliefs, then surely that is not his fault and certainly no reason not to vote for him.* Is that a good description, Richard?" Despite himself, Ferguson permitted himself a quiet smile. Catherine was, certainly, most certainly, one class act.

"What a smart lady you are, Catherine. Very smart. I knew you were too smart to refuse us this favour." It was not a question, but it got an answer.

"Actually, Richard, my answer is no. Absolutely no. And, please excuse me, gentlemen, but I have a debate to run." Catherine rose to go, but it was not yet over.

"I'm very, very sorry to hear that, Catherine. You are making a very big mistake." Catherine turned back. She smoothed her skirt, as if cleaning off some just-glimpsed dust. Maybe *she* was not finished after all.

"Talking of mistakes, Richard, what a curious choice of shirt and tie? A red stripe on black. Now, let me think, just where I have just seen that distinctive combination?" Actually, she had only just made the connection. *The British People's Party?* Surely not? Surely so. The flag had only just been unveiled. What on earth was the connection? Richard Ferguson smiled smugly, but without humour. However, he did give her an answer.

"Solidarity, Catherine. Solidarity, and compromise, in the pursuit of power. I think, perhaps, that you have underestimated us a little. Yes, not all our politicians are quite the stereotypes you so vividly described. We did not put all of our eggs in the one basket. Certainly, The Cause has helped to break the mould in this country, but the job is only half done. It is time for us to go to the next stage. Time for this country to move on, and to do that it needs strong leadership. As you might have guessed, Catherine, we do have a new leader in mind." He was right: she had underestimated them. There was more to them, much more. Careful, now.

"A new leader, Richard? Perhaps a photogenic, charismatic leader, young, and tall? Perhaps the new stereotype: the non-smoking, non-drinking, vegetarian, atheist leader? Mr. Daniel D, why not, indeed? He certainly fits most of your criteria, even more, if it turns out that he is not really interested in women. But be careful, Richard, for it has been tried before. And, in case you've forgotten, The Fuhrer lost the war, and eighty million people were slaughtered in the process." Ferguson knew only too well that Adolph Hitler was – apart from the odd, characteristic lapse - history's only example of a teetotal, vegetarian, atheist leader. A fact that The Cause had worked hard, and long, to hide. No, he would rather not dwell on that. It was infuriating, all the more so for being true, and Ferguson did not like to be reminded of it. Now he was angry; really coldly, deeply, angry.

"You really must understand, Catherine, that history does not always repeat itself. Figureheads can remain figureheads, as they were meant to. Anyway, the process is now underway. It is time for some security and order. We will start by getting the beggars and the gangsters off our streets."

"I am sure you will." Catherine acknowledged. "Yes, I am sure that you will. After all, that's what fascism means. You take the beggars off the streets and kill them. You take the gangsters off the streets, and you put them into power. Give them a country to terrorise, why not? And, after that?" Ferguson shook his head, angry, his words final.

"I'm sorry to hear this from you, Catherine. I thought you'd want to be one of us."

"*One of us?* No, I'm sorry, Richard, it's not as simple as that. Just because you shave your legs it does not make you a woman." Catherine's tone was acid. Ferguson was equal to the taunt.

"Correct, Catherine. As long as I have the capacity for rational thought, I will remain a man."

"I know, darling. It's so disappointing. Sometimes life is *such* a bitch, is it not?" With that, Catherine pouted a kiss, and was gone.

'Well,' Peter Bradshaw thought, 'It could have been worse. At least she wasn't wearing a basque.'

ELEVEN

The Small Studio, BBC Headquarters, London: Nine p.m.
December the Twenty-Third

It was forty five minutes since The Cause, and, superficially, Catherine Connor looked much as she had done for the other debates. In other words, glamorous, spectacularly so. But, this soon after the impromptu meeting, she was still raging, and it showed. She positively *sparked*, more alive, more *charged* than the previous nights. The audience, too, she noticed, had changed. They also looked more awake, more energised, more positive. Awake: how could they not be awake? So much had changed for everyone in the last five days! Change? Things had changed faster than a politician's past. And, speaking of politicians, Senator William Gladwin. How much had changed for him? *'One of us?'*. Well, it was time to find out, for real. No more characters, no more plays. Time for the simple truth. As if. Well, it was the stroke of nine, and time, so Catherine got the proceedings underway.

"Ladies and gentlemen, I will be brief because I am sure that we are all familiar with the format. The charge that we will debate tonight is as follows:-

"The West is charged with dishonesty, the failure to admit to their own beliefs."

"Tonight's sequence of advocates is William, Anne-Marie, Krishnan, Anwar and Andrew. William, can I please ask you to begin?"

As Senator William Gladwin rose to his feet, he sensed – no, knew – that he was a man on the way back. The long distance runner, closing back in on the last couple of laps. Time to make his move. He started to speak.

"Ladies and gentlemen, I think we have all heard some bizarre statements in the last few days. Some bizarre, absurd, ridiculous nonsense. But this statement, this so-called charge, is right up there with the very best of them. The failure to admit to their own beliefs? If the people of the West are guilty of anything, it is of honesty and openness about their beliefs. Openness, tolerance, diversity. Many beliefs, and the freedom to express them. This is the very essence of the West." A pause.

"*For God's sake, ladies and gentlemen, this is enshrined in the first amendment of the constitution of the United States of America!* That's right: many beliefs, and the freedom to express them! This charge is so patently ridiculous that I feel there must be some mistake, some confusion. OK, it is true that the very diversity of the West means that our beliefs are not simple, not easy to compartmentalise, maybe even confusing for an outsider to understand. But, ladies and gentlemen, dishonest, *come on!* And do you know why, ladies and gentlemen, do you know why we of the West are so open about our beliefs? Why we are so *honest* about them?" Gladwin's face had reddened with anger, and it was obvious to everyone that it was real, not mere theatrics. He had almost hurled the question at his audience, most of whom found other places to look than his face.

"Do you know why?" he demanded again. " Why are we so honest about our beliefs?" The audience, intimidated, remained silent. Gladwin lowered his voice, forcing them to listen carefully to catch his next words.

"Because we are proud of them. Because we are proud of our openness, our tolerance, our diversity. Because we are proud of the values of the West. And rightly so. Ladies and gentlemen, congratulate yourselves on belonging to the West. Applaud yourselves, for you have much to be proud of." Gladwin, seemingly unselfconscious, lead the clapping, looking around the studio as he did so. He liked what he saw: he could see that he was hitting the right notes, so he went back to hit some more.

"Ladies and gentlemen, I, of all people, have never been afraid to criticise the excesses of the West. I have long been known for my sympathies towards the Second and Third Worlds. Now, in fairness, I think it is time to look beyond those failings of the West. I think it is time to take a hard look at those who accuse us. What was it one of my colleagues quoted in an earlier debate? Let him who is without sin cast the first stone? *Well, perhaps it is time to look at those who throw the stones!*" A challenge, strident and loud. A pause, a more conciliatory tone.

"It is only fair, is it not, to consider our standards against those of our accusers? Ladies and gentlemen, it is the West that stands accused. But what if we should find that our accusers are guilty of the greater crimes? What then should we do with these so-called Trials of the West? It is a fair question, is it not? So which of our accusers should we start with? Surely those who accuse us the most, ladies and gentlemen? Who else, ladies and gentlemen, but what Anwar calls the World of Islam! Ladies and gentlemen, let us pause for a moment to consider the World of Islam." Senator William Gladwin spat the words out, viciously, venomously. Gladwin was warming up just fine. Closing in, making up the lost ground.

"In the World of Islam you can be executed for adultery. Does anyone here think that this is reasonable? In the World of Islam you can be executed for the crime of being born gay. Or being a Christian, or a Buddhist. Does anyone here think that this is reasonable? In the World of Islam children are brought up in death cults, their lives but a hymn of hate against anyone and everyone their semi-literate imam does not agree with. Muslim or non-Muslim alike. Does anyone here think that this is reasonable? Or the fact that, oil wealth or no oil wealth, most Muslim countries live in dire and needless poverty? Without any decent level of education? Does anyone think that it is reasonable for women to be second class citizens? That they have to cover themselves from head to toe lest they lead poor innocent men astray? Come on, ladies and gentlemen, *come on!* Put it all together. Does anyone really think that the World of Islam has any right to judge anyone?" A pause, a silence, a shake of the head, then a continuation.

"No, I do not think so and neither do you. No, I have another suggestion. I think that it is the West that should be judging them!" The words were almost snarled out. A short silence, laden with tension and menace. Then, unexpectedly, a softer tone.

"Except that we are not without sin." A pause, a nod. "And we are honest enough to admit it. So let's move on, and take a look at Anne-Marie's world. Let's take a not-too-close look at Africa. Tyrants and dictators. Wars, genocides and child soldiers. Oil and diamonds, gold and minerals, and grinding poverty." Gladwin did not spare the people of Africa, not at all. Mercilessly, he continued to expose the failings, the corruptions, the weaknesses. And then he posed a question.

"Ladies and gentlemen, let me ask you a question. Now, no matter how bad a hand the people of Africa have been dealt, does any of us really think they share no responsibility for this at all? Really? So who are they to be judging us? *Are they the ones who are fit to throw the first stone?*" The voice of outrage, anger, derision. The studio audience flinched: they were intimidated, uncertain, cowed. Not a single howl of outrage, as yet another taboo went crashing. 'How far have we come?' thought Catherine. 'Who could imagine anyone saying this five days ago, never mind a character like William Gladwin? *One of us*, indeed?' The Senator had more to say.

"India? Let's look at India. Poverty, corruption and the caste system. Superstition, disease and religious atrocities. No, ladies and gentlemen, they're not much better. Not fit to throw the first stone: no way. I could talk about South America, or China or the rest of the Far East, but, good people, I think you have heard enough. It is time for these people to take a good look at themselves before they attack the West, and its freedoms." A long, considered pause that almost became an ending. But not quite.

"Ladies and gentlemen, we all know the West can be an infuriating, frustrating world. We are home to so many shades of belief and opinion that it is hard to say what we do NOT believe: because, somewhere in our unimagined diversity you can be certain that someone believes it. No," and Gladwin smiled ruefully "it would be easier to herd cats than to define what the West does and does not believe. But, ladies and gentlemen, there is certainly a core to the West. There are some overriding beliefs that we all share. Firstly, the belief that we are all equal, regardless of race or creed. Secondly, and the reason that we are all here today. We believe in free speech, and in everyone's right to agree or to disagree. In that spirit, ladies and gentlemen, I exercise my right to disagree. This motion is nonsense. The West is not afraid to admit to what it believes, and nor should it be. Remember that, and stand proud, people of the West! Thank you." With that, Gladwin sat down.

Some of the studio audience loved it, but most were unmoved. Gladwin spoke in favour of the status quo. But now there was no status quo. Everyone had moved on. They wanted to know what happened next. This was, after all, the Trials of the West: no-one was really interested in the Third World or the Second World or anything in between. And they were long past being told their world was wonderful. They knew it wasn't and the rest of the world's faults were of no great interest to them. They applauded, certainly, and there were no cries of outrage or righteous indignation. However, it was clear that Gladwin had missed the target. Was it was moving too fast?

But if the target was not the studio audience, but the bonfire, and the braziers, and the men in ski-masks, then Senator William Gladwin surely and certainly hit, dead centre. Somehow, through some invisible choreography, the volunteers of the British People's Party had assembled into three lines of perfect military precision. In the front rank, a huge blonde giant proudly held aloft their black and fire flag. Facing the three lines was Daniel D, two new faces to his right and left. As the word 'proud' left Gladwin's lips, they all saluted, as one, their double arms all hurled aloft in fierce acclaim. Around the other braziers, away from the militants, many stubborn individuals had held to their posts, determined to protect the BBC and the rights and principles that Gladwin had just spoken of. They watched their military neighbours with a mixture of horror, fascination and fear. But, for the most part, they held to their posts. Sometimes freedom has a price.

It might be that others were about to pay it. The BBC barricades were not the only place where the black and lightning now held sway. Chillingly, at the major barricades around the Muslim ghettoes of Britain, regiments of the British People's Party had echoed the same manoeuvres in time-slipped synchrony. Their performances were a little more extended, however, as their web-cams duly and faithfully broadcast to all those who were interested. At these barricades, the regiments followed the last double-armed salute with a march, double-time, towards a gap in the ghetto boundary, newly created and flanked by two ski-masked veterans. These veterans held SA-80 A2 rifles, the latest British Army issue, and they stood guard over a heaped array of weapons from the many ages of war. As each soldier reached the impromptu arsenal he was handed the first weapon that came to hand. In military terms, it was not standard procedure to mix swords and rifles, spears and pistols, but that was hardly the point. This was the stuff of propaganda, the newsreel footage of history, and the images were potent beyond measure. *And what rough beast, its hour come round at last...*

Back in the City of the Infidels, Ahmed Ali Khan was both angry and elated. Angry at the words, and the insults. But elated at the foolishness he had heard. Let the West choose isolation, yes, *please* choose isolation. The West against the Rest. Let us narrow the odds. We can deal with the other infidels afterwards.

"Anne-Marie, questions?" Catherine prompted. Anne-Marie did have questions, of a sort.

"William, darling, what a friend you have been." Anne-Marie began sweetly. "Above all else, not the kind you can turn your back on. Well, good luck, darling, especially with your *new* friends. Just don't turn your back on them, either." On reflection, Catherine did not think this was really a question. But was it a statement of fact? In any case, Gladwin did not dignify it with a response.

"Krishnan?" Krishnan was quick to respond to the prompt.

"I am trying hard to understand your arguments, William, and to ignore your provocations. That is not easy to do, especially since they come from a politician we had regarded as among the more enlightened. Still, let us consider your argument. You say that the West represents all shades of belief, and is proud of it. Is that correct?"

"Yes, Krishnan, that is correct. It is unfortunate if some of what I have said offends you. However, everything I have said is true, and needed to be said. Someone needed to restore balance to these debates. We all know that the West is not the only society with problems. Is that not correct, Krishnan?"

"Let me stick to the point, William. If the West represents all shades of belief, do you not see that that can be the same as representing none? That all the competing beliefs may cancel each other out, and their sum may be therefore zero? It seems to me, William, like the story of the gambler at the horse races. He bet on every horse in every race, but could not understand why he lost money, even though he always had the winner." A wry smile from Krishnan, a faint echo from the audience. But Gladwin was equal to it, and came back with his own analogy.

"Not so, Krishnan. When you add many spices to a dish, do you not get a fine curry?" Krishnan came back, again.

"Sometimes, William. But you must not add them all, for then all dishes will taste the same. And when everything tastes the same, nothing tastes of anything." With that, Krishnan sat back, satisfied. He must remember that analogy: it really was most apt.

It may have been a smart answer, but for David Blenheim, watching amongst his colleagues in the Cabinet Room, it did absolutely nothing. Cleverness for the sake of it. Blenheim wanted substance, and he wanted answers. What was behind Gladwin's change of direction? The man almost sounded like a patriot. And he knew that there was a lot of truth in the old saw: patriotism was often the last refuge of scoundrels. Blenheim's attention drifted off onto the Gladwin puzzle, and then onto the many related matters. Anwar and Andrew's questions had been and gone – or never happened – when he was snapped back into the present. Snapped back by the sight of Anne-Marie Sesoku, sinuously and sensuously uncoiling to her feet. She looked magnificent, but then again, she always did, even when she was not angry.

"Ladies and gentlemen, he's right." A pause. "Or she, or they. It's time to talk, freely. Nice try, William, but I'm going to go ahead and say whatever I think needs to be said. Seems to me that is what friends are supposed to, anyway." A wry smile, a pause, a continuation.

"Ladies and gentlemen, *show me the money!*" A pause, silence.

"That's right, ladies and gentlemen, *show me the money!* That is the real truth that lies at the heart of the West. Or, put another way, *it's the economy, stupid!* The real core values of the West are wealth and progress. There's no need to deny it. It's nothing to be ashamed of. Speaking as an African woman, we'd love to have more wealth and progress ourselves. Why not? There's nothing good about poverty, believe me. Your problem is that you seem to have lost sight of almost everything else. Your lives are driven by the relentless cycle of advertising, purchase, and dissatisfaction. You are always just that one purchase away from making your life more fulfilled, more complete. You have to keep moving on, to a better model: a faster car, a bigger house, a more attractive partner. A never ending cycle of striving and disappointment. It certainly drives your economies to be productive, but, deep down, it makes people feel a little empty, a little unfulfilled. Am I so very far wrong, ladies and gentlemen?"

'No, you're not that far wrong." thought Catherine. 'It is the economy, stupid. And it is a never-ending cycle.'

"So then you fill the void with religion. Well, except that most of you don't. A religious life can be a little uncomfortable at times, especially if you are serious about it. And most make you feel too guilty about your pursuit of wealth. But you do need some kind of religious outlet. Something to let you see the bigger picture, and feel virtuous and good. Well, the West needed a new religion, and, ever creative, you made one." Some puzzled looks. Impatience, as Anne-Marie paused, and made them wait for clarification. What new religion? Had they not finished with such foolishness?

"The Environment. Conservation. The worship of nature in all her glory. The earth as a Mystic Paradise. The nobility of animals, and the divine interplay of ecology. Only spoilt, of course, by that terrible pestilence, man. Ladies and gentlemen, that is your new religion. Four legs good, two legs bad. Plants before People. Animal Rights."

Anne-Marie paused to let the audience digest her words. She had a point, Catherine could not help but agree. But so what? There was nothing wrong with respect for the environment, surely? But there was no time for an answer, for Anne-Marie was in full flight.

"Good people, I come from a land that is still wild, and untamed, *and I can't begin to tell how much all this foolish nonsense makes me mad!* Most of the world is still starving, or being plagued by disease, and you want to worship the wonders of nature? Of pitiless nature? Let me share with you some of my beliefs. It might make an interesting contrast to yours." A stern look at the audience, then she started on them.

"The principal purpose of the Earth is to provide a home for as many human beings as possible. People are the Earth's greatest fruit." Silence, but in the pause that followed, Catherine could sense the unmistakeable undercurrent of disagreement. Perhaps more than that: antipathy, thinly-veiled hostility. She did not believe that people were a virus on the face of the planet, but she knew those who did. 'Greatest fruit' was not quite how they saw it, not at all.

"Animals are mostly a source of food, although they can also be beautiful to look at, or can make useful labourers." A pause. "Animal Rights is a nonsense. Animals, especially, do not recognise animal rights. Try debating animal rights with a hungry lion, and you'll find that it does not recognise *human* rights either. Just food. Prey. You." The anger of the audience was almost tangible. Faces were reddened, teeth were clenched, people muttered to themselves. How dare she? 'Be careful, Anne-Marie.' Catherine thought. 'Taboos: these are powerful taboos. You've certainly got guts, woman.' Anne-Marie continued. Maybe she liked shattering taboos, for she certainly looked like she was enjoying herself.

"Trees make good firewood, and can provide good food."
"Better one hundred dead lions than one dead baby."
"No pet should eat while a child is hungry."
"Compared to humans, dolphins are stupid."
"Sheep are for wool, or for eating."
"Our ancestors wore fur. It's still the best."

"You killed off your wild animals to stop them from eating you. Bring them back, and put yourself back on the menu."

"The world was never a paradise. It never will be."

"Recycling just moves pollution somewhere else."

"Environmentalism is a tax on the poor."

"The world is not dying. It is not fragile at all."

"If the world is warming, why is the Antarctic ice getting thicker every year?

"Things are always going extinct. Let's just make sure it's not us."

There were more; lots more. Anne-Marie hammered them good, real good. Example after example; she was utterly relentless. Until she knew, and they knew, that they had got the point. It was time to get real. They had been foolish, but they would change. It was time for Anne-Marie to make a last summary.

"Ladies and gentlemen, I don't think it really matters what the West did or did not believe. I think what matters is what you believe now. Believe in wealth and prosperity, for they are better than the alternative. But believe in people too, for love really does make the world go round. And it's silly to be sentimental about the planet, it's just a resource for us to exploit. To summarise? *People before money, and nature in its place.* There, it's not that complicated, is it?" The trademark smile, the liquid flow of her long limbs, and Anne-Marie was again seated.

Except for a few diehards, and there were some, the audience applauded, tentatively at first, but soon swelling into a sustained, but cautious appreciation. Catherine let them vent their feelings, waited until the applause had died out naturally, before she prompted for the first questions.

"William, do you any questions for Anne-Marie?" Unsurprisingly, Gladwin did.

"Anne-Marie, we appreciate it is not always easy to put environmental concerns in the right perspective, particularly when people are still struggling to get enough to eat. Is it not true, however, that your somewhat hostile attitude to the environment really just reflects that Africa is at an earlier stage of development than the West?"

"You may well have a point, William." Anne-Marie replied, with a smile that, dangerously, never reached her eyes. "Africa may well be at an earlier stage of development. We are certainly at a stage where we understand that people are *part* of the environment, if that's what you mean. We are certainly at a stage where we are not too civilised to endure the inconvenience of children, for one thing. Unlike much of the West, where women seem to find child-bearing just too much of a burden. Still, no doubt the West has convinced itself that a declining population is good for the environment. Well, who am I to argue, darling? But I can assure you that there will be many Africans who are more than happy to fill the emptiness of your environmental paradise."

Pacing the cheap carpet of his modest lounge, Freddy Wilson, the most ordinary man in Britain, suddenly snapped. Like most people, Freddy wanted to do the right thing. He had endured the endless recycling demands, sifting glass and plastic and paper and seemingly everything and convinced himself that, somehow, all this work saved energy. He had suffered the endless rises in petrol duty, the road usage charges, the punitive parking tariffs. If the environment meant he could barely afford to use his car for anything other than travel to work, then what choice did he have? Like many others, he had been badly hit by the massive increases in travel tax. It hurt him that foreign holidays were, once again, the exclusive privilege of the rich. But it was the wind turbines, the god-awful windmills, that he found the hardest medicine to swallow. They loomed from the chimney stacks, whining and humming and doing nothing anyone could detect to reduce their heating bills. A visual and auditory pollution, and the death of the urban birds that brightened his early morning. Finally, the last patch of green in the area had now succumbed to their assault. Where once eager, jostling lads staged endless cup finals, there now loomed a menacing, alien forest of blade-whirling invaders, loud and unceasing in their hums and their whines and their slaughter of his pigeons. And now he understood. He had been conned. They all had. She was right, the earth was not fragile. Had he ever managed to tame the weeds in his driveway? Had anyone ever managed to exterminate the rats that still infested the building sites where we worked, rats that were bigger and fatter it seemed, every year? No, he'd been conned, and he knew it, and now he was going to do something about it.

To earn his modest living, Freddy Wilson drove a bulldozer. By some quirk of fate, the night before his yard had been closed while he was still out on site, and his huge Cat had been parked outside his house overnight, occupying two parking spaces and the attention of awestruck little boys. Yes, Freddy had had enough, and what's more, now he had the means to make that very clear.

Not pausing to grab a coat, Freddy stormed out of number eighteen, Cedar Road, fired up the massive Cat, reversed it into the centre of the street, and took aim for the forest of windmills. Curtain after curtain parted, as people heard the mighty roar and shake of the big 'dozer as it charged past in full chat. Smiling maniacally, Freddy waved his happy acknowledgement. Straight as a die, Freddy headed the beast straight towards the accursed windmill farm. Above everything else, the windmill was *the* symbol of the Environmentalists' tyranny: what better target could there be? Freddy's neighbours, astonishment gradually dawning on them, now saw just where the Cat was going. Like burning embers in a forest fire, the news leaped from house to house, until almost the whole street knew and had streamed out in his wake. They were expecting something, and they were certainly not disappointed. Howling with the fires of righteousness, Freddy crashed the great beast over the last pavement. and hurled it onto the security fence. The thundering Cat burst though the fencing as if it was paper, roaring on the first line of turbines with all the berserk fury of Freddy's Viking forbears. The air was rent by the bellowing scream of the diesel on full throttle, the screech of the blade on the towers, the crash of the turbines as they fell one on other under the juggernaut's relentless charge. It was not a battle but a slaughter, and inside five minutes it was over. Not a blade was turning, not a turbine humming. Freddy reversed the Cat from the forest of wreckage, killed the engine, and surveyed his neighbours. He looked like he was about to say something, but that he was searching for words, or still in the spell of the berserker. As he grappled with the spell, an old woman, thin but active, stepped silently from the crowd. Eyes locked onto his, and she reached up to offer Freddy a coat. It was a brownish fur coat, fox fur, not expensive, but it had been her father's loving gift fifty short years ago. She had loved it, but been afraid to wear it these last years. Of course, it was not his size, although he was not a big man, but he would be cold and he had earned it. In instinct and understanding Freddy took the coat, and surprisingly, found it almost fitted him. He had still to have his say, and somehow, it eased his nerves. After the chaos of the slaughter, the silence was almost absolute. Freddy's voice, therefore, carried to them all.

"I've had enough of our damn environmentalist rulers, folks. I'm off to kill some windmills. How about it?" A roar of approval, a bellow of delight and anger and anticipation and it had begun: The War of The Windmills was underway. In this world of webcams and chaos and virus, it soon spread. By the end of the day, across the length and breadth of Europe, the windmill hunt was well underway. On the internet, www.warofthewindmills.com was very much the hip place to be, and fur coats were, once again, very much the garment of choice.

Meanwhile, back in the BBC studio, and back when Freddy was just opening his front door, Gladwin had decided let it go. Although his speech had been short, and he had the time, he was digging a hole and he knew it. The other three advocates were more than happy to signal their perfunctory agreement with Anne-Marie, and with the studio audience. They had little enough time as it was. Catherine knew that it was ridiculous to imagine that the environmental taboo had been shattered, but there was no doubt it had at least sustained some powerful blows. In any case, it was time for the next speaker.

"Ladies and gentlemen, our third speaker, Mr. Krishnan Narajan." The familiar Nehru suit, the calm, ascetic features. Nothing to betray the inner turmoil that Krishnan most certainly felt. He was, after all, a scientist, and this was what he was born to do.

"Ladies and gentlemen, like you, I've greatly enjoyed listening to my colleagues today. However, I cannot help but think that they have not really answered the charge that we are here to discuss. Please bear with me for a minute or so while I read to you the full text of this morning's accusation." Krishnan put on a thick black pair of reading glasses, and started to read from a single typed sheet.

"They say they believe that we have evolved from raw chemicals through the laws of chance and the interaction of the environment. It would be easier to drive from Moscow to Paris at night with a blind driver, no map and no destination, but still, they say that this is what they believe. However, ask them about genetic engineering and they are utterly opposed. How so? Do they believe that the best efforts of their best minds, with the best of intentions, will be worse than raw chance? That a sighted driver with a map is more dangerous than a blind one without? Of course not. They say that they believe these things, but really

they do not. They only pretend to. Why will they not admit what they really believe?" The audience listened patiently as Krishnan read the accusation in full. Krishnan put down his notes and removed his reading glasses.

"Ladies and gentlemen, I think that this charge is about science. I think that this charge accuses the people of the West of not being honest about what science they really believe. Actually, ladies and gentlemen, I do not think you are alone in this. I'm almost ashamed to admit it, but I, too, am guilty of not being completely honest about some kinds of science. I'd like to ask you to show an old man a little patience, while I confess to you a little of my problems." Narajan paused a little to apparently gather his thoughts, then continued.

"Ladies and gentlemen, I am a physicist by profession, and I have devoted much of my life to science. To the hard, precise science of the West, the kind of science that believes in experiments, numbers, equations and predictions. From the numbers we get the equations and from the equations we can make predictions. Given confidence by our predictions, we can go on to develop technology from our science. Anything from the television to the space ship, from penicillin to the telephone. I was once – and, believe me, those days are long gone! – quite eminent in my field. That is why, ladies and gentlemen, that I find myself embarrassed to confess that I struggle with much of the new sciences. You know the kind of sciences I mean: the sciences of ecology and sociology and weather and so on. I've spent too much time with measurements and numbers and equations and I fear I am now just a little too old to really understand. My greatest difficulty, ladies and gentlemen, has been with the science of Darwin, the theory of evolution. I just have so many problems with it, and am yet unable to really understand. Well, ladies and gentlemen, I think it is now time for this old man to confess his difficulties. Hopefully, some young man will then be able to help me with my difficulties, and help

274

put this old scientist out of his misery."

Catherine was suspicious of this newly-humble old man. He did not seem quite like the Narajan of the last few days. Well, at least this time he had got their attention, although God knows how he was going to keep it.

"Ladies and gentlemen, as far as I understand it, the theory of evolution tells us that the first life was created by the interaction of electricity and radiation on some vast soup of primordial molecules. Something like that, anyway. These primitive organisms then mutate in a random fashion, and natural selection favours the good mutations to survive, and the bad mutations to die. Each step of the evolutionary path is random. There is no plan, no plan at all. For a mutation to survive, each step must be in a beneficial direction. The theory is very clear on this point: evolution is judged *step by step*. That means, you cannot make a step which is negative today, but beneficial tomorrow. No, ladies and gentlemen, it must be beneficial *today*. *Immediately*. So, the theory says that all the extraordinary life on our planet is the result of a series of random steps, each of which was immediately beneficial. The action of time and natural selection has done the rest." A slight pause, an almost imperceptible intake of breath.

"It is a beautiful theory, ladies and gentlemen, but I confess that I find it very difficult to come to terms with. I've spent just too much time with numbers and equations and experiments. I ask myself foolish questions, like what are the chances against life starting? What are the odds against this many varieties of life? Is it a billion, billion, billion to one? Or what? A number with a billion zeroes? I know it is wrong, ladies and gentlemen, but I still cling to my numbers. And to experiments. I ask myself why no-one makes the fundamental experiment? To try and create simple life from a soup of chemicals, radiation, and electricity. I know that if that experiment succeeded once, *just once*, then I,

275

and many like me, would be so much reassured. Yet, as far as I am aware, unfortunately, no evolutionary scientist ever makes the attempt. I suppose the odds must be too great, ladies and gentlemen? And I guess their faith is too strong for them to need to waste so much time? What would our religions give for such faith, I wonder? But, still, I do not understand why they do not just do the experiment. When it succeeds, as we all know it must, then the evolutionists would silence their doubters forever. *Forever*. No, I do struggle to understand, ladies and gentlemen. However, after all, I am now an old man and not what I once was." Krishnan shook his head sadly, then continued.

"Ladies and gentlemen, I wish that were my only difficulty, but I am afraid that it is not. As I understand it, for evolution to work, there must be a way to evolve. There must be a way to pass on a successful mutation. That means that we need more than a just a simple organism. There has to be a mechanism for inheritance, a way to store the successful adaptations. That mechanism is what we call genes, and DNA. Up to this point, ladies and gentlemen, even this old man, addicted to numbers, can understand. But here is the part I just cannot get. DNA itself cannot have evolved in stages, since there was no DNA to allow DNA to evolve. It is a catch-22, a chicken and egg situation. How did we get DNA without already having DNA? The answer? DNA must have appeared, in all its fabulous complexity, completely, magically, perfect. By chance. Now I am sure that they are right, ladies and gentlemen, but this does seem to me to be such an extraordinary, impossibly unlikely event. A gamblers last dream. A number with what – a billion, billion zeroes? I keep thinking of the numbers and the odds and the experiments that have never been done. But then again, I am now an old man and not what I once was. Thankfully, I am sure that there must be someone out there who can help this old man out with this difficulty."

Krishnan paused to take a breath, but more to let the

audience catch up. As if. They were just starting to realise that the old man was not quite so very old. Catherine, brilliant though she was, was just beginning to digest the subtleties of his presentation, but Krishnan had already started to speak again. For sure, she would come back to it. She would find the flaws in his reasoning.

"There is one last point about the theory of evolution, ladies and gentlemen, and the one I struggle with the most. As I understand it, the real engine of evolution is sexual reproduction. Male and female, and the mixing of genes to make better combinations. The stronger of the gene pair surviving; the female choosing the strong male and so on. The eternal dance of the mating game. But I remember that every mutation is random, and must survive by the immediate benefit that it brings. So how did males come into being, without females? What advantage is it to be male in a world with no females? And vice-versa? How did the process get started? Even the slightest adaptation towards being male is a disadvantage in the evolutionary competition. A significant disadvantage, because the adaptation consumes energy, but is useless. And all these further steps towards maleness are still useless, even when they are complete, and you have a fully functioning male organism. So, it would appear that a male gradually evolved, step by step, even though each evolutionary step was a disadvantage. *To me, ladies and gentlemen, this is, in complete defiance of the most basic principle of the theory itself.* Somehow, females also managed to defy this most basic principle of the theory. Somehow, they also managed to become more and more female, even though each step was an evolutionary disaster. Until, ladies and gentlemen, both males and females existed, fully formed, and finally, one fateful day, they met. *Ladies and gentlemen, I don't know about you, but that is quite the most romantic story I have ever heard."* Subdued laughter, mostly nervous, as if people were afraid they had not seen the real joke, and were afraid to

277

attract attention to themselves. Narajan had not finished, and silenced them with an upraised hand.

"Ladies and gentlemen, it *is* true, after all. *Love conquers all.*" Even Catherine had to laugh. It was a great line, and the audience loved it too. This time their laughter was unselfconscious, immediate, and unafraid. Narajan seemed happy to let it die out gradually, happy to take advantage of the time to gather his thoughts once again.

"Actually, ladies and gentlemen, it summarises for me the whole theory. It is not a theory of *evolution*, but of *revolution*. It is a theory that breaks its own rules. *Ridiculous*. But then again, I am now an old man and not what I once was. What is wrong with this simple-minded analysis? Is there no-one out there who can explain to this old man just where he has gone wrong?"

Narajan looked around the audience in appeal. Only deep silence in response, and he resumed his confession.

"I can accept, ladies and gentlemen, that natural selection is a powerful mechanism in evolution. However, I just do not think we understand the real engine of evolution, nor how the whole process got started. In my foolishness, I think that we should be honest about what we know, and what we don't know. Just because I may not understand how a petrol engine works, that is no reason for me to think that it is by chance."

Surely, everyone felt, this must just be theatre. Some kind of intellectual game, a joke yet to be revealed. Surely he must be missing something. Why on earth did they not have answers for him? With something so fundamental to their beliefs, surely someone must have some answers? Was it all really so ridiculous as it sounded?

"Ladies and gentlemen, it is true that I am old man, but surely I am not the only one who struggles with this theory? Surely I am not the only one that worries about the lack of numbers and equations and experiments? So how did it happen that we are all being taught this evolutionary proposition as if it were a proven fact?" A pause. Many thoughts, the sound of silent questions being asked: unusual questions. Krishnan continued.

"I can only make a guess, a foolish guess, but let me share it with you. In Darwin's time, the West was at the peak of its imperial greed. So much so, ladies and gentlemen, that the Christian churches had started to raise some awkward moral questions. What justified this conquest and slaughter? Was this really Christian? The religions were proving a problem, an obstacle, and Government needed to deal with them, and finally. The scientists, too, had a problem with religion. For them, this was the age before Einstein, and Quantum Theory, and they believed in Newton and his mechanical universe. A world where all was predictable, and there could therefore be no hand of God. Given enough data, you could solve all the equations. But the people did not really believe them, for the scientists could not yet explain the origin of life itself. With Darwin, and the theory of evolution, the political and scientific establishment finally got the weapon they were both looking for. Who could object to empire, when it was but evolution in action, the survival of the fittest? What other justification was required? And what need of religion? Science could now explain the origin of life itself, and the rise of man, and that there was no God involved. No God, but only chance. Ladies and gentlemen, who could argue with a theory that was so deceptively simple, yet so powerful? And if you did, that made you a religious fanatic, or a Creationist, someone with an irrational agenda. In the feebleness of my old age, ladies and gentlemen, it seems deceptively simple. The dominance of the theory of evolution is largely the result of a pragmatic alliance between politicians and scientists. An unholy alliance, perhaps." A pause for a quick sip of water. No-one's attention wandered, and Krishnan resumed.

"Ladies and gentlemen, I've already said more than enough, but I may as well be hung for a sheep as a lamb. As I said, I am now an old man, not what I once was, and have little to lose. I wonder if the theory of evolution is not the only example of the unholy alliance in action? If it is not the only example of the government feeding you propaganda dressed in a cloth of science? Science without numbers, and experiments, and scientists claiming to understand more than they do. Like genetic engineering. You've heard their assurances, but you're not convinced. You know it could all go horribly wrong, and this old man thinks you might be right. You might want to ask yourselves some more questions. What other new theories are your governments urging you to believe? What new scientific truths have you been fed these last few decades? And why? And how many of these truths are still true?" A last pause, a small sip of water. A little time for people to think. And little time left now, but endings can be everything.

"This old man thinks you are right to be careful, ladies and gentlemen. Whenever you hear your government has adopted some new scientific belief, think. Be suspicious. Is this science, or politics, or their unholy alliance? Why do they want you to believe this? Yes, you are guilty of not saying exactly what you believe. But there is no real sin in that. After all, we know that the truth can be a dangerous business, and especially now. It's time to talk, freely, but dangerous. Like an old man talking too much, and making a fool of himself." A wry smile.

"Ladies and gentlemen, the last words of an old scientist. Retain your scepticism. Exercise your powers of reason. Nourish them. If you do not understand something, admit it. Do not be so lazy as to call it chance. Life is a little more wonderful, and a lot more dangerous, than that. Thank you."

In the cabinet room of Number Ten, outrage grappled with disbelief, in silence. Politicians tend to be lawyers, or businessmen, or the products of privilege and wealth. They do not tend to be scientists. Science was a little too black and white for a politician to ply his trade. Well, traditional science anyway. The new sciences of environment and weather were more fertile territory. There, the absence of numbers and equations gave them sufficient scope to weave their honeyed spells. But this? Cast aside the irony and the mockery and the thin cloak of theatre, and what had they heard? Hard logic, and reason, and no place for a politician unless there was absolutely no alternative. But surely this was an attack on one of the cornerstones of their beliefs? Surely there must be someone with sufficient courage, and science, to counter this nonsense?

There certainly used to be scientists of courage and reason, and Alfred Herald was one of them, although now he was no more than a mad crank with a great future behind him. Alfred lived in Shrewsbury, England, ancestral home of Darwin, and he had followed in the master's august footsteps. One of the most brilliant biologists of his generation, he was also one of the first to confront the orthodoxy of Darwin, and he had, ultimately paid with his job and his career. Alfred, however, was not a bitter man, and he continued to pursue his theories with modesty, and his life with a certain detached humour. Hearing Narajan's very public demolition, Alfred saw an opportunity. In the square outside the former cathedral of Shrewsbury, there stands a great statue of Darwin, mighty brows furrowed in thought. It was more a shrine than a statue, and tourists still came daily to worship at the feet of the great man. Leaving the debate early, while everyone was still glued to their screens, Alfred Herald headed for the shrine. Half an hour later, the statue had a new legend, and it read, in bright white lettering, 'Love Conquers All'. The Darwinian humour quickly caught on. Evolved, even. The next Darwin statue to fall victim was in the Natural History Museum, in London. This august statue also got a new legend, a fine echo of the fierce concentration on its stern visage. It read 'I believe in Luck, in Luck Almighty'.

Back in the studio. and in the present tense, Senator William Gladwin thought he might be the one to see the weakness in Narajan's arguments, and he was happy to open the questions.

"Krishnan, a most impressive piece of reasoning. And a fine piece of theatre from an old man who is, apparently, not what he once was. Unfortunately, I do not have sufficient scientific background to be able to expose the specific flaws in your arguments, as subtle as they must be. But, in a general sense, I think we can all see the weakness of your approach. I think you are being too literal, too *binary* in your reasoning and in your faith in numbers. This is, after all, nature we are talking about. Not everything in the natural world can be expressed as clearly as it can be in physics. That does not make it wrong, just different. Surely you must appreciate, Krishnan, that it is not always just about counting?" Krishnan hesitated for a second or two to consider his answer.

"William, you really should have more respect for numbers, for they really are the basis of almost everything. Without numbers there is no technology, no agriculture, not even any building. Without numbers we would still be living in caves and planting seeds at the first false dawn of spring. But, still, I do agree that counting does not always matter. After all, Senator, I can count a politician's promises, but that does not matter very much at all. Not to me, and even less to the politician."

If Gladwin was hurt by the jibe, he didn't show it, but immediately came back.

"Fine words from a scientist, Krishnan. But perhaps you are little more politician than scientist?" It was better than nothing, but not much, and Narajan dismissed it with a simple smile of contempt.

"Anne-Marie?" Catherine prompted.

"A clever analysis, Krishnan, but maybe too clever for most of us. Maybe there's another, simpler, way to look at this apparent

282

belief in evolution. How can the West claim to believe in evolution, and the survival of the fittest, when they spend so much time and energy to stop this same evolution? To preserve the environment, just as it is? Surely, the story of evolution is as much about extinction as it is about adaptation? Why would the West strive so passionately to defeat their own irresistible theory?" No answer was required: Narajan had only five seconds left anyway, and offered none. Anwar declined Catherine's invitation, and she moved on to Andrew.

"Andrew, any questions?" She didn't show it, but Catherine was as nervous as a kitten in a kennel. She knew it only took just the one slip, the one error, and Andrew could be utterly undone. She knew he was, and looked, exhausted. It would be so easy to blow it. Andrew, however, was tired, but calm.

"A remarkable argument, Krishnan. I'm surprised to find that I know so little about evolution that I just can't agree or disagree in any meaningful way. It really makes me wonder: what else I do not really understand as much as I thought? What else do I take for granted that I ought to think a little more about?" Again, it was hardly a question, but it did certainly raised some in the minds of the audience. Catherine, mindful of theatre, gave them a few seconds to answer them before she had to move them on. They had a long way to go, they would have time enough, later, to think more deeply.

TWELVE

"Ladies and Gentlemen, our fourth speaker, Mr. Anwar Abbat."
The rugged warrior face seemed a little less intense than the day
before. The bearing was just a little more relaxed. The voice,
however, was still deep and menacing.

"Ladies and gentlemen, but especially, people of the West.
The last few days have been, for you, most extraordinary. The
foundations of your society are under scrutiny and threat like
never before; and rightly so. It is time. You have watched many
of your beliefs be exposed and ridiculed; and rightly so. It is time.
Today you are charged with failing to admit to your beliefs. Well,
I have to be fair to you. There is one belief that you still hold,
and are proud to admit to. Your belief in your system that you
call democracy. The democracy that you believe allows you to
speak freely, to be honest with yourselves, and amongst yourselves.
But that is not the only belief that you still hold. These last,
historic, few days, who among you has not believed in, and been
proud of, the BBC? The first, and greatest, defender of that
democracy, is it not? Ladies and gentlemen of the West, you are
still proud to believe in the BBC, without whom none of this
incredible process would be possible. Ladies and gentlemen, let us
applaud not ourselves, but the ladies and gentlemen of the BBC."

Anwar led the applause, and, to a man, the audience
followed. Who among the many thousands at the BBC did not
feel that wave of thanks and appreciation? Even Peter Bradshaw,
alone at his desk, felt the welcome glow of satisfaction and pride.
Anwar gave it a few seconds, then lowered his hands, palm
downs in a clear gesture of enough, time to move on.

"Not that the BBC is alone, even in this country. When I use
the words 'BBC', I do not mean to be too literal. I include many

of the other television stations, newspapers, the different branches of the media. Not all of course, but many, perhaps most. Across Europe, every country has their equivalents, even if no-one has quite the unique freedom that the BBC has. To be funded by tax and not be beholden to advertisers, or to your own viewers, is that not freedom indeed? But everyone does have their own equivalents. Even in the United States, there are BBCs, and many of them. You know better than I, ladies and gentlemen, that their role is essential. Your democracy absolutely depends on an independent media, powerful enough to challenge the propaganda of the state, able to counter their arguments, to dispute their facts, to bring them to account for their lies. Ladies and gentlemen, it is clear that you are proud of your belief in the journalists of the BBC. Of course, they cannot always be accurate in every detail, because they do not have access to all the facts that they need, and you recognise this, and give them the benefit of the doubt. If they have to embellish the occasional report, add in the occasional half-truth, then you can accept it, knowing that it is necessary to expose the truths that lie beneath. Do you not marvel, ladies and gentlemen, at where these journalists come from? Who are they, these fearless, principled champions of democracy, and how are they found?"

Catherine was not the only one to feel a little tremor of unease. This is Anwar Abbat speaking. What was his purpose? Where was he going with this?

"Ladies and gentlemen, I think you know that the BBC is more than just the defender of democracy. The BBC is also the passionate enemy of imperialism, and especially the imperialism of your American friends. In your Western wars of aggression, it is the BBC that helps to balance the scales of the uneven contests. No matter how few are your casualties, or how many are those of the enemy, the BBC is still able to admit that you are losing. Lose one of yours to ten of the enemy, the war is madness. One to a hundred, it is unacceptable. One to a thousand, it is unsustainable and you will surely lose, in time. And it is the BBC that will highlight the collateral damage of your bombs and guns and missiles. It is the BBC that is unafraid to proclaim it excessive, unnecessary, probably a war crime. It is the BBC that exposes the conditions in your prison camps, and the unacceptable treatment of your prisoners. Fearlessly, in the headlines, and without any great burden of verification. And it is always the BBC that proclaims you are losing the propaganda war. A statement which then becomes, by definition, true. Yes, we all owe the BBC a great debt of gratitude."

Catherine felt the ambiguity start to crystallise. Some of the audience too, sensed it, and looked a little uneasy. Peter Bradshaw felt the first hairs stand up on the back of his neck. '*I come to bury Caesar, not to praise him...*', he remembered.

"Ladies and gentlemen, I will not treat you like fools. The World of Islam is well aware of the power of propaganda. It is the only way we can confront the overwhelming material power of the West. I admit that we are well aware that our real battleground is in the media, the BBC, and that this battle is the only key to our victory. I admit that, at a practical level, the BBC is a friend to Islam, even if only because we share the same enemy. Even if only because my enemy's enemy is my friend. However, I have to confess that some things make me a little uneasy. Like why our casualties are so much less important than yours? Why does one of your dead mean so much more than one of ours? I tell myself that this is not racism, just asymmetry. Something, obviously, completely different. I ask myself how it is that we can site our weapons to maximise collateral damage - in schools, and mosques, hospitals - yet you do not report it? Is it that you do not think we are really worthy of western standards, what else can you expect from Muslims? I wonder how it is that, when necessary, we can kill women and children, torture our

286

prisoners, use suicide bombers, yet none of this will attract the headlines like your mistreatment of Muslim prisoners? I tell myself that this is this not because we are considered barbarians, and unfit to be judged against by Western values, but I am a little uneasy. Yet I comfort myself that you feel so superior that you must never torture a prisoner, no matter how many of your sons' lives it may save. I comfort myself that your military values the lives of their prisoners above those of their own comrades. That they no longer understand the real meaning of the word WAR."

By the last sentence, Abbat's reasonable tone had become savage, sardonic, mocking. Abbat once again exuded his customary menace, stark and uncompromising. He let several seconds tick away, let the tension build, but then let it drain away again, as he reverted to his earlier, reasonable tones.

"Still, the BBC is our weapon, and we must use it, even if we feel just a little insulted. At a practical level, the BBC *is* a friend of Islam, even if we do not fully understand why. But ask yourselves, ladies and gentlemen, who are these journalists who so cleverly weight the scales? Where did they come from, these journalists who apply the standards of the West with such elegant discrimination? How do you find such fearless enemies of imperialism?"

'He knows!' Catherine realised. 'The Cause. He is talking of The Cause!' In his cold eyrie, Peter Bradshaw shared the same thought. A bead of sweat popped onto his brow, distracting, annoying, as Abbat, smiling, continued. His mockery was now turning more to anger, his tone lower, more intense.

"Ladies and gentlemen, there is yet more to the BBC. It is more than just the defender of democracy, more than just the enemy of imperialism. Who is it that has taught you to feel shame for your imperial past? Who is it that has highlighted the emptiness of your culture, and the glories of multiculturalism? Who is it that has forced you to respect women's rights? Of their rights to abortion, and the sanctity of the single parent family?

287

Who is it that has encouraged you to seek eternal youth, and made heroes of those blessed by an early death? Who is that has freed you from your prejudices against gays, and highlighted their contributions to your values and society? Who is it that has opened your eyes to the rights of animals, and the need to maintain this Earth unchanged? Who is it that has liberated you from the chains of religion, ridiculing its priests and its foolishness? Who has driven this social enlightenment of the West? Who are these social architects and engineers? Who is responsible for this dramatic transformation of your society? *Who is it that has created this mad dog that threatens us all?*"

Abbat hurled the challenge into utter silence. Jaw pulsing, he scanned his audience, head nodding slightly in unconscious muscular release. It was unbelievable, but Catherine sensed that the audience was now beginning to turn. To turn his way. To ask the question, Who? Maybe Abbat knew of The Cause, maybe he only guessed at it, maybe he just assumed that everyone at BBC was the same. The thought angered her, hell had she not just made her independence clear? Meanwhile, the assault continued.

"Yes, ladies and gentlemen, it is the BBC, and its values. The BBC: yes, the British Broadcasting Corruption. Yes, for that is *exactly* what it is. It is BBC values that drives Islam's hatred of the West. It is true that – today at least – the BBC is the tool of Islam. But only because they do not have any real respect for our enmity. We, however, are under no illusions. We recognise that, above all, it is BBC values that are Islam's greatest enemy. Ladies and gentlemen of the West, you must stop and think. You say that you believe in democracy. It is true, you can vote for your politicians. You can listen to them, watch them, pry into their lives. But only through the eyes of the media. You see and hear only what the media want you to. They feed you propaganda spiced in a dish of drama or documentary. They sift and spin their propaganda, weaving their views into your news. Yes, you are free to cast your vote, but it is the media who have moulded your choice. It is the media who are really in charge. So who are these people? Who are these mysterious, faceless, anonymous, unelected creatures? Where do they come from? What do they believe in? Where are they taking you? Ladies and gentlemen, you must wake up! You are all asleep on a speeding bus, you do not know the driver, and you have no idea where he is taking you. *Wake up! Stop the bus, get out, before it is too late!*"

A silence in which Abbat gathered his thoughts one last time. He knew he had almost said enough. Gazing around the audience, his manner was still intense, but no longer mocking or angry. He desperately needed them to understand.

"Ladies and gentlemen, this debate is about truth, and the truths that you will admit to. Ladies and gentlemen, I ask you, I *beg* you, to recognise and admit just this one truth. That your democracy has been stolen, and that you no longer know who is really in charge. Admit this, and unmask the thieves, before it is too late. Perhaps then you may find again the world's respect. Thank you."

The audience were rising in applause even as Abbat was still sitting down. He had told them something that they had desperately needed to hear, and they were grateful. Some of them felt a little embarrassed at the insult to their BBC hosts, but after all, it was the people's money that paid for all this, so was it not the people who were the real hosts? Outwardly, Catherine was as poised and unmoved as ever, but inwardly she felt a delicious delight. 'Two defeats for The Cause in the one day. Who would ever have imagined it? Life can be such a bitch, Mr. Richard Ferguson, can it not?'

In the still remoteness of his office, rage and anger roared loud in Bradshaw's ears. How could he? After all they had done for them? How could they ever trust sectarian bigots like these? Loud thoughts, strident thoughts, but not loud nor strident enough to drown out the ring of the little-used red mobile. 'Well, Mr. Abbat,' he thought, 'your words cannot be unsaid, but they can certainly be *regretted*.' His caller agreed, even if he was angrier, much angrier.

However, in the cabinet room of Number Ten, the reaction could hardly have been more different, the honourable members rising with the audience in implausible synchrony. Cheers and shouts of 'Hear-hear' echoed from a dozen throats. There was not one of them who had not been tormented and terrorised by these BBC bullies over the years. How sweet to see them finally on the receiving end! Their delight swelled and grew, merriment spreading like an impromptu end-of-term party, as if they were back at the boarding school that they had so long ago survived. David Blenheim shared their delight, but he had more to think about. Which, despite the clamour and distraction, he did, until Abbat's questions were over, and Connor was about to invite Westlands to speak. Blenheim was now only too aware that his heart was pumping, *hard*. There was so much at stake now, and no going back. 'Don't blow it, Andrew' he found himself wishing.

At the barricades, at the braziers where the black and fire did not hold sway, confusion now did. Confusion, doubt and anger. Mary Elizabeth Thornton, veteran of a thousand protests, stood transfixed by Abbat's words. Mary was forty seven years old, small, plump and romantic, and for as long as she could remember she had worshipped the BBC with all the force of her considerable passion. She was in good company, for so many at the barricades had so much in common, this community of the caring and the committed and the defenders of freedom. She had always lived for these moments of righteous excitement, the romance, the partying, and all, always, for a good cause. Right now, Mary Elizabeth was as shattered as her idol. It was hard to believe just how much had changed, and so fast. The debates had already caused her to question much of her comfortably-held beliefs. The idea that, somehow, their barricade protests had played some part in the rise of the fascists made her very uncomfortable. Not to mention that it had raised just a few, troubling, questions about the BBC. Stirred her very fine conspiracy antennae. But Abbat had exposed what, deep down, she was starting to fear. That her faith had been misplaced, and the BBC was not the paragon she had thought they were. Far from it, very far from it, and she was horrified. What had she done? What had she been doing all these years?

Back in the studio, Catherine Connor made her last introduction. "Ladies and Gentlemen, our last speaker, Mr. Andrew Westlands." As Westlands rose to his feet, she echoed Blenheim's wish: 'Don't blow it, Andrew.' Andrew, she feared, might do just that. He was definitely a little more worn, a little more stressed. The flowers seemed like an age away, but the very thought did bring her back an inward smile. 'Never underestimate this rogue ...' she thought, as Andrew started to speak. She might yet be right, for his delivery was as calm and confident as always.

"Ladies and gentlemen, People of the West, I don't know exactly what it is I believe in. But, for as long as I can remember, I've been getting told what I *should* believe in. By the grace of God, I've managed to retain enough sense to reject most of it. I am sure we are all in the same position. But, for the record, I'd like to run through just some of the stuff that I, at least, have been fed. If you're older, you've heard more: if you're younger, then you'll get some laughs.

We were threatened that:-

The earth will be consumed in a nuclear war; America will be a dust-bowl by nineteen eighty; oil will run out in the late eighties; overpopulation is the greatest danger to the human race; we must consume more in order to stimulate production; nuclear power is the greatest danger to the world.

Now the threats are:-

Islam will destroy the West; it is not food production that is the problem, but distribution; oil will run out in twenty-fifty; we must recycle to minimize production; the population of Europe is in terminal decline; nuclear power is the only real answer to our energy needs.

The nutritionists told us:-

Milk is good; butter is bad; margarine is good; wine is bad.

Now they tell us:-

Milk is bad; butter is good; margarine is bad; wine is good.

The sociologists lectured us that:-

Single parent families are good; gay is good; a criminal is a failure to himself; multiculturalism is good.

Now the gospel has changed to:-

Single parent families are bad; gays die young; a criminal is a failure of society; multiculturalism is bad.

The scientists and economists assured us that:-

The Earth is entering a new Ice Age; global trade is essential to relieve the poverty of the Third World; intelligence is a product of education, not genetics; travel broadens the mind, and spreads wealth; computers will soon have consciousness.

Now they're certain that:-

The Earth is undergoing Global Warming; global trade is cultural imperialism; intelligence is a product of genetics, not education; travel is economic imperialism and an environmental disaster; computers will never have consciousness.

"Ladies and Gentlemen, I don't know about you, but it certainly makes my head spin. Doesn't really do much to convince you, either, does it? Four legs good, two legs bad. Four legs good, two legs better. And back again. Nonsense, mostly, and mostly of the doom and gloom variety. The sky really is going to fall on our heads. Really. Ladies and gentlemen, I won't pretend to you that I'm always certain of what I believe in, but I do know one thing. *I don't believe them*. Even if I wanted to, I wouldn't know which *part* to believe in, and which *contradiction* to ignore? No, like you, I know better, and I don't believe them. There are times, ladies and gentlemen, when I wish I had Senator Gladwin's nerve. I'd love to be able to ask you to join me in the one great shout of 'We don't Believe You!' Hell, I really wish I did, because it just so needs saying. Aye, *we don't believe you, and we won't get fooled again.*

"Like you, however, I have not always had enough courage to tell them that. I admit that I've been intimidated. They have been too good at weaving their message into something moral, so that to disagree is to be somehow backward, small-minded, a little evil. Political correctness, slick and effective. Moral or immoral tyranny, take your pick. Until this week, ladies and gentlemen. After all this time, we've finally got our voice back. And we have heard rather a lot this week, have we not? We are ruled by fear and greed. We have no heroes any more and no values beyond money. Our laws are not fit for purpose, and we cannot protect our innocents. Environmentalism has gone mad, we are surrounded by junk science, and the media have corrupted our democracies. It's time to talk, freely, but the truth can be painful. No argument. Well, let's deal with it. Let's get ourselves out of these chains of contradictions. To start, let's keep it simple. Let's ask: what do we believe in?

"What do we believe in? Well, pretty much anything, I'd imagine. But the one belief we absolutely have to share is a belief in democracy, or we do not belong in the West. We need to believe that, ultimately, democracy is the least worst political system. That we need to take back control of our democracy from those who have corrupted it. We need to take our democracy from those who only let us vote on slogans, while they make the laws. Those who failed to protect our innocents, or to respect our wishes. Those who drove the social revolution in our society, but never, ever, consulted us! Anwar is basically right: our real enemy is not Islam, but those forces who corrupted our democracy. Islam's real enemy is not the West, but those very same forces.

"Ladies and gentlemen, we are all agreed that it is good to talk, again. I think it is also time to act, again. I think that it is time to get some sense of values back. To find some heroes. To protect our innocents. To scrap our laws and start again, with the laws that *we* want, not them. To make sure the public stays in control of the law-making process. *To let us vote on laws, not slogans.* To ensure that we know who is in control of our media so that we can filter their message accordingly. To demonstrate that we understand that democracy, like everything else, sometimes needs to be renewed.

"Ladies and gentlemen, let's start again. The West has made some horrendous mistakes in the last fifty years. Let's admit that, learn from it, and now show the real strength of West: integrity; adaptability; creativity." Another silence, this one punctuated by nods from the audience. Andrew resumed, his voice lower, deeper.

"Ladies and gentlemen, I know there is revolution on the streets. We can all see it and hear it. Bonfires and barricades and the siren calls of chaos. Fascists and flags and the seduction of the gun and the glamour of war. Ladies and gentlemen, resist it. Let us not let loose the dogs of war. Let us not march the hard march of the nailed boot. Let us not shout the hymns of hate. *Let us lower our voices, and whisper together. Let us whisper our song of change. Let us whisper together, and whisper up a wind. A wind from the West, and a wind of change, and of Renaissance. Yes, ladies and gentlemen it is time for a Renaissance of the West. Are you ready?*

'Oh my God....' Catherine thought. "I think they are. And so am I. But for what?' Andrew, however, was clearly not finished, and might just be about to tell them.

"Ladies and gentlemen, one last thing. I know that I've had a lot to say in the last few days. Now I'm going to put my life where my mouth is. If you want to be part of this Renaissance, then join me. Join those of us who believe it is time to talk, freely. Who believe that talk is good, but that action is *better*. Who believe that we must be able to vote for laws, not empty slogans. Ladies and gentlemen, tomorrow will see the launch of the Party of Western Renaissance. A party that will put the people back in power. A new political party that will respect the values of democracy. We need to do this, ladies and gentlemen, and before it is too late. Remember what the wise man once said. *All that has to happen for evil to succeed is for good men to do nothing.* Ladies and gentlemen, *do something*. Take a stand, do your duty, and join us. Join us in the Renaissance of the West. Thank you."

It was forked lightning in a clear blue sky, and its product was confusion and disbelief. Had Westlands really just said what he had said? A new political party? *The Party of Western Renaissance?* What madness was this? Surely he *could not be serious?* Of the billion plus audience, those in the studio were the first to reach a consensus. Initially, a few isolated ripples as the boldest were first to rise, hesitantly, to their feet: a swell of reinforcement from the less bold, but still brave: finally, a tide of people rising to their feet in approval. This was no madness. They knew he was serious, and so, they had decided, were they.

At the barricades, an animated Mary Elizabeth Thornton was suddenly busy. Grabbing one of the last stock of white sheets, she reached for paint and brush. Daubing frantically, she was the first of the veterans to finish. The first to unfurl over her brazier, in crisp red letters on white, '*Party of Western Renaissance*'. Captured by her web cam, the banner snapped out across the ether, onto the news, and into history. Within minutes, most of her community of braziers had joined her, realigned in synchrony like the dust on a magnet. And then they did the most unexpected thing. Picking up their small rucksacks of personal items, they formed into a little ragtag column, and began to walk away. Behind them, their braziers still burned, and their banners proclaimed their new message of 'Party of Western Renaissance'. All except one, for it proclaimed, perhaps with unconscious humour, 'Won't Get Fooled Again!'

A world away from the barriers, but in walking distance, the Cabinet Room of Number Ten had reacted to the studio scenes with rising horror. Soon followed by anger, and outrage. Democracy? Demagoguery was more like it. This audience was not people, but sheep. One stunt had been followed by another and now they had arrived at the final pièce de théâtre. It would never stand the cold grey light of dawn, and they all knew it. The right honourable member for Surbiton spoke for them all, when his strong, polished tones rose high over the babble of voices, compelling them to silence and to attention.

"Gentlemen, this idiot theatre, this foolish stunt, is the last and final product of the BBC. For once they have become one of the casualties, not that any of us here will shed any tears over it. Not one. Nor should any of us lose any sleep over this *Party of Western Renaissance*." An unveiled sneer. "The Party of Western Renaissance? *A new political party that will respect the values of democracy.* What schoolboy nonsense: a facile madness that will come to nothing. We are in the real world of politics, my friends, not in the theatre of dreams. What man of reputation would ever join with such naïve foolishness?"

Smiles of agreement, heads nodding in reassurance, suddenly broken by the clear tones of David Blenheim.

"Actually, gentlemen, I rather think I might. Perhaps some of you might care to join me?"

THIRTEEN

The chrome and steel and mirrors were as sterile as the people who drank there. A cocktail bar in an international hotel, it's name unimportant, nothing but a characterless way-station, independent of place and context. A bar that is too light and too bright for magic, or intuition, or even some modest insight. However, tonight is no ordinary night, and, in the wake of Westlands' words, the bar is now a hubbub of noise and emotion. But not everyone participates. Seated at the far left of the long black marble, Solomon N'Chenga gently nurses his ice and bubbles in a gossamer halo of silence. For once, there is enough *something* in the air for Solomon to be able to think just a little clearly.

'What propels you, Andrew, so far and so fast? Is it luck, or fate, or am I chasing the wrong man? Luck, just how could anyone even begin to measure this richness of luck, Andrew? Are you a luck *millionaire*? No, certainly more. A luck *billionaire*? More? No, Andrew, I need a more rational explanation. So just what - exactly - did you do, all those years ago? And, for that matter, what did Red Michael do?' And the corollary, obvious. 'And just what did Eldon Harker do, for that matter?' Solomon continues to think, or, more accurately, *to muse*, while his right hand swirls the bubbles and ice in an unconscious incantation. It is some ten minutes before the tap on his shoulder, and the swirling comes to an end. Ten fruitful minutes. But after thought, action must always follow. His contact is tall, and lean, and stamped with the mark of the hunter. Eager for action. Soon the dark Rome night swallows them, talking as they walked.

Less than a mile away, and the debates' words have shaken Ahmed Ali Khan to his very core, threatening to shatter all faith in his divine mission. What if – as Abbat said – it was not really the West that was the enemy, but the BBC elite? What if Westlands succeeded, somehow, in bringing Britain back away from its abomination, back into some kind of normal, wholesome existence? Would the rest of Europe then follow? Would even the Great Satan follow, too? Why strike at the West, just when it was beginning to change? Ahmed Ali Khan's head pounded with questions, questions, questions, but no answers. He hardly heard any of the stupid questions that followed Andrew's startling announcement, barely registered the fiery exchanges between Westlands and the foolish, traitorous American. But, mercifully, the infidel woman drew him back to the debate. The *unattainable* infidel woman, with the sinful, irresistible beauty. The infidel woman who summed up so much of what he despised, and hated, and yet wanted so very badly.

Nine hundred miles away, Catherine Connor's clear, confident tones signaled the end of the debate.

"Ladies and gentlemen, the motion for the fifth debate is:

I charge the West with fear, with being too frightened to look deeper than the surface of their lives.

Thank you, ladies and gentlemen. We look forward to seeing you all again tomorrow. It's time to talk freely."

Fifteen minutes later, Catherine Connor had just reached make-up and chimed her mobile back into life. Somehow, she was not surprised to get the text from Andrew. The message was short, and sweet, and it immediately raised all the hairs on the back of her long and graceful neck.

"*Be careful, Catherine. The BBC is no longer safe for you. Do not trust anyone. Sorry to alarm you, but necessary. Will see you ASAP. X Andrew.*"

Catherine stared at the message for two long minutes before

298

she came to a conclusion. 'Men,' she thought 'always assuming that women are fragile. Well, Andrew, you've certainly got a surprise coming.' And she smiled to herself, pleased with her reflex bravado. Pleased, but not fooled, as her actions soon made very clear.

Half an hour later, as she was driven out through the dimming braziers, Catherine knew she had used the last of her favours with the gentlemen of BBC security. Well, not quite, she was too pretty for that; for a woman like her, there would always be favours. However, as she glanced nervously down at the bag that lay at her feet, Catherine knew that, for now at least, her favours bank was empty. She just hoped she had done the right thing. And she gazed out the side window, into the BBC night, at the braziers and the barricades, so familiar, and yet so alien, so unreal. Could all this really be real? What was the eternal cycle of the Hindus? Samsara, moksha, samadhi. Illusion, awakening, bliss. Then illusion again. Real? The big car was warm, but, despite herself, Catherine shivered.

Leather and brass and old wood: comfortable, familiar surroundings framing unfamiliar faces. The Sanctuary – where else could they go for a meeting such as this? Such as this! Chamberlain was only too aware that his clients were not people who thought much of national boundaries. No, they were much too powerful to be so tightly bound He also knew - only too well - that they enjoyed a challenge, the noise and heat and smoke of battle. But this? This was the stuff of comedy. 'Have you heard the one about the Englishman, the Frenchman, the Italian and the German?' The whimsical thought raised Chamberlain's spirits a little. Well, he was always game for laugh.

"Gentlemen ..." he began.

The introductions were not really necessary, but Chamberlain went through the formalities anyway. It was probably the strangest group that The Sanctuary had ever hosted. Jacques Ducrocq, small, dark, plump and late fifties. French, razor sharp and quick to let you know. Berndt Kessel, dark Bavarian features in a tall, spare frame. Middle to late forties, academic, slow of speech but deep and quick of thought. Paolo Canera, blonde, blue-eyed Milanese: medium height and restless, relentless mind. Thankfully, there was no need for interpreters, as they all spoke perfect English. Unusually for a French politician, Ducrocq was quite happy to admit to the fact. After all, as he would say, I am Norman. And are the English not just the illegitimate children of Normans?

Completing Chamberlain's full hand of clients were David Blenheim and Andrew Westlands. All five were dressed formally, suits and ties ensuring no disrespect was given nor taken. The cool air of the Sanctuary crackled: expectancy woven tight with excitement and a thin thread of weariness. 'Yes,' thought Chamberlain. 'I have given my clients their meeting. But their goal, surely, is not attainable? The key people are here, that is true. But the differences are too great, their divisions surely too wide. What foolishness did they all now indulge?' David Blenheim was the first to break the silence. His voice was bold and clear, and his words immediately engaging.

"Only a fool, gentlemen, tries to build trust from silicon and video. That is why we are here today, as men. To build trust: trust in each other. If we can but trust each other, then, together, the Party of Western Renaissance can sweep Europe. Divided, we are doomed to isolation and failure. And failure, my friends, is not an option. As Andrew has said: the choice is Renaissance or Revolution. All of us are here today because we have chosen Renaissance."

It was, thought Chamberlain in hindsight, a master class in negotiation. On the face of it, agreement should not have been possible. There was no real Party of Western Renaissance, even in

Britain, much less in Europe. No constitution, no rules. Perhaps that was what made agreement possible, the unblemished potential of the blank canvas? Certainly a factor. And desire, passion: they were all clearly, passionately, committed to their Renaissance. And there was no issue of leadership. By whatever twist of luck or fate, Westlands' leadership was beyond question. Westlands himself, Blenheim, Ducrocq, Panera: their words had certainly all contributed to their agreement. But it was Kessel, the almost taciturn Kessel, who had, early on, set them on the right track, when he had said:-

"Gentlemen, we are not here to agree on policies. I think all our peoples have had quite enough of committees and policies. We are here to agree on the mechanics of our democracies, nothing more, nothing less. To ensure that, once again, our people get to make their own policies, their own laws. And continue to do so. Let us define the framework for that democracy. And what will our people do with their democracy? Whatever they choose. And in our different countries, be sure that they will not all choose the same. For me, gentlemen, I think that is no problem. As you might say, Jacques: Vive la Difference!"

'Yes, Kessel set them on the right track.' thought Chamberlain, surveying the now-empty wood and brass and leather. 'In any case, it would appear they have done the impossible. What was the joke again? *Have you heard the one about the Englishman, the Frenchman, the Italian and the German? No, what about them? They **agreed**.* Actually, it was funny. And some of his clients might just appreciate the joke. Especially since they had got what they wanted.'

In the vast and dimly-lit office, the large projection clock showed five past twelve, London time. Peter Bradshaw, lifted from the gloom by the twin pools of his art-deco desk-lamps, is still frozen in quandary. It had been worse than he had anticipated, and now he had difficult decisions to make.

Richard Ferguson had arrived half an hour earlier, his black shirt and red tie somehow more prominent, more aggressive than before. Not the vastness of Bradshaw's office, nor, indeed, the status of Bradshaw himself, did anything to dim either his arrogance or his fury. As always, Ferguson got straight to it.

"I've spoken to my people, Peter, and they are not happy. Not happy at all. We cannot unsay what Abbat has said. But there must be consequences. As a start, we expect that he will be removed from the programme. As a start. After that, removed from the limelight, we will have time and space to consider a more complete course of action. Can I take it that we are in agreement, Peter?"

The arrogance. The casual assumption of power. The disrespect for his position. No, nothing unexpected, then. But not this time. This time, it simply could not be done and Bradshaw realised - and not to his surprise - that he was delighted. It was time. His time: his turn.

"Richard, you must realise that that is simply not possible. These debates have the focus of the world. They have that focus because - how shall I put it? - it's time to talk, freely? It's working, Richard. Of course, I regret the offence that is caused, but, in the long run, it is a price worth paying. In any case, any attempt to restrict what is said is going to blow up in our faces. All our faces. It will not serve your purpose. I am afraid that the BBC, and The Cause, will have to take our medicine just like everyone else."

There, it was said, and it was out, and Bradshaw felt a wave of relief. Not so bad, after all. Overdue, but at least he had done it, finally. However, Ferguson met the speech with silence. A continuing silence. And the longer the silence lasted, the more Bradshaw's relief evaporated into the gloom. By the time Ferguson spoke, Bradshaw had more than started to regret his premature relaxation. But not his words, not yet. Ferguson's words, however were positively dripping with menace.

"Please do not make too many assumptions, Director General. It is true that many things have changed in this last week. Many, many things. You think, perhaps, that The Cause is not what it was a week ago. In that, you are indeed correct. It is not. It is now something quite different indeed. The wheels of history are now turning very fast indeed, Director General. The Cause is dead. Long live the British People's Party!"

A pause. A long, slow smile from Ferguson that was nothing but a display of teeth. Bradshaw, shocked at the bluntness of the words, waited for the continuation. He had only seconds to wait, as Ferguson leaned over the great desk and hissed his next words straight into Bradshaw's face.

"Please do not think, Director General, please do not *dream* that The Cause has been at all diminished. Please understand just who is driving those wheels. The Cause is now something greater. Something more powerful still. Not something for you to offend, Peter, old friend. Not at all."

His meaning was clear, and the threat clearer. Chilled though he was, Peter Bradshaw was still bolstered by reality. Yes, reality. In real life, there was no way for the BBC to remove Abbat, much less anyone on the debates. What they had said, they had said. The Cause, or the People's Party, or whatever, would just have to recognise that reality. He came back at Ferguson, just as bluntly.

"I am sorry, Richard, but what you ask is simply not possible. You must recognise realities, like it or not!"

"And do you expect me to take back that message to my colleagues, Director General? Not possible? These are the people who now command our streets. Who are bound for the highest power. Do not be foolish enough to underestimate my colleagues, Director General. Do not be fooled by dreadlocks and drama. Mr. Daniel D is not someone to be crossed lightly. He does not recognise your rules nor your realities. You talk to me of realities, Peter? It is you who should recognise the realities. The reality of power, for a start. Real power."

"The reality of power, Richard? And what might that be?" shot back Bradshaw, openly angry now. Was not the power of the BBC *real*?

"The reality of power, Peter? *Power grows from the barrel of a gun*. Believe it. It always has. Please remove Abbat from the debates. Or some of my colleagues might just do it for you. Good-night, Director General."

And he was gone, and Bradshaw was left with his quandaries. It took time. But Bradshaw remembered the man he had been, many compromises ago. The man he still was, in some imperfect way. He was still a man who recognised duty, and responsibility. Would Ferguson cool down? Would his so-called colleagues? *Do things usually cool down in a furnace?* No. But to do nothing was to be complicit in this. Well, OK, there was no middle way now. *The centre cannot hold. What dread beast?* Time to decide. And he knew that he already had, for he had not fallen all the way, not yet. Time to make the call. And he did, and he spoke to his good friend in the Metropolitan Police. It was only after he had put the phone down that he realised the assumption that he had made. Too late?

Midnight, Santa Eularia, Ibiza

The crash of the sea and the smell of the salt and the cool of the night breeze helped speed Robert Alexander in his race against time. The lounge of his fourth floor apartment is an isolated brick of light in the dark December night. Robert himself, wrapped in a thick grey sea-wool jersey, is hunched at his desk, eyes fixed on a large flat-screen monitor. Despite his evident concentration, Robert Alexander is acutely conscious of the time: he now had only thirty four hours left, maximum. Realistically, it was much less than that, for what good could a virus solution be, if it arrived too late for anyone to receive it? Pressure? No pressure: he had been here before, many times, and he knew the secret. Do not be rushed. Be careful in your preparations. Start slowly, move in the right direction, and - always - the speed will come, inevitably. Without doubt, this was his greatest challenge yet, and he had stuck to his method religiously. Already he was beginning to see the first signs of his preparations bearing fruit. Not tangible enough to call progress, real progress, more a sense that this puzzle was created to be solved. Yes, that was it. There was a solution and it could be found. That meant that he, Robert Alexander Scott, had to be a contender. Pressure? No pressure, only opportunity.

London: One Minute to Midnight, December the Twenty Third

Mary Elizabeth Thornton and all the rest of the amateurs were long gone from the fiery ring that surrounded the BBC. Their places had been filled - more than filled - by hundreds of eager foot-soldiers of the British People's Party. To their disappointment, little action marked their arrival, save that of cheering and flag-waving and the occasional fight in the queue for 'rations'. 'Rations', despite being limited in variety, were of a surprisingly high quality, especially the vegetarian ones. In honour, no doubt, of their inspirational leader. Still, to those who craved action, it was a little disappointing.

In the barricades that encircled the urban Muslims, there was no such disappointment. Birmingham was typical. In the streets that surrounded the central mosque, night had turned to fiery day as whole streets burned. The air was rent by screams of anger, and pain, and the slap of the high velocity rifle. Dead and injured littered the streets, as BPP and Islamists fought corner by corner, barricade by improvised barricade. Striking a blow that was at least as much psychological as military, the BPP used a pack of attack dogs - a mixture of thirty or so Rottweilers, Dobermans and Bull Terriers - to dislodge, in stark terror, some Islamists who had been foolish enough to dig-in on the corner of Hill street and Bryant street. Dogs: unclean, abominations! Attack dogs?! There had to be a response, a psychological response, and it was swift, and brutal. A cheering group of masked Islamists draped the headless corpse of an unnamed BPP unfortunate above the entrance to the Lowell Road. The BPP counter -attack was also swift, and especially savage, as a still living Islamist jihadi was fed to the slavering pack of attack dogs. They tore him limb from limb, ripping open his entrails and eating him, alive, even as he screamed in his last futile agonies. Worse still, the whole terrible scene was filmed and broadcast live, with powerful projectors beaming high definition images onto the walls of the frontline tenements. The whole grim and dreadful tableau was, in turn, broadcast and re-broadcast worldwide. The nightmare images were perhaps the last straw, the high water mark of the unbridled violence. For, ten minutes later, and before another spiral in the horror, the first rumble of the tanks was heard.

The British Challenger 2 tank is seventy tons of gun, machine guns, steel and reactive armour. It is not something to be stopped by dog nor rifle nor building nor anything less than a shaped charge projectile of perfect fabrication and application. The first Challenger was greeted - by both sides - with mute and staring disbelief. The second Challenger was greeted with the first symptoms of what second world war generals had long ago termed 'tank fright'. The knowledge that the rampaging beast that approached was several hundred times your weight, was invulnerable to anything you possessed, and could crush everything in its path faster than you could run. A tank in full charge is a truly terrifying sight, an awesome juggernaut of noise and metal and menace. Even before it opened fire. After which, the gates of hell beckoned. It was a long time since the days of blitzkrieg, but 'tank fright' proved to be just as real as ever it had been. Inside fifteen minutes, tanks patrolled the now-empty streets in and around the Birmingham ghetto, occasionally flattening barricades on an apparent whim. BPP and Islamists melted away into the night, licking their wounds and venting their frustrations on the weak, the foolish, and the defenceless.

It was just after two a.m. when the first rumours were heard. A Challenger 2 had gone missing, so they said. It was around half an hour later that the first internet pictures appeared. A Challenger 2, rather expertly daubed in the fire and lightning, its top hatch thrust back and open. Standing tall from the hatch was a familiar figure, and the dreadlocks streamed in the wake of the wind and the night. The BPP had just moved ahead - way ahead - in the urban arms race. People waited for the official denials, but they never came. Unofficially, the story was that a tank had got trapped, its crew, unwilling to kill civilians, forced to surrender their monster. But few believed it. Trapped? Trapped by what? What could hope to trap one of those monsters? No, they knew the real reason. Most people only whispered it. Mutiny. God Forbid. Mutiny. Whose side was the army now on?

By three a.m. there were rumours of a second tank missing. And that it had to be mutiny. Who else but the crew could control one of these beasts? Who else but the crew would know how to disable the GPS tracking that protected the creatures from such a change of ownership? By four a.m. there were no more Challengers on the streets of Birmingham. It was, simply, too risky. The streets, however, remained quiet. The BPP had withdrawn back to their own lines, and were busy rebuilding their barricades, or catching some rest. The attack dogs had been returned to their meshed pens, where untiring web-cams broadcast endless images of their snarling abomination. Clearly, there was a lull in the fighting, but only the better to fight tomorrow.

Despite the chilling scenes, and the many, harrowing, deaths of the faithful, Sheikh Mohammed Omar Al Nasran was overjoyed, quietly triumphant. It was almost as if he dwelt in a different, parallel, universe. But no, Sheikh Nasran was very much here, and now. He had to be. Sheikh Nasran had the honour to be the most senior Al Quaeda commander in Britain, and he was a very focused man, indeed. Casualties, however, were of no account to him: no more than the necessary currency of war, never mind of jihad. Blood was nothing more than the price of victory. Of no concern whatever, and certainly no cause for emotion. But the news, the news that he had just heard, that was cause for emotion indeed. Emotion, and thanksgiving, and prayers to Allah the most merciful. For now he knew, for certain, of the great blows that were to be struck. And that they would be a part of it, and also in dealing - publicly ! - with the apostate, the renegade, Islam's traitor-in-chief. Tomorrow - no, it was no longer tomorrow, but today, tonight! Yes, tonight, the world will see what price is to be paid for disrespect, and treachery. *It's time to talk, freely?* No, not always, infidels.

Mayfair, London: Two a.m.

The Talisker 25 has just started to cast his healing spell on an exhausted, but adrenalin-soaked, Andrew Westlands. Exhausted, truly exhausted, but as yet no chance of sleep. But, like Robert Alexander Scott, Andrew was a man who had faith in his process. A glass or two of the island amber and the adrenalin would give way to the sleep that his body so badly craved. But his mind, over-stimulated, could not stop flashing up thoughts and scenes and images of his day. To calm them, smooth them, order them, Andrew tried to review his day systematically, objectively. Tried to replay it, as if watching some movie in which strode this

308

character of Andrew Daniel Westlands. What a day had it been? How could he make sense of it, never mind assimilate it? Eighteen hours ago he had awakened, rested, smiling with thoughts of Catherine, and romance. Since then a whirlwind had swept him into Chamberlain, Omnibox, the debate and, finally, *President of the Party of Western Renaissance*. What kind of day was that? Unbelievable, incredible, the stuff of comic books. President of the Party of Western Renaissance: the thought was dizzying, narcotic, stirring the yet unslaked thirst for power that, deep down, all men have. Careful, Andrew, he warned. *Those whom the Gods would destroy they first drive mad with pride.* Careful. Stay grounded. You need to stay grounded, now of all times. You need....

And it came to him: a mate. Yes, a mate. Not a romance, but its potential result. Yes: however high the fates might propel a man, nothing grounded him quite like a mate. A mate: his mate: Catherine? What would it be like waking up to the same woman every day again? Thinking of it, picturing Catherine, where exactly was his problem? His problem? His age for one. His other marriages, for another. Still, there might just be that aphrodisiac of power that they all talk about. Really? And what power do you actually have, Andrew? Still he had a chance: she was interested, definitely. *He made her laugh*. And they were booked for coffee, tomorrow, at ten. Sure he had a chance, but he had to be positive: faint heart never won fair lady. Anyway, was he not always positive? His father, long dead, had put it better than anyone:-

To be negative is to have felt the pain of events that never happened. To be positive is to have taken pleasure from events that were never more than a dream.

Yes, he'd be positive, as always. And he'd enjoy the romance. Hell, it was for a woman to think of choosing a mate. Men needed to keep things simpler... And Andrew smiled, and took a larger sip of the Talisker. Yes, keep it simple, Andrew. Fate will do the rest.

And, with that thought, Andrew began to relax. As he relaxed, he slowed, and his fatigue overtook him, swiftly. At first his sleep was deep, and restful, but then it gave way to the dreams. In counterpoint to his day, they were vivid, startling, and very real indeed. It would be a pity when he woke up, in the morning, and remembered that not all dreams come true. But meanwhile, in his sleep, Andrew smiled.

Santa Eularia, Ibiza: Three a.m.

Standing at the far right corner of the sea-balcony, the chill wind tore at the rough grey of Robert's jersey and he clutched the warm coffee mug tightly between his cupped hands. Fifty feet down and a hundred feet out, the liquid blackness of the unseen sea thundered rhythmically up the beach. Rhythm, ebb and flow, the pulse of creation. Now, especially now, he had to respect his own creative rhythm. Now was the time to digest, to assimilate, to impose order before the next explosion of ideas. Too much order: no creation. Too much creation: only chaos. And he was so very close. But he had time to choose only one path. It must be right, first time. He must be sure of where he was, before he chose that path. And, as he considered the last few hours, there was so much still to understand.

Robert Alexander was using, naturally enough, a UNOS computer. Thankfully, you did not need to be running U-Sys in order to create U-Sys. Not that such a paradox would be in the least surprising, given the events of these last few days. He did have a U-Sys computer - or was it not U-Heat! - waiting in the corner. A waiting test-bed, which was all that it was fit for. Anyway, it was now some seven hours since he had completed the download, opened the source code with the U-Soft assembler, and verified that it did, indeed, compile into the U-Sys kernel. As had almost everyone else, no doubt. But then Robert Alexander did something quite different to - he supposed - everyone else. He opened the source with his own assembler. It was an unknown quirk of history that Robert Alexander had almost sold his assembler to the U-Soft start-up, all those years ago. At the last minute he had lost out: the winning assembler was considered marginally superior because it included 'Optimising Features'. To the layman, 'Optimising Features' meant that the U-Soft assembler was able to remove bits of code that were defined, but never used. Which it did: Robert could not deny that the U-Soft assembler - as it came to be - produced code that was a little smaller than his own. To Robert Alexander, however, 'Optimising Features' meant interference. It was his source code, not the compiler's. *What I have written, I have written.* Anyway the rest was history, except that Robert, stubbornly, continued to use his own assembler. He just could not trust a compiler that interfered with his code. He still used his own assembler, up to and including last night. That was why, just under seven hours ago, he was astonished - shattered! - to discover that his assembler refused to compile the U-Sys source. It was inexplicable, baffling, and immediately raised waves of emotion in a mind that absolutely had to stay cool. But Robert calmed the waves, and stayed cool. First of all, working carefully, methodically, he determined that the problem was that the U-Sys source included a little-used format of comment. In layman's terms, comments had to be specially marked to indicate to the assembler/compiler that 'this text is only to remind me how this works'. In this case, the marking of the U-Sys comments was subtly different. Of course, Robert could have removed the comments, but that meant changing the source, and any change, at this stage, was simply not acceptable. He had to be able to compare - precisely - the output of the two compilers. So Robert then had to redress

311

the situation by modifying his own assembler. This was not so simple a task as it was many years since he had worked on the program, and it proved to be many archives before he could locate its source. All in all, it took over four hours to bring it all together, and then implement the changes. Four precious hours! And then, finally, he was able to compile the U-Sys source, and check.

And compile it again. And check, again. And compile again. And check, again. But there was no error, and no doubt. His assembler produced a kernel that was seven per cent smaller than U-Soft's! Never, ever, had his assembler produced smaller code! It was theoretically possible, of course - given certain strange behaviours - but he had never, ever seen it. Typically, he would expect his code to be one or two per cent bigger, although it depended entirely on the efficiency of the source code. But smaller?! Seven per cent smaller! At a practical level, impossible. But true. After that he had made his first, brief visit to the balcony. That was now two hours and many discoveries ago. So here he now was, on his wind-swept balcony, trying to digest it all. The wind was cutting through his tired grey wool, and the coffee was cold, but Robert started to feel a warm inward glow. Anticipation, or what? Yet there was still so much to do, and so little time left. Thankfully, the sea and the coffee and the salt air had accomplished their task: he knew what his next step had to be. He also knew that, above all else, he had to stay focused on the puzzle, not the prize. There would time enough to dream of prizes, soon enough.

Ahmed Ali Khan, faced with the certain knowledge of his imminent death, was consumed by an overwhelming, voracious hunger for life. Time for dreams? There was not time enough for anything, much less dreams. There was so, so much he wanted to do and see and experience. He wanted to eat life whole, gorge himself on all the experiences he now knew that he would never have. He was not ready to die! And they had promised him a wife, a good Muslim wife to comfort him and help him though his last hours. But no message had come - this virus that is our saviour, is also our curse, Insh'Allah - and no wife to comfort him. No comfort and no soft kisses and no prospect of immortality in this life. His adrenalin and testosterone and all of his chemical messengers positively screamed for life, and flight, and a woman, a mate. He wanted to pace the Rome streets, to wander the ancient city, to experience anything and everything that came. But, now, so close to his duty, he could not. He *dare* not. Who knows what could happen to him in such a foolishness? No, he could not, he must fulfil his sacred mission. To be awake, even here, in this infidel room, was that still not life, and sweet, too? Then that meant that sleep was now his enemy, robbing him of his last sweet morsels of experience. But he had to sleep, for he had so much still to do, and would need all of his faculties, his intelligence, his skills. He dared not be too tired. And what if the Jihad Code, like the promised wife, did not arrive? How would it get through the virus? Fool! Was it not *our* virus? Would we not have made sure of a way for this, the key to our final victory? No, the Jihad Code would come, and his life would end, soon, even if it was to be glorious end. Insh'allah.

A brief pause in his thoughts, a rueful reflection.

As always, the elders had been right. They had warned him that, come the time, he would be sorely tested. That he would not see that he was really *entering* life, not *leaving* it. Entering Eternal Life. They had warned him that he might need the help that they had given him. The sleeping pills, strong and irresistible. Take them, they said, take them and get the rest you will so sorely need. Take them and save yourself from temptation. 'Yes, temptation. To wander out into the Rome night, and away, and into life ...'

And then, just at the moment of his greatest temptation,

Ahmed Ali Khan knew the full glory of Allah's mercy. He realised that he had already passed his test. He had already conquered his temptations. It was clear. Even if he were to wander into the Rome night, and away, did he imagine that they would not find him? Did he imagine that they would not hunt him down? Did he imagine that they would let all the lives they had sacrificed go to waste, and that there would be no reckoning and no punishment? No, Ahmed Ali Khan understood, clearly and finally, that he was already dead. It was for him now only to choose the manner of his death. To ensure the full measure of his worth; to earn his eternal salvation; to receive his heavenly reward. Yes, Allah was Most Merciful. Martyrdom was so much easier to bear, when you were already dead.

Calmer now, Ahmed went into the bathroom and located the dark glass bottle of sleeping pills that lay in the bottom compartment of his toilet bag. A brief struggle with the lid, and Ahmed had two of the large brown capsules in the palm of his left hand. He strode straight to the mini-bar, lifted the nearest can - Fanta, or some such cheerful name - and popped it open. A quick swallow of the sugar, a gulp of the pills, more sugar, and it was done. The pills were strong, and within ten minutes he was sleeping. It was some three hours before the dreams started. Terrible, terrible dreams. Agony, and death, and blood, blood, blood. Ahmed knew these dreams, and knew that they are only sent to strengthen him, and stiffen his resolve. Beyond the restless figure in the great baroque bed, in the still Roman night, the winter sun had already started to think about rising. When it did, it would be Christmas Eve. Did any children still expect presents?

FOURTEEN

Six a.m. Santa Eularia, Ibiza. The long balcony, facing south-east, is bathed in the dawn rays of the winter Mediterranean sun. In the centre of the balcony is a long stone bench, its crude lines softened by faded vines of still-plump grapes. The view from the balcony is of a benign blue sea, barely restless enough to throw occasional waves up the shore. Robert Alexander Scott is draped on the hard and unyielding bench: unkempt, unshaven, oblivious to the light or the beauty or the discomfort of the cold stone. Robert is gripped by shock, and disbelief, and a sense of utter unreality. Even - how ridiculous was this? - anxiety. Yes, what if he had made a terrible mistake? But, rationally, he knew that he had not. Anything but! He had done it! He had cracked the virus: fame, fortune and glory would all be his! Rationally, intellectually, Robert knew it was true, but emotionally he just could not grasp it. He simply could not connect with the fact. But, at a practical level he knew he had to act. He must claim his reward, now - surely he was the first? - before anyone else cracked it too. He knew he would have to prove what he had done. Fine, no problem. But would the legendary U-Soft accept his proof? Would they play fair with him? For one hundred million dollars? Knowing what he now knew of the virus, surely the thought was ridiculous? Who and what was U-Soft, anyway? How could he trust U-Soft at all? Much less for - and he said it out loud - "One hundred million dollars"?

So there it was: another problem to be solved. Another layer to peel from the onion. Such perfect timing: a welcome jolt back to the real world. Solve this problem, this small problem, and the glory and the fame and the endless money would be his. Just one more problem before he became The Man Who Killed the Virus.

Perhaps. Five minutes later, Robert Alexander made the first of his two phone calls.

U-Soft European Headquarters, London: Five Fifteen a.m.
Christmas Eve

It was a cubicle. To say anything more about it would be to deny its essential nature. A cubicle is a cubicle is - in this case - Christine's cubicle. Christine was a slightly plump, blue-eyes, auburn haired woman of twenty six. She would never be beautiful, but would probably always be attractive. She was also sweet-natured, and it shone through every aspect of her being, and most especially in her voice. It was sheer chance that had placed her on one of the U-Soft validation lines: the special lines that U-Soft had set up to vet the freaks and nuts whom they knew would rush to claim the one hundred million dollars. They could not have chosen a better voice, a kinder nature, to somehow sweeten the news of their almost-inevitable failure. In fact, there had been far fewer claimants than U-Soft had anticipated, and this was only Christine's third call.

"U-Soft Validation; Christine here. Who am I speaking to?"

"Robert." A careful one. No problem.

"OK, Robert. Now, do you wish to report a solution to the virus?"

"Yes, Christine." To be polite, he used her name. Like everyone else, Robert had instinctively softened in response to Christine's tone.

"OK, Robert. Now, have you downloaded and run our U-Validate software? Do you have it running right now?"

"Yes, I do, Christine."

"Great, Robert. Now, can you see a large blue dialogue box with a number in it?"

"Yes, Christine. The number is eight-five-three-two."

316

"OK, that's fine, Robert. Can I just ask you to repeat that number?"

"The number is eight-five-three-two."

The procedure was now simple, but, as with everything U-Soft, clever. To save themselves from being inundated with false claims, U-Soft had written the U-Validate software. The claimant had to run the software. When he did so, it generated a number. That number told a U-Soft operator - in this case, Christine - whether or not the claimant was really running U-Sys, what date the computer was set to, and what kind of power the computer possessed. In this case, when Christine entered eight-five-three-two into HER validate program, it came back with 'U-Sys valid. Seed seven-five-three-zero-one. Please click to start timer.' So far, so good. Christine now had to read the numbers out to the claimant, get him to enter them into his computer. She would then count to three and they were both to click their computers in rough synchrony.

"OK, Robert. Now, I am going to ask you to please type in some numbers, but not to click your mouse. OK?"

"OK, Christine."

"OK, Robert. The numbers are: seven-five-three-zero-one."

"OK, Christine, they're in."

"Now, Robert, please type them again, and then tell me what you see. I repeat: the numbers are seven-five-three-zero-one."

"They're in, Christine. I now see a message which says 'click to start'."

"OK, Robert. Please do not click just yet. After a count of three, I am going to ask you to click your mouse. After you do, your computer will try to generate a ten digit number for you to give back to me. The number will appear on your screen digit by digit. Be patient, it may take several minutes for the first digit to appear. You must read out the digits to me as soon as they appear. Is that clear, Robert."

"Yes, Christine. I will read out the digits as they come. I'm ready." This was the point at which her other callers had fallen apart. Lost patience before the first digit appeared, as she had been told to expect. It was a clever test, indeed. The U-Validate software contained some very complex equations. When a number was entered, these equations would start to generate a unique, ten-digit answer. If the computer were free of the virus, then it would come back with the answer fairly quickly. Otherwise, with computers running so achingly slowly, the poor claimants would have to wait for hours. Which neither of her two previous clients had done, choosing instead to guess the wrong answer. Maybe Robert would prove to be more patient. In any case, as he called out his digits, she had to enter the same digits on her own computer. On the tenth digit, she would see a 'PASS' or 'FAIL' message. She would LOVE to get that far, even just once.

"OK, Robert. Three-two-one-click."

"Eight-nine-four-seven-seven-three-one-zero-six-two."

Oh, my God. Even with her typing speed, she could hardly keep up, was not sure she had got them all correct, but, there it was, indisputable: 'PASS' Christine felt faint, light-headed, dizzy, speechless. But she knew that she was being recorded - big time - and could not screw this one up. Her voice may have faltered a bit, but it held up.

"Very good, Robert. I am pleased to inform you that your answer is good. You have passed the first stage of claim validation. Please hold the line while I connect you with someone more senior." Then, unable to resist it, she added. 'Good luck, Robert!"

In fact, and unknown to Christine, but her computer had automatically sent a message up the food chain the moment she had entered the tenth digit. Far up the food chain, and it was only a delay of a few seconds before Robert heard the brusque tones of Carl Sorensen, Head of Research and Development, U-Soft Corporation.

318

"Good afternoon, Robert. My name is Carl Sorensen, and I am Head of R&D at the U-Soft Corporation. I understand that you have passed the first stage of our validation process. I have some brief questions for you. You are, no doubt, a highly intelligent man, and will appreciate the need to keep your answers as precise and as succinct as possible. OK?"

"OK."

"Do you work on your own or are you part of a team?"

"I work alone."

"Have you modified the U-Sys source code in order to effect a solution?"

"Yes."

"If you were to upload your source code to me, now, would the U-Sys assembler, without any other changes, compile this source into a virus-free kernel?"

"Yes."

"In your considered Judgement, would the nature of your fix be clear to us?"

"Yes."

"What scale of side-effects is your fix is likely to cause?"

"None."

"None? *None?* A bold statement, Robert. OK, I think we now need to see you and your source code. Where are you, right now?"

"Santa Eularia, the island of Ibiza."

"Please give me your full address, including post-code. We will send a helicopter and then fly you onwards to London from the mainland."

"Actually, Carl, my address will be of no use to you, because I will not be there. Here are the details of where and when I will be ready..." And he told him. If Carl Sorensen was surprised, he gave no sign of it, but confirmed that the helicopter would be there.

Christmas Eve should have been an early Christmas for connoisseurs of journalese. The debates, the launch of the PWR, the continuing virus, the threat of civil war, the attacks on the taboos of Western science: too many to list. That was, no doubt, the problem: who on earth could distil all that down into one short headline? Still, they tried.

The Times led with 'PWR SEEKS POWER AMIDST BPP SAVAGERY'. Beneath the headline was two pictures: on the left, Westlands in full flow: on the right, a graphic close up of the BPP attack dogs. The Telegraph had 'BLENHEIM AND WESTLANDS UNITE TO SEEK RENAISSANCE', but a smaller headline half way down the page asked 'PWR OR BPP: THE ONLY CHOICE?' The Independent had the dramatic 'PWR FOR RENAISSANCE: BPP FOR REVOLUTION'. Below the headline were two contrasting images. On the left was an animated Westlands, Catherine Connor neatly framed in the background. On the right, standing in the turret of the Challenger 2, Mr Daniel D, dreadlocks streaming: for all the world the very image of the pagan warrior charging into battle. The Sun struggled to maintain its signature theme with 'PWR : 0 BPP : 0 (PLAY JUST STARTED)'. On page four, however, it was more inspired, with a large image of Darwin to the left of 'THE ROMANTIC GENE (IUS)? ' The Express went for maximum impact, 'LET LOOSE THE DOGS OF WAR!' accompanying a graphic image of the BPP attack dogs in full flight. The Mirror, taking an uncharacteristic position, asserted 'STREETS IN FLAMES AS WEST SEEKS RENAISSANCE'. In the rest of the world, the headlines, unsurprisingly, echoed the same themes. The Washington Post was uninspired, with 'EUROPE: RENAISSANCE OR REVOLUTION'. The Delhi Times had 'WEST IN CHAOS AS TABOOS SHATTERED'. In Iran, the headlines thundered 'INFIDEL ABOMINATION'. Their image of the BPP attack dogs, and the unfortunate, screaming jihadi, left nothing to the imagination.

In any case, inspired or otherwise, the headline-writers would soon get plenty of opportunity to redeem themselves, for this Christmas Eve was going to be one of those days.

Mayfair, London: Eight a.m. Christmas Eve

It was two hours since Andrew Westlands had wakened, rested and well and absolutely, utterly, brimming with anticipation. To say that he faced a challenging day was the master of understatements: the world was on the brink of a catastrophe, a return to the Dark Ages, and he was one of the few people in a position to turn it around. But he was positive, and confident. He sensed - no, knew - that today was going to be *his day*. He was going to rise to the challenge. This day would be his day more than any other day had ever been. And he was old enough, and wise enough, to make sure that he took time to savour it, not just let it blaze past him in a rush of action and decisions. Confident, yes, why not? But just why did he feel this *good*? Was it the aphrodisiac of power, or the aphrodisiac of woman or both? Even the realisation that his new mobile - its number known only to a select few, he was told, and only for the most urgent issues - already had fifteen texts, that realisation hardly scratched the surface of his good humour. His yoga stretches done, his chilli omelette consumed, Andrew steadily worked through the messages. In fairness, they were all urgent. But he refused to be rushed. First things first. And the first thing was his coffee with Catherine, as promised. For some reason that prompted the thought that this might just have been the last time he would ever start the day in his quiet, civilised bachelor ritual. 'Well, so be it.' he smiled to himself. 'I'm ready.' Then, catching his eye from the soundless TV on the kitchen wall, the dread images of the BPP attack dogs. The shock of it. Childhood's End, sure enough. 'Yes, I'm ready for you, too.' he thought. 'Wolves eat dogs, fools.'

When he opened the front door of his flat, some five minutes later, another shock. A large, well dressed male figure of forty odd years and the ingrained stamp of authority.

"Sorry to surprise you, Mr. Westlands. My name is Detective Inspector Bendle of the Special Branch. I have been instructed to organise your personal protection. I regret the intrusion, sir, but I am afraid that it is, unfortunately, necessary. With your co-operation sir, we can keep our presence as discreet as possible. For the time being, two of my colleagues will be assigned to you at all times. I'd like to introduce .."

Detective Inspector Bendle had had plenty of time to rehearse his little speech. He'd been wakened from the urban bower of Fernbank, Govanhill, Glasgow, at the sharp end of four o'clock. To be told that they had information that someone had cracked the virus, and that, if correct, there would be no more messages and no trail and no reason for him to be sunning himself up there. They had another job for him, and he had ten minutes to be ready for it was a long journey by helicopter. When he had arrived, half an hour ago, he made a key realisation. Mayfair might be richer than Govanhill in money terms, but it was far poorer in terms of hot bacon rolls.

Andrew was happy enough to co-operate with Bendle. For one, he had no choice. For two, he knew he had better get used to it. 'It might,' he thought, dryly, 'impress the lady ...'

Santa Eularia, Ibiza: Nine Thirty a.m. Christmas Eve

The island of Ibiza is an eclectic mix of just about everything and anything and anyone. 'A List' celebrities: artists: ageing hippies and New Age freaks: manic clubbers, drawn to the 'Club Capital of the World': family holiday-makers: and the amused, or bemused, Spanish who kept it all running. At a profit. Ibiza was also an island with a gift for presentation and promotion, and was

322

probably home to more semi-pro broadcasters than teachers. And in the Santa Eularia morning market, that Christmas Eve, it seemed like most of them must be there. Not that they were at all interested in the hand-made jewellery or the leather-work or the tarot readings or the artists or the oils or candles or hippy crafts. No, they were all focused on a plain stall, on whose rough surface sat a large computer and monitor. The computer was clearly running the characteristic U-Sys media player, but at a rate that seemed outrageous to people who had already become habituated to the virus-induced crawl. To the right of the computer was large brown envelope, elaborately sealed with wax - a wax, according to its nearby vendor, that was ideal for liberating inhibitions and guilt. Above the stall, a large sign said 'The Christmas Virus: Fixed'. Behind the stall sat a plump, middle-aged man, unshaven, unkempt, his curly salt and pepper hair even wilder than normal. Robert Alexander's second call had certainly been successful.

If Robert Alexander was fazed by the media circus, then he certainly did not show it. He seemed happy to wait patiently for the arrival of the Santa Eularia Mayor, due in five minutes. He would then formally hand over the sealed package, with its instructions, in Spanish and English: 'To be opened, in public, at eleven fifty nine this evening, in the event that I do not instruct otherwise.' The helicopter was due in fifteen minutes: they had cleared an area of the nearby beach, less than fifty yards away. 'That should raise some sand.' Robert thought. 'Anyway, it all makes for excellent theatre, and just as fine an insurance policy as I can imagine. I will be ready for you, Mr. Eldon Harker. I think I am ready for you now.'

The handover and the beach-landing drama both went smoothly, and twenty minutes later Robert Alexander was staring out of the rear window of a six seat Lynx. The pilot told him that he should be in U-Soft London within three hours, and that

Eldon Harker would be waiting. Robert realised that Harker must have left around the time he had finished his call to Sorensen. 'I wonder,' thought Robert, 'what he'll think of my solution?'

Central London: Ten a.m. Christmas Eve

Question: how is it possible for two of the world's most recognisable celebrities to enjoy a quiet and intimate coffee in the centre of London. Answer: choose a small, intimate coffee bar, and ask the owner, your friend, to close it for an hour or so. That was why Andrew was sitting in a small booth in Italian T's, alone except for his bodyguards and the large latte that steamed away in front of him. It was ten minutes later when Catherine Connor arrived. Made an entrance, might be more accurate. Made an entrance in the way that glamorous women always do, whether they want to or not. A light blue coat, dark blue trouser suit, yellow boots, and matching gloves,. And, of course, her perfect eyes, cheekbones and hair. Andrew's bodyguards, seasoned professionals that they were, tried manfully not to stare, but only succeeded in making themselves even more conspicuous than they already were. Andrew made to rise from his booth, but Catherine waved him down as she walked over.

"I see that you've brought along your chaperones, Andrew. Am I really that dangerous?"

Well begun is half done. Thirty minutes later, and Andrew realises that he has done almost all of the talking. And that it has been serious talking. He had wondered how he - in the face of the insane pressures he was under - just how he was going to keep things light, and romantic. *You make me laugh*, she said. Well, Catherine was not so foolish. History was being made. How on earth could they *not* talk about what was happening. What *was* happening, Andrew? Is there a plan? What is the plan? So he had talked, and she had listened. Engrossed, but not the engrossment of a mere journalist, surely?

But now he was just about out of time.

"I hate to say it, Catherine, but I'm due elsewhere in ten. I really must apologise: you've hardly had the chance to get a word in."

"No apology necessary, Andrew. I was interested. *I am interested.*" As she said, the thoughts. 'Interested in what? Him? What about his age? Come on, he was as vital as a man half his age, and with none of the childishness. And his track-record? His ex-wives? What about them: maybe he was just poor at choosing wives? Wives? Wife? Is this about Andrew, or is this about power, and is there a difference?'

Andrew had no clue what she was thinking but did catch the words. *Interested.* Before he could find a response, Catherine had moved on.

"I really don't want to delay you, Andrew. I'll see you tonight at the debate. That's something else on your list. '*Afraid to look beyond the surface of things*' Are you afraid to look beyond the surface of things, Andrew?" The answer was out before he meant it.

"Not at all, Catherine. In fact, I'd very much like to get the chance." And he raised a theatrical eyebrow, his favourite, perennial-rogue look. It was a mistake, for there was no answering smile.

"Really, Andrew? Well, I think you have quite enough on your mind already. And, believe me, I do not intend to be a distraction. OK?"

It did not require an answer. She stood up, put on her coat. He'd blown it. And then, a last remark.

"Anyway, there'll be plenty of time for that later" and she gave him a smile, and was gone. It was a fine exit, and she knew it.

London: Ten Thirty a.m. Christmas Eve

It was now two hours since Robert Alexander Scott disappeared into the U-Soft helicopter, and, to the internet rumour engines, two hours is a very long time indeed. If anyone actually still believed that U-Soft would honour their offer, and pay out *one hundred million dollars* to some unknown, unkempt, middle-aged programmer, then they were keeping very quiet indeed. The internet consensus was that Robert Alexander, and all the occupants of his U-soft helicopter, had already met with some tragic 'accident', and that the sealed brown envelope had already been exchanged for a U-Soft fake and a large personal donation to the Major of Santa Eularia's pension fund. Apparently, the helicopter had suffered rotor failure somewhere over the Ibizan interior, and a search for survivors was already underway. Not that everyone was fooled by a story so facile and obvious, so lacking in that element of surprise that was the hallmark of real life. Many viewed the controversial images of the U-Soft Lynx and had, in justice, to acknowledge the weight of the visual evidence. It was clearly apparent to any fair-minded person that the helicopter's markings had, indeed, been subtly altered. The helicopter that Robert Alexander so foolishly entered was not civilian at all, but military. There was no conclusive proof that it was U.S., but there was a huge Nimitz-class aircraft carrier conveniently - and suspiciously - within range. The U.S.A., apparently, intended to be sole beneficiary of the virus fix, at least for the time being. However, a significant - and growing - number of people, thought a little deeper. Were not '*afraid to look beyond the surface of things*' Was the whole incident not just the latest, dramatic demonstration of alien abduction at its most public? Who, above all, benefited most from the Christmas Virus? And where had it come from?

The U-Soft statement, made on the stroke of ten-thirty, should have quelled most of the rumours.

The U-Soft corporation confirms that they have received details of what is alleged to be a fix to the Christmas Virus. At the present moment, all relevant U-Soft resources are engaged in the attempt to validate this claim. We will hold a press conference at our London headquarters at three o'clock this afternoon. We hope to be able to present our conclusions at that time.

Some of the rumours did indeed shrivel and die. But some of them were reborn, Phoenix-like, and stronger than ever. Think, people! Who was *really* responsible for the statement?

The City of the Infidels, Noon, Christmas Eve

Ahmed Ali Khan, languidly poised on the steps of the Excelsior Hotel, faced the slavering hounds of the press with his characteristic cool and urbane good humour. He would now be proceeding to the Circus Maximus, he told them. That was much the better place to get a decent shot of him, and against the spectacular, newly-arrived backdrop of the Sky Galleon. And would they please be so kind as to remember which was his good side? If you will just excuse me, gentlemen, there will be time enough for you all later...

He had been warned just over an hour before, the apologetic hotel manager only too regretful, desperate to offer Ahmed whatever assistance he could, anything to help Ahmed avoid the worst excesses of the press pack. Ahmed, however, reassured him that he had remained here incognito for longer than anyone could reasonably have hoped or expected: and anyway, it was time for him to endure the publicity for the sake of his cause. He would appreciate it if he could complete his check-out in his room. After that, he would be ready to face the gentlemen within the hour, if they would just be kind enough to wait.

"After all, Signor Di Giacomo, my mission is not exactly a secret, is it?" he asked, rhetorically, and they both smiled.

Despite the performance, deep down Ahmed wondered just how he would pull it off. The tick-tock, tick-tock was back again, drawing and holding his thoughts in rapt fascination, filling his every sense with looming dread. Tick-tock. Twenty five hours of life left. Time is running out, Ahmed. Make the most of your most precious life…

The Barricades, Birmingham: Eleven a.m. Christmas Eve

It was a bright, cold, morning in Birmingham, and the rays of winter sun seemed to probe the crude barricades with a forensic distaste. The barricades are organic, non-uniform, typically six feet by fifteen of rubble and timber and burnt-out motors. Every hundred feet or so looms a higher structure, a timber tower, perhaps fifteen feet high and twenty feet square. The towers have clearly been built to a set pattern. At the front, there is a small window, around one foot square and latticed with wire mesh. Both sides of the tower are solid, but the rear is open, giving access via a crude wooden ladder of questionable construction. The inside of the tower is lined with rough stone blocks, crudely cemented into place in a triumph of function over form. From the top of the nearest tower juts an impromptu flag pole, bearing - in the still December air - a listless square of the black and lightning. In the way that people do, the tower has been given a name. Hardly a triumph of the imagination, but on the near side of the tower is daubed, in crude white letters 'Fort Apache'. Around the barricades, and especially close to the towers, are small groups of men, drinking tea and swapping tales and looted cigarettes. Just on the stroke of eleven, their tea is rudely disturbed, as Fort Apache finds out that the Indians were coming. *Fast.*

Sixty miles an hour, or thereabouts, as far as Mehmet can make out, but it was only a reflex glance, a gesture of habit. Even in this darkest of moments, humour! 'Are they really going to charge me with speeding?' It is less than a hundred yards to the barricades and the nearest fort and the black and lightning that is his target. 'Three seconds, Insh'Allah'. The battered Ford five tonner bucks and swerves over the rubble-strewn road, but Mehmet wrestles it back into line, forces himself, against all his instincts, to stay off the brakes, to resist the rising internal scream that said 'BRAKE! BRAKE NOW!' A high pitched bullet whined past on his open drivers window, then another, then another. Fifty yards to go, and Mehmet knows he is already dead, now. Already a martyr and Paradise awaits. He slips down the seat: no need to see: only to keep the wheel straight and his right foot on the pedal. Aloud, he shouts.

"Death, infidels! Death and Hell for you! Death and Paradise for me!"

A burst of automatic fire shatters the windscreen, too late, bullets burying themselves in the lifeless fabric and steel. The truck hit Fort Apache at just over sixty miles an hour, but the effect was a world more dramatic than that. A split second earlier, as Mehmet's foot came off the accelerator pedal, five tons of potassium chlorate and sugar ignited. The colossal, deafening, explosion hurled Fort Apache skywards in a gigantic mushroom of flame and smoke and deadly debris. Two minutes later, and Fort Khyber, two miles down the road, met the same spectacular fate. Watching it all from the safety of his command post, Sheikh Mohammed Omar Al Nasran permitted himself some exultant words:

"Did you think we were defenceless, infidels? Did you think you *amateurs* would succeed against us, when all others have failed? Allah wills it, infidels. Death is coming to you all. After that, hell awaits."

It was another shocking escalation, and a dramatically successful tactic. Two gaping holes now appeared where once there were forts. The barricades had been breached. A victory had been won. However, in other respects it seemed that it might yet prove to be a disaster.

Strategically, it defies all military doctrine for the besieged to escalate the fighting. The besieged are playing for time, trying to hold out long enough for the attackers to lose heart or for help to fight its way in. It is almost never in their interests to increase the rate of battle, the burn rate of their limited ammunition and supplies. Why make their supply problems worse?

Politically, it seemed like a disaster too. The people of Britain were inured, accustomed to the images of suicide trucks: it was a modern cliché. But not in this country! In Palestine, Beirut, Iraq, Chechyna; you name it, wherever the Islamists waged war. But here? It proved all of their worst fears. Britain was now no different. Al Qaeda, the Taliban, call it what you will, they were here. It was a propaganda gift for the BPP, and they certainly made the most of it. *Who organised the suicide trucks? Who drove them? Where had the explosives come from? How long had they been waiting their time? Well, if war had come to the people of Britain, then so be it. Who still wants to listen to the feeble counsel of the Renaissance fools? Have you no courage?*

The logic was feeble, but in any case, logic is no match for passion. And it was passion that drove thousands of new recruits to the barricades, lusting for blood and revenge. They would have to wait their time, for their first allotted task proved to be construction: building a second ring of barricades, one hundred yards back from the first, outer ring. It was a text-book response: now there would be two rings to pierce, and rather more than twice the difficulty.

It was an hour later when the fascists made their first offensive response. In a carefully co-ordinated series of actions, cables were severed and pipes were sealed and all supplies of electricity and gas into the Muslim ghetto suddenly came to a halt. It was a beautiful Christmas Eve, bright and clear, but cold.

Tonight it would get colder, and dark. Perhaps Christmas Eve would bring them fires?

South London: Eleven a.m. Christmas Eve

"The patterns of history are but the signature of man. The people change, but the pattern remains the same. Cool, man, is it not?"

'Up close,' thought Richard Ferguson, 'you are one scary, *magnificent* man. But where are you going with this?' Up close, Daniel D was, indeed scary. His height, his incongruous 'Arjan Dread' locks, his staring blue eyes, his strange mixture of High English and Jamaican street jive. The thinly-veiled look of a man who would risk all. The man who was willing to face them all down, who would burn Korans and Bibles and everything else and dare them to war. Up here, in the top floor of the fearsome tower block, past the thousands of BPP foot-soldiers that roamed around its graffiti rich corridors, up here Daniel D was in his kingdom, and holding court. Up here, in the vast open space that was once six separate homes. The vast space, full of computers and television screens and wall charts and nobody else but them. Daniel D lectured his court: Ferguson, and Ferguson alone.

"Waaaay chill, myaan. Alwaaays de saaame people, always de saaame pyattern. Hiiistory. You dere yet, myaan?"

"Sure, Danny. And history is what we are making. Together."

"Ya, myaan. We done pleynty tooge'der." Then a change of tone: Dread gone, High English back. "Yes: we have indeed, Richard. And we are indebted to you, and to The Cause. Do you know the one thing, above all, that I will remember you for?" A chill ran down Ferguson. *Remember?* He guessed, rightly, that he was not meant to interrupt. Later.

"Your corruption of history. The myth of the religious war. *Imagine there's no religion.* All the millions who would not have died in the foolish religious wars. Yes, the terrible, inevitable

331

consequences of religion." Daniel D paused, smiled, resumed.

"And, in the last hundred years of war, in the last hundred *bonanza* years of war, what *religious wars*? The First World War was fought for Empire, Christian on Christian. The Second World War was our first, heroic attempt to create the Arjan World. And we were so close! Our atheist leader defeated only by the efforts of the Great Atheist himself, Comrade Stalin. Korea, Vietnam: capitalist versus communist. What religious wars have there been? None! But you, Richard, you and your colleagues, pulled it off. *Religion is the prime cause of war in the world today. Fact, and the BBC tells you so.* Unbelievable, remarkable, and you have my deepest respect. Joseph Goebbels in all his glory could never have pulled this off. Respect, myaan. But time to move on, y'know. You cool with this, myaaaaaaaan?" This did need a response, and Ferguson, alternating between the glow of praise and the chill of fear, knew it.

"Cool about what, Danny?"

"Some stuff gotta go, myaan. Some o' d'at nancy-boy stuff gotta go, myaan. Like before, myaan."

"Nancy-boy stuff? *Nancy-boy stuff?*" Anger started to rise in Ferguson. He needed the anger to stoke up his courage. Now was not the time to let this gutter trash dominate him. He needed to assert himself, to put this madman back in his cage. But carefully. However, Daniel D, strangely empathetic, moved to reassure him. Lowered his head a little, almost in apology, as he wrapped one long arm around Ferguson's left shoulder. Keeping his head lower, and talking closely now, close enough for Ferguson to feel the hot breath and the moisture. Was this *the moment*? The moment that Ferguson had been waiting for? Daniel D whispered now, intimate.

"Chill, myaaan. We always be tooge'der. Until deeyeth us do pyart …" And as he felt the long knife enter his guts, and the shock and the pain hit him, Ferguson made the connection. Long

332

knives. Like before. *History is written by men with long knives.* And the pain stopped, and his eyes closed.

Daniel D gave it a few moments to make sure that the man was absolutely dead. Then he withdrew - lovingly - his trusty, treasured, hunting knife. It never failed him. It never failed to please him. And he had people to clean up for him now. Lots and lots of people. Life was a *blast*. Daniel D wiped the blade on the sleeve of Ferguson's blue cashmere suit, and replaced it in his leather shoulder holster. Well, now he had his duties to attend to.

MI-5 Headquarters, London: Eleven Fifteen a.m. Christmas Eve

What did you do when your country was descending into anarchy, armed fascists and Islamists were locked in open warfare, the loyalty of your armed forces was subject to question, your industry and institutions were paralysed by a computer virus, and now *this*? If you were John Nightingale, the Director-General of MI-5, you kept your head and made your plans and waited for a break to come your way.

John Nightingale is seated behind a modest leather-topped desk, still very much the image of gentlemen's club cool. The grey Aquascutum pinstripe suit, the white shirt, the dark blue tie. Facing him is Hector, and he is still very much in character. That is to say, he was still very much the kind of man that made women foolish. 'M' started to speak.

"Thanks for being prompt, Hector. As you know, things are moving a little quickly. It does rather look like we might just have a solution to the problem of the virus. We think that U-Soft will confirm this at three. Given that, there will be no reason for anyone to send or receive our customary evening message. We will therefore suspend the hunt for Red Michael - or whomever - for the time being. I do stress, Hector, that I do mean just that: *for the time being.* Right now, I have more urgent need of your talents. *Andrew Westlands*. He is becoming a key political figure. And, in the light of what we have just learned, he is about to become even more so ..." Hector took his cue

"*What we have just learned*, sir?"

"David Blenheim is about to resign as Prime Minister. He will then propose a vote of no confidence in Her Majesty's Government. All our indications are that the vote will succeed. By early this evening we will no longer have any effective government, and will not get one at least until after the results of the General Election. This, I understand, will be set for the third week in January. By that time, David Blenheim will be deputy leader of the Party of Western Renaissance. Andrew Westlands will still be its President. Provided, of course, that you, Hector, manage to keep Westlands alive. Do I make myself clear, Hector?" He did. *Keep Westlands alive while all around descends into anarchy and he is the number one target of almost all concerned.*

"Clear, sir. And perhaps make a close observation of him, too?"

"Absolutely, Hector. There is so little we really understand about the virus and the sudden anarchy and Mr Westlands' role in all this. Which might just be an accident of fate, the right man in the right place at the right time, who knows? Anyway, why not come back to me in half an hour with a proposal on the resources you require? Our American cousins have a stake in this, too, so for once the budget might be adequate."

John Nightingale had not, of course, told Hector everything. Most European parliaments had evolved along similar lines. The no-confidence vote was an example of that: a device whereby a government can be forced - in extremis - to go back to the electorate to renew its mandate. A mechanism to trigger a general election. Of course, they were not all the same, but they produced much the same results. There were already hints to suggest that it was not just Britain that would be facing a new general election. Well, he'd pass that along when he had something a little more tangible.

How do you prepare to meet the world's cleverest man? In Robert Alexander's case, with nerves - fear, even - but also with a growing sense of anticipation. To meet the legendary Eldon Harker, talk with him: how amazing was that? What would it be like to talk with a truly, genuinely brilliant man? What would he really be like?

Robert Alexander Scott was alone in the large U-Soft training theatre, save for the hundred or so empty seats and the half dozen steroid-enhanced U-Soft guards. Even though they had kept him busy during his flights - BUSY! - the adrenalin has obliterated any shadows of fatigue from his face or manner. He fidgets relentlessly, twisting his unruly hair into ever tighter curls; rubbing at the dark, heavy growth on his chin: scratching his ears and squirming relentlessly on a seat which - despite Robert's behaviour - is actually soft and comfortable. Thinking.

'Busy, yes they kept him BUSY. What was the password for his computer? Where was the source code? What approach did he take to the problem? What tests had he run? Had he investigated date changes?' They had even linking him directly to Sorensen, video conferencing while they flew, testing while they talked while they flew. Yes, of course, the tests must be well advanced by now. They must know.' And, in a sudden jolt to his memory...

'That means the money is mine. One hundred million dollars.' The thought ought to have made him leap with joy and triumph: was worth, surely, at the very least, a broad smile. But no leap and no smile. 'This might,' Robert realised 'prove to be a problem. A real problem.' Robert Alexander Scott knew that he already had enough money. More than enough to make him a little guilty, especially at the end of the season when the junkies ran out of easy tourists and money and the hard winter started to embrace them. 'What will I do with one hundred million dollars?' Robert Alexander asked himself. 'What do I need that I don't already have? Well, a wife, for a start. A wife: perhaps kids? Surely one hundred million dollars bought a lot of dresses and handbags and shoes and therefore a lot of wives?' and Robert Andrew smiled as his own wry humour. 'As if.' It was just at that moment that Eldon Harker strode through the front left doorway.

"Congratulations, Robert. Indeed, you have much to smile about. Our testing is not formally finished - we do have procedures, I'm afraid - but it is obvious to me that you have the solution to our problem. I can therefore confirm that you have won one hundred million dollars." There is no way to say such a thing that can even begin to make it real. Other than just to say it, and let time do the rest. Robert Alexander Scott, however, had already started to devalue his prize. That made it much easier for him to remember his manners, and to find his voice.

"Thank you, Mr. Harker." The words were a bit weak, but, given the circumstances, better than he had expected.

"Please, call me Eldon. I understand, Robert, that you found yourself in a somewhat advantageous position in respect of this problem? It has been suggested that you were - let me put it directly - a little lucky, perhaps?"

"Yes, Eldon. I had written my own assembler many years ago…"

"Which we declined to use. A most unfortunate choice. Perhaps. But not for you. So what will you do with the money, Robert? What will you do with the hundred million dollars?" Robert had expected the question, had had time to prepare his answer. Not that it showed.

"Hmm.' A pause. A scratch of the ear. A crossing of legs. 'Hmm. It's a problem, yes. Indeed." Ten, twenty, thirty seconds of awkwardness, fidgeting, and silence. "Interesting that I did not think through the implications of the helicopter at the time. You know, the publicity. I can't just .. Hmm. Obviously, I was excited, but I'm sure there must have been a better solution..."

'He's not interested in the money.' thought Eldon Harker. 'Definitely not. He's on to another problem. Encouraging.' And unusual. Over the years Eldon Harker had created countless millionaires. Several billionaires. And what had they done, most of them? Cars; yachts; islands; fancy women. Luxury; leisure; drugs, some of them. Lives of ever-gilded boredom. Squandered their talent, and their time. Eldon no longer expected too much. But this was encouraging...

"Perhaps, Robert. Perhaps you were just not quite so lucky with that particular problem. But I understand you have been, shall we say, lucky, quite a few times over the years. For example, you provided the 3-D firmware for the Qtel graphics workstation?"

"Yes, I did Eldon. Some time ago."

"For the princely sum of fifteen hundred dollars, Robert. Was there any particular reason why you had to price your work quite so ridiculously low?" Despite the words, the way that Eldon said it, there was more humour in it than mockery.

"I was happy with it, Eldon. Maybe they just drive a harder bargain than you..."

"Touche, Robert." and they shared a smile. "You also wrote the BIOS for the XCESS computer. Fine work, if I might add. Pity it wasn't U-Sys compatible. Also wrote the first on-line search engine. But forgot to patent it. There is quite a list, Robert, of problems you have been lucky with. Or unlucky, depending on how you look at it."

"Hmm. I suppose there is. Hmm." A scratch of the ear. A pause. A shift on the seat. "I'm happy with my work, Eldon. Who wouldn't be? I get to choose what problems I work on. And how many people can say that?"

'And how many people would think to say that?' thought Eldon.

'*When they have just won one hundred million dollars.* Maybe. Just maybe. Just maybe Robert Alexander Scott might be the one we're looking for. The Arthur to take the sword from the stone. Amazing what one hundred million dollars can find for you.' So he asked.

"I have an another problem you might like to help solve, Robert. A problem that - I confess - I myself find quite challenging. A rather significant problem. Would you perhaps like to hear a little about this problem, Robert?"

A problem that Eldon Harker found quite challenging? And the downside was what, exactly?

"Absolutely, Eldon. Absolutely." This was going better than Robert Alexander could have even begun to imagine. The solution to the virus, the money, Eldon Harker, and now …

"We have given the problem a name, Robert. Omnibox."

And Eldon talked, and Robert Alexander listened, and then they talked together. To Alex Reynolds, the longest serving of the bodyguards, it seemed like it had been a very long time, if at all, since he had seen Eldon Harker so animated. No doubt there would be consequences. No doubt at all.

Curious, though, that they had dismissed the matter of the virus so quickly. They had a solution. But what? And why no discussion about how the virus had got there in the first place? About who had put it there? It just was and now it would just not be. They would just ship the fix out to the waiting world, and that would be that. No, that did not make any sense, not at all. Who was responsible? Responsible for the chaos and the deaths and the anarchy that was still out there, for God's sake! No, for them or he or she or whomever, there would have to be consequences. For what the world had just been through, there *had* to be consequences.

338

FIFTEEN

Winter light daubs the cobbled street from its palette of grey and rain. Puddles, liquid and glistening, radiate raindrops in perfect, effortless, circles. Under a carapace of nylon, a young couple spin a cocoon of shelter and shared promises. On the wet stone of an ancient doorway, a beggar cowers, eyes fixed on a time too far distant and too long gone. Above the wintry tableau, the blue-eyed man turns from the window in unexpected emotion. Life is relentless, and fleeting, and chances must be seized while there is yet time. He has much to do, and turns back to his computer. The time is just past noon and the screen is filled by a text box. It reads:-

"Explain this to me." he asked. "They know that chance is woven into the very thread of life. The lucky meeting, the healthy child, the accident that just passed them by. They know full well that without this unpredictability, there can be no life at all, nothing but a dull mechanical whirr. Yet they will not recognise that this unpredictability is but a cloak for the Will of God. How foolish! Where better for the Will of God to hide but in that very essence of life? Where better for the Will of God to hide, but in that which can never be proved, nor disproved? Is this also but an accident? A lucky accident?"

I did not understand all that he had said, but still I understood. I charge the West with fear, with being too frightened to look deeper than the surface of their lives.

He closes the computer, and quickly starts on his packing.

London: One Thirty p.m. Christmas Eve

The press industry had taken to on-line newspapers like a duck to water. Advertising revenues were through the roof: production costs were disappearing into the mist of history. At times like this, however, the model presented some unexpected challenges. It was only one-thirty in the afternoon of Christmas Eve, but already there had been a weeks' worth of headlines. Take The London Times, for instance. The first issues had blended together the debates, Andrew's political declaration, and the battle of barricades, to produce 'PWR SEEKS POWER AMIDST BPP SAVAGERY'. Uninspired, but at least appropriate. The rumours of Blenheim's resignation, coupled with the dramatic scenes of the Ibizan market, were distilled into 'BLENHEIM ON BRINK AS VIRUS VANQUISHED?'. Better. And that had been followed by yet more iterations. And now, the latest, startling news. Blenheim had not resigned. He had called - and won - a vote of no confidence in his own government. At the present moment he was en route to the Queen to formally request the dissolution of Parliament, and the announcement of a new General Election. Naturally, in this election he would be proud to be vice president of the Party of Western Renaissance. Running in parallel to this, the rumours of a fix to virus were now all but confirmed: U-Soft had so many people testing the proposed fix that it had sprung a thousand security leaks. There was widespread footage of U-Soft computers bouncing back into rude health. Some enterprising reporters had even got hold of the fixed code, and were broadcasting live demonstrations of computers being revived from their cyber-coma. The bulk DVD manufacturers refused to confirm - or deny - the rumours that their production had already been booked - usurped, was more accurate - and that they now waiting for confirmation of the final, master disk. The latest - but surely not the last - headline of the day went 'VIRUS

FIXED BUT DEMOCRACY PAYS DEADLY PRICE'. It covered almost all the bases: the barricades, the Islamists, the vote of no confidence and the now-confirmed fix. It might even be good for a couple of hours. Since the U-Soft conference did not start for an hour and a half, that it was at least an each-way bet. The conference was bound to last more than half an hour, and no-one was likely to file copy before it was over, surely?

Well, yes, there was another, growing, story. An event that had been long planned, but - and unsurprisingly - overshadowed by the Virus and the Chaos. Today, in Rome, the first of the Sky Galleons was to be unveiled. Tomorrow, 'The Green World - as she had been named - would commence her maiden, deeply symbolic voyage. A symbolism that was only too necessary in the light of the now-fevered tension between the West and the World of Islam. The Italian press would be there today in force, and soon they would have copy to file, headlines to write. Well, it was better than being bored, although, for most journalists, boredom seemed a very distant memory.

The Circus Maximus Rome, Two-Thirty GMT, Christmas Eve

The Circus Maximus: it's name said it all. The Greatest Circus. Over two thousand years of spectacle and drama and the occasional heroic death. The thunder of the hooves and the chariots was heard no longer, but the roar of the impassioned crowd still was. For where did the fanatical football fans gather to celebrate their triumphs, to salute their heroes, and to taunt their rivals? Two thousand years of frenzy and adulation. Truly, the Greatest Circus. It would be reasonable to imagine that, in two thousand years, the Circus Maximus had seen it all. But you would be wrong. It had never seen anything quite like the Sky Galleon .

The Circus Maximus is an elongated oval on the south bank

of the Tiber, close to the ancient - and modern - centre of the city. It is a huge grassy area, some six hundred and fifty yards long and one hundred yards wide. Occasional, ancient trees dot its perimeter, a couple at its midway point, but its shape and function are still unmistakable. An oval built for racing, and sport, and for people to gather in their tens of thousands. Today the crowd is almost all on the southern half of the oval, facing towards a small stage that is roughly at the half way point. Behind the stage, the entire northern half is bounded by a twelve foot-high fence, whose razor wire top make it clear that it is not to be viewed as merely a challenge. Immediately in front of the small stage is an enclosed perimeter, inside which, betrayed by the size and density of their cameras, are the gentlemen of the press. More crowds surround the far outer perimeter of the northern half, held back by the forbidding fence. Just beyond the fence, police and dogs survey the crowd with dispassionate, anonymous suspicion. But they are mere dots, dwarfed by the real contents of the northern half: the Sky Galleon, the extraordinary product of genius and deep, deep budget. A technological triumph, certainly, but that is not what holds the audience in rapt and awe-struck silence. An aesthetic marvel, but it is not its beauty which entrances the gaping crowd. Not its beauty, but, its size. Its sheer, incredible, *unbelievable* size. The Sky Galleon is two hundred and ninety yards long, seventy five yards wide, and seventy yards tall. Eight hundred and seventy feet long! Up close, it is overwhelming.

To the layman, Sky Galleon most resembles a vast, green airship, but with small wings and tail plane that hint of aeroplane. The top surface of the helium-filled cylinder is dominated by the dull black of the super-light, latest-technology solar panels. Two small, stubby wings, one close to the nose, one close to the tail, are internally joined to the titanium spine. It is this enormously strong spine that bears the stresses of the wings and the network of internal cables that maintain the shape of the helium-filled envelope. On each side of the Sky Galleon, around the centre line, are four gleaming titanium masts, their silver purity interrupted by fabric wrappings of green, as if decorated by some designer scarf. The masts run parallel to the length of the cylinder, close in to its surface. Two masts are to the front of the ship, just behind the small wings. They are placed symmetrically about the centre line of the ship, one forty yards above the other. The other pair are similarly located, but are just behind the small rear wing. Front and rear wings both have four propellers, two on each side. The vertical rear tail wing is eighty foot tall and forty feet long. The whole helium-blessed structure is, despite everything, still lighter than air, and is tethered some forty feet from the ground by a network of chains. Suspended underneath its belly, wheels just touching the ground, is the passenger compartment. Sleek, aerodynamic and large, designed to carry at least one hundred people. The Sky Galleon is indeed something to marvel at. But to really understand the marvel, it is necessary to understand more about why, and what, it really is.

The Sky Galleon existed because, fundamentally, travel was an environmental disaster. Especially air travel: airliners criss-crossing the skies, seeding the atmosphere with thousands of tons of carbon dioxide, warming the planet and distributing a host of other pollutants as they went. As the West woke to the real dangers to the environment, increasingly the question was asked: *is your journey really necessary?* More than that, the new awareness was beginning to affect trade, too. Sure, it might be cheaper to buy North African fruit, but what about the damage done to the environment as it is brought over? Would it not be better to source produce locally? Why did we need exotic or un-seasonal products anyway?

This new environmental purity was all very admirable, but it threatened to have catastrophic consequences. What was to happen to the Second and Third World countries whose main industry was tourism? Who relied on the money that the tourists no longer brought? What would the people live on? And what about those countries that had invested in agriculture - at the behest of the World Bank, and the United Nations, and all the rest of the advisory agencies? Would their oranges and grapefruit and bananas be left to rot where they grew? Would that be their only food? And subtler problems: did not travel broaden the mind? What would happen if the eco-friendly West retreated within its walls? And, withdrawn from everyday dialogue, routine cultural exchange, what would be their attitude to the environmentally-unfriendly ways that much of the Third World was still enforced to employ? After all, the environment was a global concern. Would the West permit them to damage their precious environment?

The environmental Puritanism was a huge, and growing, threat to the rest of the world. But, most of all, to the World of Islam. It was World of Islam who had invested most in the new economics, looking ahead to the days when the oil, finally, ran out. It was they whose culture, now isolated from the West, had most to fear from attack and holocaust. The Sky Galleon was their answer. It was, therefore, the world of Islam that had funded the Sky Galleon. To understand why, it is necessary to understand more about the wondrous mix of technologies that lay beneath its sleek surface. The technologies that would enable The Green World to fly around the World, in less than ten days, with no consumption of petrol or gas or fuel whatever.

It was easy to see that the Sky Galleon was powered by sunlight: who could not notice the vast black area of solar cells. Certainly, they could generate enough power to drive the Sky Galleon, albeit slowly. Two tons of the latest generation lithium-ion batteries provide a store for the electricity, smoothing out the peaks and troughs of the sunlight. And enabling night flight. But what the crowd could not see - but certainly knew about - was how The Green World would be transformed into a galleon. For the eight titanium masts were a brilliant blend of ancient and modern technologies. Each mast was actually hinged into the side of the ship. Once underway, small electric motors would 'raise' the mast, folding it out from the side of the ship just as a mast might be raised from the deck of a ship. The masts therefore, would jut out from the side of the ship, much like the wings. As a second stage, barely visible Kevlar rigging would unfurl the green sails that were wrapped around each mast. They resembled more the cups of a wind gauge than sails: cups/sails on Kevlar ropes. The inner core of each mast was fixed directly to the ship's super-strong titanium spine. The outer ring, to which the Kevlar ropes were attached, was free to rotate. The Kevlar ropes would be gradually unfurled. As the wind hit the cups they would billow, the Kevlar rope would stretch taut, and more would be fed out, gradually, ensuring it remained taut. The rope, taut as a steel rotor, driven by the wind-filled vanes at each end, would spin. This, in turn, would spin the whole outer core of the mast. Which was linked, within the body of the ship, to a generator shaft. The wind produced electricity that turned the propellers. The revolving shafts were mated to the generator with a sophisticated revolving joint. This meant that the masts, unlike those of ship, could be angled - up and down and left to right - always catching the best of the wind. Small electric motors made the adjustments automatically. Any surplus wind power was stored in the batteries. It was expected that a Sky Galleon would be able to maintain average speeds, even under full load, of seventy-five to one hundred miles an hour.

Unsurprisingly, safety was also paramount. Unlike the Hindenburg, the Green World simply could not burn. Helium is inert, and the surface of the gas envelope non-flammable. Should the winds get too strong, it would become necessary to wind

345

back in the sails. This was done by electric motors, which would simply wind back in the Kevlar ropes and then fold the masts back into the side of the ship. It did not matter how strong the wind got: as the wind got stronger, so more of its power would be routed back into the rewinding operation. The stronger the wind, therefore, the stronger the force available to combat it: elegant, effective, and safe. The vanes in the wings and tail plane controlled the direction, attitude, and altitude of the craft, much as they did for a conventional plane. Directional and vertical stability were, in fact, better than that of a conventional aircraft: not only that, the speed could be reduced to zero, making it safer by far than any aeroplane or helicopter could ever hope to be.

It might have been the 'sails' that had given the Sky Galleon its name, but the way that its 'sails' worked reminded people more of a Mississippi paddle-steamer. But it all came to the same thing: galleons and paddle steamers were both stately vessels, and icons of their age. So too, would be the Sky Galleon: a technological, environmentally-friendly, iconic marvel. Not only an icon, but also Islam's emphatic response to the environmental problems of air transport. The emphatic, *practical* solution to tourism and trade, but without the environmental damage. The icon of the age, most certainly.

Fittingly, The Green World's first, symbolic voyage would be tomorrow, Christmas Day. Fittingly, too, it would bear a message, written on the programmable display screen on its starboard side. Unsurprisingly, the message would be 'Peace and Harmony'. Unfortunately, the Sky Galleon was still too unproven to allow any passengers to make her inaugural flight. Her only occupants - other than the tons of instruments that would record her every breath - would be the two pilots that were necessary to maintain her in twenty four hour flight. Fittingly, too, the first pilot was to be the man who was the principal driving force behind its creation. The man with the contacts, the energy: the man who badgered and harried and somehow, eventually pulled together all the funding. That man was Mohammad Ali Khan. And the second pilot to help take the great ship through the rest of her voyage was also deeply symbolic. A man who, above all, had come to symbolise the ideal integration of Islam and the West. A young, charismatic, photogenic man. Mohammad's adopted son, Ahmed Ali Khan.

London: Two p.m. Christmas Eve

There is nothing quite like being in the BBC for keeping on top of the news - if you wanted to, which Catherine Connor most certainly did. 'On top of the news? At this time? And just how would you hope to do that?'

How indeed, at this time? The collapse of the government, the rise of the PWR, the BPP on the streets, the fix to the virus... for a journalist, it was an embarrassment of riches, just too much happening all at the same time. What exactly was going on, now? Just what was going on with the PWR? Blenheim and Andrew? What would be the impact if the virus really was fixed? What would be the impact on she, herself? Would tonight's debate go ahead? Even if it did, would she still be the presenter, given the publicity around her public - and growing - relationship with Andrew Westlands? They might say that she was too close. That she had an inside track. And she *did* have an inside track. The most inside of all inside tracks. Damn, it was tempting; so, so tempting. But so confusing too: where did the journalist stop and where did the woman begin? How could she balance the two demands?

'Don't be daft.' thought Catherine. 'You're a woman, for God's sake. That's what we do.' So she wrote the short text. 'Thinking of you. Talk? X. And she added a smiley face, and sent it. 'There. What was so hard about that?' she thought.

The Circus Maximus, Rome: Two-Thirty p.m.
GMT, Christmas Eve

Three thirty, Rome time. Twenty hours, thirty minutes to go. *I am ready to fulfil my destiny.* The press conference had gone well and he had done well and Ahmed Ali Khan was renewed by the sense of his own importance. He *was important*: fated: destined. Had they not all told him so? Had he not been able to acknowledge it, *to the world*? "Yes, I am proud to be a symbol." A symbol, infidel fools, of you know not what. "A new beginning for relations between the West and the World of Islam?" Oh yes, infidels, a new beginning. And I, Ahmed Ali Khan am the symbol and the focus. How sweet it was. How sweet was *life*. Glancing at his watch - again - Ahmed saw that it was three thirty three. All the threes. Twenty hours, twenty seven minutes to go. *How sweet was life.* And, just like that, it was back, more terrible than ever. The doubts, the fear, the terror. The end to his life, many, many lives. And for some reason, the image of the little blonde boy. The boy with the ball. What if he was wrong?

'Oh, father, Allah be praised that you are here! *Please*, finish with these technicians. We need to talk, father. Now! I have such need of your faith!'

The passenger cabin of the Sky Galleon is almost empty of seats, but is instead - at this moment - a jumbled mound of instrument boxes and recording apparatus. Thirty feet away, separated by a large fortune in scientific equipment, Mohammed Ali Khan is talking to a technician. As if hearing of his son's silent plea, Mohammed Ali Khan brings the discussion to an abrupt end.

"The risk is acceptable. It is too late to replace the unit, and the risk is too small. Matter closed."

'The risk is nil.' Mohammed sneers to himself as he picks a careful route through the equipment. 'Now, My Son, I am ready for you. And I think you have great need of me. Well, not for so much longer.'

U-Soft London, Conference Room One: Two Fifty Nine p.m. Christmas Eve

To Peter Hawkins, the better half of the Odd Couple, it seemed like old times. Gone were the steroid-fattened guards - well, most of them. Back were the U-Soft robots, who had verified their identities in an effortless, digital blink, then ushered them politely to their pre-assigned seats. Like old times. Back to normal. The virus was most obviously neutralised, resolved. All over bar the shouting. Like hell it was. Not for Hawkins it wasn't. He - and he was no different from every one of this roomful of restless reporters - he needed to understand just what this virus was. Where it came from. Who put it there. Where it was going. The world was on the verge of chaos, people were dying - and there had to be consequences. It could not just cease to be. Someone had to held responsible. Punished. And then there were other questions. More difficult questions, perhaps. Old times: well, perhaps. Old times in Sarajevo, Bosnia, perhaps. Tanks on the ridges, snipers on the hilltops, people starving in the streets, and no-one responsible. Until, finally, they got tired of the same questions, and did something about it.

Precisely on the hour, Brian Dempsey and Mohan Nehran, strode in and took up position at a lectern to the left of the stage. Brian Dempsey glanced briefly around the audience, waiting for them to settle, then started right in.

"Ladies and gentlemen, I'd like to dispense with the formalities. Eldon Harker would like to speak to you about the virus himself." On cue, the vast screen behind him stirred into life, and the face appeared. The long narrow face, the shoulder length hair, the continuous silver eyebrow, and the luminous green eyes. The voice is characteristically brusque.

"Ladies and gentlemen, the Christmas Virus has been eliminated. I would like to now explain the nature of the virus, and how it had arisen. In recognition of my audience, I will make this explanation in layman's terms. A more technical explanation will be made available on U-Soft.com, after this conference." A pause that racked the tension another notch higher. A brief, incongruous smile, as the alien mask delivered its astonishing assessment.

"The Christmas Virus was so difficult to find, ladies and gentlemen, because - in a sense - we were looking in the wrong place. The Virus is not in the U-Soft source at all. The Virus is in the assembler that U-Soft purchased, twenty one years ago. You could say that our source code awakened the virus that had always been waiting, dormant and patient. You could also say that the assembler's real purpose was to introduce the virus into the U-Soft kernel. Let me explain further."

You could suggest that it was sheer shock that restrained the hall from pandemonium and chaos. But, to anyone familiar with the gentle men and women of the media, such a suggestion would be ridiculous: the gentle people's reaction to shock was invariably noise and clamour and frenzy. The real reason was practical. It was the knowledge that the electronic Eldon was only a recording, about to continue, and that none of them dare miss a word. So the audience gaped and stared and exchanged looks of deepest outrage, but in silence. The electronic Eldon, as if anticipating this, had paused for perhaps five seconds, no more, and then resumed.

"Ladies and gentlemen, to understand what follows, you must appreciate that writing computer software is a very highly creative task. Not at all the dull, featureless assembly line of the popular stereotype. This task attracts, therefore, not only the very clever, but the very creative. And creative people, ladies and gentlemen, all tend to have their own style. They produce work

350

that is not merely functional, but has a particular identity. Style: yes, programmers tend to have their own characteristic *style*. Let me give you a couple of simple examples, to make this clearer. To explain how style can exist in an object whose sole purpose is efficiency." A pause. A closing of the eyes that was too long to be called a blink.

"Many of the tasks that a piece of software does is repetitive. Take the act of drawing a picture on the screen, for example. If the screen had one hundred lines, you could tell the computer 'from one to a hundred, draw the next line'. However, you could just as easily say 'from zero to ninety-nine, draw the next line.' That will also draw one hundred lines. There are, in fact, an infinite number of ways to express the command to count one hundred items, and all of them with *precisely* the same result. In the example I have given you, programmers tend to prefer to work either counting from zero, or counting from one, and this then becomes a style issue for them. Others, in order to clearly mark 'their code' will use something less obvious like counting down, not up - but, again, whose effect is precisely the same. This is a simple example. Let me give you another, slightly more complex example. Frequently software will have to answer questions like 'which of my database records contains the name Eldon Harker?' The answer to the question was the *number* of the correct record: whether it was the first record in the file, or the second, or whatever number it was. Of course, such a record might not exist, and so one answer must symbolically indicate that no such record was found. In this case, some programmers would choose 'zero' to represent this. Others would choose minus one. Still others would choose more exotic numbers. Again, all these symbols would be perfectly equivalent in terms of function. There are many more such examples, ladies and gentlemen, and the net result is this: if he wants, a programmer can write his source in such a way that has a unique signature.

The principal trigger for the Christmas Virus was a very specific software signature. The signature of one of my ex-colleagues, Mr Michael MacDonald. I trust that we are clear so far?" An enquiring raise of the right hand side of the monobrow. Hawkins, surprising himself, was clear. It was surprising, and interesting, and clear. And an absolute bombshell! Oblivious, Harker continued.

"There were other triggers. Every piece of software must assert its ownership through a copyright notice, or the copyright is lost. A secondary trigger for the virus was a copyright notice that identified the owner to be the U-Soft Corporation. There were - are - others, but I see no value to the enumeration of them all. Thankfully, the mystery now seems to have been unravelled. The name of the man who unravelled this mystery is Robert Alexander Scott. Robert was in the fortunate - and almost unique - position of being able to compile our source code with both the U-Soft assembler - the one we had bought in - and with his own assembler. He noticed that the compiled U-Soft kernel was bigger than it ought to be. Bigger than its source alone ought to make it. Robert deduced that the compiled kernel must contain additional code that was not in the source at all, but had to be taken from elsewhere. And where else could it be taken from, but the assembler itself? Yet how could this trap be hidden? How could the assembler know when to spring its trap, to add its virus code, and yet otherwise behave exactly as the user expected? What signal would be well-nigh undetectable, yet never be likely to happen by accident?" A pause, giving them just the smallest of opportunities, before the continuation.

"Robert Alexander Scott posed himself the same problem. Thankfully, he came up with the same answer. What signal could he use for a trigger? What would he choose? Answer: a unique, embedded source code signature. Perhaps also the copyright owner. So Robert examined the kernel source code for characteristic signatures, and found them. Three of them. Robert then standardised these signatures - or enough parts of them - into a new signature. His. A signature that the virus could not be familiar with. In summary: Robert modified the source code to become different from - but functionally identical to - the original source code. And, ladies and gentlemen, it worked. The assembler no longer got the hidden signal. The compiled kernel now does exactly what its source code commanded: no more, no less, no virus. For his brilliance, Robert Alexander Scott has won the U-Soft reward of one hundred thousand dollars. And, I am sure, the eternal gratitude of us all."

A pause. Thunderstruck, Peter Hawkins nevertheless thought that he had understood. *Harker was saying that the source code had no virus, but it was the compiler that added it in. The virus was in the compiler all along. When it saw source code of a certain style, and owner, it sprung its trap. That meant...* But the pause was over, and Eldon Harker was about to tell them.

"That, ladies and gentlemen, is the explanation of the how. How the virus was introduced, and why it was so hard to find. It also gives us the when. The virus was written at least twenty one years ago. The question now, is by whom? Did someone anticipate a specific signature in source code that was yet to be written? Did one of the authors of the assembler know of the U-Soft project? Did he also guess that someone he knew - whose software signature he was familiar with - was going to be working on the U-Sys project? Or did he know that he was going to work on the U-Sys kernel himself? That he himself would be able to give the source code the signature that the assembler was looking for? The secret signal?" There was no way to ask the question without a natural pause, so the image of Eldon Harker deliberately paused. And there was no way, at this critical moment, to take a pause without the tension becoming almost unbearable. It was theatre, the *highest of theatre*, but it was *natural*. Just the nature of the beast. But the pause - the agonising pause - was followed by...

"At this stage, ladies and gentlemen, unfortunately, we cannot be sure which of these possibilities is true. U-Soft purchased the assembler from a small Rhode Island company called BaseSoft. At least one person worked for both BaseSoft and for U-Soft. That person is Michael MacDonald. We know this because I myself hired him from BaseSoft. But I stress, ladies and gentlemen, that the virus could also be the work of someone else who worked on the development of the BaseSoft assembler. Someone who knew Michael MacDonald, knew his style, and guessed that he would be unable to resist the U-Sys project. At that time, ladies and gentlemen, the world of the personal computer and its operating software was small. Very small. This scenario is not as implausible as it would be today. In any case, we - and the authorities - were already looking for Michael MacDonald, and that search continues today. We are also now looking into the background of the BaseSoft Corporation. Unfortunately, the BaseSoft corporation ceased to exist many years ago. We are presently hunting for its personnel records, and we will inform you of developments when they happen." Another pause. 'And if you don't find them?' Peter Hawkins asked himself. Anger rising, neck and cheeks flushing deep red. '*What if you don't find them?*' But Eldon was forging on, and he had to focus, focus. Miss nothing.

"I have not addressed, ladies and gentlemen, the apparently topical nature of the messages. Really, there is no need. The messages were written twenty one years ago and that is a fact. Believe in conspiracies if you will, but understand that the facts do not support them. But I will say, ladies and gentlemen, that to the author of the virus - the brilliant author of the virus - the issues that the virus messages address today were no more the logical outcome of the issues that had already arisen back then. They were no more than intelligent extrapolations. In any case, the messages were written twenty one years ago. It is true because that it's the only possible interpretation of the evidence." a slight pause. Peter Hawkins felt sick, ill, his heart pounding in chest. Too agitated. Blood pressure too high. Thankfully, it looked like Harker was about to finish.

"The last issue I have to address, ladies and gentlemen, is where we go from here. Short-term, we are distributing a clean kernel, using the modified source code and the existing assembler. However, we can never be certain what other viruses might lurk in this assembler, what viruses may be waiting - in the kernel, or in any other of our applications - to be triggered. We have, therefore, purchased from Robert Alexander Scott his assembler, together with its source code. Since we have the source for the assembler, this means we can be certain that it, itself, has no hidden viruses. We expect to issue a long term fix to the kernel in around one months' time. This fix will use the original kernel source code - unmodified in any way, unless we find an error in the ten percent we have still to check - but compiled with Robert's assembler. This will give us a clear audit trail for all elements of the kernel, and will enable us to prevent a repeat of anything like The Christmas Virus. It will also do one more, important thing, ladies and gentlemen. It will establish, beyond any doubt, that U-Soft source code was not at fault in any way. That means that U-Soft can direct its money into research and development, into the search for progress, and not into the pockets of parasitic lawyers. That will enable us to be able to say, 'Never again!' Thank-you, ladies and gentlemen." Click, a dark screen, and bedlam.

A layman might imagine that the mood among the media would be jubilant, celebratory. The Christmas Virus had been defeated: the chaos could be overcome. Who knows, life might even go back to the way it was before the virus. Well, no, that was not going to happen, but - bottom line - the virus had been defeated and people could go back to work and when people went back to work things went back to normal. But the media were not jubilant, but raging. The news that the Virus had been defeated was not news at all: hell, some of them even came to this conference with their U-Sys laptops. Their *working* U-Sys laptops. Anyway, everyone in the media knew that good news was no news, unless it happened to be in sport. No, they had come here for the kind of story that their audience wanted: the solution to the mystery and the identification of the villains responsible. A chase to be followed by blood and revenge, that was what the mob wanted. And how was this now going to happen? Most of the first few questions were little more than snarls of rage and outrage, and Robert Perry was perhaps the first to be coherent. He addressed his question to Brian Dempsey.

"Brian, are we to understand that you consider that BaseSoft are the ultimate source of the virus, and that all the U-Sys code is - in itself - clean of infection?"

"Yes, Robert, that is precisely our position. In the near future we will release a new kernel, using the same source code, but compiled by Robert's assembler. The kernel will be clean of the virus. Ergo, our source is clean."

"So, the guilty party must be an employee of BaseSoft? Someone who knew the style of Michael MacDonald's code, right?"

"It would appear so."

"Or indeed, anyone who knew the style of Michael MacDonald's code, and who was able to gain access to, and modify, the BaseSoft assembler. Correct?"

"Yes, it is also possible that someone outside of BaseSoft was able to gain access to, and modify, the code. Unlikely, but possible."

"So let me sum up my understanding, Brian. In order for us to be sure that Michael MacDonald is guilty, we would have to locate ALL of the previous employees of this long-lost corporation - living and dead - and have them convince a jury that at no time - ever - could anyone other than BaseSoft employees have had access to the source code for their assembler. Ever. And that none of these employees - living or dead - had themselves ever worked on the assembler, and thus might potentially be the guilty party. That the only person who could ever have worked on or modified the assembler was Michael MacDonald? Correct?"

"Again, it would appear so. But I am no lawyer, Peter."

"Lawyer, Brian? Gentlemen, what would you not give to be Michael MacDonald's lawyer today? *What court on Earth could find his client guilty?* Believe me, gentlemen, I am not a rich man, but hell, even my lawyer could get him off! And - as we all know - with lawyers, you only get what you can afford." A bitter smile, and the end of the exchange. Robert Perry's forensic analysis left nothing more to be said on the subject. He had been a lawyer himself, back in the deniable mists of time, and the training had never left him. His analysis was sound. *Not Michael MacDonald, not anyone would ever be found guilty of this crime.* This monstrous crime. The pack were going to be cheated of their prey. Forever.

Unsurprisingly, this proved to be the cue for a torrent of abuse, barely and thinly disguised as questions. To their credit, Dempsey and Nehran bore them with quiet patience. They were professionals, on the biggest stage of their career, and they were going to do themselves justice. Finally, Peter Hawkins was able to get the nod. His anger was now cold, contained, and he enunciated his words with a patient fury.

"Mohan, I am interested in the last remarks that Eldon Harker made. From my notes, I quote: *That means that we can direct money into research and development, into the search for progress, and not into the pockets of parasitic lawyers. That will enable us to be able to say, 'Never again!* Are my notes accurate, Mohan?" Mohan was certain that he was. He had good reason for to be.

"Yes, Peter. You are word perfect."

"Great, Mohan. So we have just all been dragged to the edge of chaos by you good people of U-Soft - not your fault, mind - and now you tell us that you will make sure that it never happens again? Never again? And why on earth should anyone, ever, give U-Soft the chance to endanger us all again?" He spoke for them all. What needed to be said. No-one was responsible? Well, U-Soft were. Why on earth would anyone give them the chance to screw up again? Nehran was silent; instead Dempsey replied.

"A very good question, Peter. One that Mr Eldon Harker would very much like to address himself. One moment, please." Click, and there, again, was the electronic image of Harker. The recording started to speak immediately."

"A very good question, ladies and gentlemen. And the answer is... Omnibox."

So Eldon Harker told them about Omnibox. Their own computer, available anytime, anywhere. A physical computer that could not be written to by viruses, but only appeared to be 'their computer' through data stored on a remote server. But was still 'their computer' in any meaningful way. He told them that the data would be defined in an open way: they could use U-Soft for their Omnibox - or anyone else that wanted to compete. It was more like a service, run on vast servers. Servers that were protected from viruses by dedicated technicians - of course - but also by the cleansing focus of competition. Competition that could use radically different software. He told them about software that could make real progress as there were never any older versions to be compatible with. Only ever one current, version: what incompatibilities could there be? He told them about pay-per-use. About how, if you didn't like U-Soft, you could just switch your Omnibox to someone else just like you did for your cable or satellite company. Eldon talked and - despite their determination not to - they listened, and heard, and were fascinated.

It was four fifteen before they swarmed out to file copy. It was not what they had expected, but they had plenty to think about. Plenty to write about, that was sure. It was just a pity that they were a little light on the *bad* news.

The Piazza Navona, Rome: Four Fifteen GMT, Christmas Eve

Hell would freeze over before Solomon the Hunter abandoned a hunt this close to his quarry.

Back in London, the journalists had just started to stream out from the U-Soft conference, clear in the knowledge that no man would stand trial for the Virus. Solomon was, of course, ahead of them. He had already known about BaseSoft. He now knew what they did not: that BaseSoft had had two employees; Michael MacDonald and a Bruce Tiller, alive and well and living in Albuquerque, New Mexico. Legally, the best it could be was one man's word against another, and no jury could make that kind of choice. Beyond a shadow of a doubt, Red Michael MacDonald was safe from prosecution. But Solomon N'Chenga was not a lawyer, but a hunter, and he was not much interested in trials one way or another. But he was interested in his quarry, Red Michael MacDonald. Sitting in the cold of the half-empty December square, Solomon cupped his hands round the large, still-steaming cappuccino. 'I need to meet you, Michael MacDonald' he thought. 'I need to know what you know. Help me to understand why the work of the Virus really is over? Help me to understand about you, Michael MacDonald. Help me to understand just what was your goal, and what else you have set in motion. Understand, Red Michael, that I will hound you to the Gates of Hell, if I have to.'

Then Solomon N'Chenga reviewed his preparations. It is not legal, even in Italy, to use the tiny, hidden wireless surveillance equipment that now studded the churches of Rome. The fifteen hundred transmitters deployed into, and around, seventy five churches. The painstaking work of twenty highly-trained U-Soft technicians. Red Michael was a man who liked fancy churches. 'Well, Christian, where you will go, on Christmas Eve?' Solomon asked himself. 'Yes, I think I already know. Anyway, sooner or later, Michael, I most definitely will know.' With that, Solomon took a great, scalding gulp of coffee, put some coins on the table, and was gone. He strode quickly, for he was eager for the hunt, as always.

BBC Headquarters, London: Four Fifteen p.m. Christmas Eve

'The Cause is dead, long live the Cause!' thought Peter Bradshaw, bitterly. But his bitterness was more than a little tempered by the sweetness of his rediscovered courage. He had agreed, finally, to their demands, but then he had always intended to. In any case, they were not The Cause, but other, more mainstream, politicians. What had happened to The Cause, anyway? Part of the BPP now, sure, but he would have expected to see more of Ferguson now, not less. An odd time to disappear, surely? In any case, The Cause or no Cause, he had made his point. Set down his marker. He - and the BBC - had been kicked around too long. Been too long the unwitting tool of the packs of pressure groups and lobbyists and peddlers of who-knows-what nonsense. *No more*, and he had told them. Leaning back, hands driven by habit to the sides of his sleek scalp, he reviewed his last words.

"I will agree to your request, gentlemen, but please listen carefully to what I have to say. It is now obvious to me that the BBC has become too sensitive to the demands of our many and vocal special interest groupings. Because of that, the BBC has failed in its requirement to serve the interests of the majority of our customers. It is my firm intention to now address that failing. In order to do so, the BBC must be seen to be above any possible taint of bias. It is in that light that I agree to your request.

However, be warned: I mean what I say, and look forward to an opportunity to prove it to you."

Yes, that was what he had meant to say. It was up to them to hear him or not. A couple of minutes to gather his thoughts, then he would make the call. It was the right thing to do.

The Circus Maximus Rome, Four-Thirty GMT, Christmas Eve

Earlier, Ahmed Ali Khan had watched his last sunset, and as the great golden sun sank behind the Roman hills, he did not think he had ever seen a more beautiful one. In fact, it had been a beautiful day, cold but dry and bright, *and* a perfect sunset, and Ahmed thanked Allah for his mercy and his gifts. But now, Ahmed had allowed himself to become distracted. There was a young family on the North perimeter, just an average young family. The parents were perhaps in their late twenties, the child walking, but only just, and something about them had caught his attention. They were just so engrossed in themselves, in the moment, in the shared wonder of the child who could not stop pointing at the great green Sky Galleon. So engrossed, so complete, so happy - not that they probably realised it. Suddenly, Ahmed was hit by a great wave of longing for this future that he would never have. Hit by the overwhelming sense of a life never quite led. But surely, he had been chosen for the highest of honours, the greatest of glories? That meant he had been chosen to make this sacrifice, and he must bear the sorrows that went with it. And then the thought, subversive.

'Then again, who chose me for this sacrifice? Surely it was not *my* choice, for ever since I was a child, my life been directed to this end? My whole life has been but the shaping of a terrible weapon. My life has never been mine to dispose of, to make choices with. No, my choices have all been made for me. By my father, and his friends, and their beliefs. If I had been asked -

361

myself - would I have chosen to make this sacrifice?' And then another thought. 'What if the code does not come? We have only...'

And Ahmed stares down at his watch again. His beautiful, expensive, watch shows five thirty. *Tick, tock.* Eighteen and one half hours left. *Tick tock.* Dragging his eyes away, as Ahmed looks up he catches his father watching him. 'Does he suspect what I am thinking?' he asks himself. 'And what looks so different about him?'

To those who knew Mohammed Ali Khan, he did look subtly different. He is still the tall, rangy, physical man of his North Western genes. His beard is still full, his grey suit still sharp and his green roll neck jersey entirely typical. His grey hair is - yes, that was it - his grey hair was less grey. *Darker.* My father is trying to look his best. It is so unexpected - so worldly, so - and Ahmed freezes on the thought. *Not worldly at all. My father is looking his best for Paradise.*

The watching Mohammed Ali Khan has seen enough. His son needs him, again. Mohammed knows that it is going to be a long night. And still no sign of the code. Yes, a long night. Fine then, all the more for him to savour.

London: Five p.m. Christmas Eve

By five o'clock, most of the people of Britain had started to believe in Christmas again. In London, crowds started to mass in Trafalgar Square, Covent Garden, Piccadilly Circus. They were still cautious, but the news was finally beginning to sink in. The Christmas Virus had been defeated. Life was going to get back to normal. Well, not perhaps normal, but certainly better. The BPP and the Islamists were still facing each other down at the ghettoes, the Party of Western Renaissance - and the General Election - was on everyone's lips, but - hey - not all of that was bad. Things had been going wrong for a while, and at least now matters were coming to a head. People were now, at least, talking freely. Sure, despite everything else going on, they might soon be back at work - or school, God forbid! - but this was Christmas Eve, and no-one was going back to work today, believe me. The same scenes, the same crowds, were being repeated in all the major towns and cities across Britain. Everywhere, more and more people came out, gathering in the corners, squares, shopping malls, and talking. About their relief at the virus fix, about the chaos at the barricades - and what was the government doing about it? - and about politics in general. They talked about the debates, and perhaps they had not been the worst thing? They talked about tonight's debate? Would it still go on? Why not? And its motion, and the virus text: what exactly did it mean? And what about *"Where better for the Will of God to hide, but in that which can never be proved, nor disproved? Is this also but an accident? A lucky accident?"* Was it lucky that we had the luck without which there could be no life?

Across mainland European the mood was also of relief and celebration, although still far from festive. Events on the mainland had lagged behind those in Britain, and they had more reason to be a little cautious yet. Berlin, Paris and Rome were all in the throes of their own version of the 'No confidence' vote. People *did* expect there to be elections - they demanded them, and for the PWR to be in them! - and they looked forward to the impending announcements. *But you never know with politicians.* And, like their fellow-citizens in Britain, they also looked forward to the night's debate.

Catherine Connor had also been very much looking forward to the night's debate. But not any more. The call was not entirely unexpected, and the Director General had been at pains to point out it was not personal, but the result was the same and quite utterly devastating. She was off the debate, and so was Andrew Westlands. Not negotiable. On the very last night - and hell, on Christmas Eve! But she was too disappointed even to be angry. Disappointed, deflated, defeated. And then she got another call, this one from Andrew. His tone was positive, and he certainly didn't waste time on small talk.

"Well, Catherine, it would seem that we have both had our last debate on the Sins of the West. That's good news, because it's time for us to move on. Right now - for some reason - the action seems to be centred round me. Why don't I send a car and you can join me? You can share the experience, or you can report on it, or any mixture of the two. Why not? Now, how often does a young woman get an offer like that?"

Andrew's mood, she sensed, was not as confident as his words. 'Share it or report it?" Or both. Well, as a woman, and a journalist, this was hardly the most difficult decision she would have to make.

Thirty minutes later, Catherine Connor was heading down the Marylebone Road in a rather large and comfortable old car. For the record, Andrew had actually said just a little more.

"I promise you, Catherine, these are going to be quite some days. You're going to meet some rather interesting people, not to mention some of your colleagues in the media. Now, where should I send the car to?"

At least he was old enough and smart enough to give her some warning. That was why the car was heading first to her flat, and her wardrobe and her suitcase. 'I love you, Jimmy Choo' Catherine smiled to herself, while she mentally scanned her wardrobe. Well, there was no way this lady would not be ready for battle. The debate? To hell with the debate. This might just be a lot more exciting. Business and pleasure. What fool said it was a man's world, anyway?

It was six o'clock by the time the car arrived at its destination. It was a nondescript house in a nondescript street and anyway Catherine had hardly arrived but she was leaving. As the car had pulled in, her driver had motioned her to stay put. Less than a minute later, the rear door had opened and Andrew Westlands had leant in, smiling yet apologetic.

"I'm so pleased that you've come, Catherine. *Really delighted.*" A big, genuine, heart-warming smile. Andrew was good at that smile, and Catherine had no choice but to smile back in response. Then his gesture of apology. "Unfortunately, things are moving just a little too fast for comfort. We have to head for the airport ... em ... *now*. Hope to be in Rome for ten, local time. It's a private jet, so we'll be working as we fly. You didn't happen to bring your passport, Catherine, did you?" '*Men!*' Catherine thought. 'How on earth was I supposed to have thought of that?' But she had, not that she was entirely sure why.

"Yes, Andrew, it just so happens that I did. And I normally travel with a little more than a passport, Andrew ... but don't worry, I thought of that too. Now tell me, Andrew, just why we are going to Rome?" With that, Catherine moved over on the seat to let Andrew in. It was a limousine, and the rear seat was vast, but a gesture is a gesture.

A minute later a convoy of four cars pulled out from the nondescript street, bound for the airport. David Blenheim was in one of the cars, talking animatedly on his mobile. Detective Chief Inspector Bendle was in another, together with two of his colleagues. He was rather looking forward to the private jet, and Rome. Anyway, anything had to be better than Mayfair. Hector was in the last car, alone but for his driver. Special Branch and MI-5 might have to work together, but they never mix.

Central London: Six Thirty p.m. Christmas Eve

By six-thirty, it was not just Catherine Connor who knew why she and Andrew and Blenheim and the rest of the circus were going to Rome. For in Rome, Paris and Berlin the results of the no-confidence votes were now in. Their governments had all been voted out. Elections had been called. It was now time for the Party of Western Renaissance to present a united front. The leaders needed to meet: they needed to focus their actions and their policies and the focus of the media. They needed a conference, a showpiece conference where they could present their unified vision of a truly democratic Europe. Where could such a conference be held? Not London or Paris, because the British - or at least, the English - would never agree to Paris, and the French would rather give up wine than consent to London. Berlin, then? The Reichstag? No, not possible. Absolutely not possible, *not at any time.* And with the black and lightning back in the streets? No, the very image sent shudders down the spine.

And what rough beast, its hour come round at last,
Slouches towards Berlin to be born?"

So it had to be Rome. The ancient heart of the first great Western Empire. *Senatus Populusque Romanus.* Strength and Honour. Could there be a better choice, anyway?

So, even to the man in the street, it was obvious. To the gentlemen of the media, there was another, equally obvious reason. What better event for the PWR to hook onto the inaugural flight of *The Green World*? The symbol of a new dawn for the environment, the new dawn for co-operation between Islam and the West? In addition, the media were already gathering in Rome, swarming all around the Circus Maximus and the next day's route. A PWR conference to follow on would be ideal. Convenient. Very convenient: and as everyone in the media knew, if you made their job easy, then the media would make your job easy too.

In Trafalgar Square, the crowds grew deeper and denser as people were drawn to the streets by the excitement of the still-unfolding events. The mood had become exhilarated, jubilant, celebratory. *Like Christmas was coming.* Even the freezing cold of the fountains could not deter some of the hardier ones, although it is true that not very many of the bathers were entirely sober. Nor entirely willing. Yet, the cold and the crush and the noise seemed only to add to the festive mood. *Christmas was coming. Renaissance was coming.* What was not to celebrate? OK, there were still problems, but they were over the worst and surely they were nothing they could not solve?

There were certainly many problems, and many of them continued to flock to the barricades. However, although the volunteers continued to arrive, and to build, and to keep up their vigilance, and to hold to their discipline, there was a rumour. Of course, there were actually many rumours, but one in particular grew more.

The Barricades, Birmingham: Seven p.m. Christmas Eve

'I am a battlefield commander. I lead my warriors from the front. What else can I do, for without their respect, I am already dead.'

The lights pick out the tall, distinctive form of Daniel D, a mere ten yards from the outer ring of barricades. In the still night there is no wind to whip his long dreadlocks, and they hang down his back like a Teuton warrior of old. It is madness to stand so close to the barricades, to present their enemies with the chance to take him out so easily. But the image is compelling, the stuff of history, no shot has rung out, and now it is almost done. Despite the cold, Daniel D wears only a thin black and lightning shirt above the black ski-pants and military boots. His face is still vivid with passion, his eyes light-sabre bright, and he has said enough. The rumour is confirmed. With one last salute, he turns and his volunteers follow his lead. They do their best, but the formation is ragged, their march still amateur. Still, they follow their leader, as they always will.

It was an hour earlier that Daniel D had made his decision. He was a battlefield commander: how else had he got where he was? But - and it was a new realisation for him - much more than that. He was a natural strategist too: perhaps, a brilliant strategist. It was strategy that his warriors needed now. He had not been surprised at the negotiations, but was surprised at how much the fools would concede. Just how much power did a few volunteers give? How much progress could be made with just a few willing killers? More, much more, than he could ever have imagined. Still, Daniel D knew that his position was weaker than those fools realised. Battlefield tactics would only get him so far. Strategy was what he needed, and strategy had called for the negotiations; the spoils of talk, not of war. So, now he had to lead his troops back from the barricades. Put his guns back in their holsters. Well, they would not be far away, when he needed them. More than that, Daniel D knew something the other negotiators did not. Something important.

That was why, an hour later, it was an impassioned Daniel D who had asked his warriors to be patient, and to trust him, and to follow him away from the barricades. Which they did, and headed back to their homes and their pubs.

An hour later, on the military stroke of eight o'clock, Lieutenant Jamie Howland bulldozed his Challenger 2 tank through the inner barricades, and led the small column of Warriors into the Birmingham ghetto. Unmanned drones had been over flying the area all day, and they had all been told what to expect. But no amount of preparation could have readied them for the sight that greeted them.

Loughal road was normally lined by row upon row of shops as many and as varied as the bazaars that inspired them. Now all that remained of the shops were blackened and barbed-wire husks, impromptu barricades, improvised quarries for the supply of brick and stone for the barriers that were urgently needed elsewhere. Standing at the side of the husks were sullen and masked young men, many of them sporting Kalashnikovs, one even proudly brandishing a grenade launcher. Green crescent flags flew everywhere, and there was no hint whatever of the girls or women that must surely still live there. As the great Challenger turned the column right at Barry Road, the destruction became less general, more specific. Here, many of the shops were undamaged: halal fast food outlets, mini supermarkets. Some of these were even open. Almost all the internet cafes and travel agents and money transfer shops were closed and barred, but not all. However, while these were still open, the masked Islamists that lounged from their doorways did nothing for any passing trade. Where there had been DVD hire shops, music shops or - God forbid! - any recognisable chain store, nothing remained but an empty and blackened shell.

Finally, as the column halted at George Square, the first furtive sightings of women, and small children. But the women were more of a blur of black cloth, hunched and clutching their children to their billowing folds. The children were dirty, hungry-looking, and stared with frightened, red-rimmed eyes. But only glimpses. Older men, too, seemed to have vanished. But these were details, noted almost subliminally and recorded as background data. The immediate effect was something entirely different. George Square was festooned with huge posters of Sheikh Mohammed Omar Al Nasran, and the Great Martyr Osama. Some of them pictured sitting together around a campfire, clearly friends. At the far end of the square there was now a large, rough wooden stage. Improvised floodlights lit the stage, although it looked as it had just recently been emptied. The lights glistened on its dark red boards, and in the far corner light glinted off something that glittered. It was a ring: a ring that is still on the hand that lies severed in its mute testament to sin or perhaps just disobedience. It had to be deliberate: a signal that no-one could fail to interpret. This, then, was where the punishments were administered. Here, in the full glare of the lights and the crowd, those who offended them could lose their hand or their head. As an example, to encourage the rest. The air around the stage absolutely reeked of fear and menace and the memory of evil.

Behind the stage, a huge white screen had been erected, no more than just white sheets on a wood backing, but no doubt effective enough. Good enough to show the punishments in gory closed-circuit detail. Banks of speakers to the side, currently playing something alien. Good enough, too, for the debates, the Trials of the West, that were no doubt at least as popular here as everywhere else. And, as Jamie's eye was drawn upward by the screen, he saw them. Face after anxious face, crammed desperately at the windows of the upstairs flats. The terrified faces of children; the terror-filled eyes of the women, that no veil could mask; the desperate faces of the older men, hanging back in fear of being of the summons to prove their allegiance. The poor, wretched - doubly wretched - innocent, ordinary people who a week ago went about their ordinary lives in ordinary content. The meat in the sandwich. Fascists on the outside, fascists on the inside, and the innocent caught between the two.

'This is not Birmingham!' Jamie protested to himself. 'Who could possibly think this is Birmingham? Who could possibly think this is Britain? Beirut, perhaps, or - better - Kabul. But not that either.' To Jamie, this looked like a city that had been captured by bandits, brigands.' It did indeed, and he was not far wrong. A city where the innocent huddled in fear and in hiding and the streets were ruled by the cruel. *All that has to happen for evil to succeed is for good men to do nothing.*

Half an hour later, the first gentlemen of the media were admitted. Brian O'Donnell, of the BBC, was the first to reach George Square. Shell-shocked, angry - raging! - at what he had seen, he was determined to broadcast. Moving his crew to the right of the entrance to the square, under the baleful barrel of the Challenger, Brian felt sufficiently secure to start his broadcast. The scenes were stark, shocking, horrifying, and he knew that the BBC would never broadcast them. The scenes were lacking in cultural sensitivity, done without the co-operation of the community leaders, that kind of thing. Community leaders? These are the oppressors of these people! The cameras rolled, and Brian made his presentation to the audience that would never be. But, to Brian's disbelief, the BBC did broadcast his piece. Apparently, the Director General wanted changes, big changes. 'Publish and be damned' was a rough translation. *It's time to talk, freely,* might be a better one.

SIXTEEN

The God of Small Things had not been on their side, and at nine o'clock their small plane was still minutes from landing at Ciampino airport, Rome. Small delays in traffic, small delays in getting their paperwork cleared, small delays in pre-flight checks, small last-minute delays as they were already on the runway. When you added them all up, then they would be still mid-air when the last debate started. That meant they must either waste time at Ciampino while they waited for it to finish, or interrupt their viewing while they landed and cleared customs. Damn.

'Still,' Andrew thought, 'it's been a good flight.' And, with a smile, 'I feel a little more grounded.' It was true, he did. Catherine had made a difference. The big problem with the media, he was beginning to realise, was the tempo of their process. Continual, rapid, relentless questions, as all the while the cameras recorded your every gesture. It was a process which was designed to ensure that you had no time to *think* out your answer, only to respond by reflex. Like the game where you had to repeat the same phrase, over and over again, and the winner was the one who went longest before he made the inevitable mistake. They were not looking for answers, but news, and the easiest way to get news was to pressurise you into a mistake. Catherine knew the process, inside out, and it made a difference. Limit your exposure. Set the tempo of the interview with the first question. Use facial gestures to play for time. When a question begins... She knew her business, and it made life easier. There were times, however, when she was a distraction. Like when she moved her long legs a certain way, or leaned over a little too close, or a dozen or three things that would suddenly make him see her quite differently indeed. But, there was no doubt he felt better for having her along. Some of that was probably practical. When she had told him that he looked terrible, and that he was no use to anyone exhausted, and why didn't he close his eyes for half an hour, he hadn't resisted too hard. And it worked, he felt the difference, felt ready for the next whirl of the wheel. His thoughts were interrupted by the touch of long slender fingers on is shoulder.

"Andrew, we're getting ready to watch the debate. If you want a ringside seat, I suggest you come now."

Andrew smiled, and followed Catherine to the lounge at the rear of the plane. Blenheim and Chamberlain were already there, their personal secretaries standing behind them. It felt strange to be going to watch the debate, not to participate in it. For he and Catherine to be the spectators, not the players. Despite that, as if by habit, the adrenalin started to kick in. 'You can't teach an old dog...' Andrew thought to himself, and smiled.

The virus may have been defeated, but the debates now had a life of their own. Everywhere, people gathered to watch the debate, just as they had done for the last five days. People wanted to see the last debate. They wanted to hear what the speakers had to say. *Perhaps they wanted to look beyond the surface of things?*

In George Square, Birmingham, the debate seemed to have brought the women and the children - but not the older men - out from their hiding places. Thousands of people were now clustered around the big improvised screen, and a high powered projector cast ten foot heads across the square. Brian O'Donnell had a journalist's sense for a story. The audience would be the players, for a change. He started to film.

In among the still-strewn passenger cabin of the Sky Galleon, one of the technicians had rigged up a miniature satellite dish and a small plasma screen. Ahmed Ali Khan, his father, and a couple of the sweat-streaked technicians were now gathered expectantly around it. Without Catherine and Andrew - and their absence was now public knowledge - it would be different, Ahmed thought. Without the glamorous infidel, more respectful, for one. Less... tempting. Yes, that was the word: tempting. Ahmed Ali Khan, impatient - but yet not impatient, glad for time to slow - glanced at his watch. One minute to ten. Tick, tock.

The Small Studio, BBC Headquarters, London: Nine p.m. Christmas Eve

There is a time for glamour and a time for gravitas and a time when your choice has been long made and only a fool would try to change it. That is why Alastair Smith had tried desperately - but unsuccessfully - to resist the BBC's offer, and why he now stood in front of the studio with an acute sense of being in the wrong place, at the wrong time.

It is nine o'clock in the familiar BBC studio, and the scene that Alastair Smith faces is just as familiar to him as it is to the rest of the world.

A studio audience, exactly one hundred, overwhelming white, perhaps five or six brown or black faces. Eerie.

To his left, the long narrow table with the advocates and the clocks. The advocates, as familiar as family.
Senator William Gladwin: tall, handsome, well-dressed and distinguished.

Krishnan Narajan: thin, grey-haired, ascetic, bifocal and clever
Anwar Abbat: dark, thick-necked, black-bearded and menacing
Anne-Marie Sesoku: tall, black, beautiful and earthy. 'Still some glamour, thank God' thought Smith.

Andrew Westlands: not there, the space below his clock empty. Well, he would explain.

"Ladies and gentlemen, it is my pleasure to welcome you tonight to the last in our series of debates. As you are aware - and can no doubt see - due to an unfortunate conflict of interest,

374

neither Catherine Connor nor Andrew Westlands are eligible to take part in tonight's debate. The BBC has regretfully concluded that the role which Andrew Westlands has so capably played could not be filled, at this late stage, by a new participant. The role of presenter is, however, essential, and it is with gratitude that I, Alastair Smith, stand in front of you tonight. It is my hope, and expectation, that this last debate will prove to be at least as stimulating and thought-provoking as any that have gone before.

"Ladies and gentlemen, let us proceed. The motion for tonight's debate is: *I charge the West with fear, with being too frightened to look deeper than the surface of their lives.* The sequence of speakers is: Anwar Abbat, Krishnan Narajan, Anne-Marie-Sesoku and Senator William Gladwin. Anwar, would you please now get the debate underway."

The Muslim would have the first word. But the American would have the last. Unease. Connor gone. Westlands gone. Unease. Were things still the same? What else - under the surface - had changed?

Certainly, Abbat, on the surface had not. The barely suppressed emotion, rippling ceaselessly under the surface. Aggression; passion; sincerity. The neck muscles bulging. And now relaxing, as he took a deliberate breath. And tensing again, as the deep tones once more cast their familiar spell.

"Ladies and gentlemen, you are accused of being *too frightened to look deeper.* Well, ladies and gentlemen, tonight I must ask you not to be too frightened to look a little deeper. I want you to imagine: to imagine with me..." A pause, a gathering of thoughts.

"Let us first imagine a world without chance. A world without luck. A world where, if you knew enough, you could predict everything that would ever happen. From your first faltering step, to your last dying breath, all can be predicted and known. Imagine this world that whirs like a great mechanical toy. Imagine this world where everything that happens is entirely the result of the

375

way that the machine was constructed and set into motion. Is there life in such a world? How can there be life when all is predictable? No, you are just mechanical mannequins, acting out your parts according to the script you were programmed with. No, ladies and gentlemen, you have imagined a world without life. Take away chance from life, and you take away life itself." It was - for Anwar - an unexpected beginning. But it had *insight*. Already, there were signs that the audience were beginning to recognise this, and to respond.

"Ladies and gentlemen, is there free will in such a world? Of course not! How can there be free will when your every action is already known, ages before you make them? The tone is of derision, mockery. "Your choices had been made long ago, and not by you. No, free will is gone. You have taken away free will. And, without free will, how can there be sin? How, indeed, can there be religion? How can there be a God? Well, perhaps there can still be a God, but his only role can be to construct the machine, and then to set it into motion. After that, the world - and we ourselves - are just a dull mechanical whirr. Imagine such a world, and - admit it! - it was hard for a God to be real. Imagine such a world and - face it! - you have imagined a world without God." A pause, a glance around the audience. This was deeper, faster, and the response was wary, cautious. *Where are you going, Anwar?* said many of the looks.

"But ladies and gentlemen of the West... *your scientists were not afraid to look beyond the surface of things, and this mechanical world is exactly the world that they discovered.*" The words were almost shouted, the enunciation resonant in deep force. *Where, indeed, Anwar? Deep.* The audience uncomfortable. A pause - enough for Abbat to savour it - a continuation.

"They looked - Newton, Faraday, Darwin, I will name but three - they looked and this is the world that they discovered.

Given enough information, and a few more equations, and all - *everything that could ever happen!* - all would be known. They looked beyond the surface of things, and they saw the machine. A complex machine, an *enormously* complex machine, but still a machine. They saw that there was no God, but only this machine, and your world has never been the same since. The rest of the world was not convinced - and especially not the World of Islam - but you people of the West believed in your equations and your science and your *machine* and you would not listen. But at least your scientists continued to look. They were not yet afraid. They looked *deeper*." A pause, slight but still there. *Tension. Expectancy.*

"And they found Quantum Theory. And Chaos Theory. They discovered that they had been wrong. Discovered that the world could never, ever, be mechanical. That, deep down, things were unpredictable. Unknowable. Chance was woven into the very fabric of life. Why? They did not know, and they did not want it to be true, but the experiments proved it. Again, and again, and again. Yes, your scientists looked deeper and they saw that unpredictability - life - was woven into the very fabric of the universe. So your scientists threw away the machine, and brought back life. Brought back free will. Brought back... but no, they did not bring back God. For they had a new name: chance. So they tell us that *chance* is woven into the fabric of the universe. All that happens is, ultimately, down to *chance*. Where there is life, there is *chance*. Where there is *chance*, there is life. An inseparable duo." The audience, silent, absorbed, thinking. Deeper.

"Ladies and gentlemen, I ask you to again imagine with me. Imagine that we do not use this word 'chance'. Imagine, instead, that we use a different term. Imagine if we used the term 'The Will of God' 'Insh'Allah'. Imagine if we said '*The Will of God* is woven into the fabric of the Universe'? Imagine if we said that 'all that happens is, ultimately, down to *The Will of God*. Where there is life, there is *The Will of God*. Where there is *The Will of*

God, there is life.' *Ladies and gentlemen, what is luck and what is the Will of God?* Can we ever know the difference? Are they actually one and the same?" No-one stirred, move, spoke, replied. This was not what they expected from this particular Muslim. Any Muslim. *Deep, deep...* and getting deeper, as Abbat resumed.

"I think we cannot ever really know, ladies and gentlemen. I think that we cannot ever prove what is luck, and what is the Will of God, and what is the difference. *Is it therefore the Will of God that we must have faith? Faith, Insh'Allah?*" A pause, just beginning.

"INSH'ALLAH!" Unexpectedly, impossibly it rang out around the BBC studio. The response: adrenalin, instant, senses on maximum. Who would echo this phrase? Danger: but from where? The wrong place at the wrong time? Yes, and it all unfolded so very fast. A cameraman stepped out from behind his rostrum camera, the one nearest the speakers. A tall man, middle-aged, clean-shaven, white cameraman, clutching some kind of keypad or remote control. His eyes were wild and his lips were wide and his words were hurled loud into the horror-struck studio.

"YOU ARE A TRAITOR, ABBAT! TRAITORS MUST DIE! INSH'ALLAH!"

And die, Abbat did, as forty pounds of C4 exploded in a blinding white ball of light and heat. The C4 had been shaped so that the full force of the explosion would be directed outwards, not above or below. Which it was, and the entire studio was engulfed in a searing wave of shock and flame and deadly shards of white hot metal. Directed or not, the force was too great, and the floor above and the floor below and everyone in them were lost in the smoke and fire and dust. Abbat did not, unfortunately, die alone. The last debate was over, and none of its speakers would ever speak again, freely or otherwise.

At twelve minutes past nine, London time, the screens of three billion viewers flashed white and then went out and for several seconds the world was as quiet as it had been for a very long time. After the silence came the fury, and the storm. Everyone felt they now knew the characters of the debates *personally*, that they were, if not exactly friends, then certainly people that they knew. People who had been brave enough to speak their minds. People with a right to free speech, and to life. And what gave these Islamic fascists the right to snuff these lives out? Just because they did not agree with their views? People felt that the loss was personal: their response was, therefore, emotional. After the sorrow, the reaction. Rage, violence, and revenge swept through the crowds like some new virus. *What were they going to do about this?*

Even in the World of Islam, there was more anger than jubilation. Anwar had become something of a cult figure to many of them. The Good Muslim. What right did these mullahs have to kill him? What good did it do? What was going to come next? Those who did erupt into cheers and chants - and they were, in most places, a minority - were viewed with not-always-well-disguised contempt. What exactly did they think this did for their Great Faith? Was their faith really the same as ours? Come to that, was not Anwar Abbat a martyr for our faith?

At fifteen minutes past nine, London time, in a small jet high above the Rome skies, Andrew Westlands and Catherine Connor were still staring into each other's faces, silent. What had not passed in that long look? Disbelief, shock, sorrow, anger but above all disbelief. It should have been them! Why was it not them? What was happening to them? Why? David Blenheim, finally, was the one to break the spell. He had to. As he spoke, he looked from one to the other.

"Well, it seems like you have both been spared. You can call it luck or fate or The Will of God or anything you like, but the name changes nothing. Your lives have been spared. Now, I think, you both have the chance to make the most of them."

It said more than the words alone did and it broke the spell and Catherine suddenly crumpled. A woman, with a woman's tears, suddenly, *maddeningly*, vulnerable. The effect immediate: Andrew moving to her, holding her tightly to him, stroking the long hair as he felt the heat of the wet tears soak through the shoulder of his shirt. Well, right now she had to do the crying for both of them. Things were just simpler that way.

By the time the small jet touched down at Ciampino, ten minutes later, Catherine had recovered, as women quickly do. She had things to do, and plenty of time later for tears. Glancing across at Andrew, she was inwardly delighted at the grimness of the look on the slightly-worn face. Andrew, it was clear, was not going to let her down. Or anyone else for that matter. As it happens, Andrew was thinking much along those lines. He was determined to do what he had to do. For everyone. But he was under no illusions. They were still *nowhere*. It still looked - he hated to admit it to himself - an almost impossible task. He would do his best. But would it be enough? Well, what more could he do: the rest was fate, was it not? Or was it?

Sitting in the row opposite them, were David Blenheim and Chamberlain. Sitting together, Blenheim thought, and probably thinking much the same things.

'Time to be the practical politician. If you want to do something, then you must first get the power to do so. We need to get you that power, Andrew. For all of us.' Looking across at Andrew and Catherine, the overwhelming thought. 'What an opportunity for you, Andrew and Catherine! What an incredible opportunity! The sole survivors. *Spared by the Will of God*. The focus of the world on you - now more than ever, and just when you most need it! The Renaissance survives in this glamorous couple.

Destiny's Chosen. The Chosen Couple. Oh yes, Andrew, I think I can get you power. And just what power will that give you, Catherine, if that is what you choose?' That was an unexpected thought, and interesting, and Blenheim stayed with it for a while.

Television is show business, and when you have the world watching, the show most certainly must go on. The BBC rapidly rose to the challenge, and within five minutes of the explosion, the screens were once again filled with dramatic images. The images, dramatic and powerful, were of the reaction to the slaughter and the outrage. The images were shot from George Square, Birmingham, and they were supplied by Brian O'Donnell, whose turn it was to be in the right place at the right time. Twenty fours ago, the BBC would not have shown them, but this twenty fours had been a very long time in the life of the BBC.

The images, shot from the entrance to the square, panned around the posters and the banners and the huge white screen and the seething mass of cheering, chanting, young men and women. The real-time soundtrack of the Allu Akbars and the high scream of the ullahs and the sharp crack of the Kalashnikov tracers as they lit the night sky in fiery celebration. The young man, face wrapped in a green shawl, advancing towards the camera and the Challenger. In his hand a petrol bomb, unlit rag protruding from its top. He is taunting the camera as he advances, deliberate, confident. The images a catalyst for other images. The Trafalgar Square crowd roaring in fury and anger, the cries of rage and the chants of 'BPP! BPP!' as a large black and lightning is unfurled. A mob on the verge of becoming a pack of killers, and the scene repeated across the country and across the streets and squares of the civilised West.

Too late, Sheikh Mohammed Omar Al Nasran gets the message and reacts. Just as the young man's hate-filled face comes within a few yards from the camera, two men burst from the crowd behind them. Two men in camouflage suits, faces robed in black, screaming, Kalashnikovs gesticulating in unmistakable anger. Bewildered, the young man drops the petrol bomb, glass shattering, petrol spilling around his feet. Frightened, now as camouflage jackets force him to his knees. His face is hidden, but 'What have I done wrong?' is briefly written in his pitiful gestures, before his face is hidden forever by the clip of bullets that shatter his head into a thousand shards of bone and brain and blood.

'Act in haste and repent at leisure." Daniel D smiled to himself. 'One mistake leads to another. I have the initiative now, you fools. You will never regain it, believe me.' Daniel D had, indeed, planned well. He knew, as every terrorist knew, that their most potent weapon was propaganda, and the media was the battleground. *Propaganda, propaganda, propaganda. Media, media, media.* Daniel D echoed the mantra. Daniel D also knew that propaganda was not like an ordinary weapon, such as a gun or rifle or a sword. A sword was a weapon in itself. It would always be a weapon. But an event, that was different. Today an event might be a weapon: tomorrow the same event might be nothing, or - even worse - a weapon only for your enemy. Today's sword could be tomorrow's landmine. To win the propaganda war, you had to move quickly, always. Anticipate, act, anticipate. How many troops had this propaganda victory given him? Millions? That was the key to ultimate victory, for, in the end, Daniel D knew that propaganda could only go so far. 'How many divisions does the Pope have?' as Great Stalin had asked. No, sooner or later you needed troops. Divisions. Well, he would have them. Perhaps soon. Insh'Allah, and he smiled at the irony of it all.

The Circus Maximus Rome: Eleven a.m. Christmas Eve

'It was a mistake,' thought Ahmed 'watching the execution with the infidels. They just did not understand that it was justice. Had no stomach for justice, anyway. And the irony...' It had been almost too much. It had been hard enough not to scream with joy at the great strike against the traitor Abbat. Harder yet to express outrage at the majesty of Allah's justice. But the irony, when the poor fool infidel technician had said:-

"It puts all this into context, Ahmed. I'm so proud to be able to work for *peace* between our cultures. And I'm even more proud to know you, and your father, and just to be a part of this great adventure. Soon - God willing - those madmen will be consigned to the footnotes of history.' With that, he had got up and gone back to work. Back to work!! *Consigned to the footnotes of history!* The irony, the almost unbearable irony. He did not know. The infidel did not know what he was working on. And when he did know, would he then feel quite so proud? Anyway Ahmed now had to concentrate. It was ... and Ahmed glanced at his watch. Eleven o'clock. Thirteen hours of sweet, sweet life. Tick-tock. Then Paradise. Hopefully. *Anyway, I am already dead.* Glancing up, Ahmed caught his father's eye, the unspoken question. He nodded reassurance: 'I am ready, father' he said to himself. 'Ready to do my duty to you and to Allah, The Most Merciful.' But the final code was still to arrive. Thirteen hours. Tick, tock. It would arrive, Insh'Allah. Here, as Ahmed looked out at the dark night, death felt nearer. More intimate. Less alien. It was the bright noon day that he feared. How many hours away? Tick, tock, and before he could stop himself, he glanced down again.

The Excelsior Hotel, Rome: Eleven a.m. Christmas Eve

Rome is in Italy, and in Italy they still know how to value a politician's friendship. That is why Signor Di Giacomo had to perform to the heights of his considerable talent earlier this evening, as he smoothed his dear Hollywood friends from the edge of riot, into acceptance, and understanding, and into the kind keeping of their sister hotel which was in any case at least as good. That is why the entire top floor of the Excelsior hotel was now occupied by Westlands, Connor, Blenheim, Chamberlain and party.

There are three suites on the top floor of the Excelsior: the Goethe, the Proust, and the Shakespeare. Chamberlain was shown to the Goethe: Blenheim to the Proust: Di Giacomo, with evident pride, ushered Westlands to the Shakespeare. The Shakespeare was a vast suite, the entrance hall leading into a huge lounge, off which there were two cloakrooms, a kitchen and - thankfully - *three* bedrooms. Naturally, Signor di Giacomo, with the instinctive romantic optimism of the Italian male, had booked Catherine into the same suite as Andrew. But of all the nights that Andrew would have chosen for romance, this would have to be the last on the list, and - worse - Catherine had not been given a vote. But *three* bedrooms ... and Andrew glanced towards Catherine. She was in front of him, already walking, and he could not see her face.

"I'll take the one on the left, if you don't mind, Andrew. And right now, I'm going to have a brandy, and a bath." The door closed and the awkwardness passed and Signor Di Giacomo shrugged his shoulders at Andrew in a sympathetic gesture of regret.

Five minutes and two calls later, and there was at least an outline plan. The Shakespeare would be the centre of their operations and they would meet here in half an hour's time. They all knew that there was too much to do and too little time, but that they had also to be fit for the conference tomorrow. And vaguely presentable. So they set a deadline: come three o'clock, the meeting is over and they grab a few hours' rest. Tomorrow was the day. Renaissance Day.

'Well,' thought Andrew, 'I've got half an hour. Good enough for a shower and shave and a chance to write my Christmas list.' He would have loved a Talisker 25, but that would have to wait. 'Put it on your Christmas list, fool!' he mocked himself, and headed for the shower.

Hector and Bendle were also happy with the arrangements. The entire top floor was now theirs to isolate and secure. The stair entrances were now both guarded by two armed officers and also under remote visual surveillance. The lifts had been reprogrammed to prevent any access to the top floor. That is, except for the one - discreet - lift that goes directly from the ground floor to the top. Very discreet, since its entrance is behind an unmarked door. Two of Bendle's finest were stationed - clumsily, in Hector's opinion - close to this door. Two more waited at the top. The lift itself had been embedded with cameras and scanners, and these broadcast their encrypted images directly to the handheld monitors that Hector, Bendle and everyone else now carried. It was not perfect, but it was all that they could do in the circumstances. That left Hector free to roam the top corridor, alert, suspicious, and thinking.

The Circus Maximus, Rome: Midnight, Christmas Eve

The Circus Maximus is not an elongated oval, but the blade of a spear, and it pointed right at the very heart of Rome. Ahmed Ali Khan had seen that - *immediately* - the first time he had looked at a map. Insh'Allah, it was so fitting, so perfect, so obvious he wondered why no-one else had noticed it. But here, on the very stroke of midnight, all he could see through the glass of the gondola was his reflection.

It was a unique feature in the design of the Sky Galleon that the passenger compartment - more properly, the gondola - was detachable. That meant that the transformation of a Sky Galleon from a first class liner to a basic freight workhorse was as simple as detach/attach. *Clunk-click*, they called it. The clunk-clicking was done by four titanium tubes that secured the gondola at each of its corners. The hollow tubes also sheathed the power cables that ran to and from the solar cells, the wind-driven turbines, the propellers, and the batteries. The particular gondola that Ahmed now stood in was a mere sixty feet by forty feet. Its upper half was formed from a transparent plastic composite, its lower, load-bearing half was fashioned in an aluminium/magnesium alloy. The front of the gondola was almost identical to the flight deck of any modern airliner, a couple of seats, a joystick, bank upon bank of dials showing everything from the basics of speed and altitude, to the Galleon specific esoterica such as effective wind power and cell charge rate. Behind that was - and now that it was almost empty, it finally looked like it again - a lounge area: seats, coffee table, plasma screen. Further back there were two single beds, and at the end of the gondola, a small toilet and a galley kitchen. In the interests of privacy, the rear half could be screened from the outside by a dark green semi-circular curtain. The whole gondola was carpeted, save for a small six by four area just rear of the lounge area. This was the hatch to the battery compartment, and was kept clear to ensure that battery maintenance was kept as simple as possible. Which was just as well, because one of the twelve state-of-the-art Nickel metal hydride cells was faulty, and they were waiting on the arrival of its replacement.

As Ahmed Ali Khan turned away from his reflection, he could see only two other people on the gondola: his father, and one - last - technician. The delivery of the replacement battery had been delayed - the lorry broke down, or got caught in traffic, something - but there was no reason for any more technicians to wait. The battery was being delivered by specialists, who were fully trained in its fitment. And there was nothing else to do, they knew that. The Sky Galleon had already flown. It had already undergone the final ministrations of its Bavarian craftsmen in Munich, and had arrived here this morning under its own steam. Everything worked, and it did not take two dozen PhDs to change a battery, however special. So only one remained, but not for long. Ahmed would send him away soon, he could come back early tomorrow if he really needed to. Because the people who would arrive with the battery really were specialists. So was their battery. It was made of lead, Americium, Cobalt, and C4, and, to many, it was worth far more than the Sky Galleon itself. This last battery was the perfect specimen of the poor man's atomics: a dirty bomb. A *sacred* bomb. A bomb fashioned from three key ingredients: americium, for the alpha rays that could provide a lethal radiation dose so immediately; cobalt, for the gamma rays that would render a place toxic for a century; and C4 to create the avenging Cloud of Allah, and to spread its dread rain as far and as fast as possible. Not to mention the fiery storm of molten, flesh-shredding, metal shards that would mean instant death to any its path. A bomb indeed. A bomb that would change history, and would start the Final War that was to come.

'Judgement is coming, infidels.' So close now, Ahmed liked the sound of the words. Revelled in them. 'Judgement is coming, infidels. Soon.' Without thinking, he glanced down at this watch. Tick, tock.

The Tiber, Rome: Eleven a.m. Christmas Day

"Why do you run from me, Christian, when you know I can't harm you? Why won't you just stop and answer my questions?"

Solomon N'Chenga had wandered down the labyrinth of back

387

streets that led from the Pantheon, and now stood leaning on a railing looking down on the dark Tiber. The night is clear, bright and cold, and Solomon is wrapped against its chill by a full-length leather coat, gloves, and a dark cap. Solomon N'Chenga had posed himself the question, because he now knew just a little more than he had an hour ago. In fact, he knew all there was to know about BaseSoft Inc. That there had been two employees: Michael MacDonald, and a Harry Falk, now deceased, killed in a car accident this past two years. No court in the land could touch Red Michael MacDonald. His wife Karen had said he would be back, and he would. But why not now? Waiting until the heat had gone down? Probably, it would be the smart thing to do.

'But I don't want to wait, Christian. So I will find you. And I know just where to look for you, Christian, tomorrow.' Solomon then corrected himself. 'Not tomorrow, Christian. Today.' Solomon looked up at the night sky, especially bright. Where was the star that led the magi, all those years ago? Do I need you, star?' Almost imperceptibly, Solomon shook his head. 'Hell no, I don't. I know fine just where to find the Christian. Today.' Solomon wrapped his coat tighter against the water-borne cold, and strode towards the bridge.

At the same moment, Red Michael MacDonald was just over a mile away, in the Santa Maria Maggiore, and still at Midnight Mass. If any of the congregation notices the unusual fervour in his singing, or the rapt attention of his prayers, this is Rome, and in Rome it can happen. Nor do the five remote cameras pay him any attention, as Solomon's people relentlessly scan the audience for faces. For what is that they see? For Red Michael MacDonald is invisible, and in his place is a white-bearded Fransciscan, familiar and comfortable in his brown robes. His head is hidden - although it is still clear that he does not have much hair - by a clerical hat, but in any case he is a brown-eyed man. Half an hour later, the brown-eyed monk strides down the via Orissimo, heading towards the cold of the river and beyond. If he is tired, then the signs are subtle, for he walks fast and his look is purposeful.

SEVENTEEN

The Circus Maximus, Rome: Two a.m. Christmas Day

"Please enter access code:" Ahmed's laptop asked.

'This one I do know.' Ahmed thought, smiling grimly.

"One seven four five" he typed.

"Invalid code. Please re-enter:" his laptop replied. 'So far so good', Ahmed thought.

"Two eight five six" he typed.

"Please wait" was the response. *Please wait*. Exactly what had he been doing this last two hours, and still he needed the real code?

Ahmed Ali Khan was on the right hand side of the flight deck of *The Green World*, his laptop plugged into a USB port. The design of the Sky Galleons was every bit as computer friendly as you would expect a twenty first century marvel to be. With a laptop, cable and the right access codes, you could download - or set - almost every aspect of the great ships history or behaviour. What specifically interested Ahmed tonight, however, was not speed nor distance nor charging rates nor any of the other ordinary elements of this extraordinary creation. He was interested in the batteries. Not in their charge level - which one of the dials showed anyway - but in the hidden access into their advanced configuration. More specifically yet, he was interested in access to the one battery-that-was-not-a-battery that had arrived fifteen minutes ago, and that he must now test to make sure that it was correctly installed.

"Please wait" it bleeped again. Then the display cleared.

"Bomb status operational. Please proceed to enter activation codes manually."

Codes, always codes, it was the world they lived in. The bomb had to be code protected - if not, even some of their own might be tempted to find another use for it. Or, more likely, sell it, for what was its worth? To the infidel gangsters? To the heretic Shias? Ahmed knew how the bomb was designed. The steel container, and the lead lining to protect the faithful from its invisible - but lethal - radiation while the bomb was in transit. The C4 shaped around the six kilos of Americium, which they had got from their oil exploration interests. Slowly, carefully, undetectably, over the long years. And the C4 shaped around the Cobalt-60, painstakingly gleaned from the cancer wards of a hundred or more hospitals. *If they have cancer, then let them die*, was how his father put it. *They will never know the difference*. But the codes: the codes would do two things. Firstly, they would spring apart the steel and lead sides of the bomb. Without the codes, the sides would stay in place and much of the bomb's power would be lost, absorbed by the lead and steel. A waste of a bomb. If you were not trying to use the bomb, but to steal its contents, without the codes any attempt to open the case would just trigger a small explosion with the protective lead and steel still in place. You - and much around you - would die, but the contents would be transformed into little more than small-but-lethal cloud of dust. *It was the codes made the bomb useful as a bomb, and only as a bomb*. Yes, his great father knew the first trigger code. But no-one was trusted completely. It was not personal, but what if the infidels were to get to work on them with their drugs, and their suggestion, and their magic with lies? No, the second code was only to be sent when their great leader knew that *The Green World* was operational, and that Ahmed Ali Khan and his father were both on board, and ready. It was the one final bit of insurance. But now it was getting late! There was so little time! There was only … and, before he could stop himself, Ahmed glanced at his watch. Again. Tick, tock. *Tick, tock.*

"Ahmed, my son, there is time enough. Have faith. Ready your computer, and let us go to pray, on this, our last night before Paradise."

He was right, as always. So Ahmed Ali Khan disconnected his laptop and left it on the pilot's seat. The Sky Galleon was equipped with an excellent satellite-based internet connection, and his laptop would check for mail every minute or so. When it got mail, it would send an alert to his mobile phone. Yes, why not go to pray? After all, what better thing to do, on this the last night of your life. And then - like a bolt from the blue - it was there, again. *Prayer? I can think of better things to do before you leave this sweet, sweet life. Prayer? I thought martyrs always went to heaven, anyway, did they not?* Ahmed shivered, and, under his breath, uttered his incantation.

"Allah, the Most Merciful, please give me strength."

The Hotel Excelsior, Rome: Three Thirty a.m. Christmas Day

"The people want excitement, and drama, and glamour: give them it, combine it with politics, and they will give you power. They will give us all power."

With that statement, Jacques DuCrocq had won the argument, and the conference was going to go ahead, at three o'clock this afternoon. The European leaders were all gathered here: Jacques Ducrocq from Paris, Berndt Kessel from Berlin, Paolo Canera from Rome, and David Blenheim and himself. Initially, Andrew had suggested that they postpone the conference. That the intense public focus on himself and Catherine, their perceived romance, their last-minute reprieve from the slaughter at the BBC, *the whole thing*, was a distraction from their serious goals. That they should wait until the people focused again on the fundamental issues, were not so swayed by soap opera drama. Blenheim had disagreed - strongly - and Canera had asked him to please listen

392

to the advice of professional politicians. Kessel had yet to speak when Ducrocq had cut through the crap, and put the argument to rest. *The people want excitement, and drama, and glamour: give them it, combine it with politics, and they will give you power.* He was right and the conference - the show? - would go on. So what about the conference? What were the key themes? Who was to say what? Would they speak as individuals, or only as members of a group? How long should it be? When should it start?

Actually, given the scope for disagreement - limitless, and traditional - they had made remarkable progress. They had also, more or less, stuck to their pre-assigned schedule, and left not long after three. Catherine - who had texted Andrew hours ago to tell him she was not going to reappear until the morning - would be long asleep. Andrew was, he knew, exhausted, but adrenalin is easier to turn on than off, and sleep was nowhere close. Well, it was Christmas Day, and he had made his list. That meant he was allowed one Talisker Twenty-Five, large. Which he did and, as always, it did the trick. By four a.m. Andrew was asleep, and already dreaming. Of power, and all that it made possible.

Actually, Catherine had not been sleeping that long before him. She had been more shocked than she had realised, and more confused than she could remember. Shocked at the carnage at the BBC, at their lucky escape, and at all those who had not been so lucky. Especially her characters. *The prophet, the philosopher, the demagogue and the Siren Queen*: dead, incredibly, all dead. Gone. She felt a terrible sadness at the sheer waste of it, lives suddenly extinguished and for what? Only the revolutionary remained - what did that mean? And, of course, herself, and somehow they were now *The Lucky Couple.* Were they a couple? Was she here as a journalist, or as part of a couple? Was she a politician? A politician's partner? What role was she to play and how did you play it, anyway? The confusion, the shock, the never-quite-far-away emotion, that might at any time betray her. No, this was a time to be on her own, to gather herself, to soak, and to sip her brandy, and to make herself ready for the morning. Not a time to be meeting politicians. Anyway, the politicians would still be there tomorrow, and they could wait. After all, it was a woman's privilege, was it not? By tomorrow, however, she would need to have made her mind up. Which role was she to play? Another thought: did she really have a choice?

The Circus Maximus, Rome: Six a.m. Christmas Day

Perhaps, after all, this is all just the mercy of Allah, The Most Merciful. That no code will come, and He will find another way to His Will. Perhaps all the deaths will not be necessary. Perhaps He will spare the innocent young, at least.

It is dawn, but Ahmed Ali Khan is in that twilight world that lies between prayers and dreams. His phone has not rung and his laptop - as he looks over - still lies dormant on the pilot's chair. The night has been long - and is long good or bad, now? - and his mind has struggled to find any peace. Yes, martyrdom awaits, and all the pleasures of Paradise, but life is sweet, too. For everyone, not just him. Why must he be the man who pulls the trigger on a war that will kill millions upon millions? Infidels and believers alike. Men, women and children. Like the little blonde boy, with the ball. Dead, tomorrow, and why, most merciful Allah, is this the only way? No, perhaps the code will not arrive in time, or - a new thought - it might not work? Yes, was it possible it would not work? What was it his teacher had said? *The problem with puzzles is that so many clever people are attracted to solving them?* Ahmed Ali Khan considered the puzzle of the codes.

The brilliance of the code breakers of the NSA and GCHQ was legendary, and greatly intimidating. Not only that, this brilliance was now allied to the power of the computers that could just analyse a message, over and over and over until it made sense. People always leave patterns, and eventually those patterns will betray you. And if your computer can go fast enough …? So Al Quaeda, like many terrorist organisations, now relied heavily on pictures, because the computers were *no good* at reading messages embedded in pictures. Steganography, to give it its formal name. Where the font was nothing specific, where the angle and shape of the character was unusual, where there were dots where they should not be. Drunken writing. Drunken writing was just so very hard for the computer to read. However, you needed more: much more. The words themselves needed to meaningful only in the light of some secret, shared knowledge that the code breakers could not have. For example, what was the name of our local shop? What was the name of your favourite aunt? Who did you walk to school with?

From these principles, the Al Quaeda process had evolved. To send a message, write something innocuous and attach a number of pictures at the same time. There could be several pictures, but usually two. Use a specially written program - *Caliph*, and well named! - to lay the pictures on top of one another, *as you combine two negatives to make a positive*. The new positive image would then contain embedded characters, the characters written in the drunken scrawl that computers found so hard to read. *Caliph* would display this positive picture, and you - a human operator - would then find and read the characters. Next, you would enter the characters into the box below the picture. *Caliph* would translate, transform, and expand these characters, and, finally, reveal the message. It was beautiful, almost impossible to crack, but there was one weakness. What if the characters you read were unclear? It happened. Normally, there be some kind of self-check, so that the *Caliph* software would tell you it was not possible. But did that always work? And, in this case, when the answer was so very short. Fourteen characters. *Fourteen numbers.* What if he did not read the characters properly and there was no self-check? *What if - through the mercy of Allah, the Most Merciful - he got the wrong fourteen numbers?* Life, sweet life, for me. For everyone. But no, Ahmed, you fool! *For you are already dead.* They may be spared, but you will not. Surely, if he was to die, it should not be for nothing? How much time did he have now? The unstoppable glance: six hours. Tick, tock. Fighting down his panic, Ahmed Ali Khan went back to his prayers.

The Circus Maximus, Rome: Nine a.m. Christmas Day

It was the one hundred and first Surah that he had turned to in these last few hours. Al Qari'ah: The Calamity, *The Stunning Blow.*
  'The Day of Noise and Clamour.
  What is the Day of Noise and Clamour?… '
The Bomb: the alchemy of alpha and gamma and plastique. Plus one, last, deadly ingredient. The Distribution Vector. Or, in this case, more simply: height. The alpha particles were deadly if ingested or in contact with the skin: not immediately deadly, more the long slow torture of the cancers and the sheer utter *inevitability* of it. Unfortunately, the alpha rays were easily blocked: unless, of course, they came down on a cloud from above. The gamma rays, on the other hand, would not be blocked easily and they would last a hundred years, but it was essential to distribute them as widely as possible. Like from a cloud from above. *The plastique, the cloud-maker.* Their great bomb, therefore, would come from above, and it would be exploded above their heads. Specifically, their bomb would be altitude-triggered at a height of one hundred and fifty feet. That meant that the bomb could only be armed when they were safely above that height, or it would explode when they were going up -

here, above the Circus Maximus, *in the wrong place.* Nor was the arming of the bomb the only thing that had to be left to the last minute. Unfortunately, even when Ahmed Ali Khan - finally! - received the promised message, he still had much to do. To decrypt the message - *correctly*, Allah be merciful! - to enter it manually into the bomb, to load the other messages into the huge, computerised display screen, to prepare the decouplers, to... prepare himself. So little time, now. Ahmed looked around the gondola, now once again buzzing with overalled technicians, checking this, checking that, focused, intense, seemingly efficient. Fools. *Today is The Day of Noise and Clamour.* Ahmed glanced towards the flight deck, and his laptop, sitting on the pilot's chair... *but it wasn't!* What fool had moved....panic rising, Ahmed leapt to his feet and barged - rudely, roughly, he had NO TIME! - past a gaggle of overalls and on into the flight deck. His laptop...? There, on the co-pilot's wide window ledge. Safe! Allah be merciful! Safe, and off. Screen blank and no power cable protruding from its rear! Power saving mode. *Sleeping. No message received because his laptop was sleeping...*

Feverishly, Ahmed Ali Khan brought the laptop - slowly, achingly slowly - back into life, past the wake-up password, past the system restore, back onto the broadband network, back into mail collection and - tick, tock, tick, tock - connected to the mail server and... *two messages waiting.* The first - agony! - spam, always spam! The second, '*Good luck on your momentous Day*', and two attachments. The words of the Surah One Oh One echoed:-
   '*It is a day whereon men will be like moths scattered about,*
   And the mountains will be like carded wool.
   Then he, whose balance of good deeds will be found heavy,
   Will be in a life of good pleasure and satisfaction.
   Be he whose balance of good deeds will be found light,
   Will have his home in a bottomless Pit.'
But he must move, *now.* He must take the laptop to the back,

find himself a private area. The message must be decoded before he was forced to join in the formalities of the flight ceremonies. The ceremonies to mark this momentous journey. *For this short journey, fools!* How long did he have? The irresistible glance: two hours fifty minutes. Tick, tock.

The Hotel Excelsior, Rome: Nine a.m. Christmas Day

Catherine Connor was a morning person: every day starts without any mistakes in it. Whether it was really anything to do with adopted mental attitude, or the phase of her birthday moon, or just the way she was built, the net effect was the same.

'Bright, shining, cheerful, amusing…' Andrew thought. 'I cannot deny it. It is nice to have a woman around in the morning, again.'

She had wakened him over an hour ago, one small dark mocha square poised perfectly beside a steaming, aromatic espresso.

"Rise and shine, Great Leader' Catherine began brightly. 'Try the chocolate. You look like you need it. First meeting is booked for eight forty five. Let's try and look our best, now. This is theatre, Andrew. Mustn't disappoint your audience. And definitely not me, darling, is that not right?" A perfectly brilliant smile, and suddenly Catherine's fragrance was all that was left behind.

Never forget to lock your bedroom door, Andrew thought. Still, Catherine did a most charming wake-up call, even if it was a little early for him to be taking orders. Thinking about it, Andrew wasn't entirely convinced Catherine's threats were empty. A sip of the espresso, a bite of the fine dark mocha, a slurp of the rest of the liquid caffeine. It melted the mocha *just so*. 'Hmm, not the worst way to do your coffee,' thought Andrew. He could not resist his well-used mantra. 'But I need to be careful. For, after all, I am an old dog and this *is* a new trick.' And it was, but then again Catherine was, too. An involuntary smile to himself. She was most definitely in his sights, and she did fill them so very beautifully. Then the first real kick of adrenalin, and the last vestiges of the easy comfort of sleep firmly left him. 'And so is all of today. Entirely new. Entirely difficult. You have no time to indulge yourself, old man. No time at all.' Andrew listened to himself and was ready by eight forty. Perhaps he might even have thought that he was ready enough.

The Circus Maximus, Rome: Eleven a.m. Christmas Day

'Not all killers are *stone-cold* killers.' thought Ahmed Ali Khan. 'It is a mistake, an easy mistake. Shock and confusion can give the illusion of coldness. Inside, he may have been on fire.'

Ahmed is *on fire* inside, inside his head. It was almost two hours since he received the message and rushed his laptop into privacy. Almost two hours since he had sat down in the only private area of the bustling Sky Galleon, the small toilet at the rear. If it appeared to the technicians that he was the victim of fear, then who cared what the fools thought anyway? They were Dead Men Walking. But then, he had almost been unable to remember the password to start *Caliph*, his mind stubbornly refusing to yield the name that he knew almost as well as his own. And then, finally, it came back to him, and he was in, and *Caliph* was busy. The message, the two images, the endless visual manipulations, objects appearing and disappearing, and, finally, the drunken words appearing - but only if you knew how - and where - to look. Where? At the bottom left of the screen, just where your eye wandered least. How? Not always easy. The letters 'h', 's', 'u' - so far, not bad - 'L', 'r', 'm', 'q' - clear enough - 'k', 'i' - no, 'j' , surely - no, 'i', definitely - 'o', - no, zero, surely? - *do not be foolish, no numbers, remember?* - 'd', 'h', 'k', 's', 'a', 'B', 'Z'. 'hsuLrmqkiodhksaBZ'. Or 'hsuLrmqkjodhksaBZ'. 'Allah, be merciful, I cannot be certain! 'i' or 'j', it is not clear! Is there a check sum? There must be a checksum: if I enter the wrong characters, surely *Caliph* will tell me and ask for a different set. But perhaps not? Which one to try? First thoughts or second thoughts? Allah, the most Merciful, please help this poor sinner. I am so short of time. I have only ... ' - and again the irresistible glance. *Tick, tock.* 'Please, Allah, the most Merciful, please help this poor sinner, NOW?'

Perhaps Allah the Most Merciful did help Ahmed Ali Khan. Perhaps there was a check-sum, something that would have warned him, if he had not read the characters correctly. But he could not be certain, for *Caliph* had just given him its answer. Perhaps the characters he had entered had all been correct, but perhaps also there was no self-check. But dare he go back and try again? Did he have the time? Did these numbers that *Caliph* now displayed look they were The Numbers? Ahmed had stared fervently at the fourteen digits, commanding their apparent randomness to reveal their true pattern. *All patterns reveal the Will of God, if you are so blessed.* But Ahmed saw no pattern, just fourteen digits: '84625329076513' What was this number, really? Really, *in itself*?

Now, it was eleven o'clock and Ali Ahmed Khan had glided through the ceremonies behind a mask of panic-induced shock. Not waving, but drowning. Not wishing me good luck, but saying good-bye. The Cool One who was really - *red hot* - frozen in fear. Now, only fifteen minutes of private-yet-public prayer, fifteen minutes for the last checks, the last formalities, and then they would cast off. Off, and up, and onwards. Paradise awaited Ahmed. Tick, tock. Not only that, but right now, in the great square, the infidels would be revelling in their idolatry. The very public idolatry of the Great Infidel.

"La llaha illa illah wa Muhammad rasul Allah" Ahmed chanted soundlessly to himself: "*There is but one God and Muhammad is His Prophet*"

But the little blonde boy would be there, and his parents, and many like him, and Allah was Merciful, surely, above all things?

The Circus Maximus, Rome: Eleven Fifteen a.m. Christmas Day

Their Time had Come.

It is measure of the respect in which the Italians hold their politicians, that Westlands, Connor, Blenheim and Canera were able to look down onto *The Green World* from the vantage point of a circling Bell helicopter. They were not permitted too close, of course, but even to be this close to the Sky Galleon?! Certainly, no journalist could hope to gain that kind of clearance, and - right now, at least - no other politicians had sufficient future that they even dare risk ask.

It was, Andrew thought, quite a most remarkable sight. The sheer size of the brute. The sheer ambition of its entirely renewable - well, almost - propulsion. The size of the crowds, must be two hundred thousand at least. But Andrew knew that the most remarkable aspect of the Sky Galleon was invisible: it was the reason behind its existence. The attempt at rapprochement between the West and The World of Islam. The rapprochement - so their advisers hoped, anyway - that would come to be seen as a key symbol of the Renaissance that would now unfold. The Second Chance. It was not mere tourism that had Andrew flying today, no, far from it. This was a press opportunity, an historic one, and - today, of all days - every opportunity had to be taken. Today was their day. Their Time had Come. The Bell banked as the pilot swung it to the great ship's starboard side. There, the huge electronic bulletin board, carried its message of conciliation. 'Happy Christmas and Peace to All Men'. The Sky Galleon and the board and the message and the Renaissance chopper: yes, it made for a great shot, Andrew thought, cynically. He was not entirely comfortable with something so stage-managed, so manufactured, and had said so. Catherine had told him to act like a professional, and to do his job for all their sakes'. It was a fair point, he had to admit. Damn it.

The Circus Maximus, Rome: Eleven thirty a.m. Christmas Day

The Circus Maximus is the blade of a great spear that points right at the heart of St Peter's Square. At eleven thirty on the morning of Christmas Day, half the blade of that spear was about to be despatched towards its target.

"Sugar Golf one, you are cleared for lift-off."

"Roger, ground control. Commencing lift-off."

Not take-off, but lift-off, and despite his mission and the fear and the *tick tock* Ahmed Ali Khan was brought back briefly to the everyman's wonder of the Sky Galleon and the proposed voyage and the pride and glory to be taken even from the least part of this day. Was that a sin, Merciful God, was this the pride that could lead me astray?

To the massed crowds of the Circus Maximus, there was a barely perceptible click as the anchor chains were detached and then nothing: silence, pure and empty and deep with the impossible cadence of failure. Watching in the hovering helicopter, two hundred feet to starboard and one hundred feet above, Andrew looked at Catherine and she shook her head in impatience. *Too early* it meant. *Keep looking*. It was the deep, expectant silence that made it so deceptive: in reality, watched later, and dispassionately, it was clear that *The Green World* had hardly hesitated. But, to the expectant onlookers, the silence and the emptiness meant... until the first gaps started to appear between the gondola and the ground and then got bigger and were then taller than a man and growing and within two minutes the whole great structure was fifty foot in the air and then one

402

hundred then two then at two hundred and fifty feet the engines went on and the blades of the propellers started to turn. By that time the silence was now the thunderous roar of a crowd in acclaim, and the propellers may as well have been powered by elastic as by the one-less-than-twelve state-of-the-art batteries that were full charged and eager to do some work.

It took fifteen minutes for Ahmed Ali Khan to get the great spear aloft and turned towards its target. That left fifteen minutes. So little? *Tick tock.* The first task, the gondola escape interlocks.

The Sky Galleon was an inherently safe design, not least because the only way that the great helium envelope could deflate quickly would be if it were utterly destroyed by some huge impact. The helium was utterly inert, and in the normal way of things, the envelope was largely self-sealing. Even under the pressure of dozens of large ruptures, the Sky Galleon would still be able to descend at a rate safe enough to protect the occupants of the gondola. On land. At sea, however, it was a very different matter, and most of the Sky Galleon's time would be spent over sea. Certainly, the gondola would hit the waves in good shape, but after that, as the gas envelope continued to deflate, the gondola would start to sink of its own weight. Not only that, but as the envelope deflated enough, it would become like a great water-gathering skin, collecting the water from the waves and sinking under the surface and dragging the gondola deeper and deeper at an ever-accelerating rate. For safety, therefore, the gondola could be detached from the gas envelope, even while the Sky Galleon was in flight. But to do so, Ahmed had to disengage the interlock: to disregard the altimeter-driven warning that said:

"Caution: you are two hundred feet high. Are you sure you want to disengage the gondola safety interlock?" Ahmed was sure, and he did. When he pressed the disengage button itself, fifteen minutes from now, two things would therefore happen. Firstly, the gondola would drop from the gas envelope and from the rest of the huge structure. Secondly, the battery release chamber would be opened. Just like a bomb bay. Sending the heavy batteries down to the ground like a stream of rectangular bombs. It was meant to ensure that the gondola would float. But while the gondola would float on water, it would not float on air. They would join the batteries, but in their own time, and not before Ahmed would be sure of his victory. And the start of the Final War that was to come.

The great electronic message board still showed 'Happy Christmas and Peace to All Men'. That was Ahmed's next task. After that, he could join his great father and Paradise. Beneath the Sky Galleon, the Tiber started to appear, bright, eternal, and unsuspecting.

To the right of the Sky Galleon, the Bell helicopter buzzed around like an fly around an elephant.

The next seven minutes passed so slowly yet so very, very quickly. The alternate messages were loaded and his laptop disconnected and *Caliph* run yet again but this time it was 'hsuLrmqkjodhksaBZ' that he entered and there was again no self-check message and instead again the fourteen numbers. '84625329076513' Exactly the same as before, when he had entered 'hsuLrmqkiodhksaBZ' The *Caliph* software was smart, perhaps. *All patterns reveal the Will of God, if you are so blessed.* Perhaps. But there was the number and that was the end of all doubt and now he hurried to join his father in the battery storage compartment. *The bomb bay, in fact.*

The Circus Maximus, Rome: Eleven fifty five a.m.
Christmas Day

Muhammad Ali Khan is standing over what looks like a large stainless steel case, on the surface of which is revealed a recessed keypad, a small LED display, beside which are two LED indicators. Muhammad has entered the first code - his code - and the first LED is green. The LED display says 'First code correct. Second code:', and the second LED indicator is red. Behind Muhammad stands Ahmed Ali Khan. His left hand is under his laptop, his right hand stabilises it by the right-hand edge of its screen.

"Your code, my son?" asks Muhammad Ali Khan. Just as he spoke, the great starboard display board started to change.

It had started as a public relations gimmick, but they soon realised that the messages of ever-changing display board could play a key part in the whole propaganda exercise that was *The Green World's* maiden voyage. Who would not be affected by its expert prompting? Thus far, its messages had been the slow, steady, beginning, but the media had been alerted that the messages would change, would become a talking point, and many expectant cameras were trained on the great board. Some of the stations had even prepared templates that interleaved the messages with images of the great galleon itself. The first new message was not that unexpected, because usually what can go wrong, sooner or later, does.

> *Americium.* Someone has screwed up.
> *Alpha.* Embarrassing. Puzzling. Wait: is there a connection?
> *Cobalt.* Cobalt? *Cobalt?*
> *Gamma. Oh my God!*
> *We have a radio-active bomb on board, and it is primed*
> *to explode.*

Do what we instruct or we will explode the bomb.
Do what we instruct and we will not explode the bomb.
No-one must leave the Circus Maximus.
No-one must leave St Peter's Square.
La llaha illa illah wa Muhammad rasul Allah
There is but one God and Muhammad is His Prophet

Two hundred yards above and two hundred yard to starboard, elementary geometry fought with poetry for control of Andrew's thought. By the laws of Pythagoras, the Bell of Westlands, Connor and Blenheim was two hundred and eighty yards away from the Sky Galleon. By the intuition of poetry:

'And what rough beast, its hour come round at last,

Slouches towards Bethlehem to be born?'

Not Bethlehem, *Rome*. Two hundred and eight yards. Hector, sitting behind Westlands as he should be, as he intended to be for the foreseeable future, somehow senses the thought. *How long to get to the gondola and what could they do?* A large, broad hand on Andrew's shoulder.

"Don't even think it, Andrew. If the bomb is real, and is armed, you will only make them detonate it. If it is not, then you will probably die in vain, and we need a little more from you than that. We must wait, sir. Patience" Yes, patience, the policeman's best friend.

Eleven fifty-six a.m. Below the great ship, St Peter's Square had just come into view. The Christmas Mass is now at its climax, the communion. Either the images had not been relayed to them or they had obeyed the command to stay put or maybe they did the only thing it made sense to do now. It was already too late.

406

Above them, the board had a new message.

Surah One Hundred and One
The Day of Noise and Clamour

"Your code, my son." Muhammad asked again.

"*Father, why, when Allah is The Most Merciful, do so many have to die?*"

A chill stole over Muhammad. Not now, son. Be strong. But he is not strong, is he? He loves life too much. *He who grasps life too tightly between his fingers will find only death.* But I must reason with him. It is Paradise at stake; for us both.

"My son, it is because Allah, The Most Merciful, requires us to slaughter the unbelievers. To show them the terror of His Vengeance. So that we turn all people to the Right Path."

"We slaughter even the children, father? Even the innocent?" *Even the little blonde boy that waits, unknowing, below us even now?*

"Yes, my son. Even the children. It is, unfortunately, their fate."

"But, father, after this bomb, their vengeance will be terrible. Many, many, Muslims will also die! Surely that cannot also be His Will?"

"My son, my son! Many, many Muslims deserve to die! How many good Muslims are there, really? How many Muslims really follow the true path of Islam? How many are little more than lip-serving infidel dogs, bound for hell with the rest of the infidels? How many more are the God-accursed heretics of the Shia? Trust me, my son. I am your father. I have guided you all these years. You are my chosen son. God's Divine Instrument. This one last time, Ahmed, I ask you to trust your father."

"Am I really your son, Muhammad? Or am I, perhaps, only your weapon? What am I really to you, father, other than an instrument of war?"

"My son, my son, do not weaken now! You are so very close

407

to Paradise. Give me the code. Let us now do what has been so long planned. We can laugh at the infidels - together - from the comforts of Paradise."

Tick, tock. The long seconds raced away. Outside, on the great electronic board, the Surah had reached:

What is the Day of Noise and Clamour?

And What will explain to thee what the Day of Noise and Clamour is?

Something passed across Ahmed Ali Khan's face. Acceptance. Resolution. Conclusion. He is ready to do his duty.

"Eight. Four. Six. Two. Five. Three. Two. Zero. Seven. Six. Five. One. *Eight.*" *Eight, not three.*

As he calls the numbers out, Muhammad enters them on the key-pad and responds 'check'. On the last 'eight', the LED indicator starts to flash slowly. *But it is not green. It is red.* Muhammad fights the surge of panic, keeps his voice steady and his anger in check.

"There must be some error, my son. Quickly, while the time is still right."

"Eight. Four. Six. Two. Five. Three. Two. Zero. Seven. Six. Five. *Nine.* Eight." *Nine, not one. Eight, not three.*

Muhammad - slowly, carefully, deliberately - enters them on the key-pad, again confirming each, one-by-one, with a 'check'. On the last 'eight', the red LED indicator still does not turn green. Instead it started to flash more quickly, more *urgently.* Its meaning is obvious: *warning.* How many wrong entries will it accept?

Below the great ship, the great square and the great dome. One minute to noon. Still time enough for the code and the disengagement and for the bomb to open and for the weapon to throw off its lead shield and to bare its dread teeth. Time enough for the plastique to create the Cloud of Allah. Down below, these will be the last Christians to stand in this square for at least four generations. One minute is still enough. Anyway, if we are a little late, it is only God's will, Insh'Allah. Still perfect. Still perfect time for his son to do what he must do to claim his martyrdom and his eternal prize. Still enough time for his son to do what he has to do. *One way or another.* The gun is now in Muhammad's hand as if by God's will and as if it should never have been out of it. A Makarov, modern and deadly, the last gift of the dying Russian officer, who no longer had anything left to offer to the Jihad but delight in his agonies.

"You are going to die, my son. That, at this hour, is not negotiable. All you can choose is the manner of it. Please, my son, accept the gift of martyrdom with me."

On the circling helicopter, another hand on another shoulder. The hand is long and thin and feminine and the broad shoulder is Hector's.

"Hector, Andrew is right. It is by staying here that we will die in vain. We need to get close. You are trained. Now is the time for you to do what you are trained to do. You will never get a better chance."

Hector was torn between responsibilities. How is it possible to think clearly? You will never get a better chance? The Sky Galleon, the radioactive bomb, the life he had been entrusted to protect, the massed humanity below ... and the long-barrelled Beretta in his pocket, with the image-intensifier sights. To see better what was going on inside the semi-opaque gondola of the *The Green World...*

"Pilot, get me as close as you can." and Hector reached for the Beretta.

On the great screen, the words now read:
It is a day whereon men will be like moths scattered about,
And the mountains will be like carded wool.

409

Ahmed Ali Khan looks steadily at his expectant father.

"Father, I know I am *already dead*. I have been already dead since the day you chose me. You are right: the only thing I can choose now is the manner of it. And I choose martyrdom. I choose to be martyred for Allah, The Most Merciful, and to spend my eternity in Paradise." Relief and delight flash across Muhammad's face, but the urgency remains. It is the first stroke of noon, and down below, in the great square, the blessing has started.

"Quickly, my son. Give me the code, for it should be now!"

"No, father, I will give you no code. Yes, I have chosen martyrdom to my God, Allah the Most Merciful. *But my God is not your God*. Your God is not merciful, but cruel. Your God is not kind, but vengeful. Your God is not understanding, but savage. I do not know the name of your God, father, but I know what he is. *It is not Allah you worship, father, but the God of Death*."

Outside on the great screen , the Surah now reads:
Then, he whose balance of good deeds will be found heavy,
Will be in a life of good pleasure and satisfaction.

Fury rages across Muhammad's face. Fury, and a hint of savage joy. He would be as strong as this adopted infidel was weak. But he would not lose his cunning...

"Give me the code or I will shoot, my foolish son! Please do not force me to send you to Hell!"

"Will you really shoot, father, while I hold the laptop? Will it survive the fall, for you to get the code that you need? Or will you kill me to gain nothing?"

The question has been asked and the impasse has been identified. No way back and no way forward but through the power of will, and will alone. Who - father or son - has the greater force? It is an inevitable battle, a battle that is long, long overdue, but - finally - the eyes of father and son lock together in the timeless challenge. Who, now, is the stronger? Silence, only the faint hum of the propellers. *Tick, tock*. My son is weak,

Muhammad knows. My will is strong ...Tick, tock. His son must weaken, Muhammad knows, because he is too kind. Too soft. The distant hum of the propellers. Do I see the first hint of weakness? *Tick, tock....*

Blam, blam, blam, BLAM! The cupola is like a great tensioned drum as the bullets of the Beretta hammer at its now transparent shell. Transparent, that is, through the lens of the intensifier, as Hector looses the last of the clip at the standing, gun pointing figure of Muhammad. Blam, blam, blam, BLAM! But it is no good: the cupola is too strong for his bullets, long barrelled or not. But...

...But Ahmed Ali Khan seizes on the distraction. That bit younger, that bit quicker, than his great father.

"Catch, father!" and he hurls the laptop high in the air towards his still-reacting father.

In that instant, Muhammad Ali Khan makes the only decision that he can and drops the Makarov to clutch the laptop from the air and to save the life of the code that will bring them salvation and - Allah be praised! - he catches the laptop, and...

"Put the laptop down, father. I will shoot." Does he really think I believe him? He who worships weakness and kindness?

"You will not shoot, son. You cannot shoot." Despite his confident words, Muhammad knows that he must make the gun safe. *He must make sure.*

"So give me the gun, my son. The crisis is past. Let us put this behind us now."

They are still in the battery compartment, barely two feet apart. Muhammad reaches out his right hand for the gun.

"Give me the gun, son!" shouts Muhammad, suddenly and - it was time! Insh'Allah - lunged for the weapon. He misses with his right, but swings on the balls of his feet to bring his left arm around and round Ahmed's neck and to grip Ahmed's wrist in his own strong right arm, and to pull the gun towards him and to prise apart the fingers and he had just enough time to register his shock at the explosion of the gun and the smell of the cordite and the great gouts of blood that poured onto the Great Bomb and the hole in his chest and the look of horror on the face of his Chosen Son. Who has made him a martyr, Insh'Allah.

Outside on the great screen , the Surah now reads:
Then, he whose balance of good deeds will be found light,
Will have his home in a bottomless Pit.

Ahmed Ali Khan knew that the danger was not yet passed, so he fought the shock and grief and did what he had to do. Fourteen random codes - quick, quick, who knows what can happen - and the LED went red, both LEDs went red. Quick, quick, to the flight deck.

Two minutes later, a billion eyes of a horror-struck world saw a new message on the great electronic board of the Great Green Beast.

"Happy Christmas. Peace to all men. The bomb has been disarmed. The danger is now passed. You are now all safe. Insh'Allah."

It was almost a miracle of the photographers art, but as the cameras framed the words of the electronic screen, what gave the picture its dynamic was the helicopter that hovered, outlined by the weak orb of the noon-day Christmas sun, at the top right of the frame. It was a shot that said all that had to be said, and more.

EIGHTEEN

St Peter's Square, Rome: Two p.m. Christmas Day

It's a great thing to be already dead, for you have nothing further to lose.

It was now an hour later and the Sky Galleon was cruising serenely towards the Mediterranean but Ahmed Ali Khan knew they would board in five minutes and they would be taking him back with them. He did not know exactly who they would be, but they would be military, and they would ask him lots of questions and he would tell them everything. Of course, they - the other *they* - would get to him some day. Sooner or later. They would kill him, that much was surely certain. Well, at least he would die a real martyr. A martyr to Allah, The Most Merciful, and not another offering to some pagan God of Death. Nor would Ahmed Ali Khan go easily. *Not easily into that good night, no not at all.* Life was sweet, and he would savour it now. A wife - a blonde boy- was it too much to ask? Yes, probably, *but you never know.* Didn't matter, for his life - all of it - was now given back to him. What was it they called it? *Renaissance.* Yes, that was it. He was a Renaissance Man, too.

St Peter's Square, Rome: Two p.m. Christmas Day

The Sky Galleon was now out of sight but hardly out of mind.
Probably never out of mind.

Solomon N'Chenga had dreamt last night of the Caribbean, and rum, and pretty young women who made him laugh and he was - he hoped - soon going to be on his way. Surely this had been the climax of the Christmas Bug? Surely this was the last act in the play, and surely now he was going to meet the playwright, and get to see the unwritten script?

Solomon N'Chenga is standing some ten yards back from one of the turnstiles that controlled the exit from St Peter's Square. There was no rush, no panic. Most people now accepted that it was over, and many of them had stayed, gone into the great cathedral to offer up their thanks and their relief. But not the blue-eyed man, whose back is just about to emerge from the turnstile and whose broad form is even now being ushered towards Solomon by two of his large and grim-faced gentlemen.

"Good afternoon, Michael." opened Solomon. "My name is Solomon N'Chenga, and I am delighted to meet you. Finally."

The broad figure is wearing a hat, and the head is bowed, but now Michael removes the hat from his red stubble and looks up, directly, into Solomon's eyes.

"Ah yes. You must be the Solomon who has been sent to judge me."

The words seem without a proper ending and the tone is deep and powerful and unusual and the eyes are impossible. For the first time in a very long time, Solomon is hit by the jolt and he is afraid. Who is this man and what is this man? Do I really dare to judge him?

The blue eyes in the deep face know what he is thinking, of that Solomon is sure.

414

U-Soft Headquarters, Washington D.C.: Three p.m. Rome time, Christmas Day

The planned launch of the Party of Western Renaissance went ahead, as planned, at three o'clock local time, Rome. Eldon Harker watched the proceedings on a large screen in his familiar office on the forty-third floor. As Andrew Westlands took the floor, Eldon felt a surge of pride in his erstwhile protégé. He has done so well, he thought, as Andrew opened.

"Three hours ago we were all already dead. Now we have been given a second chance. A Renaissance. Let's make the most of the privilege."

Eldon listened to the whole speech, and it was as brilliant as Eldon had hoped it would be. His favourite protégé: had he not done so well? And his other - more brilliant - protégé, what of him? Eldon considered the blue eyed man, a little, but really the conjectures were pointless. A waste of time, and he had no time to waste. For Eldon Harker had a new project, and new protégé, and Robert Alexander Scott was waiting for him. They had so much work to do, together.

A Mountain Cave, Afghanistan: Four p.m. Rome Time, Christmas Day

Have we been tricked by the infidels, or has someone betrayed us?

That was the first question that the Great Sheikh had to address, after he picked himself up from the agony of their defeat. They had been so close - so close! - and yet defeated, at the last, *in the City of the Infidels, and on Christmas Day! Allah, the Most merciful, what have your servants done to deserve such a terrible defeat?* How had it happened, when the plan had been so perfect, so careful, so patient?

But, the more the Great Sheikh thought of it, the more obvious the answer was. The infidels could not have tricked them: how could they, when - up to the very last minute - the faithful could have succeeded? How could the infidels have let them get so close to rendering the abomination of Rome into a wasteland, and to triggering the Final War that still awaited? No, not possible, and neither could they have been betrayed, for the same reason. Not unless the betrayal was by Ahmed Ali Khan - Allah curse him into eternity! But that would have meant a long betrayal, and the weak infidel would never - never! - have been able to hide it from them. No, he knew the real reason for their failure. *It was not His Will.* Why had we been so sure it was His Will? After all, the Will of God is deeper than the blackest of nights in a star-empty sky. That had been their sin: pride. We had been too sure of His Will. They had not shown enough humility and now they were being punished. Insh'Allah. Thankfully, there was already another opportunity, and their preparations were far advanced. This time, they must make sure that it was His Will. Above all, they needed to pray, and to pray as never before.

416

The Tower Block, London: Six p.m. Rome Time, Christmas Day

I have built an army in a week... how much longer will it take me to build a Reich?

But the words were written before noon, and The Great Escape, and Daniel D is now gripped by a violent, towering, murderous rage.

"Tink I a batty myaan?" he screams. "Who tink I baaatty?" There is only an echo for an answer, for apart from Daniel D, there is only one other in the room, and he is in no position to talk. Daniel D is still stunned at the opportunity that had come and gone *even before he had known of its existence.* He had known nothing – *nothing!* – of the Muslims' attack – but, now, knowing how close the fools had come - he cannot believe in his misfortune. *How could they have come so close and yet failed! War is the locomotive of history.* War was the locomotive that his movement waited for. Not just any war: they needed a cruel, pitiless, God-less war. *Blood is the rich wine of war, and power is its fruit! Wars are won only by those who drink deepest of its wine. Wars are always won by those who drink the most blood.*

Daniel D, struck by the truth of the thought, turns from the window and strides to the poor blood-stained figure that slumps against the ropes binding him to the cheap plastic seat. Blood, yes, that was the answer. *If he could not yet have war, at least he could have more blood.* Daniel D again unsheathed his faithful attack knife. 'Well, you might have no more to tell me, Muslim. But you still have plenty of blood. If I am careful, then I can make you last. After that, the dogs need to be fed.'

417

The Hotel Excelsior, Rome: Eight p.m. Christmas Day

They say that well begun is half done and Andrew knew that it had been well begun.

There was absolutely no doubt that the conference had been a success: a tremendous success. How could it fail to be, given the events of the last twenty four hours, and especially those of the last three?! The power was near now, so near Andrew felt it - and its fascination - and it frightened him just a little. When you only gain power to give it away, is that really power?' Andrew asked himself, again. 'What is power that can never be used?'

"Well?" her voice demands.

Andrew is started from his fine reverie on the nature of the power, and looks up at the voice. Catherine is standing at her bedroom doorway and "Well?" is a very good question. She is wearing a long black sleeveless dress that makes no attempt to disguise the swelling of her breasts or the elegant grace of her long slim arms. The dress sweeps open at the knee to show the length and grace of the shapely legs that are tipped by the bright red of the high glamour heels. Her blonde hair is fixed up and down the nape of her long and graceful neck, accentuated by the pendants of stone and gold that hang from her ears. Catherine's make-up is minimal, her skin is clear, her eyes are bright, and her smile is full of gentle mockery.

"Well, Andrew, will I do?" she prompts again.

"Do?" Andrew manages. "For just about anything, Catherine, believe me. You look - how can I say it? - *absolutely fabulous.*" He had to stop staring at her. He needed a comeback line.

"So now, Catherine, now that you are clearly ready for *anything*, would you mind letting me know just what *are* our plans for this evening?" Andrew's banter was cool, but its effect was destroyed by the fact that he still couldn't tear his eyes off her.

"Certainly, Andrew," Catherine smiled. "I've cancelled the

late press conference and our meeting with the Europeans. I've told…"

Ding-dong. The bell. 'I thought security …'

"I'll get it.", and Catherine swept gracefully towards the door. 'The realities of power …' mused Andrew. 'The reality of the power of a woman's beauty. That is real indeed. And a power that *can* be used, God save us all.'

And then Catherine is back again, smiling as if she had guessed what he had been thinking. Or maybe because of the champagne bucket that she held in those elegant hands. A champagne bucket, with a fine bottle whose price even Andrew might think twice about.

"Ah yes, Andrew, our plans. Well, I thought we'd start with some champagne. After that … well, who knows where the champagne might lead?" And Catherine smiled that most perfect smile.

'Who knows indeed?' thought Andrew as he - suddenly almost embarrassed - returned the smile. Well, looking at Catherine, he was more than ready to take the chance.

'After all,' he told himself. 'After all, I might be an old dog, but this is also a very old trick.'